TRICKSTER

TRICKSTER

SAM MICHAELS

An Aria Book

First published in the United Kingdom in 2019 by Aria,
an imprint of Head of Zeus Ltd

A CIP catalogue record for this book is available from
the British Library.

Printed and bound in Great Britain by
CPI Group (UK) Ltd, Croydon CR0 4YY

ISBN (PBO): 9781789544428
ISBN (E): 9781789542172

MIX
Paper from
responsible sources
FSC® C020471

Aria
c/o Head of Zeus
First Floor East
5–8 Hardwick Street
London EC1R 4RG

WWW.ARIAFICTION.COM

TRICKSTER

For Andrew Sydney Blofeld, my beautiful baby boy.

You've always astounded me, from the day you were born until now, to see the extraordinary man you've become. I couldn't be prouder of you and I know you'll continue to amaze me. I'm the luckiest woman, to have such a caring, brave and gorgeous son – I love you.

This one is for you, darling, because you're simply the best!

Love always, Mum xxx

Prologue

'Leave it out,' the man protested. 'We don't want to be messing with the likes of Georgina Garrett. She's dangerous, some say she's mad, and if we don't want to end up in body bags, we should stay well away from her.'

'What are you, a bleedin' fairy? She's a woman, and I ain't letting her stand in my way.'

'Sod off, Liam, I ain't a fairy! I like women, not men, but that Georgina is one woman I'm not messing with.'

'Fine, suit yourself. I'll find someone else to do the job with, someone who ain't yellow-livered like you.'

'Do that! It's your funeral,' the man snapped, thinking as he marched out of the pub that if the idiot was stupid enough to go up against Georgina Garrett, that's how he'd end up. In a coffin.

From what he'd heard, and rumours were rife, Georgina had been born on the day that the war had been declared. Though she may not have come out fighting, she was a force to be reckoned with now. He didn't know what it was, but something must have happened to turn her into the ruthless, heartless bitch who ruled the streets of Battersea.

He would have liked to know the full story – to know what happened to Georgina Garrett from the day she was born, but of course that was impossible. You didn't ask questions about her – not if you expected to live.

PART 1

THE BIRTH OF GEORGINA GARRETT

London, Battersea, 4 August 1914

Sissy Garrett doubled over in agony as another contraction ripped through her skinny body. She grabbed hold of the butler sink for support, panting hard as beads of sweat formed on her pallid skin.

'Gawd help me,' she ground out through gritted teeth, and rubbed the underpart of her hugely swollen stomach. Her violet eyes were wide with fear and her heart-shaped face was contorted in pain. At twenty-two, this was her first child, and it had been long waited for.

She looked down at the puddle of water that was seeping through the worn floorboards. Her contractions had come on quickly and taken her by surprise. Now, as she stood in the small, shared scullery, her heart hammered in panic. Mr and Mrs Linehan lived upstairs with their toddler, but Sissy knew they were out. Alfred Linehan would be working, running errands on the streets, and his wife, Lillian, had said she was going to stay at her sister's for a few days.

Sissy was all alone, on the cusp of giving birth, and silently cursed Jack again. Her husband frequently did a disappearing act and came and went as regularly as the tide on the Thames. She'd often tell him he was as much use as a chocolate fireguard, and on several occasions his petty thieving had failed to pay the rent. This would leave her having to hide from the landlord in the cupboard under the stairs. Still, she loved Jack dearly, and prayed he would come home soon.

She slowly walked across the scullery as cockroaches darted for cover. With just one cold tap and a range stove in the room, there wasn't a table or chair available to steady herself. Discoloured wallpaper hung off the walls and hand-washed, ragged clothes were draped over a makeshift washing line that ran from one side of the room to the other. Black mould covered the back wall, which housed a draughty door leading to the yard and outside privy.

It was squalid, basic and cheap, but Sissy preferred to grin and bear it rather than live with Dulcie, her mother-in-law. The woman lived with Percy, her drunken second husband. He wasn't Jack's father but had taught his stepson the art of larceny. They had the rare luxury of a two-bedroom house, but as Percy's alcoholism had left him incapable of grafting, Sissy always wondered how they managed to pay the rent.

When she'd first married Jack, Dulcie had offered them a home, but Sissy had politely declined. She found Dulcie to be a hard woman and feared her quick temper. No, she could never live under the same roof as her. She thought about her own parents who had been dead for several years. She wished her mum was with her now, to hold her hand and tell her everything would be all right.

Sissy paused in the hallway as another wave of pain gripped her body. 'Jack bloody Garrett,' she gasped, steadying herself against the wall, 'where are you when I need you?'

She took several deep breaths and waited for the contraction to pass, eventually managing to get to their one room which, like the scullery, was almost bare, except for two wooden chairs, a rickety table and a large bed on which she desperately wanted to rest. It crossed her mind to bang on the wall and attract the attention of her neighbour, but Miss Capstone was a godly woman and it was no secret that she despised Jack and his unlawful ways. Though Sissy was afraid, she didn't want to face another scornful lecture and instead lowered her aching body onto her lumpy mattress.

It was hot. The late morning sun shone brightly through the window, illuminating the dilapidated room. Her nostrils twitched at the musty smell, and she wished she'd opened the window. A cool breeze would be welcome, but Sissy felt too weak and knew she should conserve her energy. She lay back and stared at the flaking paint on the ceiling. She wanted this baby so much, but worried about the sort of life she was bringing it into. Money was sparse, and their home was almost derelict, infested with bugs and vermin. All she could offer the child was her unconditional love.

A lone tear slipped from her eye and trickled down her face to rest in her ebony hair, which was now damp with sweat.

The sound of the front door opening snapped Sissy from her worrying thoughts. She heard her husband's heavy footsteps and sighed with relief as their door flew open. Jack charged into the room like a strong gale bursting open a barn door.

'Sis, you ain't gonna believe this… we're at war!'

Sissy pushed herself up on her haunches and looked at her husband as he waved a newspaper in front of her face. She couldn't read, but Jack emphatically pointed at the headline.

'See, it says here: "War declared on Germany".'

'Yeah, well, never mind about that… the baby's coming.'

Jack's eyes widened, and the colour drained from his face. 'Oh blimey, are you all right? Wh… wh… what do I do?'

Sissy smiled weakly. It wasn't often she saw her husband in a flap, but he was now, and it had nothing to do with the war. 'This ain't no place for men, Jack. Go and get Mrs Blundell at number seventeen. Give her two and six and tell her to hurry up!'

'Mrs Blundell!' Jack spat the name through his crooked teeth. 'The old girl's always drunk. How the bleedin' hell is she gonna help?'

'She's the handywoman round here, and a darn sight

cheaper than the doctor. Just go, Jack… get a move on,' Sissy urged, wincing as pain began to rack her body again. She was aware childbirth wasn't easy, but she hadn't expected it to feel like torture.

Without another word Jack dashed from the room and soon after Sissy heard the front door slam. Her knuckles were white as she gripped the blanket beneath her, and she tried to stifle a scream. Please hurry, she thought frantically, and writhed as the pain became almost unbearable. Jack was right, Mrs Blundell was drunk a lot of the time, but she'd helped most of the local women to give birth. *Blundell's Babies* they were affectionately called. If you paid her a shilling, she'd lay out the dead too.

Sissy quickly tried to push that thought from her mind. Childbearing was a dangerous time for a woman, so she wouldn't allow herself to think of death. Instead, she tried to focus on names for the baby. She'd wanted Ernest for a boy, after her father, but Jack insisted on George. Well, she thought, it was bound to be a boy. It had certainly kicked her bony ribs hard enough, and fancy being born on the day war broke out!

The door opened again, and to her relief, she saw Mrs Blundell follow Jack into the room. Thankfully the last contraction had eased, though Sissy knew it wouldn't be long until the next one arrived.

'Oh, my dear, look at the state of you,' the old woman said as she leaned forward and placed her chubby hand on Sissy's moist forehead. 'Jack, fetch me a bowl of cold water and a cloth to wipe her brow.'

Sissy tried to turn her face away from the woman's foul breath. She was sure the stale alcohol fumes must be toxic.

'How quickly are the pains coming?' Mrs Blundell asked, rolling up the sleeves of her dark grey dress. The material was stretched tightly across her enormous chest, and as she turned away from the bed to walk towards the window, Sissy gazed in awe at her huge hips.

'I dunno… quickly… every five or ten minutes I suppose.'

'And have your waters broken?'

'Yes… I… erm… I thought I'd wet meself,' Sissy answered coyly.

Mrs Blundell drew the curtains, but the thin material was too short for the window, so the room was still quite light. 'We don't want any prying eyes now, do we? Is this your first?'

'Yes.'

'In that case we'll probably have a good few hours to wait. Best you send that old man of yours off down the pub or something. We don't want him hanging around making a nuisance of himself. Don't worry, I'll get word to him when the baby's here.'

Sissy nodded, but she didn't want Jack going to the pub. They could ill afford him supping away what little money they had, and Jack wasn't very good at holding his liquor. In fact, once he got a taste for it, there'd be no stopping him and he'd carry on drinking until he passed out.

'You look very thin. Have you been eating properly?'

'I try, but you know how it is. Bread and jam most nights, and if I do manage to get my hands on any decent meat, I like to make sure Jack gets a good plateful. After all, he's the one out there grafting for us.'

The door opened again, and Jack walked in carrying an enamelled bowl of water.

'Good man. Now pull up that chair for me and bugger off. Your wife is going to be busy for ages yet, so you go and wait in the Cedars and I'll send one of my boys to come and get you later.'

Sissy looked at Jack and covertly shook her head.

'It's all right, Mrs Blundell, I'll stay here and help out.'

'You'll do no such thing! A man in a room when a woman's giving birth… I've never heard the likes of it!'

Jack looked sheepish and threw an imploring look at his wife before reluctantly agreeing to the woman's orders. 'All right, but I'll be outside, on the stairs.'

This was one of the reasons why Sissy loved her husband so much. Yes, he was a rogue, but a lovable one, and when he wasn't out grafting, he was always there to look after her.

'I suppose that'll be OK, but I don't want you bursting through that door when you hear your missus screaming, 'cos believes me, she will. Just remember, young man, thousands of women have done this before and the pain is normal.'

'All right, thanks, Mrs Blundell. I'll be right outside, Sissy,' Jack added nervously. As he walked from the room, he didn't once take his eyes off his wife.

Sissy could feel another wave of excruciating pain washing over her. She gritted her teeth and groaned loudly as Mrs Blundell mopped her brow.

'That's it, my girl, deep breaths,' the woman said soothingly.

Sissy didn't know Mrs Blundell very well, but her reassuring manner and calming voice had quickly gained her confidence. With her grey hair in a bun, and a face etched with deep grooves, she looked to be well into her sixties and it was reputed that she'd birthed babies since she was a teenager. What Mrs Blundell didn't know about childbearing wasn't worth knowing, but handywomen were outlawed now as the government had trained midwives to take over the role. Sissy didn't trust a new, young midwife, and felt safer in Mrs Blundell's hands. Also, the experienced woman was a lot cheaper than the medical professionals.

Jack had sat on the third step up for over three hours. He'd paced the hallway, gone outside for fresh air several times, and now sat back down again. He tapped his foot as he worried about his wife on the other side of the door. It sounded like she was having a rough time and he longed to go in and comfort her. But he knew the rules, and Mrs Blundell had made it quite clear that he wasn't welcome.

He could have kicked himself. If only he'd put some money aside, he could have paid for a proper doctor. Yes, Mrs Blundell had birthed lots of babies, but everyone knew she was partial to the gin. A sudden scream broke his thoughts and he jumped to his feet at the sound of his wife's ear-piercing cries. The sound was long and arduous, then he heard Sissy cry, 'Please... I can't take any more.'

Someone hammered on the front door, so Jack rushed to open it, but was disappointed to find a very stern-looking Miss Capstone stood on the step.

'I take it from the noise that your wife is in labour?'

Jack nodded.

'Is the doctor with her?'

Jack shook his head.

'So, I assume Mrs Blundell is with her?'

Jack nodded again.

'Get out of my way,' his neighbour said, sounding irritated, and she pushed Jack to one side as she barged past him.

She was a slim woman with pointed features and thin lips. She always wore a hat and dressed in black, but no-one knew who she was in mourning for, as from what Jack had heard, she was a spinster. She lived with her brother and was known to rent out rooms, but it seemed the lodgers never stayed very long. Jack guessed they were put off by having the Bible constantly shoved down their throats. He didn't like to argue with God and even less so with women, so he didn't offer any resistance as Miss Capstone glared at him with beady, disdainful eyes, then entered the room where his wife was bringing his child into the world.

'Miss Capstone, can I help you?' Mrs Blundell asked, sounding annoyed at the uninvited visitor.

'I doubt it, but I thought I may be able to help you. It sounds like the woman is struggling.'

'No, she's fine. Everything's going as it should,' Mrs Blundell answered curtly.

Sissy wanted to pull the covers over her bare legs, embarrassed to be showing so much of herself to her neighbour, but she didn't have the strength.

'Well, yes, it's God's will. A woman's pain in childbirth is part of the suffering brought into the world through sin. He said, "I will make child bearing painful". I've no doubt He has made your pains twice as bad, as you are spawning a child of... well, that good-for-nothing thieving husband of yours!'

Sissy was shocked at Miss Capstone's words, and her haughty attitude riled her, but she was quickly distracted by an overwhelming urge to push.

As Sissy's body felt as though it was splitting in two, she saw Mrs Blundell march to the door and throw it open. 'Miss Capstone, take yourself and your self-righteous judgemental views out of this room,' the woman shouted.

'How dare you speak to me like that.'

'Oh, I dare. Now get out!'

Miss Capstone took in the thunderous look on Mrs Blundell's face, and obviously deciding that it might be better to retreat, left the room. The door was slammed behind her. Taking a deep breath, Mrs Blundell returned to Sissy's side. Her tone instantly changed. 'I'm going to take a look, dear. I think we're getting close now.'

Sissy closed her eyes as Mrs Blundell peered between her legs.

'Yes, as I thought, you're crowning. The baby is on its way. Now, try not to push until I tell you to.'

Sissy held her breath. She wanted to bear down but she'd been instructed not to. 'I must... I have to, I can't help it,' she cried.

'Quick breaths, Sissy, pant, dear... The baby is coming out a bit slowly. If he's got ears like his father, he's probably got stuck in there,' Mrs Blundell said with a chortle.

If Sissy hadn't been in so much pain, she might have laughed too. Jack did have enormous ears that stuck out, but it endeared him to her even more. She'd often joked with him, asking if his head spun round and round if he got caught in a strong wind.

'Right, push again, but gently,' Mrs Blundell instructed, and shortly after she smiled. 'Ah yes, well done.'

Suddenly, the pain subsided, and Sissy felt numb as her child slithered into Mrs Blundell's waiting hands. She'd done it. Her baby was born.

'Here she is… you have a perfect baby girl,' the woman said as she cut the cord then warmly handed Sissy her bloodied child.

Sissy felt exhausted but overwhelmed with motherly love for the tiny baby in her arms. She held her immediately to her breast and the baby instantly began to suckle. 'Can you tell Jack to come in please?'

'Not just yet,' Mrs Blundell replied as she busied herself between Sissy's legs. I need to clean you up a bit first. Oh no!'

'What's wrong?' she asked anxiously.

'Er, nothing, dear… just relax. You… um… have a little bit of tearing, that's all. I just need to fix you up a bit.'

Sissy felt reassured and held her daughter close, admiring her thick mop of black hair, just like her own. Her ears were squashed so it was difficult to tell, but she didn't think the child had inherited her father's ears, or his wonky nose. Mind you, Jack's nose was only wonky because it had been punched so many times.

'Oh, my darling, you're so beautiful,' Sissy whispered and gently kissed the top of her baby's head. As she gazed at her daughter in amazement, the sheets underneath her began to feel wet and warm. 'What's going on, Mrs Blundell? I feel a bit strange.'

'Nothing… nothing at all… you're bleeding. It happens sometimes. Don't worry, you'll be fine.'

Mrs Blundell's tone was higher-pitched than normal, and the urgency in her voice caused Sissy to panic. She'd heard of women haemorrhaging and bleeding to death after childbirth. She wasn't a believer like her neighbour Miss Capstone, but suddenly she found herself praying to God to spare her for the sake of her newborn baby.

Mrs Blundell suddenly pulled a blanket over Sissy and rushed out of the room mumbling something that Sissy didn't quite catch. Through her confusion, she instinctively knew her life was in danger and wondered if Mrs Blundell had fled in fear. Had she been abandoned to die alone? 'Mrs Blundell, come back,' Sissy shouted feebly, her strength sapping as blood spewed from her womb.

When their door flew open and Mrs Blundell appeared, Jack jumped to his feet again. 'Has Sissy had the baby?'

'Yes, but you'd better come in, and hurry.'

Jack heard the urgency in the woman's voice. Pushing her none too gently to one side, he dashed into the room. 'Sissy... Sis... it's me, love, Jack. Can you hear me?' Jack stared down at his wife's pale face. Her eyes were closed, and he noticed her lips had a blue tinge.

'Let me move the baby,' Mrs Blundell said, taking the child from Sissy's breast and laying it down beside her.

Jack briefly saw that the baby was a girl, but his eyes quickly returned to Sissy. 'What's wrong with my wife?' he demanded to know.

'She... she's haemorrhaging and I'm sorry, there's nothing more I can do.'

'What are you talking about?' Jack asked, confused. He took Sissy's limp, scrawny hand in his, and held it to his cheek. 'Sissy... wake up, darling. You've had a little girl... She's gorgeous, just like you.'

The baby was quietly gurgling by Sissy's side, but Jack had hardly noticed her as he was engulfed in concern for his wife. Slowly, Sissy's eyes half opened.

'She's awake... Mrs Blundell, she's all right. Sissy, it's me, love... you're going to be fine.'

His wife smiled a soft smile, her voice barely a whisper as she said, 'Call her Georgina, and always tell her how much I loved her. Give her my ring, Jack, make sure she...' Then, her eyes closed again, and her head rolled to one side.

'Sissy... don't leave me, darling... please... We need you. Georgina needs her mum... You can't go,' Jack begged, as tears began to roll down his rough face. But it was too late. Sissy would never hear his pleas and Georgina would never know her mother.

As Georgina Garrett lay next to the dead body of her mother, a few streets away, Billy Wilcox, a lad of four, was absorbed in the task of pulling the legs off a spider. Several doors down from Billy, Molly Mipple had been born six months earlier to an impoverished family, and was kicking her tiny legs, crying with hunger. Soon, all their lives would intertwine with devastating consequences.

2

It was early evening when Jack's mother, Dulcie, finally came to sit in the comfort of her chair in front of the hearth, pleased that the warm August weather meant she didn't need any coal for a fire. She had just about managed to find the money to pay the rent, but there was little remaining, and she worried how she would feed them both for the rest of the week.

As was usual these days, Percy was deeply unconscious in an alcohol-fuelled slumber, sprawled inelegantly across the chair opposite hers and snoring loudly. He was a short man, a little over five feet tall, and nowadays as thin as a rake. She doubted he'd be wanting any food. He'd much prefer to fill his belly with ale, but her stomach grumbled at the thought of bread and cheese. She knew there was a small stale crust left in the kitchen, but the cheese had been eaten the day before.

Percy slapped his lips together in his sleep, and she stared at him as the hunger in her stomach was replaced by a deep hatred and resentment towards the man she had once loved.

She rubbed her aching feet and sighed deeply, her heart heavy with shame. Where once Percy had supported them, she was now left to be the breadwinner, and with no education or knowledge of anything other than running a home, she'd been forced into selling herself. At forty-five years old, she wasn't as firm or attractive as many of the younger single mothers who worked the labyrinth of filthy, run-down streets, but there were still men who fancied the older woman.

To her surprise, she'd found it was often the younger gentlemen who would pay for her services. They knew she'd have the experience and skills to teach them a thing or two. She could tolerate the young men, especially as most of them got the deed done quickly, but it was the old men who turned her stomach. With their rotten teeth and bad breath, instead of lifting her skirts and parting her legs, she'd rather stick a knife in their chests. She had little choice though, and just hoped her neighbours, and more so her son, would never discover how she kept a roof over their heads.

Percy broke wind, and Dulcie turned her face away from the vile smell, then turned back to look at him with disgust. She thought his guts must be rotting. She wished he'd drink himself to death or have a fatal accident. He'd fallen off the railway bridge twice before and had once been hit by a horse and cart outside the pub, but the old git had survived, much to Dulcie's dismay.

It seemed to her that only the good died young, like her first husband, Boris. She felt a lump in her throat at the thought of him. He'd been killed in an accident at work when a kiln had exploded in the steelworks, just months after Jack was born. She'd been left devastated and penniless, but Percy had willingly taken her and her son on, and up until a couple of years ago, had provided well through poaching and stealing.

Compared to most of the families in this part of London, she'd thought her life with Percy had been charmed. She wasn't burdened with several children's mouths to feed, and Percy's ill-gotten gains had comfortably furnished their home. She'd kept a good figure, and her chestnut hair hadn't greyed. But her bones were feeling age creeping in, which left her joints aching and her hands beginning to gnarl prematurely. Dulcie tutted to herself. Who'd have thought it would have come to this? Where once she had looked down her nose at prostitutes, now, at her time of life, she was one of them.

She heard a tap on the front room window and knew it would be Jack. He was the only person who knocked on the window instead of the door. Her hips felt stiff as she pushed herself up from her chair, and as she passed Percy she gave him a kick in the shins. The good-for-nothing so and so wouldn't feel it in his state, she thought, and she plastered a smile on her face to greet her son.

She opened the door but was surprised to see Jack holding a bundle that looked like a baby. She studied her son's face. His puffy, red-rimmed eyes told her all she needed to know. 'Come in, Son,' she said, opening the door wider and trying to get a glimpse at what he held.

'Sissy's dead, Mum. She died minutes after having the baby.'

Dulcie gently took the child from her son's muscular arms. The baby, who had started to cry, was wrapped in a cut-off from an old patchwork quilt, which she recognised as one she'd given Sissy months earlier. 'Does the baby have a name?' Dulcie asked, attempting to hide her emotion. She could see her son's heart was breaking, which broke her own.

'Georgina... it's what Sissy wanted,' Jack answered, his voice beginning to crack as he was obviously doing his utmost to hold back his tears.

'That's lovely, a girl then, and she looks just like her mum,' Dulcie answered softly, and rocked from side to side in a bid to calm the child. It didn't work. Georgina continued to cry incessantly, hungry for her mother's milk.

'I dunno what to do, Mum. She needs a feed...'

Dulcie chewed her lower lip as her mind turned, but then struck by an idea she said, 'Don't worry, Jack, I know someone who might be able to help. There's a jug of ale in the kitchen. Go and pour yourself a glass. I'll be back as soon as I can.'

Dulcie left her house and hurried along the narrow

street with the wailing baby in her arms. She could ill afford to feed Percy and herself, let alone this poor little mite, and a wet nurse didn't come cheap. However, if her idea panned out, she wouldn't have to part with a penny.

Fifteen minutes later Dulcie was in the roughest part of town. This was an area no person of good virtue would dare to frequent. Women hung out of windows with their bosoms on display, vying for business, while others were drunk, vomiting openly in the filthy streets. In a dark corner behind a cart, Dulcie glimpsed a woman bent over with her skirt up, a punter behind her, trousers round his ankles as he pounded hard for his pleasure.

This wasn't the sort of place where Dulcie felt comfortable carrying a small baby. She held her granddaughter protectively close to her and tried to muffle the child's screams in the hope of avoiding any unwanted attention.

The sun was still high in the sky. Dulcie was grateful, as she would have been worried if it had been dark. A short, skinny man with bare feet and a bent back walked towards her. His leering eyes unnerved Dulcie and she could see he was trying to peer at the child she held. He stood ominously in front of her, blocking her path. If she hadn't been carrying Georgina, she wouldn't have given a second thought to kneeing him in the crotch.

With an evil sneer, he licked his lips, nodded towards the baby and then asked, 'How much?'

'This child is not for sale,' Dulcie said firmly, then sidestepped the man and marched on. It was no secret that in these streets, any desire could be bought for the right price, but it turned Dulcie's stomach. It wasn't unusual for a prostitute to fall with an unwanted pregnancy, then sell the child on, no questions asked. Dulcie didn't believe it was something any woman wanted to do, but the desperation of poverty forced them into it. Gawd knows where those helpless babies ended up, or what they went through, Dulcie thought, and shuddered. She reckoned the women would be better off killing their babies – something she suspected her friend Ruby had recently resorted to.

She had seen many young women turn to drugs or booze to numb the pain and block out the memories of what they'd done. Some went out of their minds and ended up in institutions, a fate worse than death, and it was something she didn't want to see happen to Ruby. The girl was only sixteen, with bright ginger hair and a sprinkling of freckles across her nose. Her fair skin was the colour of porcelain, so when she'd turned up on the streets one day her purple and yellow bruises had really stood out.

Dulcie had taken her under her wing and learnt that Ruby was homeless after running away from her abusive father. Her mother had died when Ruby was seven, and her father had forced her into his bed to fulfil the role of his wife. When he'd filled her belly with a child, he'd beaten her until she miscarried, then thrown her out to fend for herself.

Dulcie did her best to protect the girl and would steer her away from the customers she knew had a liking for wanting to rough up the women, but it hadn't been long before she'd noticed that Ruby was trying to hide a growing bump in her stomach. She'd had a quiet word with her and found that Ruby was distraught, fearing her secret would be discovered and she'd be sent to the workhouse. Dulcie felt sorry for the girl but, struggling herself to make enough money to live on, she could only offer a shoulder to cry on.

Less than a week ago and well into her pregnancy, Ruby disappeared, but then she'd turned up again two days ago, her stomach flat. She refused to discuss the fate of the baby, but Dulcie noticed her demeanour had changed. Where once she'd been a chatty young woman with a wicked sense of humour, she was now mostly silent, her eyes veiled in a darkness that Dulcie couldn't penetrate.

Ruby lived in the basement of a shared house at the end of the street. It was decrepit, with the roof caved in and the stairs to the upper level broken. Dulcie thought the whole house looked unsound and had never been inside, but she had to speak to Ruby and hoped to find her in. She took a deep breath and braced herself for what she may find, then slowly walked down the stairs that led to the basement door. It was open, so with trepidation, she stepped inside.

As her eyes adjusted to the dim light, she searched for Ruby. Several people were scattered, asleep on the dirty floor. Flies buzzed around, and Dulcie was sure she saw a rat the size of a cat scuttle around the edge of the room. Bile rose in her throat at the stench of soiled bodies and human excrement. She spotted a woman huddled in a corner with a small child by her side. She didn't look old enough to be the mother, though the grime covering her face made it difficult to tell.

'I'm looking for Ruby,' Dulcie said quietly to the woman.

The woman pointed to a doorway. Dulcie had to step over an unconscious boy, dressed in rags and probably drunk. He couldn't have been any older than about five or six, but this wasn't an unusual sight in these slums. She tried to block out the image of the horrors of his life, then nervously walked through the doorway that led into an even darker room. As she struggled to focus, she wondered how living in these conditions could be worse than the workhouse, but she reasoned, at least these vagrants, prostitutes, drunks and orphans had their freedom.

'Dulcie.' She heard her name in the gloom and instantly recognised Ruby's voice.

Ruby climbed up from the pile of rags she was sitting on. 'What on earth are you doing here?'

'Looking for you,' Dulcie answered. 'I need your help.'

'Yeah, well, we all need help, but you've got to help yourself down here,' Ruby said dismissively.

'Listen, Ruby... I know you've not long birthed a child, so you'll still have your milk. This baby has lost her mother and needs feeding.'

'No... No... I couldn't feed my own, so I ain't feeding that one.' Ruby turned her back and went to walk away.

'I'll make it worth your while,' Dulcie called in desperation.

The girl spun back on the heel of her clogs and walked towards her. 'Is that right? How much are you offering?'

Dulcie had thought about it and knew the measly sum she could afford wouldn't be enough. However, she'd quickly formulated a better idea and now said, 'Come and live with me. I have a nice house in a decent street. You can't stay here, Ruby, it's disgusting. Feed the baby, and I'll make sure you get food and shelter. You won't have to walk the streets, and you'll have a clean roof to sleep under.'

'I'm not sure, Dulcie... I don't deserve anyone's charity, not after what I done. This is my punishment for killing my... It's God's will.'

Even in the murkiness of the room, Dulcie could see

28

Ruby's green eyes were glistening with unshed tears. 'Don't be daft. You did what you had to do, and no god would want any young woman living like this! And anyway, it's not charity. I need you... this baby needs you. Please, Ruby, come home with me.'

Ruby pursed her lips, and for a moment, Dulcie thought the girl might burst into tears, but she didn't and instead nodded her head.

'Good, now let's get out of this shithole.' Dulcie couldn't get away quick enough, and she and Ruby made their way through the grime and back towards Dulcie's house.

'I've got two bedrooms at home. You and Georgina can have one; my son, Jack, he can kip on the sofa. When you meet my old man, Percy, just try your best to ignore him. I do most of the time. He likes a drink but he's harmless.'

'Who does the baby belong to?'

'Jack. His wife Sissy died this afternoon, just after this little one was born. My daughter-in-law was always feeble, God rest her soul. Now, one more thing... It's very important that you never, never mention how we met or what I did for money. My family don't know, and I'd like to keep it that way.'

'I understand. What are we going to tell them then?'

'I'll say I knew your mum and we'll make out you got attacked by some bloke and that's how you got pregnant, but the baby was a stillborn.'

Ruby was walking alongside Dulcie now, and when she looked at the girl, she regretted mentioning a dead baby.

'I wish it had been like that and then I wouldn't feel so guilty,' Ruby said sullenly.

'I know, love, but put all that behind you now. What's done is done,' Dulcie said in a matter-of-fact tone.

The baby had been quiet for a while, but now began to squall again. There was no stopping her, so Dulcie drew Ruby into an empty shop doorway. She handed the baby to Ruby, noting her reluctance to hold her, but with no time for this sort of nonsense she said sharply, 'She's hungry and you need to feed her.'

'What – here?'

'Yes, just get on with it while I shield you as best I can.'

Once the baby was satisfied, they carried on home and though Ruby was the ideal solution, Dulcie began to worry. She thought Percy wouldn't be sober for long enough to notice there was a new baby in the house, but Jack was bound to ask questions. She hoped he would never learn the truth. Jack lived hand to mouth, a robber, though an honourable one, but she was well aware the one thing he couldn't abide were the whores who walked the streets and the perverts who used them.

Jack sat in his mother's chair, bereft at the loss of his

beautiful wife. He hoped his mother would be home soon and his baby safe and well. He couldn't bear the thought of losing her too. She was the last little bit of Sissy that he had to hold on to. Georgina, a daughter. Funny, he always thought he'd have a son, and Sissy had been convinced she was carrying a boy. He'd have been better off with a lad. He could have taught him how to duck and dive just as Percy had shown him.

He looked across at the old man who hadn't stirred, obliterated with ale. In fact, every time he'd seen him lately, Percy had been drunk or asleep. He had fond memories of the man and respected and loved him as his own father, but worried now that Percy had succumbed to the perils of the booze. He'd seen it all around him; women too, drunk, falling out of the pubs and sprawled in the streets. It was a common sight, the curse of the working classes, but until a few years ago, Percy had always appeared to be better than that.

He heard the front door open and jumped from the chair when his mother walked into the room carrying Georgina, who was now much quieter than she had been before they'd left.

'Is she all right, Mum?' he asked, then over his mother's shoulder, he noticed a nervous-looking red-haired young woman.

'She's fine, Son. We stopped on our way here and gave her a feed. Pop upstairs and empty my bottom drawer. Just put the stuff on my bed for now, and bring the drawer down here, with a spare blanket. It'll make a perfect little crib for this one.'

Jack glanced quizzically at the unknown woman as he passed her, then dashed up the stairs two at a time and came back down with the oak drawer, which he placed on a table under the window.

'Jack, this is Ruby. She'll be taking care of Georgina and staying in your old room. You'll be down here, so you'll need to go and collect your things from home,' his mother said as she lined the drawer with the folded blanket before placing Georgina into it.

He hadn't thought of moving back into his mother's house, but it made sense, though he couldn't face returning home just yet. Mrs Blundell had laid Sissy out, but he'd left his beloved wife all alone on their bed. He hadn't wanted to, but Georgina was desperate for milk. He didn't think he could face walking back into his room and seeing Sissy's lifeless body again.

His mother must have read his mind because she said, 'It's all right, love. You stay here and get acquainted with Ruby. I'll nip back to yours and pick up your things.'

Jack would have liked to allow his mum to do this for him, but he had his pride and knew he had to do it for himself. 'Thanks, Mum, but I'll go.'

'Jack, you have been keeping up your penny policies, haven't you?' his mother asked suspiciously.

'Yeah, of course, but I hoped I wouldn't need it yet.' From the first day he had his own money, his mother had installed in him the importance of paying into the Funeral Club. It hadn't always been easy, and there had been many times when both he and Sissy had gone hungry to pay the penny, but it was better than the humiliation of a pauper's burial. He never understood why, but it held such a stigma in these streets.

'Good, now off you go, and bring back any food you've got at yours. My cupboards are empty.'

Jack glanced at his daughter, sleeping soundly, so innocent and unaware yet that her mother had died giving birth. Yes, she was beautiful, and had Sissy's soft features, but once again, he thought to himself, she'd have been better off born a boy.

3

Weeks later, the sound of Georgina crying woke Ruby from her restless sleep. Her long, off-white nightshirt was drenched again with milk that had leaked from her full breasts. Dulcie had said she was like a cow and produced enough milk to feed all the babies in the street. It was probably true.

Wearily, she threw her legs over the side of the bed and yawned as she rubbed the night's dried debris from her eyes. She noticed the sun was well up, and assumed it must be past nine, then she heard Dulcie clattering around downstairs in the kitchen.

Georgina was still crying, so Ruby quickly changed her clothes, then put the baby to her breast. She loathed doing it. She'd been feeding the child for three weeks now and it still turned her stomach, though the baby didn't seem to notice and suckled happily.

Ruby turned her head and gazed out of the window at the clear blue sky. She couldn't bring herself to look at the child as she fed her. It wasn't her baby. It didn't feel natural. She should be holding and nursing her own kin, and once again she recalled the same memory that haunted her dreams at night. The image of her newborn son, his blue eyes bulging as he fought for breath. There had been no noise, just the sound of her own horrified gasps as she'd pinched her child's nose and held her hand over his tiny mouth until she was sure he was suffocated.

She'd wept when she'd killed him, tears of loss and remorse, and then sobbed when she'd buried his limp body in the lavender fields outside of town. But she'd vowed never to shed another tear and promised God she'd remain childless for the rest of her life.

Yet here she was, nourishing this baby, giving the infant life, when she'd taken away her own child's. This was her penance. She glanced down at the baby in her arms and briefly admired her soft, black hair. She didn't despise Georgina. It was herself she hated and couldn't forgive.

Georgina caught Ruby's eyes and stared into them, but before Ruby could look away she felt an odd tug in her womb. She was strangely overcome with emotion and suddenly felt a need to protect this child. The maternal feelings that she thought she'd buried with her son were suddenly reawakened, and her repulsion faded as love filled her heart.

Surprised at herself, she allowed Georgina's tiny hand to curl round her finger. 'Don't worry, little one,' she whispered, 'I'll always look after you.'

Dulcie was up early and busy boiling the large joint of

bacon that Jack had brought home the night before. When he'd given it to her with one of his cheeky winks, she hadn't asked any questions about where it had come from. As though wanting the best for his daughter, he was proving himself to be a good provider for the family, though it was clear he was missing Sissy dreadfully. He'd been brave at her funeral, but she'd heard him crying at night. It was odd to hear a man bawling his eyes out. She'd never seen or heard either of her husbands or her father cry. Some would think her son was being a wimp, but she understood his pain. She'd felt it herself when Boris had passed. At least Jack was man enough to keep his woes to himself.

Ruby walked into the kitchen with Georgina in her arms.

'Good morning, pet, you're up later than usual,' Dulcie said as she lifted the bacon from the saucepan.

'Morning,' Ruby chirped back. 'Yes, this little bundle of joy didn't wake up 'til half an hour ago. Mind you, she had me up twice in the night, so it was nice to have a bit of a lie-in. Something smells good. I take it Jack brought it home.'

Dulcie studied the small-framed girl. There was something distinctively different about her today. She had been so sullen and withdrawn, but this morning Dulcie noticed a glimmer of the girl she'd first met. The little flame-haired beaten mite, who despite everything her father had inflicted on her, had still managed to be funny, along with having an illuminating smile. 'You know my Jack. Now sit yourself down and I'll cut you off a bit of this bacon.'

Dulcie was pleased to see Ruby's smile was back, and as she sliced into the joint, her mouth salivated. It had been a while since she'd eaten this well and now it was beginning to show on her expanding hips.

'I can't say I know Jack,' Ruby said. 'We live in the same house, but I hardly see him.'

'He isn't around much, but when he does turn up he's rarely empty-handed. My Percy used to be the same,' Dulcie said, 'but those days are long gone and he's in bed as usual. He won't be up 'til lunchtime and then it'll only be for a top-up. Jack's gone off to the other side of the river. The rent's due so he's got some richer pickings in mind, not that he'll divulge much to me, but I have known him to have the odd pocket watch in his possession from time to time. He flogs them to that Jewish jeweller up near the station.'

'Don't you ever worry about him getting caught?'

'Nah, not my Jack. He's too bleedin' sharp. He learnt from the best. You wouldn't believe it now, but Percy was the most successful robbing bastard round here. He's never had his collar felt by the Old Bill, and my Jack's following in his footsteps.'

Dulcie sliced herself some bacon and pulled a chunk of bread from a freshly baked loaf. She'd lied to Ruby, but she didn't want to admit the truth. Yes, she was worried sick that Jack would get caught and thrown in jail. Her son was tough, he could handle it, but she'd have to go back to whoring, and that was something she never wanted to be forced to do again.

Jack's heart was pumping hard, and adrenaline coursed through his veins. He enjoyed the feeling of anxious anticipation before he did a job, and it helped to take his mind off Sissy. As he milled around the smarter streets of Chelsea, he was pleased to find an abundance of wealthy gentlemen adorned in their bowler hats and going about their business.

He'd dressed in his best attire this morning, and appeared somewhat respectable, though he knew he looked out of place and kept his eyes open for the police. If they spotted him, he was bound to be questioned about his intentions.

He knew the place well and was familiar with the alleys and walkways that offered good escape routes. It was an area where Percy used to bring him when he was a nipper, and where he'd honed the art of pickpocketing. He wouldn't be using his childhood skills today though, not now that his hands were too large and clumsy. His days of being a dipper were long behind him, and he rarely came over the bridge from Battersea. He thought it was quite a risk, but as he had family responsibilities, he'd decided to chance his luck.

Jack scanned the streets as he tried to appear inconspicuous. He walked with confidence and wore his flat cap pulled forward and low in a bid to hide his face.

It wasn't long before he spotted a target. A lone middle-aged man, short with a paunch stomach. He was walking towards an alleyway that led to a maze of small mews. This was good. He doubted the man would be capable of giving chase, and he had no cane that could be used as a weapon to fight Jack off.

He began to follow the man and quickened his pace. As he drew closer, he glanced behind to see a woman pushing a pram on the other side of the street. Jack silently cursed. The man was almost adjacent with the alley. If he didn't act now, he'd miss his opportunity. He quickly looked behind again. Thankfully, the woman had stopped and was busy seeing to the child. Now was his chance.

Jack purposely strode up alongside his target and shoved him heavily sideways into the alley.

'What do you think you're doing?' the man snapped indignantly.

Jack opened his arms and caged the man against the alley wall. 'Keep your mouth shut and you won't get hurt,' he growled.

'How dare you! Get out of my way at once... I'll have the police on to you, you filthy scoundrel.'

Jack didn't like to use violence, but this bloke didn't

know when to shut up. He pulled his arm back, then punched the man hard in the stomach as he hissed, 'I told you to keep your mouth shut.'

The man hunched over as he groaned in pain. Jack thought he'd probably winded him, but it'd done the job and stopped him from talking. 'That's better.' He smiled wryly. 'Now be a good man and empty your pockets.'

The wounded man handed over about seven pounds, a pocket watch and a silver hip flask.

'Turn round and face the wall. I know who you are and where you live, so if I hear you call for help, I promise you I'll come back and slit your throat from ear to ear.' Jack gestured with his thumb across the man's neck.

He looked visibly shaken, then quickly turned to face the wall. As soon as he did, Jack ran through the alleyway, and once out the other side he made his way through the mews and eventually to Albert Bridge. He paused momentarily to catch his breath, then with a skip in his step, headed back across the Thames to Battersea.

He'd been pleasantly surprised to have gained such a plentiful haul. The quality watch had been predictable; after all, no wealthy middle-class gent would leave home without one, but he hadn't expected to have profited from so much ready cash. It was unlike men of his victim's stature to carry any sizable amount of money. From what Jack knew, those sorts of chaps did most of their trading on account. Women were more likely to be carrying a purse, but he had his principles and would never knock off a lady.

An hour later, relaxed and confident he'd gotten away with daylight robbery, Jack was in the jeweller's offering his newly acquired watch and flask to Falk the Fence.

'Jack, you are a very bad man!' Falk said as he examined the goods for sale.

'I know, and I'll never get to heaven. What do you think, Falk? Quality, ain't they?'

'Yes… yes… very nice. Very nice indeed. I can give you five guineas for the pair,' Falk offered as he clasped his hands on his glass counter.

Jack spat his words out. 'Five guineas. Come on, Falk, you can do better than that.'

'Maybe,' Falk said with a friendly grin, 'but there's a war on now you know. Six is my final offer. Take it or leave it.'

Falk was the only jeweller in the area who would willingly buy stolen goods, especially high-calibre items, but he chose his customers carefully and would only trade with a select few. He'd once told Percy that he swapped the pinched gear with his cousin in Manchester who also owned a jewellery shop and was a fence too. It was perfect; neither of them ever got nicked for handling or receiving, and they both made a tidy profit.

'Well, you don't leave me much choice, you scheming old sod. Deal,' said Jack, and shook the man's hand. He'd known Falk since he was knee-high to a grasshopper and was quite fond of him. Jack smiled inwardly to himself. The bloke had a huge nose, but it seemed to be getting bigger with age. Falk must be knocking on nearly seventy, yet his dark eyes were as sharp as they had been when he was in his prime. It was known that he could spot a paste diamond a mile off.

'Jack, I'm very sorry to hear about Sissy. If there's anything I can do…' Falk offered as he handed over the money.

Jack tried not to show it, but he baulked at the mention of his wife's name. 'Thanks, but we're doing all right, and I've got a smashing little girl.'

'Yes, I heard. Congratulations. But I do know how you must be feeling. You remember when my Talia passed away? I grieved for many, many months, and still today, all these years later. Do you know, I sometimes walk in my front door and call her name? Huh, silly old man. But you are young, Jack, with a good future – it will be different for you. So, your daughter, what is her name?'

Jack smiled, but it didn't reach his eyes. 'Georgina.'

'A good name of Greek origin, I believe. Maybe one day she will meet my grandson,' Falk said warmly.

'Maybe,' Jack agreed.

The goods and money were exchanged along with sociable farewells, then Jack headed for home, chuffed with his ample pockets of cash. Many moons had passed since he'd been this well off, but he longed to share his good fortune with his wife. If only Sissy was still here to reap the benefits of his day's work, he thought mournfully. He'd have treated her like a princess and spoilt her rotten. Still, he knew his mother would be pleased when he offered up his coffers.

As he turned in to his street, he fingered the coins in his trouser pocket and a thought crossed his mind. He wondered how he could have been so preoccupied not to consider it before. With Percy being the way he was, how had his mother managed to pay the rent for all these years? He'd like to ask her, but he knew she'd bite his head off and tell him it was none of his bloody business. The woman had a sharp tongue, though having Georgina around seemed to have mellowed her... for now.

4

1915. One year later.

Norman Wilcox sat in the Cedars supping his neat single malt whisky as he perused the newspaper that had been left behind by another punter. Britain had been at war for a year now and was suffering heavy casualties. It wasn't unusual to see a young man on crutches having lost a limb on the front line. Today he was reading about a passenger liner, the *Arabic*, torpedoed off the coast of Ireland by a German U-boat. The government and papers were calling out for men to volunteer to sign up and do their bit for King and country, but Norman wanted nothing to do with it. He didn't have any passion for patriotism, nor any desire to put his life on the line for a cause. No, Norman Wilcox was all about himself and how to make the most money with the least effort.

He looked up from his newspaper as Hefty Howard took a seat opposite him. The man was at least six and a half feet tall, and almost as wide across. With his bald head, missing teeth and cauliflower ears, he was hardly an oil painting, but he instilled fear in all who crossed him, and that was the reason Norman had him on his payroll.

'All right, boss,' Hefty grunted. He was a man of few words and little intelligence.

'You're late.' Norman's answer was steely. As Hefty's governor, he had no reason to be afraid of the giant, and Hefty always showed him the greatest respect.

'Yeah, sorry. I got caught up with Carol and Joan having a bit of a set-to.'

'Them fucking whores at it again? I hope you gave 'em a slap this time. Any more from them two and they're out. There's plenty more where they came from. I've got girls queuing round the block to get off the streets and under my protection.'

Hefty lowered his head, and Norman shook his. He knew the man hadn't hit the girls; he never bloody did. He wouldn't think twice about bashing a bloke, and had snapped the neck of one or two, but he never laid a hand on a woman, even the old tarts. 'All right, don't worry about it for now. I've got something much bigger going down. Listen carefully, Hefty, you've got to get this right.'

Hefty leaned forward and rested his huge arms on the sticky table.

'I've got a fucking huge shipment of knocked-off baccy coming in next week. I need you and your cart to be at the delivery point and then stash it in my lock-up. It's coming in at night, on a boat. You're to meet under Kew Bridge.'

Hefty screwed up his large, ugly face and looked

confused. 'Kew Bridge. Why 'ave I gotta take the cart all the way out there?'

''Cos it's a lot quieter than it is round here, so you've got less chance of being seen. Stop asking stupid fucking questions and just do as I tell ya!'

'Sorry, boss,' Hefty answered, sounding like a sulking child.

Norman relayed the rest of the plan to Hefty and then made the big man repeat it back to him. 'Good, you've got it. Now don't fuck this up for me, Hefty, there's a lot riding on it,' he warned. He'd cut a deal with a mate of his cousin who had close connections with a Liverpool gang, the Portland Pounders. They were notorious in the Portland Road area, working around the docks and known for their savage and indiscriminate killings.

Norman had been reluctant to get involved with them. Just the mention of their name was enough to scare even the hardest of blokes off. But the tobacco the gang was sitting on was hot and the local police were actively searching for it. The Pounders knew if it was discovered, it would lead the gavvers back to them. They had to get it out of Liverpool and fast, so were willing to sell it on cheap. Norman couldn't resist the enticement of easy money.

His cousin had introduced him to his mate, and the deal had been arranged. Cash on delivery. It had been emphasised that no connection to the Portland Pounders must ever be disclosed, not if Norman valued his life, or that of his wife and five-year-old son, Billy.

He hadn't liked the threat – nobody from round here dared to take that sort of liberty – but this was too good a deal to lose so he'd swallow it for now.

'Ah, Ruby, look at her toddling around. It won't be long before she's talking,' Dulcie said as Georgina ran on wobbly legs towards her.

'I know, she's like a little whippet now.'

Georgina held up outstretched arms, and Dulcie painfully leaned down to scoop up the child. 'Yes, she most definitely is. Look at the state of this place. She's only been up half an hour and it looks like a bomb has hit it!'

'Oh, Dulcie. You shouldn't joke about things like that. Them blinkin' Zeppelin things frighten the life out of me! Apparently, 'cos they drop their bombs at night, you can't see 'em or hear 'em coming or nothing. Gawd, it don't bear thinking about,' Ruby said.

'Then don't bloody think about it. I shouldn't worry yourself about all that, love. I mean, the Germans ain't gonna bother bombing round here. There's nothing here for them – they'll have much bigger targets in mind. The nearest munitions factory is in Fulham, or that big one in Croydon... Nah, like I said, nothing to worry about. Just be thankful we don't live near the docks.' Dulcie sat back in her armchair and bobbed Georgina up and down on her knee.

'Yeah, I suppose. Talking of which, that's something I wanted to have a word with you about,' Ruby said, looking sheepish.

'Go on then, girl, spit it out.'

'Well... them munitions factories, I hear they're taking on hundreds of women, you know, on account of all the men going off to war. And I was thinking, now that Georgina don't need my milk no more, it's probably about time I got meself a job. I'm told they pay up to three quid a week!'

Dulcie chewed the side of her mouth, deep in thought. If Ruby went to work, it would follow that she'd find her own place to live too. If she was honest, she'd come to rely on the girl more than she cared to admit. 'Ruby, what do you want to go and do something like that for? Yes, three quid a week sounds good, but you'll be working bloody long shifts. It won't be much fun. And before you say anything, don't start spouting off about doing your bit for King and country. What's your King ever done for you, eh?'

Ruby smiled and rolled her eyes. 'Honest, Dul, I wasn't going to mention the war effort. It just seems I've done my job here now, so there's no reason for you to house me or Jack to graft for me.'

'Don't talk daft, you're like a mother to this child. Go if you want to go, but I don't want you to leave, and neither does Georgina. Ain't that right, darlin'?'

Of course, the baby didn't answer but Ruby laughed.

'Seriously, love,' Dulcie continued, 'you're part of the family and this is your home. My bones ain't getting any younger, and, well, I'm struggling, but don't you go telling tales on me. I don't want that son of mine to think I ain't strong enough to give him a clip round his earhole.'

'If you're sure, Dulcie, I'd love to stay. I've never been a part of a proper family before.'

Dulcie could see tears brimming in the girl's eyes. 'Pack it in, you soppy mare,' she said warmly, 'though how you can call this a proper family is beyond me. You've got him upstairs, snoring, farting and belching, and Jack out nicking anything he can lay his hands on. Me, well, we both know what I did. We're hardly upstanding citizens of the law.'

'We've got love, and that's all that matters.'

Dulcie handed Georgina over to Ruby. Her hips were really playing up today and bouncing her granddaughter on her knee hadn't helped. But Ruby was right. They did have love. She wasn't one for sharing sentiments, but she'd grown to love Ruby as if she was her own daughter.

It was late afternoon, which meant it wouldn't be long before the shops closed. The streets were quieter than usual, but there were still plenty of people about, and Jack had become accustomed to receiving disapproving looks from some. He'd even received a white feather from a woman, probably one of those women's rights feminists. Jack didn't mind the Suffragettes, he admired them if anything, but he'd been pissed off with the snooty bird who'd suggested he was a coward by giving him the feather.

Most folk believed a man should be fighting the Germans, but Jack held his head high. He was a lone parent; the army wouldn't want him. In fact, there were many local men who'd volunteered but had been turned down as their health did not match the exacting standards of the British army. What a joke, Jack thought. These blokes had wanted to fight for England, a country that had ignored their needs and had left them to rot in the filth of the slums. Years of malnutrition and a lack of proper medical attention had irreparably broken their bodies, and now they were left feeling further demoralised by the rejection of their own country. Stuff 'em, thought Jack. Stuff them all.

As he turned in to Battersea Rise, a number forty-nine motorised double-decker bus passed by him, and on the other side of the road, a horse pulling a cart jolted at the noise from the engine. But then Jack noticed it wasn't the bus that had unnerved the horse, but an angry-looking mob of men. About a dozen of them. They were leaning into their furious stomp and carrying heavy sticks. Jack thought they were looking for trouble and slouched against the wall of the Bucks Head opposite. He lit a cigarette whilst he surreptitiously studied the gang.

Most of the men wore flat caps, and Jack couldn't see their faces clearly, but he did spot his mate, Clyde, towards the back of the crowd. Jack threw his cigarette to the ground and darted across the road. 'Clyde,' he called. 'Wait up, what ya doing?'

Clyde spun around but continued to walk in haste to keep up with the rest of the men. 'Are you coming, Jack? We're going to get that dirty German.'

'Where?' Jack asked as he quickened his pace.

'Kovar – the baker's. Come on.'

Jack frowned. 'He ain't a bleedin' Jerry... he's Russian.'

Clyde didn't appear to hear Jack's protest and was caught up in the mounting fury of the gang. Attacks against German businesses and their families weren't uncommon. Since the sinking of the *Lusitania* and the use of gas on Allied troops, riots had broken out across Liverpool, Manchester and the East End of London. Now, someone here in the south-west must have got it in their head that Mr Kovar was a German.

Jack tagged along behind the crowd. He had no intention of joining the witch-hunt, but he was sure Mr Kovar's business was about to be smashed to smithereens, and that could mean there would be an opportunity for him to get his hands on something.

Just minutes later, and they were outside the bakery. Frightened customers fled the shop as the bullying men began chanting and swearing for the blood of the man they thought to be the enemy. Then Jack heard smashing glass, and saw bricks being thrown through the shopfront. If he was to acquire anything of value before the looters got on the scene, he'd have to push his way forward.

He elbowed one fellow out of the way, then grabbed the jacket of another and pulled him backwards. Jack had managed to get to the front, but then he saw Mr Kovar being dragged from the shop. Blood was spilling from the back of his head, and he was screaming for the men to spare his wife and children. Several of the gang had run inside and up some stairs that led to Mr Kovar's flat. Jack hoped the man's family had hidden themselves well.

As the men used their makeshift clubs to rain down heavy blows on Mr Kovar's shop and baking equipment, Jack spotted the till. He may as well help himself before someone else did, and there was nothing he could do to help Mr Kovar, not unless he wanted a beating himself.

The till opened easily, so Jack hastily grabbed what he could, then made a run for the door. The crowd blocked it, and though he couldn't see Mr Kovar, he knew the poor bloke was in the middle of the throng and would be lucky if he was still alive.

Jagged shards of glass protruded round the shopfront

window frame, but Jack managed to get through unharmed. He legged it up the street in the nick of time as he heard police whistles piercing the sound above the cries of Mr Kovar's family.

Half an hour later, Jack passed Clapham Junction railway station, overjoyed with the jingling coins in his pockets, though he did feel guilty about how he had obtained the money. There was nothing he could have done to prevent what had happened to Mr Kovar, but he was an opportunist and had taken advantage of the unfortunate situation.

He wasn't far from home and was looking forward to seeing Georgina. His daughter was always so pleased to see him, and with each day she was growing to look more and more like her beautiful mother. He still missed Sissy, and thought he would until the day he died, but Georgina had brought much joy to his life.

He noticed a woman in worn clothes sat on a wall. She had a small child with her, and Jack thought the little girl was probably about Georgina's age, though she wasn't as well fed and chubby as his daughter. As he passed, the woman looked up at him from under her dark lashes, so he offered a small smile.

'Got any spare change, sir? It's for me girl – she's starving.'

Jack had grown up accustomed to seeing beggars,

and he was aware that women would sometimes go as far as to steal a child to take begging with them. Pulling on the heartstrings was a proven tactic for better donations. There was something different about this woman, however, and Jack fished a couple of shillings from his pocket. 'There you go, love, get yourselves a hot meal.'

'Thank you, sir. God bless you and yours,' the woman said.

Jack's gaze passed from the woman's and he found himself looking into the child's sunken eyes. He unexpectedly felt compelled to ask, 'How old is she?'

'She's seventeen months, but small for her age. Say hello to the kind man, Molly.'

Molly shyly buried her head in her mother's armpit. Her mother hadn't been kidding – the poor child was starving. She was a bit older than his daughter but a fraction of the size.

Jack got on his way and tried to dismiss the image of the begging woman and her child. Falling on hard times could happen to anyone. His mother was a typical example. She didn't have a working husband to take care of her, and when he'd arrived at her house, her cupboards had been bare. But she still had the house, and once again, Jack wondered how she'd managed to pay the rent.

5

A week had passed since Mr Kovar's tragic death, and no-one had yet been held accountable for his senseless murder. Ruby wondered if Jack had been involved. It was a bit of a coincidence that he'd arrived home that same evening and given Dulcie enough housekeeping to last a month. She'd never know the truth, as Jack never spoke about his dealings, at least not to her.

She sat up in her bed and pounded her pillow. Georgina was sleeping soundly in the crib Jack had acquired, the house was quiet, but Ruby was restless. She was no longer haunted by the nightmares of her son's death, but she couldn't shake the fear of war. Of all the things that scared her, fire was the worst, and she'd heard horrific stories of people being burnt to death when bombs had dropped on their houses.

Suddenly, Dulcie's loud shrill voice broke the silence. 'Percy! Percy! What the hell do you think you're doing?'

Ruby heard a bit of a mumble from the old man, then Dulcie again.

'You dirty, filthy, fucking useless bastard! I promise you, if it's the last thing I do, I'll stick a fucking knife in you one of these days!'

Next, she heard Dulcie's bedroom door open and footsteps going down the stairs. She listened to the sound of running water, then footsteps coming back up. She was curious to know what was going on and was tempted to stick her head out of her bedroom door, but then thought better of it. She hadn't been on the receiving end of Dulcie's wrath, but had seen the woman's explosive temper on a few occasions.

It was probably best to keep out of her way, just as most of their neighbours did. Mary next door would pop in occasionally, but the woman seemed to be up to her eyes in kids. Ruby had often heard her through the thin walls, screaming at her children, and even yelling at her husband too. But when Mary did call in, she was always very polite to Dulcie.

The night dragged on, but eventually, Ruby drifted off to sleep.

The next morning, Ruby yawned as she stood over the butler sink bathing Georgina. The girl loved the water and playfully splashed her hands.

'Morning, love,' Dulcie said as she came into the room. 'You're up early.'

'Yes, you can thank your granddaughter for that.'

'Did you hear all that commotion in the night?' Dulcie asked.

Ruby didn't know whether to admit she had or keep

quiet. 'Er… yes,' she answered, but didn't ask what it was about, though she would have liked to know.

'You won't believe what that dirty sod did,' Dulcie said as she poured herself a cup of tea. 'I woke up 'cos I felt him get out of bed and wondered what he was up to. He only went and opened up my wardrobe and stood there and pissed in it.'

Ruby raised her eyebrows.

'Yes, I know, that's what I thought,' Dulcie said, obviously seeing the look of surprise on Ruby's face. 'He must have thought he was in the khazi. Honestly, I'll have his guts for garters one of these days.'

Ruby tried her best not to laugh, but the thought of Percy having the audacity to urinate in Dulcie's closet, well, it was too much, and a giggle slipped past her lips.

Dulcie looked mortified at Ruby laughing, but soon her shocked expression broke, and she joined in with Ruby.

'It's not funny – I'll skin him alive, I will,' Dulcie said.

Tears were streaming down Ruby's face now, and their laughter must have been contagious because Georgina began to belly laugh too.

'There's no better sound than hearing a baby laugh,' Dulcie said as her giggling subsided to be replaced with a warm smile.

'She's such a happy little girl,' Ruby commented, and hoped the precious child in her care would never experience anything like the horrors she'd endured herself as a youngster.

Jack walked into the kitchen to be chastised by his mother, the woman ordering him to put some clothes on. Ruby sneaked a glance under her lashes. He had his trousers and boots on with his braces hanging at his sides, but his top was bare. As he went to take a clean shirt from the washing on the line, Ruby pulled Georgina from the sink and wrapped her in a luxury towel embroidered with *Regent Hotel*. The girl became fidgety and reached out for her father, but Jack was busy buttoning his shirt cuffs. Then, to Ruby's surprise, she heard Georgina's sweet voice gurgle, 'Da, da, da, da.'

Jack's head shot up and he looked at his girl. 'Did you hear that, Mum? She said Dad!'

'I did. I knew she'd be talking early. She's not just got her mother's looks, but her brains too.'

'Yes, Mum, she really has. My Sissy would have been so proud of her.' Jack swallowed hard.

Ruby thought it was such a shame that Georgina would never know her mother's love, but at least she had a father who would never hurt her.

Later that day, Ruby had taken Georgina out for some fresh air, though Dulcie didn't think there was anything very fresh about the air in Battersea. Jack had gone to investigate the feasibility of turning over a new delivery company that had recently opened. It had left Dulcie alone to wipe down the kitchen and she was now sat in a living room armchair enjoying the peace and quiet. She loved her granddaughter dearly, but she also made the most of the respite from her.

Her peace was disturbed when she heard the stairs creaking and her husband moaning under his breath. Her heart sunk. She hated it when Percy woke up and got out of bed. Seeing him reminded her of how much she loathed the man, and what he'd done in the night was still seething close to the surface.

When Percy appeared in the doorway she eyed him up and down with disdain. What little bit of hair he had was sticking up. His vest was stained with vomit, and his trousers, which weren't buttoned up properly, had dried urine stains round the crotch. She found him disgusting and wished she didn't have to share a bed with him.

'I want some bread, toasted, and where's my jug of ale, woman?' Percy scratched his head and then his armpits.

Dulcie noticed his eyes were bleary and he was swaying slightly, still under the influence from the whisky he'd consumed the day before. 'In the kitchen,' Dulcie answered with contempt.

'Don't just sit there, you lazy cow, get it for me,' Percy slurred.

'Get it your fucking self!' Dulcie snapped, then turned her head away.

She heard Percy fumbling around in the kitchen, then one of the chairs at the table scrape back.

'Get in here and make me some toast,' Percy shouted.

Dulcie stormed into the kitchen with her blood boiling. How dare he order her around! 'I told you, if you want toast, make it your fucking self!'

'Don't start, Dulcie, I ain't in the mood,' Percy said, then leaned forward and rested his head on his crossed arms on the kitchen table.

'You ain't in the mood? Well, neither am I after what you did last night! You're nothing better than low-life scum,' Dulcie snapped and, unable to bring herself to look at him any longer, she turned and glared out of the window into the backyard.

'Huh, that's rich coming from you... acting all high and fucking mighty when we both know you were quick to open your legs to all and sundry.'

Dulcie's eyes narrowed in anger. 'Whose fault was that? I had no choice thanks to you and your drinking!' Still, she stared out of the window.

'Yeah, well, being married to you would be enough to drive any man to the bottle. I bet your precious Jack don't know about his mother being a whore? Nah, course he don't. I'm warning you now, woman, any more lip out of you and I'll tell him you're a fucking tart! Now, just make me some fucking toast!'

It was the final straw and Dulcie saw red, her anger reaching fever pitch. Without thought she reached out to the stove and grabbed her heavy iron-based pan, swinging it swiftly round until it hit Percy's head with a sickening thud. The force of the blow knocked him from his chair and he lay motionless on the kitchen floor.

Dulcie still had the pan in her hand as she stepped forward and looked over her husband's body. Blood was beginning to pool round his head. He twitched, then jerked, then stopped breathing. She stared down at his twisted face yet felt no remorse. Percy wouldn't be able to tell her son that she'd been a whore. She'd killed him. Her secret was safe. No, there were no regrets, just relief.

Ruby had been gone for about half an hour when Dulcie heard the young woman call her name. She couldn't bring herself to answer and glanced at her dead husband. Moments later, the kitchen door opened, and Dulcie heard Ruby gasp. She turned her head sideways and saw Ruby was staring at Percy spread-eagled on the kitchen floor, lying in a puddle of his own blood. Thankfully, Ruby must have left Georgina in her pram in the hallway.

Dulcie was sat at the table with the pan in front of her, and her voice was cold as she said abruptly, 'He's dead.'

'No... oh no! What happened?'

'I killed him.'

Ruby quickly shut the kitchen door and leaned up against it. She didn't ask Dulcie what had happened, but it didn't take a genius to work out how Percy had been killed. Half of his head was caved in.

'Bloody hell, Dul, what the hell are we going to do? You can't just leave him there like that!'

Dulcie offered no response. She heard Ruby take a few deep breaths, then say finally, 'We've got to get rid of him.'

'Yeah, but how? I've been sitting here for twenty minutes trying to think of a way. We can't carry him far, not without being seen, and you know what a nosy lot they are round here, especially Mary next door.'

Ruby sounded remarkably calm when she answered, 'In the yard, Dulcie. We'll bury him in that loose soil next to the coal bunker. I'll dig a hole, then we'll bung him in it.'

'Nope, that won't do. I've already considered that, but the neighbours would see the digging and get suspicious. Mary's one of them Catholics and is all *Thou shalt not kill*. Gawd, if she found out, I reckon she'd be straight round to the police station, or even worse, the priest!'

'We could chop him up and stick him in the coal bunker.'

'Nice idea, but have you ever smelt rotting meat? He'd stink the place to high heaven.'

Dulcie's eyes followed Ruby as she carefully stepped

around Percy's body and pulled out a chair at the table. 'What about Jack, surely he'd help?'

'NO! Jack must never know that I did Percy in. He loved that man as if he was his own father, and I don't reckon he'd take kindly to me killing him. We've got to sort this out without Jack ever finding out.'

'How are you going to explain Percy's sudden disappearance?' Ruby asked.

'I'll just say he went out to the pub and never came home.'

Ruby nodded. 'Yeah, that would work.' Then her eyes lit up like she'd had an idea. 'I know... that old barrel in the yard, we could shove him in that.'

Dulcie clicked her fingers. 'Yes, but do you think he'd fit in it?'

'We'd probably have to break his legs first to squash him down, but other than that there ain't much of him.'

'Bloody hell, that sounds a bit extreme!' Dulcie said, turning her head in disgust.

'Yeah, well, so is caving in his bloody head,' Ruby snapped.

'All right, point taken.'

Dulcie stood in the back doorway and watched as Ruby tipped the barrel onto its side before rolling it towards her then standing it back upright. She fetched a large knife, and between them, they managed to prise off the lid. There were a few inches of dark, gloopy water in the bottom, but the barrel was intact and after a quick inspection, the women agreed it seemed fit for purpose. They lifted the barrel over the step and into the kitchen, then, in silence, dragged Percy's body closer, leaving blood smeared across the floor.

'Right, how are we going to do this, feet or head first?' Ruby asked.

'Let's smash his legs, then stick him in head first. I can't stand to look at his bloody face any longer.'

The women baulked, but the job had to be done. With only a hammer, it was more difficult than Dulcie had first envisaged, and she cringed at the sound of the man's bones breaking, but they finally managed it. Between them they then picked Percy up, and unceremoniously dumped him into the barrel, pushing and squeezing him down until they could put the lid in place. It had taken a lot of strength and both women were exhausted, but they still had to nail the lid down before they moved the barrel back into the yard.

At last, job done, Dulcie slumped onto a chair, whilst Ruby washed her hands at the sink.

'Thanks, Ruby, I couldn't have done that by myself. And I'm sorry for putting you in this position, but if he ever gets found, I won't bring you into it.'

They heard Georgina cry from the hallway. 'It's all right, she's in her pram. I'll see to her,' Ruby said, leaving Dulcie to survey her kitchen, which was now a murder scene.

There were still the copious amounts of blood to clean up, but Dulcie thought it was funny really. It seemed killing was easy. The difficult part was getting rid of the corpse.

6

The following morning, Dulcie tapped the side of her cup of tea as she stood staring out of the kitchen window. Her husband was just feet away from her, his corpse rotting in the barrel in her yard. Good riddance, she thought, and turned away in revulsion but with a feeling of victory. Her only worry was Jack. She'd lain awake for most of the night and hadn't heard him come home.

'You're up early, love,' she said as Ruby came into the kitchen looking dishevelled. 'Couldn't you sleep either?' she asked, though after what they'd done yesterday, she thought it was a stupid question.

'No, not much. Georgina's still out for the count. Any tea in the pot?'

Ruby sat at the table whilst Dulcie poured her a cup. 'About him,' she said, throwing her head towards the kitchen window. 'We can't change what we've done, we just have to keep a cool head.'

'I know,' Ruby replied. 'To be honest, Dul, it ain't really bothering me. I know I should feel scared and guilty or something, but I don't feel anything. That ain't normal, is it?'

'Depends on what you mean by normal. Let's face it, you've hardly had a normal life. Already at your tender age, you've seen and experienced things that would turn the mind of any of our brave young men on the front line. I suppose it's hardened you.'

'Yeah, maybe. It's not like Percy meant anything to me. I hardly saw him really. I wish it was my dad in that barrel though.'

Dulcie was quite surprised to hear Ruby mention her father. The girl hadn't spoken about him since she'd been on the streets. 'If he ever darkens my doorstep, I'll get meself another bloody barrel and I'll make sure he ends up in it too, right alongside that stinking husband of mine.'

Ruby gulped her mouthful of tea down then laughed. 'I bet you would and all,' she said with a wicked smile. 'I didn't hear Jack come home last night?'

'I wouldn't worry, he'll be up to one of his tricks somewhere. But when he does come home, we'll have to make out we're worried about Percy. We'll say he went out last night and we ain't seen him since.'

'Yeah, OK,' Ruby agreed.

Just then they heard the front door open, and the women exchanged a knowing look. Dulcie trusted Ruby. The girl had proven she could keep a secret; after all, she'd never mentioned Dulcie's former line of work. Jack walked into the kitchen, and she noticed her son looked weary.

'Blimey, what are you two doing up at the crack of a sparrow's fart?' he asked.

'We couldn't sleep, love. Percy went out last night and he ain't been home since. You haven't seen him, have you?' Dulcie asked, feigning concern.

'No, Mum, but I wouldn't worry. You know what he's like. He's probably passed out under a bush somewhere.'

'Yes, probably. You look knackered. What you been up to?'

'Mum, you know better than to ask me questions like that. How's my girl?'

'She's fine, still asleep by all accounts. Why don't you go up to my room and get your head down for a few hours?' Dulcie suggested, hoping to get rid of him. She had no remorse for what she'd done to Percy, but she felt a twinge of guilt when she looked at her son.

'Yeah, I will. And don't worry about Percy. He'll show his face soon enough.'

He won't, Dulcie thought, we'll never see his ruddy face ever again. God forbid, but if anyone did see him, she knew she'd be for the gallows.

Despite being up all night, Jack tossed and turned in his mother's bed, unable to sleep. The night before, in the cover of London's blackout, he'd been about to break into a warehouse when he'd heard a policeman's whistle. He'd had it away on his toes, knowing that at any minute, the Old Bill would be swarming, like woodlice coming out of the skirting boards. Luckily, thanks to the German air raids, the darkness had aided his escape and he'd evaded being caught, finding himself hiding in a small lock-up next to the Thames.

Though he'd been unfortunate in turning over the warehouse, he'd discovered crates of what must be stolen Cope's tobacco in the lock-up. He couldn't believe his luck! He'd left it how he'd found it but had taken twenty-five crates and hidden them directly behind the back of the building. He chuckled to himself. No-one would think to look so close to home – his plan was genius! Whoever owned the stash wasn't likely to search behind the lock-up. They'd expect the tobacco to be long gone by now, and the theft was unlikely to be reported, not when it was already knocked-off gear.

All he had to do now was return but with transport. He couldn't shift all the crates by himself, though he was reluctant to involve anyone else. He didn't have an issue with sharing the profits. It was more a matter of who he could trust, especially as he didn't know who the tobacco belonged to in the first place. After all, he didn't want to step on the toes of any of London's gangsters and end up as a body floating down the river.

He heard his daughter's cries from Ruby's room, followed by light footsteps running up the stairs. It was pointless trying to sleep, so he slung the blankets off and threw his legs over the side of the bed. His mum had a mirror on her dressing table, and Jack caught a glimpse of himself. Gawd knows what Sissy had ever seen in him, he thought, looking at his ears sticking out at right angles to his head, and his wonky nose. There wasn't a day that passed when he didn't miss his wife.

As he opened the bedroom door, Ruby was coming out of hers with Georgina in her arms. The child was now pacified and when she saw her dad, she beamed with delight.

'How's my little princess?' Jack cooed and tickled his daughter's ribs. ''Ere, I'll take her, Ruby.'

He walked down the stairs but had to squeeze himself round the pram in the hallway. That's when it came to him: the ideal transport for the baccy. No-one would suspect a pram! He walked into the kitchen and though he was vaguely aware of his mother talking to him, her words fell on deaf ears. His mind was turning over the finer details of how using Georgina's pram could work. He'd have to open the crates, then fill the pram with the tins and cover them over with the blankets. It would take several trips, but that's when he realised the flaw... A bloke walking around with a pram might look a bit suspicious.

'Are you listening to me, Jack?' Dulcie asked.

'Ay? Er... yeah... no, sorry, Mum. What did you say?'

'I said, would you like a bowl of stew? I've got loads left over from the other night.'

'It's a bit early, but yeah, go on then,' Jack answered, his mind wandering back to the pram idea.

Ruby pulled out a chair and sat opposite him. He found himself inadvertently staring at her as he realised a woman pushing a pram wouldn't be given a second glance. Ruby fidgeted nervously in her seat, and Jack realised it was because he was looking at her. She was still untrusting of him, but after what a man had done to her, it was understandable. The thing was, despite this, could *he* trust *her*?

Jack contemplated more about her. As far as he was aware, she didn't have any friends and always seemed to be hanging round the house. In fact, she'd been very loyal to his family and had done a smashing job with Georgina. At the end of the day, she was unlikely to grass on him; after all, he was the one who provided for the household and fed and watered her.

Norman Wilcox surveyed his lock-up and wondered what cheeky bastard had the audacity to turn him over. But he couldn't understand why only some of the crates were missing. Surely, if someone had the front to break into his place and steal his tobacco, they'd have taken the lot. Oh well, he was grateful for small mercies, but if he ever found out who did this, he'd make sure they paid for it with their blood.

'Why are you looking so shifty, Hefty? You ain't

trying to pull a fast one on me, are you? I hope not, remember what happened to Benny Cuthbert?'

'Yes, guv, no, I wouldn't do nuffink like that.'

No, Norman doubted Hefty would try and rip him off, but the man was dim, and he could guess why Hefty was nervous. 'Or did you leave the fucking door unlocked again?' he asked.

Hefty was jigging from leg to leg and fumbling with his cap in his hands. 'No, guv, I... I... I dunno what you mean?'

'Nothing, Hefty. I don't mean anything. Get this door fixed and then I want the rest of the crates moved to Livingstone Road. Sling Joan out, use her room, then make sure you padlock it. As soon as you've done that, get yourself off to Wandsworth.'

'Yes, guv, but what should I do with Joan?'

'Just tell her to pack her things and to get the fuck out of my house.'

'But... I... erm... I don't think Joan will like it,' Hefty said fretfully.

'No doubt, so if she gives you any lip, give her a slap. The fucking whore is well overdue one anyway.'

Norman knew full well that Hefty wouldn't hit Joan, and he also knew the old tart would gob off at the big man, but it was down to them to sort it out. He almost smiled as he imagined the scene. Joan was a feisty woman, but she was getting on now, and wasn't pulling in the punters like she once did. She was jealous of the other girls in the house and was always picking fights with them.

Norman was sick to the back teeth of the other girls moaning to him about it. They didn't think Joan was pulling her weight, and truth be known, he knew it too. She'd worked for him for years though, so he'd given her a bit of leeway, but years of drinking heavily had ravaged her once firm body. She was nothing but a scrag of a woman now, and he wasn't a bleedin' charity. No, it was time for her to go, and what happened to her from here on wasn't his problem. He was more concerned with discovering who had stolen his tobacco.

7

'Please, stop whining, child! I ain't got nothing for you!' Fanny Mipple yelled impatiently at her daughter, Molly. The girl had been crying with hunger for hours, and her continual whinging was beginning to get Fanny down.

She'd gone without herself to provide a few crusts for her four older children, and now there was nothing left. Her lazy pig of a husband had made sure of that. He'd sooner see his kids starve than have an empty belly himself. She'd have been better off without him. At least she would get help from the government. The poor laws would see to it that she and her children were looked after, but she wasn't entitled to any help because she was lumbered with an able-bodied spouse.

Able-bodied my arse, she thought. Her husband rarely bothered to haul his idle, slovenly bones from his bed, preferring to wallow in what she could only describe as self-pity, though what he had to feel sorry for himself about was beyond her! After all, he'd moved quick enough when he'd taken her and put yet another baby in her stomach. She couldn't believe it when she'd fallen pregnant with Molly. She could barely nourish her existing children, but after several failed attempts at a home abortion, the child had been born. She's a fighter, thought Fanny, and felt guilty for being so abrupt with her daughter.

Mike, her husband, shouted out from behind the ragged curtain that divided the room. 'Shut that fucking girl up!'

Fanny ran to her child and quickly gathered her up, though she knew no amount of love would quieten her. Molly screamed louder.

'Shush, please, Molly, shush…' Fanny whispered in her daughter's ear. She was amazed that Molly even had the energy to cry, as she hadn't had a decent meal in weeks.

Molly wriggled, and continued to bawl, while Fanny paced back and forth in the small dark room. All five of her children slept on this side of the curtain. The four older kids in one bed, and Molly in a makeshift cot. A breeze wafted through the boarded-up window. There was no glass, only old pallet wood nailed to the frame. It wasn't so bad in the summer, but it would be bitterly cold and draughty in the winter. Last year she'd tried hanging old potato sacks at the window, but it had done nothing to keep out the chill.

Once again, Fanny felt a surge of guilt. Not only did she struggle to feed her children but come winter she'd be barely able to keep them warm as well. Three of her kids had coats, which they'd have to sleep in, but it wouldn't be long before they grew out of them.

Molly's cries slowly faded to a whimper. At last, thought Fanny, now she could sit on the steps outside the railway station and hope for a few pennies. Best of all, her husband had no excuse to hit her again. At least he never laid a hand on the kids, but she bore the brunt of anything that upset him, and it didn't take much to trigger him. Fanny had suffered several black eyes because of Molly's crying, and a broken nose when her eldest had woken up screaming with a nightmare. The trouble was, if she was hurt, they'd all go hungry. People were reluctant to give anything to a beggar with prolific bruises.

Mostly, her children knew to be quiet at home, and they all tried their best to stay out of the house as much as they could. Fanny recalled the look of horror on their little, dirty faces when they'd witnessed their father punch her to the ground, all because the siblings had been arguing over something silly. Molly was yet to learn.

Dulcie had been deeply disturbed when she'd looked out of the kitchen window and caught a glimpse of two rats gnawing at the barrel. Acting quickly, she grabbed the mop, then rushed outside and began to frantically pound at the vermin. 'Get out of 'ere,' she yelled, as the rats scattered.

Ruby came running through the back door. 'What's going on, Dul?'

'Rats, two of the little shits. I've got rid of them for now, but they'll be back. I'm sure they can smell him.'

'I'm not surprised – it is a bit whiffy. We're going to have to do something,' Ruby said, wrinkling her nose.

The women went inside and sat at the kitchen table. Dulcie wanted to heave at the thought of her husband's corpse, slowly rotting, but covered her mouth with her hand and swallowed hard. 'I didn't realise. I'm all bunged up with this bloody cold and can't smell a thing.'

'I noticed it the other day, but I wasn't sure if it was the sewers. The stench is definitely coming from the barrel, and there's a lot of flies buzzing round it too.'

'We'll have to dig a hole and bury it,' Dulcie said, trying not to think of the barrel's contents.

'But what about the neighbours? You said they'd get suspicious. I bumped into Mary yesterday and she was asking after Percy.'

'Well, we don't have much choice, do we?' Dulcie snapped, then added, 'If we do it at silly o'clock in the morning, as long as we're quiet, we'd probably get away with it.'

'But what about Jack?'

'He sleeps like a log so I'm sure he wouldn't hear us. It's been raining, so the ground is pretty soft. I think we should dig the hole next to the bunker, where that loose soil is. Is there a shovel in the lean-to?'

'Yes, there is, so are we doing this tonight?'

'The sooner the better, especially as it's smelling,' Dulcie answered.

'I've got to be honest, the thought of him turning putrid in that barrel is really turning my stomach.'

'Me too,' Dulcie said, 'but try and put it out of your mind. Just think about the barrel, not what's inside it.'

Dulcie heard Georgina cry out from upstairs.

'Georgina always wakes up at about three in the morning, but soon goes back down. We could do it then. Once she's asleep again, I could come and get you?' Ruby suggested.

'Yes, good idea,' Dulcie said, and then she was alone with her tormented thoughts as Ruby left to see to Georgina. She wrung her hands, and closed her eyes, but then quickly opened them again. Every time her lids were shut, she saw Percy's bloodshot eyes boring into her own. She'd hardly slept since the murder. Her dreams were filled with flashes of his face, dripping in blood, and she'd hear his voice, derisive and nasty, scathing in her ear.

Even in death, there was no escaping Percy, and now his decaying flesh was plaguing her too. It seemed dead or alive, her husband was her worst nightmare.

'Jane, will you please stop giving the neighbour's cat saucers of milk! The dirty, flea-bitten thing is on the sofa,'

Norman shouted to his wife as he glared menacingly at the ginger tom.

Jane came into the lounge, drying her hands on a tea towel. 'Sorry, it's Billy. He's playing in the garden and left the back door open. Come on, Rusty, out you go,' she said, gently swooshing the cat away.

'I can't believe it's even got a bloody name now,' Norman muttered under his breath.

Billy came charging into the room, and Norman noticed his son's scuffed and dirty knees. A trickle of blood ran down his shin. That's my boy, he thought, admiring the child's strength. He liked it that Billy was tough, and rarely cried, unlike the other Nancy boys on the street who'd go running to Mummy whenever they fell over.

'I'll get rid of him, Dad,' Billy offered, and ran towards the cat with his small fists clenched.

Rusty leapt from the sofa, and with his belly low to the ground, he scampered across the lounge, heading for the door. Billy swung his leg, and kicked the cat, catching him hard under his ribs. Rusty cried out, and Billy giggled.

'Billy, you mustn't do that!' Jane chastised her son.

'Leave the boy alone. You're too soft with him. You don't want him turning into a poofter.'

Billy puffed his chest out, clearly pleased with his father's approval.

'No, but I don't want him being cruel either,' Jane answered.

Norman recognised the look in his wife's eyes. The expression on her face told him exactly what she was thinking. Like me, that's what she means, he thought. She doesn't want her son turning out like me.

Billy ran from the room, probably chasing the cat, and Jane lowered her voice as she said, 'I saw Joan yesterday. She was a right old mess and slagging you off something rotten. I gave her a couple of bob – she looked like she needed it – but watch her, Norman, she's trouble.'

'I ain't worried about Joan and you shouldn't be giving her money! In fact, I don't even want you talking to her. If you see her again, ignore her. Them tarts should know better than to address you. I'll make sure Hefty has a word.'

'Yes, well, Joan no longer works for you. Anyway, I've known the woman most of my life, long before she was at Livingstone Road. You can't expect me to just cut her dead.'

'I bloody can and that's exactly what I expect you to do. I'm not having a wife of mine fraternising with old toms.'

Jane rolled her eyes and left the room, leaving Norman furious. If Joan dared to speak to his wife again, he'd have the whore killed. It wouldn't be difficult, nobody would miss her, and it wouldn't be the first time one of his ex-workers had been made to keep quiet... forever.

8

Ruby was on her way home from the chemist after buying medicine for Georgina's phlegmy chest. It upset her to see the girl feeling poorly, but Dulcie had told her to stop being silly. She'd said coughs and colds were part of growing up, but it worried Ruby. She'd seen too many mothers mourning the loss of their infants and it'd always started with a germ. Dulcie had moaned, saying they could ill afford the medicine until Jack had sold the stolen tobacco, but the woman had softened after witnessing Georgina having a coughing fit.

Ruby thought about the tins of Cope's under the stairs. She'd been happy to use Georgina's pram to help Jack retrieve his haul. It had somehow made her feel more part of the family. They all shared secrets now, though Jack could never discover the truth about Percy.

As she turned a corner, she recognised a familiar face. It was Oppo, a young lad whose mother used to work the streets with her. She couldn't help but grin broadly at the cheeky little street urchin as he hobbled towards her. He'd had a limp since he'd broken his leg and it'd never healed properly.

'Hello, Ruby, I ain't seen you in yonks!'

'Hi ya, Oppo. I know, it's been a long time.'

'Where ya going? What ya got in that bag?'

Ruby tried not to laugh. Oppo hadn't changed a bit – he was always full of questions. 'This is some medicine for a friend's baby that I look after now. I'm on my way home. I live with the baby and her grandma. How are you?'

Oppo shoved his hands in his ripped shorts and stepped from side to side. She noticed the fronts of his shoes had been cut and his toes were peeping through. 'I'm all right. Where do you live then?'

'Just a few streets away from here,' Ruby answered. The boy's blond hair was dirty, making it look more like brown. He had a runny nose and was so malnourished that his cheekbones poked out.

'Oh, right. I'll walk wiv ya,' Oppo said, beaming. 'I'm good at being a gentleman.'

'You are indeed. How's your mum?' Ruby asked.

Oppo pulled silly faces at a little boy in a pram passing them.

''Ere, look, did you see that baby laughing at me. Me mum says I've got a way of making people laugh. She said girls like that. I ain't sure how she is 'cos I ain't seen her for a few days.'

Ruby had always liked Oppo but had never had a lot of time for his mother. The woman hadn't seemed to care much about her son, and it wasn't unusual for her to go missing for days or even weeks at a time. 'Well, your mum is right, us girls do like a man who makes us laugh.'

'Watch this,' Oppo said, and did a silly walk imitating a chicken, which was all the funnier with his limp.

Ruby chuckled, but they were soon outside Dulcie's house.

'Can I come in and see the baby? I bet I can make her laugh too like the one we saw earlier. Oh, go on, Rube, say yes.'

'All right, yes, but don't be a nuisance to Dulcie.'

'Thanks, Rube, I won't,' Oppo answered, clearly excited.

Ruby showed him through to the front room and introduced him to Dulcie. She left them chatting whilst she fetched him a drink and a biscuit. When she returned, she thought Dulcie looked to be enjoying his company.

'Oppo, what sort of name is that?' Dulcie asked.

'Me name's Thomas really, but everyone calls me Hoppo on account of me gammy leg. No-one round 'ere says their aitches so now I'm called Oppo. I don't mind, 'cos Tom is a bit boring.'

'What happened to your leg, son?'

'I can't really remember 'cos I was only young when it happened, but me mum says I fell down some stairs and it broke.'

'If you were young when it happened, how old are you now?'

'I'm ten. I fink I was three when me leg broke. Can I use your khazi, missus?'

'Yes, it's through the kitchen – you'll see the door.'

'Cor, you've got an indoor privy! I ain't never been in a toilet indoors before!'

Oppo charged out of the room and Ruby quietly called after him, 'Keep the noise down. You'll wake Georgina.'

'He's a nice lad,' Dulcie said.

'He is. I've always had a soft spot for him. That story about his leg, it ain't entirely true, though he doesn't know the truth.'

'Oh, what really happened then?'

'His mother worked the top end of the street. I don't think you knew her? Kath? Anyway, she was off her face once and told me that when she was drunk, she'd fallen down the stairs with Oppo in her arms. He'd only been a toddler and his leg hadn't been the same since.'

'Ah, the poor boy,' Dulcie said. 'Go and make him a sandwich. He doesn't look like he's eaten a good meal in weeks.'

Ruby was pleased to see Oppo scoff the food she'd prepared and as he swallowed the last mouthful, he wiped the back of his hand across his mouth.

'That was bootiful. Thanks, missus,' he chirped to Dulcie.

'You're welcome, lad. Where do you live?'

'Me and me mum are in one of the dosshouses off

84

Green Lane, but we'll probably be doing a midnight flit soon. She always has us moving around staying one step ahead of the rent collector. I'd better go now, but can I come back again and see Georgina when she's awake?'

Dulcie looked at the boy affectionately. 'Come back tomorrow and I'll have a nice pie made for you,' she offered.

'Cor, thanks,' Oppo replied with eyes like saucers.

Ruby saw him out, then walked back into the front room with a smirk on her face.

'And what are you grinning at?' Dulcie asked.

'You! You're a big softie really.'

'Well, he's a sweet boy and quite the little charmer. He reminds me of my Jack when he was a little 'un.'

'He is a good kid,' Ruby said, then added, 'Shame the same can't be said about his mother.'

After being relentlessly nagged about the rent money, Jack had at last come up with an idea of how to offload the contraband in his mother's cupboard. Alfred Linehan lived in the flat above the one he used to share with Sissy. He knew the man ran errands on the street, so assumed he must know just about everyone and have plenty of contacts. Alfred wasn't well off, far from it, and he felt sure he could tempt the man into selling the tobacco.

It didn't take Jack long to find Alfred. He soon

spotted his tall, wiry frame hanging about outside the candle factory, and made straight for him.

'Hello, Alfred, how are you?'

Alfred looked surprised, but then Jack noticed the man seemed awkward.

'Oh, hello, mate. Yeah, I'm good. How about yourself?'

'I'm not too bad and my daughter, Georgina, is doing well. We're living at my mum's place. How's your nipper?' Jack asked, trying to sound casual. He wished he could remember the boy's name.

'Stanley, he's four now and shooting up. I can just about keep up with him growing out of his shoes. Listen, I'm really sorry about… you know…'

'Yeah, thanks. I can't say it's been easy. Sissy was the love of my life, but we're doing all right. Anyway, I take it you're still running?'

'Bloody mug's game this. A grown man being an errand boy. Still, it pays the rent. The army won't have me 'cos of my spastic arm, not that I'm bothered. The family who moved in after you have just been thrown out 'cos the army said the old man was a deserter. The poor sod was shot for being scared shitless. The bleedin' government then went and stopped his missus claiming a pension so now she's a widow, homeless and penniless. Seems to me our own forces are worse than the fucking Germans!'

'That's tough, mate. I'm glad they don't want me

neither, seeing the state of some of the blokes who've come home... legs, arms, eyes missing, fuck that. Talking of which, I bumped into your brother-in-law the other day. He didn't know who I was or nothing.'

'I know, it's a shame. Edwin was a good bloke but whatever happened to him in them trenches has turned his brain to mush. Me sister had to chuck him out – she couldn't handle him. I try and help her when I can but it's hard.'

'Tell you what, if you're keen to earn a few extra bob I've got an idea,' Jack said.

'Really, like what? I ain't doing nothing dodgy.'

'This ain't dodgy. Well, maybe just a bit, but nothing you'd get nicked for,' Jack answered with a wink.

'Tell me more, I'm all ears,' Alfred said.

'I've got some tins of Cope's. Somehow, they got lost in transit from their factory in Liverpool and I happened to find them. I'm up to my eyes with other commitments at the moment, so I'd be happy for you to knock 'em out on the cheap and take a cut, say ten per cent?'

Jack could see Alfred was mulling over his offer.

'Make it twenty per cent and you've got a deal.'

'Deal,' Jack said, and spat in the palm of his hand before shaking Alfred's. 'I'll drop off a dozen tins tomorrow, see how you go with that first.'

'Great, I'll see you tomorrow then, mate.'

Jack walked off feeling lighter and as if a burden had

been lifted from his broad shoulders. At least he'd have a steady income stream coming in for a few weeks, and now he could concentrate on a bit of shoplifting to fill the cupboards.

Billy Wilcox sauntered along his street with his two best friends, Malcolm and Sid, following behind. He had just turned six, yet he had the menacing confidence and presence of a boy three times his age. Maybe children feared him because of who his father was, or maybe it was because Billy was spiteful.

As he approached a small group of children playing marbles against a wall, he smiled and enjoyed the sight as they fled in all directions away from him. In the scuffle to escape him, one unfortunate lad missed his footing and tripped, leaving him sprawled on the damp cobbles. Billy drew closer and looked down his nose at the boy. Patrick was a few years older than him, but that didn't perturb Billy. His dad had always told him that the bigger they are, the harder they fall.

'Irish scum,' he sneered as he kicked the boy in the ribs.

Patrick yelped so Billy kicked him again. He relished the boy's cries. They gave him pleasure and made him feel powerful. Patrick tried to climb to his feet and run, but Billy blocked his path and pushed him against the wall. 'You ain't scared of me, are you?' he asked, looking up at the boy.

'No… erm… yes, I dunno.'

'Yeah, you are, you big poofter… Hold him, don't let him run away.' He had no idea what a poofter was, but he'd heard his dad say it.

The boys sprang to the sides of Patrick and each took a firm grip on his skinny arms.

Billy's ominous eyes roamed Patrick from toe to head, then he asked, 'Playing marbles, eh? Did you win?'

'No, Billy,' Patrick answered, profusely shaking his head.

Billy leaned in closer. 'You're a liar,' he said and reached into Patrick's trouser pocket. He pulled out three marbles, which he rolled in his small hand. 'Did you win these?'

'No, they're mine.'

'You'd better have 'em back then,' Billy said, adding, 'Kneel down and open your mouth, then I'll give them back.'

'What?'

'You heard, you can have your marbles when you open your mouth.'

'No, Billy, please… you can have 'em.'

'I don't want your stinking stuff.'

Patrick began to whimper as Billy's friends dragged him down to his knees and Sid pulled on his chin. As the boy's mouth opened, Billy found himself smiling again, this time at Patrick trembling.

'Hold his head,' he told Sid.

Sid grabbed a handful of hair on the back of Patrick's head and yanked it.

'Here you go, I said I'd give you your marbles back,' Billy said and dropped one into Patrick's mouth. 'If you want it, swallow it,' he said, giggling childishly.

Patrick tried to shake his head, but Sid had a firm grip.

'Go on, swallow it!' Billy repeated, still laughing. 'Or I'll shove it down your neck meself.'

Patrick struggled in vain, so Billy tried to grab the boy's tongue. As he did, the marble slipped down, and Billy roared. 'There, you've got your marble back now. Sid can have these two,' he said, then told his friends, 'Come on, we don't want to be near him much longer, we might catch fleas.'

Malcolm and Sid released the boy's arms and sniggered as they walked alongside Billy, leaving Patrick crying behind them. He wasn't the first boy to be terrorised by Billy Wilcox and his young gang and he wouldn't be the last.

9

'I'm glad Jack's finally getting rid of that baccy,' Dulcie said as Ruby pulled her coat on. 'Are you off out, love?'

'Yes, I thought I'd pop up the junction to get some balls of wool. It won't be long 'til Christmas so now that Georgina's better, I'm gonna try my hand at knitting.'

'Good on you. I've got some needles somewhere. I'll have a look for 'em while you're out.'

'That would be great, thanks, Dul,' Ruby said. She felt lighter than she had in ages. There seemed to be an easy, relaxed atmosphere in the house now that Percy was gone. Jack had searched high and low for the man, and asked around, but his efforts had been in vain. He'd resigned himself to assuming the old man had fallen in the Thames or some other ill-begotten fate had been bestowed upon him. He didn't seem to be too devastated by his loss, though Ruby had tried not to laugh at the crocodile tears Dulcie had shed in front of him.

A while later, Ruby felt like a proud mother as she pushed the pram through the bustling streets of Clapham Junction. Georgina was sat up, gawping at the sights round her and her large violet eyes twinkled with innocent mischief. It wasn't unusual for women to stop, look, and comment on the beautiful child in the pram. Ruby would revel in it, politely thanking them for their compliments, though her stomach would flip if she ever saw a man look at the girl. She didn't even trust the men in soldier uniforms; after all, they may be fighting for her liberty but they were still men.

There was a bite in the air, a sign that winter was on its way, so Ruby was pleased with the wool she'd purchased. She was given a small weekly allowance, funds permitting, but she rarely spent the money. She'd managed to save enough to buy eight large balls, all in different colours, and smiled at the picture in her head of Georgina wearing a jumper in soft pink.

Ruby headed up the hill towards the train station on her way back home. She had a spring in her step and was eager to get back indoors in the warm, then she heard a woman's voice.

'That's a beautiful little 'un you've got there.'

Ruby turned sideways to see a bedraggled-looking woman sat on the steps of the station. She stopped to thank her and noticed her clothes were little more than rags and she had a small child huddled close to her.

'Yes, she is, thank you.'

She would have liked to return the compliment, but the woman's child had sores on her face and sunken eyes. Her hair hung in matted rat's tails, and her nose was caked with yellow and green mucus.

'Can you spare any change, miss? I'd be grateful for anything,' the woman said.

The pitiful sight pulled on Ruby's heartstrings. If things had worked out differently, that half-starved woman and her poorly child could have been her. She searched her purse and handed the woman all that she had. It wasn't much, and she now regretted spending so much on the wool.

'Thank you, I'm truly obliged, I really am,' the woman said as she took the money.

Ruby looked again at the waif of a child and asked, 'What's her name?'

'It's Molly,' the woman answered, 'and I'm Fanny. Pleased to make your acquaintance, miss.'

'My name's Ruby, and this is Georgina. How old is Molly?'

'She's nearly eighteen months now. I've got four more at home. All girls, Gawd bless 'em.'

Ruby was flabbergasted. Molly was four months older than Georgina but half her size. She was clearly the runt of the litter. She could guess that this woman lived in dire poverty, but there was no sound of bitterness in her voice, just a friendly smile when she spoke. 'Are you here often?' Ruby asked, deciding that her weekly allowance would better benefit this poor woman and her family. If it hadn't been for Dulcie she would still be living in poverty too.

'Most days,' Fanny replied.

'I'll probably see you again then,' Ruby said, thinking that she had turned soft as she marched off before the woman could see the tears in her eyes.

Ruby's mood was sombre. She'd never forget what she did to her son, but seeing Fanny and Molly made her think that maybe she'd done the best thing for him. Taking his life had tortured her dreams and blackened her days, but if she'd allowed him to live, his life would have been a daily struggle for survival. She knew she couldn't have coped with seeing him suffer.

Georgina squealed and pointed as a trolley bus passed them. She was such a happy baby, and though she'd never know her mother, she'd never know hunger either.

Norman lived in a street in Battersea that housed a mixture of poor families crammed into single rooms, and slightly better off folk who could afford to rent a whole house. He was the wealthiest on the street, and the most feared. He'd have moved out years ago if it wasn't for his wife. The bloody woman insisted on staying close to her friends and family and refused to budge. He may have the locals abiding by his reign of terror, but the same couldn't be said for his wife. She ruled the roost, and what she said, went.

'I'm off out, Jane,' Norman said, and pecked his wife on the cheek.

'Hang on a minute, where you off to? You promised to take Billy to football tonight,' Jane said, and placed her hands on her slim hips.

'Yes, I haven't forgotten. I'll be back in a few hours.'

'All right, but if you let that boy down again, you'll be on the sofa for the next two weeks,' Jane warned but with a teasing smile.

Norman patted his wife's bottom, and whispered roughly in her ear, 'I won't. You're fucking getting it later.'

He pulled the collar of his coat up but ensured his questionably acquired 'King and Country' lapel badge was prominently on display. He didn't suppose any woman would dare to present him with a white feather, but his government-issued badge showed he was a state employee and was needed at home instead of on the front line.

There was talk of conscription coming in soon. All men under the age of forty-one would be called up to fight the Germans. He'd be all right, he had enough *friends* in high-up places to make sure his name wasn't on any lists, but he couldn't be sure about some of the blokes who worked for him. Oh well, that was their lookout. Norman wasn't going to use his power and waste favours on a low-life money collector or bit of muscle. He'd just have to replace his workers and there were plenty of blokes wanting to jump on his bandwagon. War or no war, men still wanted whores, high-rate loans, a flutter on the horses and protection. In fact, business had never been better.

Norman left his house and walked confidently along the street, thinking to himself that it was about time he bought himself a car. Mike Mipple stepped aside for Norman to pass. He didn't bother to acknowledge the man. He was a layabout, yet his wife kept pushing out babies. He had no sympathy for people like that – the sort who refused to help themselves. It was bad enough that Jane insisted on 'treating' the Mipple family at Christmas, but that didn't mean he had to be civil to them.

Norman checked his pocket watch. Hefty should be in the pub waiting for him. It was their regular meeting place, and no-one else dared sit at Norman's table. He never paid for his drinks or queued at the bar.

The pub was smoky when he walked in, but he could see Hefty through the haze. 'All right, guv,' the big man said.

Norman took a seat and clicked his fingers in the air. The landlord's wife fetched him his usual tipple of neat whisky. He savoured three sips before answering Hefty. 'Did you get rid of that shooter as I instructed?'

'Yeah, I wrapped it in a sack with a brick and...'

Norman interrupted, 'I don't need to hear all the details, Hefty. Suffice to say it's gone. I don't want that bank job in Westminster coming back to me.'

'But you didn't do it, the Maynards did,' Hefty commented, looking as confused as ever.

'No, but I took a cut to dispose of the guns and cleaned their stash through my loan business. Do I have to spell everything out to you? For fuck's sake, Hefty, you really get on my wick at times.' Norman liked Hefty, but his stupidity often irritated him.

'Sorry, guv.'

He looked over Hefty's shoulder, and his jaw clenched at the sight of Joan walking towards him. 'Oh no, what the fuck does she want?'

Hefty turned round and saw the woman too. He looked back at Norman like a frightened child, and Norman noticed the man's face had turned beetroot red.

'Don't worry, Hefty, I'll deal with the slag, but if she starts getting lippy, get her by the scrap of her scrawny neck and sling her out.'

Joan sashayed her way across the pub, then stood next to Hefty as bold as brass.

'Joan,' Norman growled, 'whatever it is, the answer's no.'

'Buy me a drink and I bet I can change your mind,' Joan purred.

'Don't try that with me, I ain't one of your customers.'

'I'm dead serious, Mr Wilcox, you'll want to hear what I've got to tell you.'

'Get her a drink, Hefty, but I'm warning you, Joan, if you're wasting my time, you'll be sorry.'

Hefty went to the bar, and Joan took a seat, leaning towards him as she said, 'That tobacco of yours that went missing... did you ever find out who pinched it?'

'How the fuck do you know about that? Let me guess... Hefty?' Norman asked, not surprised. Hefty never meant to do him any harm, he was just thick, and Joan wasn't a stupid woman. He could guess that Hefty had told Joan about it on the day he threw her out of the brothel.

Hefty appeared with a gin and placed it in front of Joan.

'I think I may have stumbled on some information,' Joan said.

'Oh yeah, what sort of information?'

'The sort that I can tell you: not only who is selling knocked-off baccy but also where he lives,' Joan answered with a smug smile that showed her yellowed teeth.

Norman sprang from his seat. 'Get outside with me, NOW,' he barked, then stomped to the door with Joan tottering behind and Hefty following in their wake.

It had been over a month since he'd been robbed, but it still grated on him to the point where his anger would keep him awake at night. Joan came out of the pub, and Norman flew for her. He pushed her up against the wall and clamped his hand round her throat. His face was just inches away from hers as he spat, 'Tell me what you know.'

'Get off. You're hurting me.'

Norman squeezed harder. 'I'll hurt you a fucking lot more if you don't start talking.'

'It's a bloke called Alfred Linehan,' Joan croaked. 'I was outside the Falcon, touting for a bit of business, and I see him selling the tins to a punter. I knew you'd want to know so I followed him home.'

Norman released his grip as he demanded, 'Where is he?'

Joan gasped for breath and moaned as she rubbed her bruised neck, but then had the audacity to say, 'I'm happy to tell you, Mr Wilcox, but I thought you might offer me something in return; after all, I've known you for a long time, and you know I've always been loyal to you.'

'What do you want, Joan?' Norman asked. He could have beaten the information out of her, but he was willing to do her a favour in return for the one she was doing him.

'I want my old room back. I'll work hard, and I've cleaned up my act. I'll even keep an eye on the other girls. Hefty's good at sorting out any of the blokes who don't want to pay up, but he ain't much cop at dealing with the women. You know you can trust me, Mr Wilcox.'

Norman smirked. The old tart did have a point.

'All right, Joan. But if you step out of line or cause me any trouble, you'll be out on your ear. Now, where does this Alfred bloke live?'

10

Jack carried a pigskin bag stuffed with tins but with some of Percy's tools poking out the top. The bag was heavier than he'd anticipated, so he couldn't wait to meet up with Alfred and unload the contraband.

As Jack approached the factory gates, he saw Alfred and smiled, but the man didn't return the gesture. Alarm bells went off in Jack's head. Alfred was always cheery, but today he looked perplexed. Something wasn't right.

Jack slowed his pace. He was just yards away from Alfred now, and he saw the man's eyes dart to the wall housing the open gates. It was a signal. Someone was there. Jack spun round and walked back in the direction he'd been coming from. He hadn't taken more than ten or eleven steps when he felt a heavy hand on his shoulder.

He turned around, expecting to see the Old Bill, but there were no coppers, only a huge man built like the *Titanic*. Judging by the mean line of the man's lips, Jack could tell he wasn't happy, and this was not going to be a friendly encounter.

'Jack Garrett?' the man asked in a deep, growling voice.

Jack thought there was no point in denying it. The

bloke obviously knew who he was. 'Yes. Can I help you?'

'Come with me,' the man replied, and gripped Jack's upper arm firmly.

Jack had no choice as he felt himself being pulled back along the street towards Alfred. Another man appeared, not as large as the one who had his arm, but equally unfriendly-looking. This man was dressed in expensive clothes, and his shoes were shiny. Jack guessed he must be the boss.

'Is this him?' the smaller man asked Alfred.

Alfred nodded, but his head was lowered. 'I'm sorry, mate. They were gonna hurt my Lillian if I didn't give you up.'

'It's all right,' Jack said. He could see these blokes meant business, and he would have done the same to protect his Sissy.

The big bloke grabbed Jack's bag and rifled through it before pulling out a tin of tobacco.

'You can have it, take it all,' Jack offered, thinking that maybe this was just a street robbery.

'That's very good of you, offering me my own tobacco back,' the shorter man said with a sneer.

Jack's heart dropped into his boots. They'd somehow found him, and now he was probably going to get the hiding of his life. He could offer little defence, but he thought he'd try. 'Look, I'm really sorry, mate. I didn't know who the stuff belonged to, and well... I chanced my arm. I'll pay you back, every penny I made.'

'Hefty, you know what to do,' the man said, ignoring Jack's offer.

Hefty dragged Jack further along the street. He knew the area well and soon realised where he was being taken. An alley, in between two factories. His heart thumped hard. He hoped they wouldn't be too brutal and at least leave him alive.

Norman heard Jack's arm bone crack as Hefty yanked it up behind his back. The man screamed out in agony, but Norman thought it was no more than he deserved.

'I've always wondered why didn't you steal all of my tobacco,' Norman said, his voice sinister. 'But all or some of it, the punishment's going to be the same.'

'I... I'm sorry...' Jack managed to groan.

'You will be,' Norman said, and slowly began to undo his belt.

Hefty was still holding on to Jack from behind, and grabbed a fistful of his hair, forcing his head back to watch as Norman pulled his belt through the loops. Norman wrapped the leather strap around his hand as he smiled wickedly to himself, thinking it'd been a good thing he'd sharpened the buckle this morning. With a small nod of his head, Hefty threw Jack forward.

The man landed on all fours and yelled out in pain

again. He'd probably fallen on his broken arm, but Norman didn't give a toss. 'You're already an ugly fucker so this won't make much difference to you, but take this as a warning,' he said, and swung the belt around and up so the sharpened buckle swiped across Jack's face.

Blood spurted, and Jack screamed, 'My eye! My eye!'

Norman looked down coldly at the man who'd had the cheek to steal from him. He could kill him of course, but at least the bloke hadn't denied it. He shrugged. His wife had been very accommodating that morning, their lovemaking nice and vigorous, just as he liked it, and it had left him feeling mellow. 'If you cross me again, it'll be your family that suffers next time,' he threatened, then spun round, leaving Jack crying and bleeding in a heap on the ground.

Hefty followed him carrying Jack's pigskin bag. Their work here was done.

'That was a lovely day out,' Dulcie commented as she watched Oppo help Ruby with the pram over the doorstep. 'We should do it more often.'

'Yes, Georgina really enjoyed having her gran with us today,' Ruby replied. 'I couldn't believe it when you had a go at that woman!'

'The snooty cow was looking down her nose at me,' Dulcie said haughtily.

'You soon put her in her place though, missus,' Oppo chuckled.

Dulcie wasn't listening. She'd noticed some drops of blood on the step, and more on the floorboards in the hallway. 'Jack,' she shouted, her stomach suddenly in knots. She heard a groan from the front room and rushed in to find her son lying on his back on the sofa with blood oozing from his face. 'Oh my God, Jack!' she screamed.

It looked as if his face had been cut in half diagonally from under his ear to across the other side of his head. Dulcie flinched at the sight of his raw flesh, gaping open almost down to the bone. She couldn't see his eye; there was too much blood. 'What happened, Son?'

'Baccy... arm, hurts...' Jack mumbled.

'Don't worry, I'll get you seen to.'

By now Ruby had walked into the room with Oppo, and Dulcie turned around when she heard the girl gasp. 'Get Georgina out of here, then bring me some wet towels... oh, and the bandages in a box under the sink. Oppo, look after Georgina,' Dulcie urged.

'Bad, feel bad,' Jack groaned.

Dulcie fought to keep her voice calm, but she was trembling. 'I'm gonna patch you up, but I need to get you to the hospital or get Ruby to fetch the doctor.'

'No, Mum... no docs. Whisky...'

'Son, this is bad. You'll need proper help.'

'No… whisky,' Jack repeated faintly.

Ruby came back into the room with a bowl of water, towels and bandages. Dulcie glanced quickly at the girl. She looked deathly pale. 'Get Percy's whisky,' she ordered.

Ruby ran to the kitchen and was back seconds later. She handed Dulcie the half-filled bottle. Dulcie positioned her hand behind her son's head, gently lifting it as she placed the bottle to his lips. Jack winced but gulped down large swigs of the liquid before Dulcie pulled the bottle away.

'More,' Jack said.

She fed him more of the booze until the bottle was almost empty. Jack lay back, quieter now. Dulcie dampened a towel, and carefully dabbed at her son's wound. He seemed to have slipped into unconsciousness.

'I can't fix this, Ruby. Get Oppo to run and fetch the doctor.'

As quickly as she wiped away the blood, more seeped from his face. She held the towel over the wound, and silently cursed whoever had done this to her son. She'd find out who it was, and when she did, she'd happily swing for him.

1 December 1918. Three years later.

It had been three weeks since the Great War had finally come to an end. Britain had defeated Germany and was still riding high on the wave of victory, though the country had paid heavy costs. Hundreds and thousands of men had lost their lives. Mothers were left without sons, wives without husbands, and children without fathers. Much had changed. Many women worked now, and some even had the right to vote.

Fanny Mipple was now one of those working women, proud to be a florist. They were still skint, her children were still hungry and cold, and her husband still beat her. But he did get out of bed these days, if only to take her earnings and blow them on the horses. Her four eldest girls had left home, desperate to get away from their father, and though Fanny understood their reasons, they rarely visited her.

Fanny stamped her cold feet and breathed into her cupped hands. Her fingertips were numb, but her palms were snug, thanks to the fingerless gloves Ruby had knitted her. She pulled her matching scarf over her head and shivered in the icy wind. December wasn't her favourite time of year. She loved working on the flower stall in the summer, but it wasn't as much fun in the winter.

'Good afternoon,' a posh-looking gentleman said. 'I'll take that wreath, and a bunch of mistletoe.'

He was Fanny's fifth customer of the day. Business was slow, but Mrs Wilcox never seemed to mind. The woman had purchased the stall and stock from Benny Cuthbert's family when the old boy had dropped dead from a massive heart attack.

Benny's son, also called Benny, had disappeared eight years earlier. It was no secret that he worked for Norman Wilcox, and rumours were rife at the time. Some said he'd run off with one of Norman's tarts and they'd taken a week's earnings with them. Others said that Benny had blabbed to the Old Bill about a heist Norman was involved in. Either way, everyone knew Norman had something to do with Benny mysteriously and abruptly vanishing.

Fanny reasoned that was why Mrs Wilcox had bought the stall. Apparently, she'd paid a lot more than it was worth. Guilty conscience, no doubt. Fanny didn't mind. Mrs Wilcox had pretty much handed the stall over to Fanny to run. She earned a commission on anything she sold, so hoped business would pick up after lunch.

*

Billy's power over the children in his street had increased with his age. Now, at nearly ten years old, his only friends were those who had passed his cruel initiation test to be in his gang. Many boys had tried and failed, and they were now on the receiving end of Billy's bullying. It was known that you were either part of his gang or you'd be viciously picked on. No-one dared challenge him, not even the older kids.

Billy sat on a garden wall and encouraged Malc and Sid to smoke a cigar he'd pinched from his dad. Sid lit it and took the first puff but quickly doubled over as he began to violently cough. Billy and Malc laughed at the sight, then Malc said, 'Give it here,' and snatched the cigar from Sid. Malc took two long drags and held his breath.

'Breathe out,' Sid harped as he watched his friend. 'You're turning green!'

Malc released the heavy smoke from his lungs and immediately threw up. 'That's disgusting,' he moaned as he wiped his mouth.

Billy turned his head away from the vomit. He didn't mind the sight of blood, in fact, he quite liked it, but he couldn't abide looking at Malc's puke. As he looked down the street, he spotted the unmistakable overweight silhouette of Timothy Appleton ambling towards them with the sun setting behind him. 'Look, here comes Apple-weighs-a-ton,' Billy said, looking forward to teasing him again. He was one of Billy's favourite boys to bully. As Timothy got closer, he looked up from the pavement and must have realised he was heading into Billy's path. He quickly changed direction and crossed the street but not before Billy had noticed a look of absolute dread on the boy's face, which pleased him immensely.

'Oi, fatty, where do you think you're going?' he called.

Timothy ignored Billy, and this instantly infuriated him. In Billy's head, it showed disrespect towards him, something he wouldn't allow from the kids on *his* streets.

'Pig face, come here...' Billy yelled.

Timothy began to run, but his large frame couldn't move very fast. It amused Billy to see the boy's fat thighs rubbing together as he attempted to flee. 'Let's get him,' he said to his friends and they gave chase.

It didn't take much effort for them to catch up with Timothy, and when they did, Billy was pleased to see the rosy-cheeked boy was already crying.

'Oi, lardy, don't run away from me when I call you,' he said, and jabbed his finger into Timothy's pudgy chest.

'I'm sorry, Billy, I didn't hear you.'

'Why's that, got potatoes growing out your ears? Nah, course you ain't. If you did, you would have eaten them,' Billy said, and sniggered as his friends laughed.

Then his smile disappeared, and he asked, 'What's the rush then, why were you running?'

'Erm... me mum... she told me not to be late home.'

'You live down that end of the street. You're running the wrong way, fatso,' Billy said.

Then Malc added, 'My brother reckons you must have got so fat 'cos your mother gave you all her war rations. Mummy's boy!'

'Is that right, are you a mummy's boy?'

'No, no, Billy, I ain't,' Timothy protested.

'Yeah, you are. I've seen you holding her hand. Bet *Mummy* wouldn't like you smoking, would she?'

'No... no... she wouldn't.'

'Prove you ain't a mummy's boy then – smoke this,' Billy said and indicated to Malc to give Timothy the cigar.

Timothy's hand shook as he placed it between his lips and Sid struck a match to relight it.

'Smoke it, fat boy,' Billy ordered.

Timothy tried to inhale the pungent smoke but soon sounded like he was choking.

'Give it here, wimp,' Billy said and snatched the cigar back from him. Timothy was an easy target and Billy was bored of him already, but he hadn't yet punished him enough for running away. Then he had a thought that appealed. 'Hold out your hand,' he instructed.

'What ya going to do?' Timothy asked, tears streaming down his face now.

'Teach you a lesson. Next time I call you, you won't ignore me and run away. Sid, hold his hand.'

Billy took a pull on the cigar and looked at the end to make sure it was burning hot. Satisfied, he sneered at Timothy and blew smoke into the boy's worried face. Then, ever so slowly, he lowered the cigar towards Timothy's chubby palm. The boy realised what was coming and cried out in protest, which added to Billy's pleasure. The cigar end was now just an inch away from Timothy's hand. Billy held it there, prolonging the torment, then ruthlessly stubbed it into his skin.

Timothy screamed and tried to yank his hand away, but Sid held tight and Billy twisted the cigar deeper. His nose twitched as he got a waft of burning flesh, and as he looked down at the injury, he smirked when he noticed Timothy had wet himself. 'Go on, you fat sissy, you can run back to Mummy now,' Billy said, pleased with the obvious terror he'd inflicted.

A couple of weeks later, Billy heard the Appletons had moved to a new house in a different borough. He thought it was a shame as he'd been fond of picking on the portly boy. Still, there were plenty more he could lord it over.

*

Since the war had ended, things had remained pretty much the same in Dulcie's house, except Georgina was fast growing up and Ruby was now working part-time in Falk's jewellery shop. The old man was on his last legs and his son, Ezekiel, was primed to take over, but due to his own business, couldn't yet commit full-time.

Ruby opened the safe and locked away two gold pocket watches, a sapphire pin, a diamond ring and three ornate gold scarf rings. Falk now had three professional thieves working for him, young lads, and good at what they did. The stolen goods were coming in fast, so Jack was being paid to do two trips a week to Falk's cousin in Manchester. There, he'd exchange the London haul for the Manchester one, and the police were none the wiser.

'I'm off now, Falk,' Ruby called. The old man was snoozing in a comfy chair behind the counter.

He opened one eye, yawned then said, 'All right, Ruby. Tell Jack I need him here first thing tomorrow.'

'Will do,' Ruby chirped, before closing the shop door behind her.

She said a quick hello to Fanny as she passed her stall, then hurried home. It wasn't the cold weather making her rush, it was the desire to see Georgina. She enjoyed working in Falk's shop, especially earning her own money and contributing to the household expenses, but she desperately missed the child.

It didn't take long for her to get home, and when she walked in, the warmth from the coal fire felt welcoming. 'Where's my girl?' she called and took her coat off then hung it over the bannister post.

Georgina came running from the front room. 'Wuby, Wuby!'

Ruby picked up the girl and kissed her rosy cheek. 'What have you been doing with your gran today?'

'We made a pie!' Georgina answered with gusto.

'Wow, I can't wait to taste it,' Ruby said, and carried the child back into the front room.

Dulcie was in her armchair, but Ruby noticed the woman looked tense. 'Is everything all right, Dul?' she asked her.

'No, Ruby, not really. Georgina, go and play with your doll's house again, there's a good girl.'

Ruby sat on the sofa and waited for Dulcie to explain what was wrong.

'Jack's on about us moving, you know, to a bigger house.'

'What's so bad about that?' Ruby asked, confused.

'Percy,' Dulcie answered, her voice low and flat. 'If whoever takes over this place digs up the garden, well…'

'Oh, bloody hell, they'll find the barrel.'

'My point exactly,' Dulcie said. 'I'll have to pretend I'm a stubborn old cow and flatly refuse to move.'

'Pretend?' Ruby giggled, but Dulcie's face didn't

crack into a smile. 'Yeah, well, Jack ain't normally one to defy you, so it could work,' she added seriously.

'He wants to ask your opinion too.'

'I'll say I'm happy here and I love sharing with Georgina, but I suppose he's getting fed up with kipping on the sofa. We could suggest putting a single bed in the living room. We could throw cushions on it during the day to make it look like a sofa.'

'Yeah, good idea. I'll also say that in his line of work, if we start being flash with money and moving to a bigger house, it could arouse suspicion about where the cash is coming from. Bloody pain in the arse, he is, getting ideas above his station,' Dulcie tutted.

'Talking of which, where is he? Falk wants him to do a run tomorrow.'

'I dunno, love, he never said where he was going. But if he's off to Manchester tomorrow, that'll keep him busy and out of my hair.'

Georgina came running back into the front room. 'My dolly bwoke,' she cried.

Ruby took the broken doll. 'Don't worry,' she soothed, 'go and get your coat and hat on. I'll take you up the shop and you can pick out a new one.'

'Weally? Thanks, Wuby, I love you.'

Ten minutes later, and Georgina was singing a Christmas carol as she trotted along the cobbled street with her hand in Ruby's.

'That's a nice song. Where did you hear that?'

'Gwanny sang it to me when the pie was in the oven.'

Ruby was just about to ask Georgina to sing it again, but as they turned a corner, she suddenly stopped in her tracks, terrified at the unexpected sight of her father walking towards her. She wanted to turn and run in the opposite direction, but fear rooted her to the spot.

His hands were stuffed deeply in his pockets, and his cap pulled low on his face, but he looked up and their eyes met. There was no mistaking him. He stopped in front of her, then lustfully eyed her up and down. 'Well, well, fancy seeing you here. You're looking good, Ruby,' he drawled.

'Get out of my way,' Ruby snapped, trying to hide her fear.

'Don't be like that, Rube, ain't you got a kiss for your old dad?'

Ruby felt sick. Her whole body trembled, and she felt weak at the knees.

'Who's this little one? Hello, treacle.'

Ruby gasped in horror. Treacle. That's what her father used to call her, but at the time, he'd have his filthy hands all over her body. She shuddered at the disgusting memory. 'Don't you dare talk to her!'

'Is she yours?'

'None of your business,' Ruby answered, desperate to get away from her vile father.

'She is, ain't she? How old is she? About four, I'm guessing.'

Ruby went to sidestep her father, but he moved, once again blocking her path, saying, 'Hang on a minute. I thought I'd kicked that bastard out of you, but it seems not. That makes her my child... you done well, girl, she's a looker.'

'She's not yours. She's not even mine. Just leave us alone,' Ruby cried, and turned round to walk away. She'd only taken a few steps, when Georgina screamed, and Ruby felt the child yanked from her grip.

'It's no use denying it, Ruby. I ain't silly, I know this girl is mine, and I'm taking her. I've got rights to her, so don't bother trying to stop me.'

Ruby desperately grabbed at Georgina, but her father's hold on her was firm.

'Give her back!' she yelled.

Her father was dismissive. 'Huh, no chance.' Then he ran down the street with Georgina screaming in his arms.

'Someone stop him... HELP!' Ruby shouted. 'Stop that man! He has my child... Georgina... No, Dad... No.'

There was no-one in the street to help, just an old woman, and a few children playing. Curtains twitched, but doors remained shut. Ruby gave chase. She ran as fast as her legs would carry her. She could hear Georgina calling for her, but her dad was out of sight, and soon, as Ruby ran and ran, Georgina's cries faded to silence.

12

As soon as Jack walked through his front door, he knew something was wrong. He could hear Ruby wailing and Georgina hadn't run up to greet him. He rushed through to the front room, expecting to find something wrong with his mother, but was relieved to find her alive and well in her armchair. 'What's going on?' he asked, taking in their mortified faces.

'Ruby's father has taken Georgina,' Dulcie answered soberly.

Ruby began to cry harder.

'What you on about? What do you mean, taken her?' Jack asked. It didn't make any sense in his head.

'Ruby's dad thinks Georgina is his child, and he's run off with her.'

'I'm so sorry, Jack... I tried to stop him,' Ruby sobbed. 'I really did... I ran after them... but, but...'

'Shush, now,' Dulcie said, and stroked Ruby's hair. The girl was sat on the floor, obviously distraught, with her head in Dulcie's lap.

Jack looked at his mother for some sort of clarification.

'Ruby's been to his house, but he doesn't live there now, and we don't know where he's moved to. Jack, we must go to the police, immediately. The man's a pervert.'

'What? You're telling me some fucking nonce has got my girl?' Jack shouted as the enormity of the situation began to sink in.

'Yes,' Dulcie answered, and broke down in tears. 'We've got to do something, Jack, before it's too late. If we knew where to find him, I'd kill him myself, but we don't. We have to go to the police.'

Ruby leapt to her feet and fled the room. She didn't meet Jack's eyes as she ran past him but kept repeating how sorry she was.

'Fuck the police, they won't be no help. I'll find him myself, and when I get my hands on the filthy bastard, I'll rip him to fucking pieces.'

'How are you going to find him, when Ruby can't? See sense, Son, please, let the police deal with it.'

Jack was raging. The thought of a dirty old man touching his precious daughter. 'What's his name?'

Dulcie blew her nose.

'MUM... What's his fucking name?'

'Henderson. John Henderson.'

Jack ran out of the house. He didn't know if he'd even closed the door behind him, but he heard his mother shouting out to him that if Henderson had touched Georgina, he should kill the bastard. Oh, he'd kill him all right! He'd chop his fucking nuts off first, but he'd definitely kill him.

*

Ruby had thrown herself face down on her bed and was sobbing uncontrollably. She was trying hard to block out the sickening images of what her father had done to her, knowing full well that he'd do the same to Georgina.

How could she have let this happen? The poor, beautiful girl was going to be horrifically violated and it was all her fault. Ruby could hardly breathe; her throat felt constricted as she imagined hearing Georgina's desperate voice crying out for help. Ruby knew her father well. Georgina's tears and pleas would further arouse the man.

She'd heard Jack leave, but even if Jack found him, it could be too late. Her father had probably already hurt Georgina. She rolled into a ball, and screamed, 'No...' The pain, the memories, the guilt. She felt so helpless. There had to be something she could do – she had to try.

Quickly jumping off her bed, Ruby hurried down the stairs, and out into the dark street. Though she'd already vainly searched high and low, she felt compelled to try again. She ran aimlessly, continually crying Georgina's name, not even sure of where she was going. Tears spilled from her eyes, blurring her vision, and after a while, Ruby came to realise she was never going to find the girl in time.

Her father had destroyed her childhood, and now he was about to do the same to Georgina, the girl she loved as her own. It was too much. Ruby couldn't bear it. Even if Jack did find them, she knew Georgina would never be the same again. Would Georgina ever forgive her? She'd never forgive herself. She was supposed to protect the child, yet she'd failed in the worst possible way.

Ruby came to stop breathlessly on Battersea Bridge and held on to the railing as she threw her head back and wailed like an injured animal. She knew she couldn't save Georgina and hate filled her soul. She pictured herself sticking a knife into her father's chest, then twisting and turning it, ripping out his unfeeling heart.

'I'm so sorry, Georgina...' she cried, and stood on tiptoe to look down at the dark gloom of the Thames below. The cold filthy water looked more inviting than living with the feeling of guilt and the wrenching in her heart. It didn't take much effort to climb over to the other side of the Moorish-designed balustrades, and resigned, Ruby didn't stop to reconsider.

In one move, she threw herself from the bridge. Her body felt limp as she plummeted towards the river. 'I love you,' she whispered, her last words, then felt the sting of the water's surface as she smashed against it. As her sodden skirts began to drag her down, she could still feel Georgina's pain and did nothing to try and save herself. The cold water stabbed at her like needles of fire and her lungs ached for air. In one last gasp, Ruby breathed in the Thames water. She coughed, choked, sucked more water into her lungs, then she knew nothing.

The tide took Ruby Henderson's lifeless body. Her short life was over, and Georgina's was soon to change forever.

13

Norman Wilcox looked at the clock on his mantel. It was teatime, and the hammering on his front door irritated him. It was probably one of Billy's friends knocking for him to come out and play.

Jane came into the lounge looking anxious, and Norman couldn't believe his eyes when he saw Jack Garrett behind her. 'Get him out of here,' he told his wife.

'But, Norman, he needs help. You've got to listen to him,' she said, glaring at him, and he knew that look. Fuck knows what Jack Garrett was doing in his house, but if he didn't give the bloke the time of day, he'd be in trouble with Jane later. 'All right. I'll listen. Now leave us,' he demanded and as she left the room closing the door behind her, he turned to Jack. 'You're either brave coming here or fucking stupid.'

'Neither,' Jack answered, 'I'm desperate.'

'What makes you think I'd help you with anything?'

'Because I know you'll do the right thing. You've got kids, a boy and a new baby girl.'

'Don't bring my kids into this. I hope you're not trying to threaten me?'

'No, nothing like that. Mr Wilcox, please, hear me out.'

'Go on then, you've got one minute, then if you're not out of my house, it'll be more than your face that's cut open.'

'I need to find a man. John Henderson. He's kidnapped my four-year-old daughter and I know for a fact that he's a kiddy fiddler. He took her this afternoon, a few hours ago. I've got to get her back, before...'

Norman stood up, which made Jack flinch.

'Come with me,' Norman said. 'Jane, I'm off out,' he called.

Norman grabbed a crank from a console table in the hallway and handed it to Jack. He jumped behind the steering wheel of his car parked outside and told Jack to start the engine. Jack turned the crank a few times, and on the third attempt, the Morris Oxford engine fired up.

'Get in,' Norman said.

'Where are we going?'

'To get your daughter back,' Norman answered.

Within minutes, he'd pulled up outside Hefty's house and tooted his horn. Hefty came running out of his front door, pulling his coat on at the same time.

'Where does John Henderson live?'

'Up the road from your gaff on Livingstone Road,' Hefty answered, looking quizzically at Jack.

'Jack, jump in the back. Hefty, get in,' Norman ordered.

Norman put his foot down on the accelerator. He realised there was no time to be wasted.

'What do you want John for?' Hefty asked.

'He's got Jack's girl and we're going to get her back.'

'Right. Why's he got Jack's girl?'

'Fucking hell, Hefty, are you really that thick? He's a fucking weirdo, he likes them young, very young,' Norman barked.

'Sorry, boss. Can I kill him?'

'Sure, if Jack doesn't kill him first,' Norman said with a snigger.

Norman didn't care who killed the bloke, but he was being taken off the streets one way or another. He had his own girl to think about, and her safety. One less pervert about had to be a good thing.

'That's it, the one with the blue door,' Hefty said, pointing to a mid-terrace house.

Norman pulled up, and all three men scrambled to get out of the car. Without saying a word, Hefty pulled his leg back and kicked the door. The frame splintered, and the door flew open with the first whack.

Jack entered the run-down house first and shouted for his daughter, while a middle-aged man and his wife came out of a room on the right. 'What's going on?' the man asked.

'John Henderson, where is he?' Norman asked.

Jack waited with bated breath for the man to answer.

'He lives upstairs.'

Jack flew up the stairs two at a time, to be faced with three doors. He pushed open the first one. It was empty. The second door was locked. 'He's in here,' he said to Hefty.

Hefty used his massive legs again to bust open the door and Jack ran inside. He knew instantly that the stocky man with ginger hair sat at a table was John Henderson. 'Where is she?' he demanded.

John looked at each of the men filling his room, then spoke slowly, 'I don't know what you're talking about.'

Jack sprang forward and grabbed the man round his throat. 'You fucking liar! I know you've got her... Where is she?'

John didn't speak.

'Tell me!' Jack yelled.

Jack couldn't see what was going on behind him, but Norman had opened a small wardrobe and called, 'Jack, Jack!'

The urgency in Norman's voice caused Jack to let go of John's neck, and he turned to see Georgina curled in the bottom of the wardrobe. Her hands and feet were tied, and an old rag gagged her mouth. He could see her dark lashes glistening with tears, and a look of pure terror in her eyes. In three steps he was across the room, then worked frantically on undoing the knots that bound his daughter. 'It's all right, darling, Daddy's here now.'

'You see to her, Jack. Wait for us in the car. We'll sort out Mr Henderson,' Norman said.

Jack looked at Norman's face, and saw sincerity. Once Georgina's arms were free, she threw them around his neck, clinging to him like her life depended on it while whimpering in his ear. He noticed her undergarments were missing, and she had dried blood smeared on her thighs. Anger surged. He wanted to beat the man to pulp, but knew he had to get his daughter out of there. He walked towards the smashed-in door but turned to John with a look of hatred.

He wanted to remember the man's face, for he knew by the time he'd reached Norman's car, John Henderson would be dead.

PART 2

THE REBIRTH OF GEORGINA GARRETT

14

April 1923. Four years later.

'I wish you wouldn't make Georgina look like a boy,' Dulcie said for the umpteenth time. 'She's such a beautiful girl, but I'm sure all the neighbours think I've got a grandson.'

'I don't know how many times I've got to tell you, please stop calling her Georgina. Her name is George, end of discussion.'

Dulcie could tell her son was becoming irritated, so once again she dropped the subject.

She'd been so disappointed when Jack had brought Georgina home with her beautiful black hair clipped so short that Dulcie could see the girl's scalp. He'd done it the day after John Henderson had kidnapped her, and on that same day, he'd thrown out all her little dresses and insisted that, from then on, she'd be known as George.

At the time, Dulcie could understand her son's reaction. She didn't blame him for wanting to protect his daughter and making her look like a boy seemed logical. But it was almost four years on, Georgina was nearly eight years old, yet still she was dressed in short trousers, a shirt and braces.

'Are you taking her out with you again today?' Dulcie asked.

'Yes, and I suppose you've got something to say about that too?'

'Granted, it's a Saturday, but the rest of the week, she should be in school. She's your daughter, I suppose, so you bring her up as you see fit.'

'Exactly, Mum, she is *my* daughter, so I'd appreciate you winding your neck in. Anyway, you've taught her to read and write, so what bleedin' use is school to her?'

Dulcie didn't answer. She knew anything she said would be a waste of breath. Whatever had happened to Georgina the day she'd been abducted had changed the girl, and Jack too. Georgina had become quiet, withdrawn, and Jack was now quick to lose his temper. He'd often fly into a rage at the drop of a hat, and seeing his anger unnerved her. She couldn't abide to see Georgina looking like a lad and out thieving with Jack, but she bit her tongue, fearful of triggering another of his outbursts. Though Mary knew better than to mention it, she guessed her neighbour must hear everything. It wouldn't do for the woman to think that Dulcie had gone soft.

She heard her son slam the front door and sneaked a look through her net curtains. He had a pace on and little Georgina was trotting alongside to keep up with him. He threw a look over his shoulder back at the house and once again, Dulcie was reminded of the atrocious attack on him. Years had passed, yet she still hadn't got used to his horrific scar. The poor boy had lost the sight in his left eye too, though it didn't seem to affect him. Thank goodness Alfred had brought him home that day. Norman bloody Wilcox may have saved Georgina, and for that she was grateful, but she'd never forgive him for hurting her son.

Jack marched down the street, pleased to be away from his interfering mother. The old girl meant well, but she got on his nerves, always moaning and nagging about George. He'd never let another man hurt his daughter, and if it meant disguising her as a boy, then so be it.

'Keep up,' Jack shouted over his shoulder to George.

She picked up her pace until she was walking alongside him.

'Where are we going today, Dad?'

'There's some toffs living up near the park, but I bet they're all out lining the streets of London to get a glimpse of Albert and Elizabeth.'

'What, are we going to watch the royal wedding too?'

'Nah, don't be daft. Why would we want to do something like that? No, we're going to make the most of today.'

'Aw, I'd have loved to have seen her wedding dress,' George said glumly.

'Bugger that, but if you do good today, I'll let you go

to the corner shop later and you can buy yourself some sweets.'

George beamed broadly up at her father, and Jack smiled back. He rarely allowed her to venture outside the house alone, but he knew it was time to give her some freedom.

Twenty minutes later, they were in a quiet tree-lined avenue of semi-detached houses with immaculately tiled front paths, and large, Edwardian bay windows.

'Cor, it's nice here,' George commented, looking at the smart homes.

'Bit too quiet for my liking,' Jack said, though today that suited him fine. 'Wait here and keep a look out for any nosy neighbour curtain-twitching,' he added, instructing George to stay behind one of the trees.

Next, Jack walked up the clean blue and white tiled pathway of one of the houses, and boldly rang the doorbell. As he'd hoped, nobody answered. He went back to Georgina and indicated for her to walk with him. 'Did you see anything?' he asked.

'No, I reckon the whole bloody street must be up town today.'

'Oi, language. Your gran would have your guts for garters if she heard you swearing. Right, round the back here,' Jack said, then dashed into the narrow walkway between two of the homes.

He gave a leg-up to Georgina, who swiftly climbed

over the back-garden fence then opened the sliding bolt on the gate for Jack to get in.

'Well done,' he said, 'keep quiet.'

They cautiously approached the rear of the house. When Jack was sure there was no movement from within, he picked George up and lifted her towards the roof of the back porch. She was used to burgling with her dad and didn't require instructions on what to do. With the strength of a boy twice her age, she pulled herself up onto the roof. She carefully edged her way over, then reached up to a small window.

'It's closed, Dad, pass me the crowbar.'

Jack stood on tiptoe with his arm extended as he handed his daughter the tool. She was well accomplished, and within minutes, she'd jemmied the window and was inside the house.

Jack waited nervously for George to open the back door. It was handy having her as his partner in crime as she could fit into the smallest of gaps and windows.

'I did it,' George said proudly when she opened the back door, 'and you wait 'til you see what they've got in here!'

Jack stepped into the house, delighted as he surveyed the array of polished silver on display, as well as several art-deco bronze ornaments that seemed to be all the fashion with *the bright young things*. He couldn't get his head around these wealthy youngsters nowadays. He'd seen plenty of rough women in his time, drinking, smoking, swearing and fighting, but this middle-class lot were supposed to be ladies, yet here they were, all over the papers, driving cars and wearing dresses above their knees. He was all for progression but it seemed to him that a lady of a certain class should be just that – a lady. Not out gallivanting in jazz clubs and acting like a man.

Jack quickly dismissed his thoughts. It was all right for the rich to lead a lifestyle of debauchery but in the meantime, his family was still living amongst the slums and there were no luxuries afforded to them if he didn't acquire them. He wasted no time, and quickly flew around the house stuffing any item of value into a sack. He thought the bronze works would be too heavy, so gave them a miss. In the meantime, George had gone upstairs, and he knew she'd be looking for the jewellery.

Once Jack had filled his sack and George had come back downstairs with her pockets bulging with gold, they made a run for the back door, out of the garden, along an alley then into a small field. There, they both paused for breath and fell about laughing.

'That was a doddle,' Jack said.

'Too right. Wait 'til Ezzy sees what we've got!'

Ezekiel was Falk's son and had taken over his father's jewellery shop, but George could never pronounce his name when she was younger and now affectionately called him Ezzy.

'Come on, let's get home and sort through it all. Ezzy won't touch the silver, but I know a man who will.'

George trotted along happily next to her dad, humming a cheerful tune. She was herself around him, talkative and funny. She seemed to be fine with Ezzy too and Oppo was like a big brother to her. But most other men appeared to frighten her, and she'd sink into her shell. Even Norman scared her, yet he'd helped to save her life.

Jack hoped that teaching her to box would give her more confidence. She could certainly pack a punch and had winded Hefty last week, narrowly missing his crotch. It had given them all a good laugh, except Billy. Jack had noticed the teenager watching from a distance, with an eerie smouldering expression and his steely eyes fixed on George. Billy Wilcox was trouble, Jack could feel it, but if he came near his daughter, the boy would live to regret it.

Later that day, George wanted to skip back from the sweetshop, but her father had warned her about skipping. Only girls acted like that, not tough boys, he'd told her, so instead, she walked while filling her mouth with a black jack. She enjoyed going to the corner shop alone. It was a rare treat her dad had only allowed her since he'd taught her how to fight. 'Stay out of trouble,' he'd warned, 'and make sure if any strange men talk to you, you punch 'em in the nuts and run back home as fast as you can.' She'd agreed, but she didn't know what nuts he was talking about.

As she rounded a corner, she saw Billy Wilcox towering over what she first thought was a pile of old clothes against a garden wall and wondered what he was up to. She didn't like Billy. He always pinched her when nobody was looking and said if she told, he'd set her house on fire and burn her gran to a crisp.

She drew closer and went to cross the road to avoid Billy but to her horror, she noticed the pile of clothes was a girl about her own age. She was hunkered down, and whimpering with Billy sniggering at her. George instantly stuffed her bag of sweets into her trouser pocket and ran towards them. 'What do you think you're doing, Billy?' she asked, as she grabbed his arm.

'She smells like shit. She must be a toilet so I'm going to use her like one.'

George stood horrified as Billy began to unbutton his trousers. 'Come on, George, piss on her,' he sneered.

'Leave her alone!'

'What's the matter, George? Too chicken?'

'No, I ain't chicken, but you can't do that!'

'I can do whatever I want,' Billy answered as he pulled his penis from his trousers.

George peered at the strange-looking thing in Billy's hands, then quickly stepped round him and yanked the girl to her feet.

'Ha, I bet you ain't got a John Thomas,' Billy sniggered. 'That's it, ain't it? You don't piss out of a dick... fucking weirdo.'

No, she didn't piss out of a dick and felt strangely confused, but ignoring Billy's remarks, she said to the girl, 'Come on,' and dragged her along the street.

'I hate Billy Wilcox,' the girl cried as she ran to keep up with George.

'I can't say I like him either. My dad and his dad are friends. I'm George, what's your name?'

'Molly, Molly Mipple. I live on the same street as him, but he's always mean to me. Thank you for sticking up for me. You're lucky Billy didn't punch your lights out!'

'He could try but I ain't scared of him,' George answered, full of bravado.

'I am and so are all the other kids on my street.'

'Well, you ain't got to be no more, I'll look after you,' George said and smiled down at her new friend. 'Billy's right though, you do whiff a bit.'

'I know, but that's his blinkin' fault. He pinched me shovel last week.'

'What do you need a shovel for?'

'Me mum gets me to follow the coal man and pick up the horse's shit. I can get a sack-load sometimes,' Molly answered proudly. 'Then me and me sister take it down to the allotments. They like it; they say it makes their veg grow bigger. I give them the manure and they give me some veg. At least we know we're gonna get a good meal once a week.'

George got the impression that Molly's family were very poor and felt sorry for the girl.

''Cos Billy took me shovel, I was trying to scoop up the manure with a tin plate, but then he came along and pushed me into it and threw me sack over a wall. That's why I smell like something that's come out of an 'orse's backside.'

If it hadn't been so horrendous for Molly, George would have giggled, but instead she asked, 'Do you want to come to my house? You can share my sweets, if you like.'

Molly nodded, 'Yes, all right, I've got to stay out of my dad's way, so I can't go home yet anyway.'

As they walked along chatting, George noticed Molly's skirt was ripped in several places. No wonder she'd thought the girl was a pile of rags. Even though the skirt was faded, she admired the pretty flowery design and wished her dad would allow her to wear clothes like it. He seemed to become angry with her whenever she asked, so she'd given up trying and accepted the short trousers and shirts. At least she could climb well in them, which as her dad had said, was handy in their line of work.

15

On Sunday morning, Mike Mipple rolled over in his bed to be confronted with his wife's massive stomach. The bloody woman was pregnant again, and judging by the size of her, she'd drop it any day soon. Feeling repulsed at the sight of her, he climbed out of the bed and stomped over to an old rocking chair where she'd thrown her clothes the night before. It was Sunday, her one day off from the flower stall, so she'd be hanging around the house all day. He couldn't stand the thought of having to look at her belly heavy with child.

He heard his wife groan as she stirred, then she asked, 'What are you doing?'

'Where's your purse?'

'No, Mike, please. You've already had all my earnings this week. I've only got a few pennies left and I need that to feed the kids.'

Fanny's squeaky voice grated on him. She was always mithering about feeding the bloody children or putting clothes on their backs. This wasn't what he signed up for when he'd married her. She'd been fun and carefree in those days, but now she'd become nothing but an old nag. 'Fuck the kids, just tell me where your purse is, woman!' he yelled, irritated and desperate to get away from her.

'It's in my shoe, under the chair,' Fanny answered quietly.

'Oh, I see, trying to hide it again. What 'ave I told you about being sly with me?'

Fanny lowered her eyes. 'I'm sorry, Mike.'

'Yeah, well, you try that again and you will be.'

He found the purse and quickly emptied the contents, stuffing the coins into the pocket of his wrinkled trousers, then he threw on the shirt he'd worn for nearly two weeks, a waistcoat, and flat cap, then stomped towards the door.

As the door closed behind him, he heard Fanny call out, 'Where are you going?'

'Out,' he mumbled under his breath. It was none of her fucking business, but he was off to visit a pretty new girl who Joan had recently taken on in the brothel on Livingstone Street.

Norman had cleared his plate of a hearty breakfast served up by his wife, and was now sat in his comfortable lounge, bored, but thankful it was Sunday. It had been a busy week. The Portland Pounders had delivered five dozen cases of counterfeit whisky, along with nearly a thousand pounds for cleaning. He'd sampled the whisky, and though it was labelled as a high-quality Scottish single malt, Norman could taste it was anything but. In fact, he was sure the bloody stuff was lethal. He hadn't wanted to touch the booze, but the Pounders weren't the sort of blokes to say 'no' to. His biggest problem now would be unloading the stuff. He didn't want his reputation ruined by selling it on to his local pubs, or risk repercussions from passing it on to any rivals up West. He was stuck with it for now and would have to take the small loss on the chin.

'You've got to have a word with that son of yours,' Jane said as she walked into the lounge with her blue eyes glaring and carrying his baby daughter.

Norman looked his wife up and down. She'd kept a trim figure even after birthing him three children. Her blonde hair was cut short to her neck, emphasising her high cheekbones and small, upturned nose. She was an attractive woman, but he'd rip the eyes out of any men who dared to look at her. 'What's he done now?'

'He's picking on Sally again. She's locked herself in the bathroom to get away from him, but he's rummaging through your tools looking for a screwdriver to undo the lock. I've told him to leave her alone, but he won't take any notice of me.'

'Tell him I want to see him,' Norman answered, and sighed. That was the end of his peace and quiet.

A few minutes later Billy ambled into the lounge and slumped onto the sofa.

'Your mother said you're bullying your sister again?'

'She asked for it, Dad! She barged in my room and stuck her tongue out at me.'

'Did she? I see. So, you're thirteen years old, but you're going to bash your five-year-old sister because she teased you?'

'I've warned her before, she needs a slap,' Billy answered coldly.

Norman sucked in a deep breath as his anger instantly rose. 'I'm the only man who will ever lay a hand on that child! You never, never hit the girls in this family, is that clear?'

Billy didn't answer.

'I said, is that clear?'

'Yes,' he finally replied, but Norman heard the bitterness in his son's voice.

'Now you get yourself out of this house. Go round to Tommy Marston's, ask for his Kenny then you kick the shit out of the boy.'

'But, Dad, Kenny Marston is older than me and twice the size.'

'So am I, so do as you're told. Go on, fuck off, and don't come back here 'til you've bashed the Marston boy good and proper. And a word of warning, if you let him get the better of you, I'll take my belt to you.'

Norman saw a look of fear flash through his son's eyes. It was the only emotion Billy ever showed, and even that was rare. But the threat of the belt was sure to provoke a reaction, as Billy knew how much damage the sharpened buckle could do. Granted, Norman had never whipped his son with it, but Billy had witnessed many men feel its force.

Billy slowly got up and headed for the door. Norman could see his son was reluctant to follow his instructions, but he had to teach the boy a lesson in bullying. If he didn't, he'd never hear the last of it from Jane.

George answered the front door and was pleased to see her new friend on the step.

'Hello, are you coming out to play?' Molly asked.

George would have really liked to, but though she was allowed to walk to the shop and back, her father had never granted her permission to play outside on the street. 'I'm not sure,' she replied. 'Hang on and I'll ask my dad.'

George left the door open and called up the stairs. 'Dad, can I go out and play with Molly, please?'

'No, not today, we're going round to Norman's later for Sunday dinner.'

George's shoulders slumped. It was the last thing she wanted to do, especially as Oppo was bringing a new catapult with him today.

'Please, Dad? Just for a while... I'll be back soon,' George pleaded, and as she saw her dad coming down the stairs, she stuck out her bottom lip and made her face look sulky.

'What's all this fuss about?' her gran asked as she hobbled into the hallway.

'I want to go out and play with Molly but me dad says I can't 'cos we're having dinner at Norman's.'

'No wonder you've got a face like a smacked arse, I wouldn't want to go to Norman's for dinner either,' her gran answered, then looked over George's shoulder and said, 'Hello, love,' to Molly.

'Good job you weren't invited then,' her dad snapped at her gran as he squeezed past her in the narrow hallway.

'Can't you let the girl go out for a while? What harm would it do?'

Her father stood still, with his back to them, and George looked at his broad shoulders. She saw him inhale a deep breath and crossed her fingers in the desperate hope that he'd agree. Then before he walked into the kitchen, he turned to her and said, 'Go on then, but I want you back here by one, do you understand?'

George gasped, and feeling excited, answered, 'Yes, yes, Dad, I will be... thanks,' and quickly dashed out of the door before he could change his mind.

She grabbed Molly's hand and ran as she pulled her along the street. Once at the end and round the corner, George stopped and released the girl's hand. 'He can't call me back indoors now,' she laughed.

'George, did I hear your gran call you a girl?' Molly asked with her brow knitted.

'Yeah, that's because I am a girl but me dad likes me to be a boy.'

'Oh!' Molly exclaimed looking surprised.

'Did you think I was a boy?'

'Yes, you've got short hair and your clothes...'

'I can fight like one and all; in fact, I could beat up all the boys round here. My dad taught me how to box.'

'You're so lucky. I wish I had a dad like yours. Why does he want you to be a boy?'

'I dunno, I suppose 'cos he wanted one but got me instead.'

'Ain't you bothered that you look like a boy?'

'No, not really. Me dad says girls are weaklings and he's right.'

'I don't care if you're a boy or a girl, you're still my best friend.' Molly smiled, and linked her arm through George's. 'Let's go to my house and get Ethel. She's my sister – you'll like her. She's a bit backward but she's fun to play with.'

George nodded and happily walked along the street with her pal. Molly was the first friend of her own age that she'd ever had. It felt special, she liked it and felt comfortable confiding in the girl. 'I'll tell you a secret, but you've got to promise not to tell,' she said with a proud grin.

'I promise, George, cross my heart and hope to die.'

'I go out nicking with me dad. We break into posh houses and everything!'

'Blimey, don't you get scared?'

'Nah, it's easy. Now you tell me a secret...'

Molly's expression changed. She looked sad and now George wished she hadn't asked.

'My dad hits my mum,' she said and dashed away a tear.

'That's horrible. Does he hit you too?'

'No, but I reckon he would if my mum didn't stick up for us.'

'If he ever does, I'll beat him up, Molly, I swear,' George said, and in her heart, she meant it.

A short time later, they turned onto Billy's street, and Molly stopped at a house that looked derelict. 'This is home,' she said quietly, looking slightly embarrassed.

George noticed the windows were boarded up, and the front door had seen better days.

'Let me check if my dad's home, I won't be a minute,' Molly whispered.

George waited outside, but Molly was quick to open the door again.

'It's all right, he's out. Come in.'

She was reluctant to go inside, but she didn't want to hurt Molly's feelings. As soon as she walked in, the musty smell of damp overwhelmed her. Faded wallpaper hung from the hallway walls, and George spotted rat droppings on the floor. She'd seen them in their own backyard before, and her gran had been livid, calling them filthy vermin. She'd never expected to see droppings inside someone's house!

Molly opened a door to the right. 'This is where we live. Me, Mum, Dad, and Ethel. Mum's got another one on the way, but I hope it's a boy this time.'

George couldn't believe how cold and dark the room was. A tattered curtain separated two double beds, but apart from a cot, a chair, and a rickety-looking cupboard, the room was bare. She'd already felt sorry for Molly, dressed in tatty clothes, but now her heart went out to her.

'I know what you're thinking,' Molly said quietly, 'it ain't a patch on your house.'

'Molly!' a voice shouted, and George turned to see a girl running down the stairs. She looked older than Molly and George could tell there was something odd about her.

'Slow down, Ethel, and mind the third step, you know it ain't there,' Molly called, then when her sister reached the bottom, she added, 'This is my friend George.'

'Hello, George, I is Ethel and I'm a big girl, ain't I, Molly?'

'Yes, you are,' Molly said, her eyes full of affection for her older sister. 'Where's Mum?'

'She said she was going up the fields outside town to see if she could find some rhubarb. She told me to stay here 'cos I slow her down but to hide at the top of the stairs in case Dad comes home.'

'If she's out looking for rhubarb again, it means we ain't got no dinner tonight,' Molly said to George and rolled her eyes.

'I thought you told me your mum works on a flower stall?' George asked, curious to know why there was no food in the house.

'She does, but it's me dad. He takes all the money and Mum says he pisses it up the wall.'

George wasn't sure what Molly meant, but she was sure not to lean against any of the walls in case Molly's dad had peed on them. Now she understood why the house smelt so bad.

'Do you want to play hopscotch?' Molly asked Ethel.

Ethel nodded enthusiastically and grabbed a coat off the bed. When she put it on, George noticed it was short in the arms and the material was stretched across her back. Her legs were bare, and the sole of her shoe flapped when she walked. George wished she could have given Ethel her clothes, but she knew if she did, her gran would do her nut. Anyway, at least the girl had shoes. George had seen plenty who didn't.

'I need to use the privy, Molly, will you wait for me?' Ethel asked, as she jigged from one foot to the other.

'Yes, go on then, but be quick and make sure you wash your hands with the carbolic soap,' she answered and as Ethel ran off, Molly turned to George. 'We have to use the privy out the back two doors down. With them upstairs, and three families crammed into next door, there's about eighteen of us sharing it. Me mum worries it'll make us ill and has a right go at us if we don't wash our hands after.'

'What do you do if you want to go in the middle of the night?'

'Hold it or be dead quiet. Me dad has a bucket, but he won't let us do our business indoors. Bleedin' thing stinks sometimes and me mum has to empty it. Mind you, it don't smell as rotten as the privy.'

The thought of it made George feel queasy so she was pleased when Ethel came running back in. Then she heard a man's voice from next door. He was shouting loudly, 'Up and over.'

'What's all that about?'

'Me mum says he's shell-shocked from the war. He's always shouting it out, something to do with the trenches, I think. I saw him the other day, he looks really scary, like a madman!'

The girls left the house, and once outside, George breathed in the fresh air, glad to be away from Molly's smelly room, though she was a bit worried about bumping into the man next door.

She'd been shocked at what she'd seen and hadn't realised people lived that way. How awful for Molly, she thought, and promised herself that no matter what it took, she would never, ever, be poor.

*

Later that day, Billy Wilcox looked over the bannister, and through the crack of the lounge door he could see George sat at the dinner table next to her dad. His own father would be at the head, and his mother the other end. Sally would be opposite Jack, so that meant he'd have to sit and face George. He cringed at the thought. He'd rather kick her head in than have to sit and eat with her, or him, whatever you wanted to call *it*.

It was a shame his father had ordered him to kick in Kenny Marston's head instead of George's – he'd have gleaned much more pleasure from seeing *its* blood smeared on his knuckles rather than Kenny's. As it happened, Kenny hadn't put up a fight. Tommy Marston had offered up his son like a lamb to the slaughter. He'd stood by and done nothing as Billy had pummelled Kenny's head, then the man had even asked Billy to send his regards to his father. It had been too easy; there was no challenge from either son or father. They were weak, not like the Wilcox men.

He slowly walked into the room where dinner was being served, and kept his eyes firmly fixed on George.

'Ah, Billy, there you are. Come on, sit down, dinner's getting cold,' his mother urged.

His voice had broken, and was now a deep growl, which still surprised him whenever he spoke. 'I'm not hungry,' he said, sounding more unfriendly than he'd intended.

'Don't be daft, of course you are. A growing lad like you needs a good meal,' his mother said, her voice a bit shaky.

Billy saw that his dad had the carving knife in his hands and was stood ready to slice the joint of meat. A sudden image flashed through his mind of him grabbing the knife and dragging the blade across George's throat. He imagined his mother screaming as George's blood spurted up the walls and across the pristine white tablecloth.

Billy's father's voice broke into his sadistic thoughts when he heard him order, 'Billy, sit down.'

Billy abruptly took his seat and stared at the thing in front of him. Was it a boy or a girl? He was pretty sure it didn't have a dick, but it looked like a boy, and acted like one too. Sometimes his parents referred to George as a girl, but always as a boy in front of George's dad.

'Mr Garrett's just been telling us how George is coming on well with his boxing lessons. You used to like doing a bit of boxing when you were his age, didn't you, Billy?'

His mother was obviously trying to make light conversation, but Billy couldn't bring himself to respond. Instead, he glared at George, and barely audibly, hissed, 'Weirdo.'

'What did you say?' his father asked, sounding irate.

'I said, well done,' Billy answered, with a charming smile that concealed what was really going on in his mind.

He turned his gaze to Jack, and the look of contempt in the man's eyes – well, one of his eyes – told Billy that Jack hadn't been fooled. Billy wasn't bothered. His father had already ripped out Jack's left eye, and if he didn't stop staring at him, Billy decided he would rip out the other one too and shove it down George's throat. He smiled at the thought of George gagging as *it* was forced to swallow *its* father's eyeball.

Once the roast had been eaten, and apple pie demolished, Billy felt it was a polite time to retire back to his room. He'd detested every minute of sitting with the Garretts and couldn't wait to get away from them. Especially George. There was something unnerving about a girl who looked and acted like a boy, and he couldn't understand why his parents played along with the game by referring to *it* as him.

As he walked upstairs, the sound of Jack chuckling carried from the lounge, and for a moment, Billy thought the man was laughing at him. He wanted to run back into the room and envisaged George's horrified face as he slaughtered her dad in front of her. Instead, he returned to his room where he could sit and polish his already immaculate shoes and allow his twisted imagination to run riot.

As he rubbed black polish into his Oxfords, in his

mind's eye he visualised the panic in Jack Garrett's eye as he slit his throat and watched the warm, crimson blood ooze from the man's body. He could almost hear the screams for mercy from George as he slowly and deliberately cut off parts of *its* body. First *its* ear, then a finger or two. Just like he'd done to Rusty, the neighbour's cat. Not enough to kill, just enough to cause excruciating pain.

George would beg, cry for him to stop, but in Billy's head, that showed weakness, something he couldn't respect but enjoyed hearing. He knew his dad had quietly knocked off blokes who'd tried to get one over on him, but for Billy, the thought of killing was more than business… it was pleasure.

16

Joan heard Mr Wilcox's car pull up, and quickly checked her reflection in the mirror. Her dyed brown hair was neatly styled in short curls, and her thin lips were moistened with red lipstick. Pleased with herself, she emerged from her room, keen to tell her boss some information she'd gleaned about the Portland Pounders.

Norman and Hefty walked in, while Beth came trotting down the stairs.

'Good morning, Mr Wilcox.' Joan smiled, then turned and scowled at Beth, annoyed at her uninvited presence.

'Hello, Joan, I hear business has been profitable this week. Well done, ladies.'

'Yes, come through and I'll show you the books.'

Joan followed them into the lounge, which was normally used as a waiting room or for Norman's wild parties. Norman rarely attended the parties, but he always ensured his special guests enjoyed themselves. Alcohol and drugs would be readily available, and the parties would inevitably turn into orgies.

The room was opulently dressed, with deep burgundy velvet curtains, and large brown leather, studded-back sofas. There was a walnut bar in one corner, which housed the finest spirits and champagne, only ever used for Norman's valued business associates. Few local men had ever been in this room, but it was often frequented by wealthier gentlemen, many of whom held influential roles within the local authorities.

Joan walked behind the bar. There was a safe hidden behind a painting of King George the Fifth, but she noticed Beth had followed them in. She had to get the girl out of the room so she could warn Mr Wilcox of what was coming. Carol had told her that she'd overheard Beth talking to Davey, one of the Pounders. She was supposed to be fucking him, but Carol got the impression they were planning the downfall of the Pounders gang, which Davey belonged to, *and* of Mr Wilcox. She'd never trusted Beth and now it seemed her instincts had been correct. 'Yes, Beth, what do you want?' she asked, irritated.

Mr Wilcox, Hefty and Joan glared at the girl, waiting for an answer. Beth looked nervous as she said, 'I'd like a word with Mr Wilcox, please.'

'Bugger off, Beth. Mr Wilcox is a busy man and doesn't have time to waste with you,' Joan answered with a shooing motion of her hand.

'But… it's important.'

'I don't care how important you think it is,' Joan snapped, but was swiftly interrupted by Norman.

'What is it?' he asked.

'I need to speak to you, but it has to be in private.'

'This is private. I trust the people in this room.'

Beth looked around at the three sets of eyes on her. She gulped. 'It's the Portland Pounders, Mr Wilcox. They're gonna have you done in.'

'Are they, indeed? And you know this how?'

'Davey told me. He works for Mr Kelly, and he said Mr Kelly is going to kill you and take over all your businesses.'

'I see. Anything else?'

'No, sir, that's all I know, except he did say it would be soon... very soon.'

'She's telling the truth, Mr Wilcox. One of the other girls overheard Davey talking about you copping it,' Joan added, surprised that Beth had turned out to be trustworthy after all.

'Thank you, Beth. Joan will see to it that you're paid extra for your loyalty. Leave us.'

'Thank you, sir,' Beth said and, looking relieved, she dashed from the room.

Joan surveyed Norman's face. He didn't look fazed by the news imparted to him, but Joan knew the man was deep and would be planning something. Unbeknown to her, Beth's small lie had put a nail in the girl's coffin, and that of Davey, her lover's, too.

Norman had given Jack a tip-off about a new shop on the High Street selling watches, but the owners had refused to sign up for his insurance. Normally, Hefty would be sent in and would persuade them it was in their best interest, but he had held Hefty back, knowing that the family had connections with Scotland Yard. However, if the shop was subject to a random robbery, the owners might be more inclined to reconsider Norman's offer.

It was lunchtime, and the shop was closed. The street was busy, but Norman had said he'd seen a back door with a small window to the side, and on two visits to the premises, the window had been ajar. Jack hoped it would be now.

Once they were at the back of the shop, Jack was pleased to find the window was again slightly open. It was small, not large enough for a man to fit through, but he had George with him, and though she was a tremendous size for her age, she was still able to squeeze through the tiniest of gaps.

'I'll get through that, Dad, no problem.'

'I knew you would, but instead of opening the back door, just grab all you can and pass it out to me through the window. I don't know if the place is belled up or not.'

Jack helped his daughter through the small gap, and just a few nail-biting minutes passed until he saw her small hand pop back out of the window with a full bag.

'Here you go, Dad,' she whispered.

Jack took the bag. His eyes nearly popped when he glanced inside and saw it was stuffed with expensive watches. 'Well done,' he said in hushed tones.

George looked for a chair to climb on to access her getaway from the inside, and once she'd clambered back through the window, they headed towards the Junction and Falk's jewellery shop.

'Ezzy's gonna bloody love us,' George squealed.

'What have I told you about your language?'

'Sorry, Dad, but it's true, ain't it?'

'Oh yes, very true. He'll have me on a train to Manchester tomorrow morning with this lot.'

Less than half an hour later, they were walking up the hill towards the train station and Falk's shop. They passed Fanny's flower stall, and Jack noticed the woman looked tired. Mind you, he wasn't surprised; after all, she looked huge with child.

'You're looking pleased with yourself, Jack,' Fanny called.

'Always, Fanny, always. When's the baby due?'

'Any day now. The sooner, the better – my blinkin' back is killing me.'

'Good luck, and give my regards to Mike,' Jack said, though truth be known, he couldn't stand her lazy and slovenly husband.

'That's Molly's mum,' George said quietly.

'You've been spending a lot of time with her lately.'

'Yes, she's my best friend,' George piped up, though Jack wasn't pleased to hear his daughter speak this way. It made her sound too girly.

They were soon inside Falk's, and Ezzy's face lit up as

he studied the gold and silver watches. 'Beautiful, Jack,' he enthused.

'You're gonna have to shift them pretty sharpish, mate,' Jack warned.

'I think I can guess where these came from, and if I'm right the sooner they're moved, the better. I've got to say, Jack, I admire your spunk. Do you know the brother works at Scotland Yard?'

'Yes, so you'd think they would have better security. Silly buggers left a window open.'

'Can you run these tomorrow?' Ezzy asked.

'Yep, I'll see you first thing. Come on, George, say goodbye to Ezzy.'

'Can I show him something first?' George asked as she jigged up and down on the spot looking excited.

'All right,' Jack agreed.

'Ezzy, come round here and walk towards the door,' George demanded.

The man's eyebrows rose, but with a good-natured smile he did as she asked. Jack knew what his daughter was going to do. He'd been teaching her to dip by hanging a small bell on a jacket. Now, after several weeks of practice, she could slip her hand inside the coat and the bell wouldn't sound. He'd been impressed at how quickly she'd learnt the skill and as Ezzy walked across the shop floor, George pretended to accidentally bump into him.

'Whoops. Careful, George,' Ezzy warned.

'I'm fine, but you should check your left inside pocket.'

The man felt inside his jacket. 'Very good! Can I have my wallet back please?'

With an accomplished smile on her face, George handed it to him.

'You can have a job with me as one of my dippers,' Ezzy teased.

'No, he can't,' Jack said sternly, and ruffled George's short hair. 'I couldn't do without him. See you tomorrow.'

They left Falk's shop in good spirits. Their haul had been plentiful, and Jack was pleased with the price he'd negotiated with Ezzy. 'Tonight, we shall eat like kings,' he said as he jangled the coins in his pocket and patted the notes on the inside of his coat.

'Good, 'cos I'm bleedin' starving!'

Jack smiled down at his daughter, and when he looked at her eyes, he was once again reminded of Sissy. 'When we get home, I've got something very special to give to you,' he said, thinking of his wife's wedding ring. 'I think you're old enough to have it now.'

'What is it, Dad?'

'You'll see,' Jack answered, holding back the sorrow he still felt, then added, 'Come on, hurry up, I reckon it's gonna chuck it down.'

By the time they arrived home, the sky had turned dark

grey and it was raining heavily. George was wet through to her skin, and as she squelched up the hallway, she laughed heartily at her dad shaking his head like a wet dog.

'It's raining, Gran,' she exclaimed when she saw her in the kitchen.

'Heavens above, look at the state of you! You're soaked through and dripping all over my clean floor.'

George saw her dad roll his eyes and knew what he was thinking. Her gran was fanatical about her kitchen floor, and even though the woman had bad hips, every day she'd get down on her hands and knees and scrub it so hard that the linoleum was almost worn through.

'Get them wet clothes off then put yourself in front of the fire and I'll get you a nice bowl of vegetable soup.'

George swapped a look with her dad and they wrinkled their noses.

'Don't moan about my soup, you ungrateful pair of buggers! Oppo called in earlier with a big bag of veg. I've made a broth; it'll do you good.'

George trotted upstairs and wished Oppo worked in a sweetshop instead of a grocer's. When she came back down, from the hallway, she saw her dad place a wad of notes on the kitchen table.

''Ere you go, Mum,' he said.

George walked into the front room and held her hands towards the warmth of the fire. She could tell her gran was pleased when she heard her say, 'Blimey,

Son, you've had a good day.' George smiled, proud of herself. It'd been down to her that they'd earned a good day's pay.

'Yeah, thanks to Norman,' she heard her dad answer. George frowned. It wasn't thanks to Norman, it was thanks to her!

'That bloody man. You've nothing to thank him for except that awful scar on your face!'

George's ears pricked again, and she walked back into the kitchen asking, 'What did Norman do to you, Dad?'

'Nothing, sweetheart, he's been very good to us.'

'I don't like him, or Billy. Do we have to go to their house again?'

'If we get invited, yes we do. You should show a bit more respect! Anyway, I reckon it was Jane who invited us. I doubt Norman would have if he hadn't been told to.'

George decided to drop the subject and remembered her dad had promised her something. 'Can I have it now? That thing you said was special?'

'Yes, I'll get it. Mum, is it all right if I go in your keepsakes box?'

'Oh! Of course,' her gran answered, and George saw her smile warmly at her dad.

Minutes later, he sat at the table opposite her whilst her gran watched from in front of the stove. Her eyes looked watery and George was curious to know what she was about to receive.

'I've been keeping something for you that your mother wanted you to have. In fact, her last words were to always tell you how much she loved you and to give you this.'

Her dad swallowed hard as he held out the thin gold band to her. 'I gave it to her on the day we got married and she never took it off her finger. It meant a lot to her, so you must always look after it.'

George took the ring and stared intently at it. 'I will, Dad, I promise.' It was the only thing she had of her mother's and instantly she treasured it.

'Good. Give it back to your gran for now and you can wear it when your hands are big enough.'

'Please, Dad, let me keep it. I ain't got nothing of my mum's.'

'All right, but you take care of it and don't lose it.'

George jumped from the table and kissed her dad on the cheek before darting out of the kitchen and up the stairs to her room. 'I can't wait to show Molly,' she called.

The rain had stopped, and George knocked excitedly on Molly's door. When she was invited in, she politely declined and waited on the doorstep. She really liked her friend, but Molly's home made her feel cooty.

'Look what my dad gave me today – it was my mum's,' George said and proudly opened her hand to reveal the wedding ring.

'Ah, that's lovely,' Molly cooed. 'My mum ain't got a ring. She had to pawn it.'

'Didn't she have any pictures she could pawn? That's what Mary next door does. I heard her telling me gran that she gets half a crown when she needs to get the doctor in.'

'No, me mum won't have any pictures 'cos she says that's what breeds the bugs. She had one once and when she took it off the wall, there were loads of lice behind it.'

'I saw your mum today on her stall,' George said as the girls walked arm in arm along the street. Ethel had run on ahead.

'Did you notice she had a black eye?'

'No, I didn't. Did your dad whack her again?'

'Yeah, last night. I don't know what me mum did to deserve it. I'm just glad he didn't punch her in the belly.'

'When is she having the baby?'

'She thinks it'll be any day now. I know she's going to want me to help, but I'm scared. I ain't never seen a baby being born. Have you?'

'No, but my gran said my mum died having me. Are you scared your mum will die?'

'No, she's had loads of us, but she told me there's

going to be lots of blood... That's what scares me.'

George fell quiet as a tirade of questions whirled in her mind. How would the baby get out of Molly's mum's belly and how did it get in there in the first place? She felt silly asking Molly, but her friend seemed to know everything.

'It comes out between your legs, George,' Molly answered.

'What, down there... where you go pee from?'

'Yes.'

George was horrified and wondered how a baby could possibly squeeze out of that small space!

'And your dad puts the baby in there but it's just a seed and then it grows,' Molly said.

George thought her friend sounded very grown-up, but she still couldn't get her head round it. 'How does me dad do that, you know, put the seed in?'

'The seed is in his thingy, which he puts in your mum's wee hole and then the baby grows.'

George thought back to the day when she'd met Molly and Billy Wilcox had his thingy in his hand. She'd seen boys peeing in the street but hadn't realised they'd been doing it through that! She'd tried to copy it once, up the coal bunker in the backyard, but wasn't able to shoot her urine up, so hadn't attempted it again. Now it was beginning to make sense. She didn't have a thingy and would never be a proper boy. She didn't mind, she was still tough, but wondered if it would upset her dad. 'Don't tell no-one that I didn't know about babies,' she said defensively.

'Course I won't.'

'And don't tell no-one that I ain't got a thingy.'

'I won't, George. Quick, we'd better run and catch up with Ethel. She's gone round the corner and I don't like to have her out of my sight.'

They picked up their pace, and as they flew round the bend, they both laughed when they saw Ethel sitting on a bit of wood that had been placed across an old pram carriage.

'Look at me,' Ethel squealed with delight as three young lads raced the makeshift cart towards them.

'Do you want a go?' one of the lads asked when the cart came to a stop next to them.

'No, thanks, and don't go running off like that again, Ethel,' Molly chastised her older sister.

'Bugger, run,' the lad suddenly yelled. 'Here comes Billy Wilcox!'

The three young boys scattered, and Molly helped Ethel off the cart. 'Come on, let's go,' she said urgently.

'No, I ain't running away from him,' George answered defiantly, and stood with her shoulders back, ready for Billy and his mates, Malc and Sid.

They moseyed towards them and George could see Billy had a derisive grin on his face. She instantly knew he was looking for trouble, but it was too late to scarper now, unless she wanted to look like a weakling.

'Having fun, girls?' he asked.

'What's it got to do with you, Billy?' George answered.

'I weren't talking to you, you ain't a girl – or are you?'

'Go away and pick on someone your own size,' George spat, and avoided answering his question. She noticed Ethel had huddled with Molly and both girls had paled.

'You gobby little shit. You've got a lot of mouth on you... for a girl.'

George clenched her fists by her sides. She could tell Billy was trying to goad her.

'What do you think, Sid, do you reckon she's a girl? I mean, I know it looks like a boy, but I bet it ain't.'

'I dunno, Billy, perhaps he's one of them queers.'

'Are you, George? Are you queer?'

George had heard about the queers but didn't know what they were. She'd heard her dad talk unkindly about them and he'd said they deserved to be in jail. 'I ain't queer,' she answered, though oblivious to what it meant.

'If you ain't queer, you must be a girl... Show us your cock, prove to us that you're a boy and we'll let the matter rest.'

George could feel her pulse quicken and her mouth went dry. It was impossible for her to prove she was a boy, but she didn't want to admit it to Billy Wilcox and his stupid mates.

'You can't, can you? You ain't got a dick. You pretend to be a boy, but I'll lay money on it that you'll grow a pair of tits soon.'

'Leave me alone, Billy,' George said, trying her hardest to keep her voice steady.

A wicked smile spread over Billy's face, then he said, 'Sid, grab its arms, let's have a look and clear this up once and for all.'

George panicked and before she could react, she felt Sid grappling with her arms. He was pulling them behind her back and though she struggled, she was no match for his strength. As she thrashed to release herself, she saw Billy coming closer and furiously kicked her legs out. Sid's grip tightened, and before she knew what was happening, Billy had pulled down her shorts to around her ankles. She stopped retaliating and stood motionless, feeling mortified and humiliated, yet she held back from crying.

'As I thought,' Billy sneered as he looked at her, naked from the waist down, 'she's a girl.'

'Let me see,' Malc said, and pushed past Billy for a closer inspection. 'Yep, she ain't got no curlies yet but that's definitely a girl,' he quipped and fell about laughing.

George glared at Billy with hatred in her eyes. She'd never liked him but now she loathed him. She pushed her chin out in an act of boldness and then Sid released his grip on her arms before brusquely pushing her. She fell forward onto her knees and now, with her bare bottom facing the world, she hung her head in embarrassment, desperately wishing they'd leave her alone.

'Come on,' Billy addressed his friends, 'we ain't got time to be mucking about with little girls. See ya, *George*.'

To her relief, she heard them walk off and wanted to burst into tears, but then she felt Molly's arms across her shoulders.

'I'm so sorry, George, I should have helped but I didn't know what to do.'

'It's all right, Molly, there was nothing you could have done,' she said as she scrambled to her feet and quickly pulled her shorts back up.

So what, she was a girl, and now Billy Wilcox knew the truth, but she was still harder than most boys. She felt angry that they'd ganged up on her, leaving her no chance to stand up for herself. It wasn't fair, and she'd never forgive Billy for putting her through the most shameful experience of her life. She vowed to get him back; one day, she'd make him pay for what he'd done.

17

A week later, Joan felt as if she was running on nervous energy. She'd hardly slept a wink the night before, and today was the day. Hefty had set up a meeting for Norman with the Portland Pounders, which was due to commence in one hour in her lounge. For the fourth time that morning, she checked the bar was stocked. She poured herself a large brandy and knocked it back in four big gulps, hoping the rich liquid would calm her nerves. She held her hand out. It was still shaking.

Carol put her head round the door. 'Mr Wilcox is here.'

Joan took a long, deep breath, and placed her unsteady hands on the bar, then pushed her shoulders back. 'Brace yourself,' she murmured.

Norman and Hefty came in, and she noticed Norman surveying the room.

'I'm surprised you haven't put any sheeting around,' he said.

Joan knew he was joking, but it showed he meant business. There was going to be murder. Bullets and bloodshed. She just hoped Norman knew what he was doing.

The grandfather clock in the corner of the room struck

one. Norman took out his pocket watch and checked it against the chime. As expected, the Liverpool gang arrived precisely on time. Carol showed Kevin Kelly and his entourage into the room, while Joan remained behind the bar, silently observing.

'Kevin, good to see you,' Norman greeted the gang leader, and shook his hand.

'You too, Norman,' Kevin answered. 'I'm intrigued to know why you've called this meeting.'

'All in good time. First, let's have a drink. What's your poison?'

'Whisky, and these ladies will have a gin,' Kevin laughed, referring to Davey and Dodger.

Joan poured the drinks, and Carol handed them out.

'I've arranged a little entertainment for us,' Norman said, and nodded to Carol. 'Sit down, gentlemen, and enjoy.'

Kevin sat next to Dodger on one sofa. Opposite them, Norman and Hefty sat on another. Davey took an armchair next to Norman. Carol opened the door, and Beth sashayed in, dressed in several silk scarves. Joan placed the gramophone needle on the record, but her hands were shaking, causing it to jump. Norman threw her a dirty look, and she silently mouthed, 'Sorry.'

As the tune of 'The Sheik of Araby' filled the room, Beth began to dance in the style of an Egyptian. She slowly peeled off her scarves, one by one, and draped them across the Liverpool men. She teased them with her wriggling hips and jiggling breasts. Joan noticed Davey couldn't take his eyes off her.

The record finished, and the music was replaced by the sound of applause. Beth, now naked, draped herself seductively on the arm of Davey's chair. Carol slipped out of the room.

Kevin's eyes roamed over Beth's slim body. 'Very nice.'

Dodger was sat upright, twiddling his thumbs. Hefty was staring him out. Joan thought the tension in the room could be cut with a knife and was anxious for Norman to get it over and done with.

Kevin leaned forward, and as his jacket gaped, Joan spotted the handle of his revolver. He turned his attention from Beth and looked Norman in the eyes. 'Are you going to tell me what this is all about? As much as I'm enjoying the view, I haven't come all this way to look at a whore's tits.'

'The truth is, Kevin, I'm a little disappointed. You see, I believed us to have become more than merely business associates over the years. I consider you a friend.'

'As do I, so what are you disappointed about?'

Joan's heart was pounding so hard she could hear it ringing in her ears. Any moment now she was expecting Norman to pull his gun and shoot Kevin in the head. She covertly fingered the gun hidden on a shelf under the bar. Davey or Dodger were sure to retaliate and go for Norman. Hefty was thick, but he was quick on the draw and she knew he'd take Dodger out. If Norman didn't get there first, it would leave Davey to her.

Norman pulled his gun and aimed it directly at Kevin. His finger squeezed on the trigger, but he didn't fire. Kevin's response was instantaneous, as he also drew his gun, and pointed it at Norman.

'I hear someone is out to finish me off and take over my operations,' Norman said.

Joan thought they were going to kill each other and wrapped her hand around the handle of the gun behind the bar. Hefty held his shooter at Dodger, and Dodger pointed his at Hefty. Davey had his gun on Norman.

'Funny you should say that, because I heard the same thing too,' Kevin said, and swung his arm round.

Joan jumped as the gun went off, then Beth began screaming as Davey's brains were splattered across her naked body.

'Shut the fuck up!' Norman shouted at Beth and walked across the room and placed the barrel of his revolver against her forehead.

Beth sat frozen, her face white with shock.

'You stupid bitch,' Norman growled at her, 'you've heard the saying, loose lips sink ships?'

Joan was confused. Kevin had taken out one of his own, and now Norman had a gun to Beth's head. The other men all replaced theirs. This wasn't the plan.

'Well, loose lips also gets people killed. You got drunk and blabbed to Mike Mipple. Ringing any bells now?' Norman asked, his voice sinister.

Beth didn't answer. She remained frozen, her eyes wide in fear.

'You told Mike all about your little plan to feed me information that would make me think the Pounders were going to kill me. You was hoping I would go after them first. Take Kevin Kelly down, then Davey could rise up the ranks. That's right, isn't it? You knew that if I killed Mr Kelly, the Pounders would have to retaliate. They'd take me down, and then Davey would move down here to take over my patch, with you by his side.'

'No... no, Mr Wilcox... it wasn't like that... I never said that... I swear,' Beth screeched.

'Norman, I can't stand her fucking caterwauling. Let's get this over with. You know what to do,' Kevin said.

Joan watched as Norman turned his head, smiled at Kevin, then turned back to Beth and pulled the trigger. There was a loud boom, then Beth's blood streaked up the wall behind her head. Her body slumped to one side, landing across Davey.

Kevin stood up, then shook Norman's hand. 'Pleasure doing business with you.'

Dodger nodded at Hefty, and then the men from Liverpool left.

Joan stood trembling behind the bar. Talk about a double bluff!

'Get this cleared up,' Norman said to Hefty, then he left too, the alliance between the Portland Pounders and Norman Wilcox now firmly cemented.

Joan never knew what Hefty did with the bodies, but sixty years later, during renovation works, the skeletal remains of an unidentified man and woman were excavated from the car park at the back of the Cedars. The cause of death was forensically determined as gunshot wounds to the head.

Billy ambled down his street with Sid to his left and Malc on the right. Between them, they took up the whole pavement and wouldn't move out of the way for anyone, old or young, man or woman. He thought he owned the street and all those who lived on it, but he was aware that most only respected him because he was the son of Norman Wilcox. Well, now he was nearly fourteen years old, he felt it was about time he made his own mark and earned his own money. He hammered loudly on the front door of an old man who he knew had lost his sight.

'What are you doing, Billy?' Sid asked.

'You'll see, which is more than can be said for the old git who lives here.'

The door opened, and the old man asked who was there.

'Billy Wilcox.'

'Hello, son, how's ya father?'

'He's fine, Mr Burt.'

'What can I do for you, Billy?'

'I'm going to make sure you don't get hurt.'

'What ya on about, son?' the old man asked as he held on to the doorframe for support.

'It's my new business, specially set up for the people on this street. You give me money and I make sure nothing bad happens to you.'

'Don't be daft, Billy, you're just a bit of a kid, and anyway, your dad would be bloody pissed off if any outsiders caused problems round here.'

Billy stepped forward and slyly kicked the man's shin. Mr Burt yelped, then asked, 'What did you do that for?'

'I was showing you what I mean. See, if you'd given me some money instead of mouthing off about my dad, that would never have happened. Do you get it now?'

'Yeah, I get it, Billy, but wait 'til your dad hears about this.'

'He won't hear about it, will he, Mr Burt?' Billy said and kicked the man's other shin, harder this time.

'You're a little shit, Billy Wilcox – your father would be ashamed of you.'

Billy threw his head back and laughed. 'He'd be proud of me for thinking for myself. Now, are you gonna cough up or what?'

Mr Burt shook his head as he walked off muttering to Billy to stay there and he'd get what he had. Billy turned to his friends, and looking smug, he said, 'Easy, ain't it? Now we can get ourselves some smokes.'

He noticed Malc and Sid exchange a glance, and neither looked impressed. 'What?' he asked, thinking his mates had turned yellow-bellied.

'I don't know, Billy, it don't seem right, picking on a blind old man,' Sid answered meekly.

'Fuck you, this is how the strong get stronger and the weak get weaker. If you don't like it, you know what you can do.'

'Sorry, Billy, you're right,' Sid answered.

Mr Burt came back to the front door and handed over some coins.

'Is this all you've got?' Billy asked, looking at the measly amount with disgust.

'Yes, if I had more, I'd give it to you.'

'Fine, but I want more than this next week.' He stuffed the money in his pocket and said farewell to the old man.

'Who do you reckon we should visit next?'

'I don't know, Billy,' Sid answered.

'What about the Mipples?' from Malc.

'Nah, they ain't got a pot to piss in,' Billy answered, thinking of bigger fish to fry.

And so it began: Billy Wilcox's new enterprise.

PART 3

GEORGINA GARRETT'S PAIN

18

December 1929. Six years later.

George stood in front of the mirror in her bedroom and looked at her developing chest. She ran her hand gently over one firm, pert breast and felt a tingling sensation. As her nipple hardened, she watched in fascination. When naked, she couldn't hide the fact that she was now a young woman, though she managed to hide it well when dressed. She pulled a tight vest over her head and wore a loose shirt. Her attire hid her blossoming bosoms, but there wasn't much she could do to disguise her voice.

Billy Wilcox had spread rumours about her being female, but if people knew, they never said anything to her, except on one occasion when a young man had dared to taunt her. He lived at the end of her street and as she'd walked past him, he'd made a lurid remark about her tits. She'd punched him in the mouth, which had quickly shut him up. Since then, she'd never heard anyone else comment, though she was sure they probably did behind her back.

George, now dressed in her usual masculine clothes, checked her reflection again. She liked what she saw.

Her broad shoulders and toned arms could throw a good punch. She knew she was different, but her look earned her respect. Unlike most of the women in her neighbourhood, George could look after herself and wasn't afraid of anyone. Not even Billy Wilcox, though she preferred to stay out of his way. The man had no scruples and that unnerved her. She'd run in to him a few times over the years, but since she matched his height and strength, he'd kept a healthy distance away from her. She preferred it that way but had never forgotten how he'd degraded her as a child. The disgraceful memory was burnt onto her mind and nightmares of the shameful event still sometimes disturbed her sleep.

Her gran's voice broke her thoughts, calling up the stairs, 'George, be a love. Pop to the shop and get me a packet of Lambert and Butler.'

George left her room and as she walked down the stairs, replied, 'Oh, Gran, you know my dad doesn't like you smoking.'

'Well, he's in Manchester, and what he don't know, won't hurt. Go on, I'll treat ya.'

'All right, but if he finds out, you'd better not tell him I bought them for you.'

'I won't, it'll be our secret,' Dulcie said.

George wrapped herself up in a woolly hat that her gran had just about managed to knit and pulled on her oversized utility coat.

With her head down against the biting Northerly

winds, she shoved her hands in the pockets and headed to the local corner shop. It was one of the few shops that she refrained from robbing. Not that there was much else locally worth stealing from. Most of them sold second-hand goods. When she walked in, Mr Peterson wasn't behind the counter and the bell above the door hadn't chimed. George could have quickly opened the till and pinched the takings, or lifted some luxury Christmas goodies from the shelves, but her father's words rang in her ears, 'Never nick off your own.'

'Mr Peterson... customer,' George yelled, assuming the man must be in his storeroom.

When there was no response, George approached the counter and leaned over, trying to get a glimpse through the curtained opening that led to the back. 'Mr Peterson... are you in there?' That's when she noticed the till drawer was open. 'Mr Peterson,' she called again, beginning to worry.

She jumped over the highly polished wooden top and ran through the curtain. 'Mr Peterson, are you all right?' She saw a door to her left, and pushed it open, again calling to the old man. There was still no answer, so she walked in, finding herself in the storeroom, and to her horror, she saw Mr Peterson laid face down on the floor. With her heart thumping, she dashed to his side, and silently prayed that the old man was alive. She crouched down next to him, but leaning in closer, she could see his eyes were closed, and noticed at the back of his head, his grey hair was caked in blood. 'Mr Peterson, it's me, George. Mr Peterson, can you hear me?'

The old man groaned, filling George with relief. Thank God. He was alive.

'Don't move, I'll get help,' she said urgently.

'Bi... Bi... Billy...'

George moved her face closer to Mr Peterson's. 'What did you say?'

'Billy... Billy Wilcox.'

His words left her stunned. She could hardly believe what she'd heard. 'Are you saying Billy Wilcox did this to you?'

'Yes, I didn't pay him and...'

'Don't worry about that now, I'm going to get help. You'll be all right, Mr Peterson, just sit tight. I'll be as quick as I can.'

George gently patted the old man's hand, quickly took off her coat and placed it over him, then ran from the room and through the shop. As she rushed out of the door, another customer was coming in, but with no time to spare, George ran straight past the woman and along several streets until she came to the doctor's house. She hammered on the door, but no-one answered.

In a panic, she started running back towards the shop, worried that Mr Peterson was all alone. As she dashed round the corner, she found herself confronted by four policemen, who on seeing her, blew their whistles and ran towards her.

'There he is,' one of them shouted. 'Get him.'

'George Garrett... STOP... POLICE,' another yelled.

George didn't have to stop. Shocked, she already had. Two of the officers grabbed her, one on each arm, whilst another stood in front. 'George Garrett, I'm arresting you for the murder of Mr Peterson...'

'No... he's not dead... I didn't kill him... I found him and went to get help... he was alive.' She could feel herself being dragged along the street, and continued to plead, 'You don't understand... it wasn't me... I'd never hurt the old man... I didn't do it.'

The policemen were ignoring her protests of innocence, and people were beginning to gather on their doorsteps, shaking their heads in disgust and eyeing her up and down with contempt.

'It wasn't me,' George cried again, but held back from telling them who the real culprit was. She hated Billy Wilcox, but she knew what his father was capable of. Whatever the law did to her, it would be nothing compared to what Norman Wilcox would do if he found out she'd grassed on his son.

By lunchtime that day, news had spread, and gossip was rife. Fanny wrapped a bunch of holly in newspaper and passed it to her waiting customer. 'I don't believe it. I know George Garrett – he'd never do something so heinous.'

'It's true, but then I'd expect nothing less from her. I mean, look at her father. He's not what you'd call a good example. I've known the family since before the child was born. He was a thief then, and he still is now. Fancy pretending she's a boy. No wonder she's confused. I was next door the day the child was born so I know full well that George Garrett is a girl. She'll swing for this, and God will be her final judge.'

'I'm sorry, Miss Capstone, but I hope you're wrong. The Garretts are a kind and generous family. Good day to you.'

Fanny saw the haughty look on Miss Capstone's face before she turned her back on the woman. So much for being a good Christian. The woman was mean, and Fanny wished she could afford to decline her business.

She chewed her thumbnail as she digested what Miss Capstone had told her. It couldn't be true, it just couldn't be. Yes, George was tough, some would say hard, but she was her daughter's best friend and Fanny thought a lot of the girl, though George preferred to be referred to as a boy. She'd always looked out for Molly and was kind to Ethel. Granted, she was a damn good thief, but Fanny felt she knew George well and didn't believe she could have attacked Mr Peterson. It wasn't George's style, but it stank of Billy Wilcox.

Fanny offered up a silent prayer, 'Please, Lord, don't let George hang for Billy's crime.'

'No way, not George,' Oppo protested to his customer.

The woman had heard the news about Mr Peterson's murder and as Oppo had wrapped her potatoes in newspaper, she'd relayed the gossip.

'I'm only telling you what I was told. You're friends with him, aren't you?'

'Yes, I am… er, sorry, excuse me, I've got to go,' Oppo said as the information began to sink in.

He whipped off his apron and shouted to his boss, 'Something's come up, I have to go. I'll see you tomorrow, Mr Kavanagh.'

As he dashed out of the door, he heard Mr Kavanagh call back, 'No you won't! You cheeky so and so!'

It sounded like Oppo had lost his job, not that he was bothered. His main concern was George. He had to get to the police station! As he ran, his disabled leg swung out sideways in a semi-circle fashion. People stared, some laughed, but he didn't care how ridiculous he looked.

He was soon at the station, and panting to catch his breath, he begged the desk sergeant to allow him to see his best friend. The man flatly refused and sent him away.

Oppo, realising no amount of charm would persuade the police officer to change his mind, reluctantly left the station feeling frustrated. He stood outside, wondering what to do next. Dulcie! If she'd heard what had happened, he knew the woman would be worried sick. He had no doubt that George hadn't committed the crime but there was nothing he could do for her here, so he headed off to check on the old girl. The Garretts were like family to him, and what hurt them, hurt him too.

George was thrown into a cold, concrete basement cell. There was one small barred window high above that allowed in a glimmer of light, and highlighted the faeces daubed on the walls. She shivered and wished she still had her coat. Her nose wrinkled at the overbearing smell of urine.

'Please... will someone listen to me! I'm innocent.' Her desperate cries echoed through the police station holding area, but no-one came to her aid.

George brushed off the silverfish crawling on the wooden bench attached to the damp wall and curled herself up in the foetal position. It was hopeless. How could she prove her innocence without naming Billy Wilcox?

She felt she'd lain there for what seemed like hours. The light was beginning to fade, and the temperature in the cell was rapidly dropping. Then she heard clanging, keys jangling and low voices. She sat up and dabbed her wet cheeks. It wouldn't do to be seen crying.

As she heard footsteps approaching, George ran towards the cell door and grabbed hold of the metal bars. 'Oi, you there, listen to me... I didn't kill the old man,' she shouted.

Three coppers came to stand on the other side of the bars, and one pushed his truncheon through. 'Stand back, Garrett,' he warned.

George stepped back, hoping they were going to unlock the gate. 'You'd better have come to let me out of this shithole 'cos I ain't done nothing wrong!'

'Well, so you say, but we have a credible witness who is willing to testify that she saw you running away from the murder scene.'

'For fuck's sake, how many times have I got to tell you? Yes, I was seen running away 'cos I went to get the doctor.'

'A likely excuse,' the youngest of the officers remarked sarcastically.

George felt as though she was banging her head against the filthy cell wall. Why wouldn't anyone believe her? 'What happens to you lot when you join the force? Do you put that poncey uniform on and turn into idiots? Or do you have to be as ignorant as pig shit to become a copper in the first place? If you had a brain between you, you'd soon work out who the real killer is.'

'You've got a lot of lip, Garrett, but who's the idiot here, eh? You're the one behind bars and it won't be long before you're found guilty and end up six feet under.'

'If I killed Peterson, why would I take the time to cover him with my coat?'

'Guilty conscience, hiding what you did.'

'I ain't as stupid as you lot,' George sneered and looked down her nose. 'If I had killed the old man, I wouldn't have been caught.'

'Or maybe you're not as clever as you think you are. The witness also claims that you're a female. Georgina, not George. Is this true?'

George gulped, unsure of how to answer. Her mind raced as she considered if she'd be better treated if she admitted the truth.

'Well? Are you one of them pretty boys or just a freak of nature?'

Before George could answer, the young copper unlocked the cell door, and all three came towards her. George backed away as she noticed a sickening look in their eyes.

'Considering the information we've been given, we were wondering what to do with you,' one of them said. 'We can't work out if you should be in the men's or women's block. You look like a man, but we need to check for ourselves.'

George was terrified, and nervously edged further back. As her heart hammered, her eyes darted from one copper to the next. She wanted to speak out and tell them she was a woman, but then they might beat her like she'd heard they'd done to the Suffragettes. No, she'd stand and fight her ground, like a man would, like her dad would expect of her.

'Strip.'

'W… w… what?' she stuttered, confused and hardly believing her ears. She'd been brought up to not trust the police, and this couldn't be right. Surely they couldn't make her take her clothes off? George clenched her fists, ready to use them. They couldn't make her stand naked and if they tried, she'd give them all a thick lip!

'I said, STRIP,' the policeman repeated, spitting the word as he leaned forward so his nose was almost touching hers.

The impact of the copper's order suddenly made George panic. It was like a repeat of what had happened when she was a child with Billy Wilcox. 'No… no… you can't do this to me,' she frantically yelled, and backed away until she felt the bench on the rear of her legs. The policemen moved towards her and George screamed. She hadn't meant to, but she couldn't help herself. The shrill noise echoed through the cold basement.

'She screams like a girl… Hold her,' one of them ordered.

George had to escape! She couldn't allow this to happen, not again, not after the embarrassing experience of her childhood. She went to make a run for it, but they had her cornered, so she screamed louder and tried to fight them off. Her arms flayed as she punched out, and as they grappled to retain her, she tried to gouge out one of the copper's eyes.

'Hold the cunt, it's going for my eyes,' the policeman screeched.

George fought with all her might but was no match for three burly coppers. It was all happening so quickly, and before she knew it, she felt herself being dragged backwards and was then aware of being pinned down to the bench.

'I'll have you for this,' she shouted. 'You're filth, dirty fucking filth!'

Her words had no effect and to her horror, she realised they were pulling down her trousers. 'NO,' she shrieked, and furiously kicked. Her boot connected with a policeman's chin, which sent him reeling backwards, but the other two still had her pinned. The injured policeman rubbed his face where George had booted him, then she saw him raise his hand. She watched, terrified, as he brought it down hard across her face.

'Wanker,' he snapped as searing hot pain burnt her cheek. George could taste the distinctive metallic flavour of blood in her mouth, then spat in the policeman's face. She glared at him with contempt as he wiped her bloodied saliva away with a look of disgust.

'You try anything like that again and I'll knock your fucking teeth out,' he hissed.

'Scum,' George answered rebelliously and continued struggling against the other two coppers.

The policeman sneered at her and then one of them tugged her legs apart. 'Get the fuck off me,' she screamed, hysterically writhing her body, but now her bottom half was stripped, except for her boots.

'She's female,' she heard a voice say, followed by laughter.

George closed her eyes, spent, defeated and humiliated. She squirmed under their scrutiny of her private parts, but now they knew the truth, she thought they'd leave her alone.

'You'd better check she ain't got her cock pushed up inside her. I've seen her sort before, fucking perverts.'

Helpless, her head fell to one side as she felt a rough hand enter her vagina and winced in pain. She wanted to cry out but gritted her teeth. There was no way she'd give them the satisfaction of showing how much it hurt.

'No dicks up here,' the copper said. 'Turn her over, make sure she ain't got one up her arse.'

Again, there was more laughter as George was thrown onto her front. They handled her roughly, but she had no fight left, and flopped like a rag doll. She tried to blot out the discomfort of what was happening, but when they attempted to sodomise her with a truncheon the agony was so great that she screamed and almost passed out. She thought they were ripping her body in two and feared she might die. As her tears dripped onto the wooden bench, she prayed death would come soon and spare her further anguish.

George's strength had been sapped, and as the horrific abuse continued, she saw Ruby's sweet face, the woman who had loved her like a mother. Ruby smiled lovingly at her, which calmed her and brought some comfort through the horror of what was happening. She reached out her hand to touch Ruby's soft skin, but she was just out of reach, and her image began to fade. 'Take me with you,' George whispered faintly. She'd never felt so alone and scared.

At last the assault was over, and one of the policemen threw a thin, rough blanket over her. She squeezed her eyes shut at the mocking faces of her perpetrators, then heard the cell door being locked, followed by heavy footsteps walking away and derisive sniggers. George was left sore, bleeding and utterly degraded.

Heart-breaking sobs escaped from her mouth as she yanked up her torn trousers, then she sat on the bench and hugged her knees as she pulled them into her chest. Every part of her body ached and felt bruised, and she feared they'd damaged her insides. Her shoulders shook as she drew long, juddering breaths and cried like she never had before. She wanted her gran and longed to be in the safety and security of home.

She couldn't sleep that night as the violation left her mind tormented. She wondered if the attack would have happened if she'd been less masculine. If she looked like a woman, would they have treated her so appallingly? She risked a beating, but that would have been better than what had happened. Cuts, bruises, they'd heal, but George wasn't sure her mind ever would. Flashbacks of the policeman's hand inside her left her feeling dirty and she wished she had Molly's carbolic soap to scrub herself.

Eventually, when her tears stopped flowing, her sorrow was replaced with a consuming hatred. It filled her being, and that hatred fuelled strength. When the morning sun rose, her mouth was set in a grim line, and her eyes were hard. She vowed to herself that she'd never allow another man to hurt her again.

19

Jack didn't arrive home until early afternoon the next day, and when he did, he was met by Oppo looking deathly pale and his mother verging on hysteria. He held her shoulders, and gently shook her. 'Slow down, Mum, I need to understand.'

After managing to draw in a deep, steadying breath, she said, 'George... George has been arrested for killing Mr Peterson.'

'Don't be daft. That can't be right.'

'They found him with his head bashed in, and she... she was seen running from his shop.'

'That doesn't mean she murdered him.'

'I know, but Oppo went to the station and they wouldn't let him see her. They're saying she did it! You've got to do something, Jack. Get her out of there!'

'I tried, Jack, I really did,' Oppo said as he placed his arm across Dulcie's shoulders.

Jack couldn't believe it. It didn't make sense. He paced the room and ran his fingers through his hair. 'I'm going to the station to sort this out. Oppo, look after me mum,' he called as he rushed back out of the door, still wearing his coat.

His mind twisted and turned as he ran to the police

station. They refused to allow him to see his daughter, but they did confirm she was being charged with murder. She'd see the rope for this! His stomach lurched. He didn't believe that George had killed old Peterson and needed to hear her side of the story, but without access to her, he felt helpless. There had to be something he could do, Jack thought frantically. One man's name came to his mind – one man who had influence – a man who claimed to have the Old Bill in his pocket.

Norman sat in his armchair with the newspaper in his hands, but he wasn't reading the words. His mind was on Billy. The young man had seemed jumpy the night before, and Jane had noticed blood on his trousers. When Norman had questioned him, he'd said he'd been in a scrap, and the extra money in his pockets was won on a bet. Norman wasn't convinced. His son was a good liar, but he wasn't so smart, and Norman had a niggling suspicion that Billy was somehow mixed up in the murder of Mr Peterson.

He heard a knock on the front door and peered through the crisp net curtains. Norman was pleased it wasn't the police and was unsurprised to see Jack on his step. Jane answered the door and showed Jack through.

'You've heard?' the man said abruptly.

'Yes. Did she do it?' Norman asked. He already knew the answer, but he had to be sure.

'Of course she fucking didn't!'

'All right, Jack, calm down. We'll get this cleared up, but don't take that tone with me again.'

'Sorry, Norman, I'm just worried sick about her.'

'I know you are, mate. Now go home, look after your mother and leave this to me.'

'I can't sit at home doing nothing. Please, Norman, let me help.'

'There's nothing you can do. I promise you, I'll have her out by teatime.'

'Are you sure? They'll hang her for this, Norman. I have to be sure.'

'You know me well enough to know I'm a man of my word. You're holding me up. Just go home.'

'OK and thanks, Norman. I really appreciate this, and I swear my George is innocent.'

'I don't doubt it,' Norman replied. He too was sure that George hadn't killed the man, but the same couldn't be said for his own son.

Joan was surprised when Hefty turned up. She hadn't been expecting to see him until the end of the week, but when he bundled her back into her room, she began to worry.

'Get off me, you great lummox,' she said, as she yanked her arm from his grip.

'Sorry, Joan, but I've had instructions from Norman to keep this dead secret.'

'What are you on about?'

'Is Rob the Roach due here today?' Hefty asked in a hushed voice.

'Yes, you know he always shows up as regular as clockwork.'

'Good. When Vi's screwing him, get her to slip this in his pocket,' Hefty said, and handed Joan a key.

'What's it for?'

'It's the shop key for Peterson's and Norman said you have to make sure Rob don't know he's got it.'

'For fuck's sake, Hefty, what's going on? I heard about old boy Peterson getting killed. Norman didn't have anything to do with it, did he?'

'Don't be daft, you know that ain't his style. I don't know the ins and outs, but I do know the wrong person has been nicked for it so Norman's putting it right. He's had a word with his mate in the nick, and Rob's gonna be lifted at half past three this afternoon on the end of this street. Stay indoors and keep your nosy beak out.'

'But Rob ain't a killer. He wouldn't have done Peterson in.'

'I know, but he's a slimy bastard and Norman doesn't like him. He's as good as any to take the blame for it. Now just do as you're told will ya, and keep your mouth shut.'

'All right, all right, but you tell Norman that me and Vi are gonna want a good handshake for this.'

Hefty left the key with Joan, and she slipped it into her bra. She'd heard a bloke called George Garrett had done the old man in and wondered why Norman would be saving his bacon. Oh well, she thought, that's another customer down the Swanee, but she knew Vi wouldn't miss Rob. Hefty was right, the bloke was a slimy bastard, and he liked to do things to Vi that his wife wouldn't allow. Good riddance to him, she thought, and patted the key against her breast.

George had lost count of the number of cockroaches she'd seen scuttling around the cell. She hated them – the bloody things made her skin crawl and so did policemen. She heard the familiar sound of gates opening, keys jangling, and jumped to her feet, ready to swipe the first copper to enter her cell. Never again would she allow herself to be so vilely abused. She'd be ready for them this time, and if she killed one of them, so what? She believed she was for the gallows anyway so she may as well take a copper or two with her.

As she braced herself, she heard a man shouting, 'You filthy bastards, you can't do this to me. I never killed the old bastard, and you fucking know it. I've been set up... Do you hear me? Framed!'

The tension left George's body when she realised the

police weren't coming for her, but it sounded like some other poor bugger had been nicked for something he hadn't done.

'I'm fucking innocent, you wankers!'

'Yeah, yeah, yeah. That's what they all say.'

George couldn't see what was going on, but she heard a gate slam shut, and the prisoner continuing to shout about a set-up.

Next, an old-looking policeman appeared in front of her cell. George flinched and clenched her fists. She'd fashioned a shaft from a piece of the bench that had splintered and was ready to jab it into the copper's neck. To her surprise, he opened her cell door and stood back, saying, 'You're free to go, Garrett.'

George wasn't sure she'd heard him correctly.

'Come on, you're getting out of here,' the copper said.

She didn't need telling again, though she was cautious as she passed him and held the sharpened piece of wood in her fist, ready to use it if he touched her. She still felt pain from the attack but as she walked through the holding area she hid her discomfort well. They'd left her feeling appalled, but she had her pride. For a brief moment, she paused as she passed the cell where the other man was being held.

'You fucking bastard,' he shouted through the bars, then gobbed at her. 'Wilcox has set me up for this to get you off the hook. You murdering fucking cunt... It was you who did it!'

'Move on, Garrett,' the copper said, then added to the man, 'and shut it, you.'

George's mind spun. She had no idea who the bloke was behind the bars, or how Wilcox had somehow got her out of that hell pit. She did realise he was being set up though. Billy had killed Mr Peterson; the old man had said so before he'd died.

She slipped the splintered bit of wood in her pocket and signed some papers for her release. At last, she stepped through the police station doors. It was refreshing to feel the weak sun on her face and a cold wind on her cheeks. She was free and ran into the waiting arms of her father. It was such a relief to be in his embrace and feel her fears melt away, though she held back from allowing herself to cry again. Her dad would ask what was wrong, but she could never bring herself to tell him what disgraceful act had taken place. For now, just being with her dad was enough.

20

'Have you seen the papers, Jack?' Dulcie asked, waving yesterday's news in front of her son.

They were sat opposite each other in the armchairs by the hearth, and George was upstairs in her room. Jack guessed his mother was referring to Robert Harris being charged for the murder of Mr Peterson. 'Yes, Mum, but it's no more than he deserves.'

'Come on, Son. We both know that poor man is innocent. He don't deserve the death penalty, and what about his wife and kids?'

'Leave it out, Mum. What would you prefer? Our George swinging for it?' Jack already felt bad about Rob; he didn't need his mother going on about it too.

'No, of course not. I just don't think it's right that an innocent man should be done up for it. The real murderer should be on the end of that rope, not Rob the Roach.'

'Yeah, well, there's nothing I can do about that, and Norman will make sure his wife and kids are looked after.'

'Norman bloody Wilcox. It's always the same name. He's left you half blind with that awful scar. That man has blood on his hands, and I wish to God you'd have nothing to do with him!'

'Say what you like about him, but he's saved our George twice now. I'd rather have him on my side and not as an enemy,' Jack said.

'Just watch yourself with him, Son. Granted, he's helped out, but I wouldn't trust him as far as I could spit him.'

Jack had heard enough. If his mother wasn't going on about Norman, then she'd be on at him about George looking like a boy and fighting the local lads. 'I'm going for a pint. I'll see you later.'

As he grabbed his coat from over the newel post at the bottom of the stairs, he heard his mother call out, 'Don't drink too much. You know you can't hold your booze.'

Jack slammed the door behind him. Living with his mother was becoming more and more bothersome. She nagged worse than an old haggard wife. He could understand why Percy had done a disappearing act and didn't blame the man. He'd considered it himself, but at the end of the day, she was still his mother, and someone had to look after her.

George lay on her bed and had been staring up at the ceiling all morning when she heard the front door close.

She assumed her father had gone for a Sunday lunchtime drink and knew he'd return later, the worse for wear.

She closed her eyes and tried to think of Ruby, the beautiful face of an angel who'd come to her in the cell, but instead, the faces of the policemen flashed through her mind. She'd always remember them, sneering, and what they did to her. She'd been too ashamed to tell her family and had vowed to carry the secret to her grave. She wished the experience had left her numb, but it hadn't. The pain and torment felt very real and though she'd tried to put it to the back of her mind, she couldn't forget. Nor could she forgive.

She was grateful she wasn't being hanged for Mr Peterson's death, but knew the wrong man was going to the gallows. Billy Wilcox had caused all this. It was all his fault. He was dangerous and far worse than his father. At least Norman had morals. It seemed Billy had none.

George opened her eyes again and stared back at the ceiling. She twisted her mother's wedding ring that she wore on her little finger, an unconscious habit she'd acquired whenever she was deep in thought. Christmas was fast approaching. She couldn't touch Billy, not yet. She'd have to bide her time with him. But the three policemen... they didn't deserve to enjoy the festive spirit or see in the New Year celebrations. George pictured them with their families, and the images left her with a bitter taste in her mouth. It wasn't right. It wasn't fair.

She couldn't bring them to justice through the courts, but she could impose her own. Revenge. George suddenly sat up and threw her legs over the side of the bed. Yes, revenge. That would work. Revenge for the disgusting way they'd treated her. She'd pay them back, each one of them. Her gran would be busy cooking dinner, whilst her dad was getting drunk, which left her with the day to plan it.

At last, for the first time since her arrest, George smiled. She could never rid herself of the awful memories, but she refused to allow them to beat her. She knew that to win, she had to defeat those who'd hurt her. It would be the only way to make her feel empowered.

21

The next day, Molly Mipple shivered in bed, and groaned out loud as she realised she was once again lying in her older sister's urine. The girl should have stopped wetting the bed by now, but their mother had told Molly it was because her sister had bad nerves and a simple mind. Molly wasn't surprised and blamed their father.

'Ethel... get up... you've wet the bed again,' she whispered, careful not to wake anyone else, especially their dad. He didn't like it when Ethel had her 'accidents' and would take it out on their mother. Molly's older sisters had long left home, and rarely visited, which left Molly and Ethel sharing a bed, with their six-year-old sister in the cot beside them.

'Oh no, I'm sorry, Molly,' Ethel sniffed.

'It's all right – just get up so that I can change my clothes before I go to work. Keep quiet. It's still dark so hopefully he won't wake up.'

Ethel quietly climbed out of the bed, and Molly followed. She'd have liked a bath, or at least a thorough wash, but there was no hot water, and boiling up pans was sure to disturb her father.

'What shall I do about the bed?' Ethel asked quietly.

As Ethel stood in front of the cold draught from the broken window, Molly saw her sister was trembling, and her eyes were filled with unshed tears.

'Wait for Dad to go out, then stand the mattress up against the wall and let it air. In the meantime, help me turn it over, and get back in. You'll have to pretend to be asleep until he buggers off.'

Ethel nodded, and between them, they lifted the heavy mattress.

'What you doing?' their younger sister piped up.

'Shush, Charlotte, go back to sleep,' Molly ordered.

'What you doing, Ethel?' Charlotte asked again, louder this time.

Then Molly's worst fear was recognised as the curtain between the rooms flew open, and she saw the outline of her dad standing there.

'What the fuck is going on in here?'

'Nothing... nothing, Dad, sorry,' Molly answered.

Ethel had dropped to her knees by the side of the bed and was cowering under the window. Charlotte had pulled her thin blanket up to her chin.

'Has she pissed the fucking bed again?' her father roared.

'Mike, Mike... come back to bed. I'll sort this out,' her mother urged as she appeared behind him.

'She has, ain't she? The dirty fucking cow!'

Molly stood rooted to the spot as she saw her father reach round and grab the back of her mother's neck. He yanked her forward with such force that she landed on all fours between the bed and the cot, just inches away from Molly's feet. Then Molly saw her dad kick at her mum's behind, and her mother cried out in obvious pain.

'Get it cleaned up, woman. I'm warning you, if she does this one more fucking time she's out!'

Ethel whimpered in the corner, and Molly instinctively stood blocking her protectively.

'She won't, I promise,' her mother said.

Her father grunted, then pulled the curtain back across the room. She was about to sigh with relief but then the curtain whipped across again and she saw her father launch the contents of his piss bucket directly at them.

'And you can get that cleaned up too,' he yelled.

Molly stood in shock as her dad's dark urine dripped from her hair. She heard his bedsprings creak, and hoped he'd go back to sleep, but the room was beginning to light up in response to the rising sun.

'Go, Molly, you'll be late for work,' her mother said in a hushed voice as she climbed to her feet.

'But...'

'No buts, just go. We'll be all right; leave this to me. You don't want to give him another excuse to kick off.'

Molly nodded. Her mother was right. Though her father had never done an honest day's work in his life, he'd go mad if she was late for her job in the match-making factory. It would be just another excuse for him to use her mum as a punchbag.

She grabbed her coat from off the bed, thankful it was dry, and Ethel handed her a crocheted turban-styled hat. She'd have liked to change her clothes and run her head under the only tap in the house, but that would mean going through her dad's room to the shared scullery. With her father already in a foul mood, she thought better of it.

'Be a good girl today,' she whispered to Ethel, kissing her lightly on her cheek. She could taste her sister's salty tears and was again reminded of how much she hated their father. Then, she tiptoed from the room and out of the front door.

The sun hadn't long been up, but the streets were already bustling with people on their way to work, or some heading home after night shifts. The cool morning air was bracing, and as Molly buttoned her coat, she noticed the smell of the urine. If she was to get to the factory before her shift started, she'd have to run all the way. At least there was running hot water in the ladies' cloakroom, and she could rinse out her skirts and hair.

Monday mornings were Joan's favourite time of the week. It was the only day the brothel was closed, and though she detested housework all the women would muck in and give the house a good going-through.

As Joan wrapped her dressing gown round herself, she heard Carol's footsteps overhead, then Vi humming as she dashed across the upstairs landing to the bathroom, followed by Annie shouting out to Vi, telling her not to be too long. Hilda had replaced Beth, but she was as quiet as a mouse, and though it had been six years, the women still weren't sure if they trusted her or not. They'd all be down soon, and then they would enjoy a chat over a cup of tea and bread with dripping. Joan licked her lips. There was always a bit of dripping left after the Sunday dinner – she made sure of that.

Joan quickly dressed but didn't bother to do her face up with make-up. There was no need as there'd be no punters today. She opened the curtains and squinted against the bright, morning sun. It felt warm for December. Christmas was only a couple of weeks away, but it didn't feel very seasonable in the brothel. Norman always banned any show of festivity. He said he didn't want the customers reminded of home and their kids.

As Joan went to turn away from the window, she caught a glimpse of Norman's car coming down the street heading towards the house. She suddenly panicked. He wasn't due to visit until Thursday, and she hadn't yet finished preparing the books. Then her mind raced. She wondered what reason would bring him to call so early in the morning.

As the car parked up, Joan hurriedly applied some

lipstick, and rubbed some on her cheeks to give her a bit of colour. She was on the better side of fifty-five now, and hardly ever saw direct sunlight. Her high cheekbones were prominent, but her pale, wrinkled skin and drawn thin face gave her a skeletal appearance.

Joan emerged from her room as Hefty opened the front door. His huge frame almost blocked the doorway, but Joan could see that he was alone, and sighed with relief.

'What are you doing here at this ridiculous hour?'

'I need a word... in private,' Hefty answered, shifting his bulk from one foot to the other.

'You'd better come to my room then,' Joan said. She could see he looked uncomfortable, and assumed he was seeking girlfriend advice again. 'So, who is she this time?'

'No, Joan, it ain't about a bird.'

'What then? Don't tell me you want me to sew your bleedin' buttons on your shirts again? I ain't got time to sod about, Hefty.'

'No, nothing like that. It's about Billy.'

'Billy... Norman's boy? What about him?' Joan asked, curling her lips in distaste. She'd never liked the lad. Years of working with men had given her a good nose for sussing the bad ones, and she'd known instantly that there was something very wrong with Billy Wilcox.

'It's a bit delicate, but Mike Mipple told me that Billy is running his own girls.'

'Oh, Hefty, you big lump of a fool. Don't believe a word that comes out of Mike's mouth. We ain't seen hide nor hair of him for years, not since he blabbed to Norman about what Beth had told him. Don't get me wrong, the man did the right thing, albeit for a good back-hander, but he's been out to get Norman 'cos he didn't get paid what he thought was due to him. I heard he went to the Maynards and offered to sell Norman up the river. The Maynards told him where to go, but I'll bet he's just trying to stir up shit again.'

Hefty sat down on Joan's chaise longue and shook his head. 'Nah, it's true. I checked it out for myself. Billy's got himself a little set-up in a house off Queenstown Road. He's got two foreign bits in there. I ain't sure, but Mike reckons they're from Belgium or Russia, but he said they ain't half on the young side. To be honest, I ain't even convinced they're you know... proper grown-ups.'

'Are you absolutely sure about this, Hefty?'

'As sure as today is Monday. I sat outside yesterday and watched. He's got his mate on the door and judging from the number of blokes I saw coming and going, I think he's got himself a good little earner. I watched for most of the day, and Billy turned up. He didn't stay long, but when he came out, he looked pretty fucking chuffed with himself. What do I do, Joan? Should I tell Norman?'

Joan flopped onto the edge of her bed. Her head

was reeling. If Hefty had got this correct, then it all made sense. Business had dropped off a bit lately, and Vi had said she'd heard there were some new Russian girls working the area. No-one gave a toss about the street girls, but another brothel in the same town was direct competition and Joan knew Norman would see it as a threat. As much as Joan disliked Billy, she was struggling to believe that he'd knowingly stitch up his own father.

'Joan, what do you think I should do?' Hefty asked again.

'I'm not sure. I don't know if Norman will thank you for telling him. Let's face it, he thinks the sun shines out of his boy's arse.'

'But he don't, Joan, he doesn't think that at all. He lets people believe that's how he feels, but he knows Billy is a sly bastard. He's told me so himself.'

'Really? In that case, you've got to tell him. If he finds out from someone else and discovers you already knew but didn't tell him, he won't be none too pleased.'

'That's what I thought. Fuck it, I ain't looking forward to this,' Hefty said, pushing himself to his feet. 'Thanks, Joan. I'll see you Thursday... I hope.'

Joan saw Hefty out, then went through to the kitchen. Carol, Vi, Anne and Hilda all turned to look at her.

'Well, what was that all about?' Carol asked.

'Nothing. Just Hefty wanting advice about his non-existent love life again,' Joan answered. The outcome of this was not going to be good, and Joan decided the fewer who knew about it, the better.

George felt frustrated. She hadn't left the house all weekend as she'd convinced herself people would look at her and would know what had happened. Now she realised that was impossible and with her mind set on paying back the policemen, she felt a renewed vigour. Her father was still sleeping off his hangover, and her gran was busy baking a Christmas cake and mince pies. Oppo had managed to charm Mr Kavanagh into giving him back his job, so he wasn't around either. The quiet suited her – it gave her time to think clearly.

Molly had called in yesterday to check on her, but George had made excuses about feeling tired, so her friend hadn't stayed long. She'd felt awful lying to Molly and had been desperate to tell her the truth, but the words hadn't come.

'Do you want to come and lick the bowl?' she heard her gran call from the kitchen.

'No thanks, I'm not seven years old any more.' She laughed, trying to sound unaffected, then added, 'I'm going out for a walk. I'll see you later, Gran.'

Minutes later, as George wandered aimlessly, she found herself passing Mr Peterson's shop. She was surprised to find it open, and saw the man's wife behind the counter. She guessed the woman couldn't afford to lose the business. George put her head down and hurried past. She knew she was innocent, but she was also aware of the culprit and felt guilty harbouring the secret. Her dad had warned her to keep quiet about it, and George agreed she would, but it didn't feel right, and she hated Billy Wilcox all the more.

It was lunchtime; the streets were busy with workers spewing from the local factories. Everyone seemed to be in such a rush, worrying about completing their business before it was time to go back to work. George stood still for a moment and leaned her head back to look at the fluffy clouds overhead. Smoke belched from the surrounding chimneys, and as she took a deep breath, she could smell the unmistakable pungent aroma of heavy industry. The bricks of the buildings were blackened with soot, as were the kids who played outside with snotty noses and dirty, scuffed knees. Her gran was right, Battersea was a stinking town, but it was home.

George continued her stroll, one moment grateful to be free without a death sentence hanging over her, the next depressed and consumed with hatred. She focused her thoughts on the three policemen. She was so intent on planning the perfect justice, that she hadn't realised she was on Billy Wilcox's street.

She was about to turn round and walk the other way, but then noticed a group of young men a few hundred yards in front of her. They'd formed a circle, and George guessed there was some poor victim in the middle being bullied. She thought about ignoring it and knew she shouldn't get involved, but for reasons she couldn't explain to herself, she walked towards them. As she drew closer, she recognised Malc and Sid along with a few of Billy's gang, then to her dismay, she realised they were surrounding Molly!

George quickened her pace to defend her friend. She knew Molly wouldn't stand a chance against these thugs.

'Oi, you lot, leave her alone,' she shouted as she charged towards them.

The gang stepped aside, and George could see Molly was distraught and in tears.

'Look who it is,' a short bloke with a face that looked as though it had melted said, 'George Garrett, the only bloke in Battersea with tits!'

The young men laughed, and George could feel her cheeks flushing. She was about to snipe back at the man, telling him she knew his face wasn't burnt in the trenches, like he claimed it was. She knew the truth, that Billy Wilcox had blow-torched him for having the bottle to backchat him. The flame had ensured he never did again. Before George could say anything, Malc spoke next.

'Piss off, George. You ain't welcome round here.' Then he turned his attention back to Molly. 'That she-man, whatever it is, ain't gonna help you, Miss pissy pants.'

Molly shot her a look and George could see her friend was terrified and noticed the urine stains on her dishevelled skirt.

'Why are you still standing there? I told you to piss off, you dickless fucking wonder,' Malc said aggressively.

George saw red. The reference to her anatomy made her feel as if she was back in the police cell again and she had so much pent-up anger. 'Who the fuck do you think you are?' she said through gritted teeth and in a blind fury, ran at him with her fists thrashing.

He didn't seem prepared, and George managed to punch him square on the nose. Blood instantly began to spurt from his face, and the shock appeared to stop him retaliating. The one with the scarred face came at George, but she spotted him from the corner of her eye and spun and lumped him in the mouth. His lip split, but he came back at her. The boxing lessons served George well. She was quick, light on her feet and gave him a left hook to the side of his head, then a strong right-hand upper-cut, which connected hard under his chin and knocked him off balance. He retreated, but Sid lashed out at her. She noticed something glint in the sun, and realised he had a small knife. He waved it furiously in front of her, but George laughed.

'You wanker,' she smirked, 'four of you against the *dickless wonder*, and still you need to be tooled up. Go on, fuck off, the lot of you. If I ever see you come near Molly again, I'll have you all, one by one.'

The men exchanged looks with each other, then Malc spoke. 'Come on, it ain't worth it.'

'Make sure Billy hears about this,' George called as the lads sloped off. Then she turned her attention to Molly. 'Are you all right?'

'Yes, thanks, George. I don't know what would have happened if you hadn't have come along.'

'Good job I did! You know Billy and his gang are just bullies. If I got any one of them alone, they'd shit themselves.'

'Yeah, I know, but they've been picking on everyone in this street for as long as I can remember. You would have thought they'd have grown up by now. Course, it doesn't help that Ethel wets the bed and I have to share with her. To top it all, me dad emptied his bucket on us too. I was on my way home to get changed,' Molly said, indicating her soiled skirt.

'Tell you what, I'll walk you back to your house, then I'll make sure you get back to work without being bothered.'

'Thanks, George, I'd really appreciate that, but ain't you got nothing better to do?'

'Not really. Now that I'm as tall as him, my dad ain't so keen on taking me out with him any more. He reckons he can do the jobs quicker without me.'

'I suppose that ain't a bad thing, especially as you've already been arrested.'

George's stomach flipped at the mention of the arrest and she felt her jaw tighten.

'Are you all right? I know you said you was tired yesterday, but you don't seem yourself,' Molly asked.

No, George wasn't all right. The memory of the abuse ate away at her day and night. The only thing that stopped the painful recollections was the idea of paying back the policemen for what they'd done. 'Yes, I'm fine,' she answered, and immediately regretted sounding so curt.

'You're not, are you? I've known you a long time, and I know when something isn't right.'

George bit her bottom lip and began to twist her mother's wedding ring.

'I'm your best friend, you can tell me anything,' Molly offered. 'A problem shared and all that.'

George felt tears beginning to prick her eyes and looked around before pulling Molly down a narrow alley, hoping that she hadn't been seen crying.

'Oh, George, what is it? What's got you so upset? I've never seen you like this before.'

George took a long, deep breath and tried to compose herself. She looked at Molly's concerned face, then blurted, 'The coppers did terrible things to me, awful, disgusting things. I'll kill them, Molly, I swear I will.'

'What did they do?'

'They... they, erm... oh God, I can't bring meself

to say… They held me down and hurt me… with a truncheon… in my backside.' As George revealed the horrors of her experience, she felt her legs go weak and fell to her knees. 'It hurt so much, I thought they were going to kill me,' she sobbed.

Molly crouched down and wrapped her arms round George as her body was racked with tears.

'Oh, George, that's despicable. No wonder you're so upset. Have you told your gran or your dad?'

George shot her head round to look at her friend. Her eyes glistened and were panicked. 'No, please, Molly, you must never tell a soul. I'm so ashamed, I couldn't stand for anyone else to know.'

'It's all right, I won't say anything, but this wasn't your fault. You have nothing to be ashamed of. It's them bloody coppers who should be ashamed of themselves. They're supposed to look after us, not do things like… *that*!'

'Yeah, well, I'll never trust another one for as long as I live. Anyway, so now you know but I'd appreciate it if we didn't talk about it again.' It had momentarily felt good to unburden herself of the terrible secret, but as George pulled herself together, she once again felt humiliated.

Molly nodded. George could see the pity in her friend's eyes and it wasn't something she liked. 'Come on, I'd better get you home then back to work before you're late,' she said as she stood up and wiped her face with the cuff of her donkey jacket, newly acquired for her by her father.

As they walked, Molly asked, 'What are you doing this weekend?'

George appreciated her friend trying to lighten the mood and changing the subject. 'Nothing,' she answered.

'I was thinking about taking Ethel and Charlotte to the park on Sunday to keep them from under my dad's feet. Why don't you come with us?'

'Yeah, I'd like that. I haven't been to the park in ages.'

'Good. It'll be nice to get away from these streets and the likes of Billy Wilcox. I don't know why he's so horrible. His mother is a lovely woman, and his dad seems all right.'

'I dunno. I ain't so sure about his dad. They say the apple don't fall far from the tree.'

'Perhaps you're right. I don't know what dodgy stuff his dad does, but I've heard Billy's lot have been taking money from the people on my street in return for not having their windows smashed, or worse.'

'I think that's how Mr Peterson got himself done in. He said something about not paying Billy. It ain't right, Molly, he shouldn't be allowed to get away with it.'

'Unless his dad stops him, I can't see anyone else fronting him, can you?'

No, George couldn't. She'd have liked to put a blade between his shoulders, and if she could have got away with it, she would have, but for now, thoughts of revenge on the policemen were more pressing.

Once Molly had quickly changed, and they'd reached the factory gates, Molly gave George a gentle squeeze. 'I'll see you Sunday,' she said.

'Yes, see ya,' George answered, grateful that Molly didn't mention the police again, though she could tell her friend felt sorry for her. It did feel better to share her secret, though it made her feel awkward and it hadn't lessened her desire for retribution.

The days were short at this time of year, and the streets grew darker as ominous clouds covered the winter sun. George pulled her collar up round her neck and hunched her shoulders as she thought about an idea she'd formulated. She'd need Molly's help to pull it off, and it meant Molly would be doing her a big favour. Their friendship went back years and George was about to test Molly's loyalty.

22

Billy looked at Sid's and Malc's bruised faces and shook his head in disgust. 'I still can't believe you let a girl do that to you. You fucking pussies!'

'In all fairness, she ain't a normal girl,' Sid said, his lip still swollen after nearly a week.

'Granted, she's a freak, but you're a fucking disgrace, the lot of you!' Billy shouted, as his eyes wandered over his gang.

'Don't include me in this. I wasn't there. I was here, looking after the girls,' Knuckles said defensively.

'Do you want us to get her, Billy?' Malc asked.

'No. It's too late for that. She's shown you all right up! Just stay out of her way, for now.'

They were all gathered for their weekly meeting in Billy's brothel. The three-bedroom house was rent-free as Billy had taken over the rent collections for the landlord's other dozen properties. He'd increased the fees, and those tenants who didn't like it, or couldn't afford to pay, had been thrown out and replaced. The revenue from pimping out the Russian tarts was all profit, apart from the few pence he paid his whores.

'Right, down to business. Knuckles, any problems this week?'

'No, Bill, only Mike Mipple trying to get in here again. 'I told the dirty bastard to fuck off. If I start letting his sort in, we'll have every fucking scumbag in Battersea knocking on the door.'

'Good, he can go and fuck the streetwalkers. Now then, Malc, Sid... I want another ten per cent added to the rent collections. You know what to do if anyone objects.'

Malc and Sid nodded.

'Knuckles, I've got twenty-odd blokes interested in the poker. I'm having a meet with Al at the Dukes Head tomorrow. He's got a big room upstairs, and it's one of the few pubs my old man ain't got covered under his insurance policies. I want you and Pimples with me. I don't think Al will have any objections, but bring your tools, just in case.'

'But I thought Al was married to one of the Maynards?' Knuckles asked.

'Yeah, he is, but his missus has been shagging some geezer from up West, so word has it that Al gave her a good hiding. She's fucked off back to her mother's. I don't know the full story, but from what I heard Al had a visit from Harry Maynard and now he can't count to ten on his fingers any more.'

The men laughed, and Billy added, 'See what I mean? Al ain't going to mind us taking over his pub twice a week. In fact, unless he wants to lose a few toes too, I reckon he might welcome us with open arms.'

There was a tap on the door, and Malc got up to open it. Varvara – a tall, slim blonde girl – stood in the doorway wearing a lacy red bra with white silk knickers and stockings. Dina, equally tall and slim, in a cream satin slip, was standing beside her.

'Are you ready for us?' Varvara purred.

'Yeah, let them in, but Sid and Malc, you ain't having a treat this week, not after allowing that Garrett slag to mark your faces. The rest of you, fill your boots,' Billy said, then cocked a finger at the girls. 'You two, come here.'

The young Russian women approached Billy and stood in front of him. He ran his hand up Varvara's thigh and dug his fingers into her buttocks. 'Come, sit here,' he said, and pulled her onto his knee.

Varvara looked uncomfortable and flashed a desperate glance to Dina. Billy's hand slipped up the side of Varvara's body and across her exposed breasts, finally resting around her long neck. He squeezed, ever so slightly, causing Varvara to flinch. 'Knuckles tells me you've been good girls. Keep yourselves clean and stay out of sight. You know what'll happen if you disobey me?'

Varvara gasped as Billy tightened his grip round her neck. 'Yes, we know,' she croaked nervously.

'Right, have fun, boys,' Billy said, and stood up, throwing Varvara to the floor.

Goodbyes were said as Billy left, and soon, as the sun

was beginning to set on the weekend, Billy was outside his home.

As he put his key in the lock, Billy thought to himself that one day, this house and his mother would be his and he'd be more powerful than his father could ever imagine. When that day came, his dad would show him the respect he deserved, and he relished the thought. But for now, for the sake of his mother, he'd have to endure his father treating him like a child.

He loathed the way his dad tried to control him, always telling him what to do and thinking he had the right to chastise him. As far as Billy was concerned, the only authoritative thing about his father was the belt the man wore round his waist. Without his sharpened buckle, his father was weak. Billy thought he was too soft on his tarts and they made a mug out of him. The same could be said for his sister. Sally had him wrapped around her little finger. It turned Billy's stomach to see how spoilt the girl was, but his father was too stupid to see it.

His mother was the only woman Billy respected. He adored her, but the thought of her sharing her bed with his dad repulsed him. He believed his mother should be cherished, admired from afar and not have his father's dirty hands all over her. He had no doubt that his dad fucked his whores. Billy thought they probably sucked his dad's cock too, then that same cock, the one that had been inside a tart's mouth, would contaminate his precious mother. He tried not to think about it, but when he did, he'd feel bile rise in his throat.

As he opened the door, he clenched his jaw, hating the pretence of being nice to his dad. He reminded himself to smile; after all, he didn't want to upset his mother.

He strode into the lounge to find his father looking impatient and tapping his foot. He recognised that look, the same expression his father always had before giving Billy a telling-off. He ignored the man's obvious irritation and casually said, 'Hello, Dad. Where's Mum?'

'Gone to visit your nan 'til Sunday. Sit down, Son, I want to have a little chat with you.'

Here we go again. His father was going to bore him with yet another lecture, Billy thought as he sat on the sofa. His dad stood up from his armchair and paced the room. Billy thought he looked nervous, perhaps of him, and he hid a sly grin.

'Now don't bother denying it, because I know all the facts. Would you care to explain to me why you think it's acceptable to open a rival brothel directly under my nose and not tell me anything about it?'

So, his father had found out. Billy had expected this and was surprised it hadn't come sooner. It just went to show that his dad wasn't as all-knowing as he thought. 'I don't ask you about your business, so I don't see what mine has to do with you,' he answered brazenly.

'You know I control this town. If you weren't my own flesh and blood, you'd have seen the buckle of my belt by now. It ain't on, Son. You can't defy me like this and expect to get away with it.'

Billy refrained from laughing. He'd grown up with the threat of that bloody belt and thought his dad might have come up with something more original by now. 'Is that right? Well, I have defied you, *Dad*. I've been getting away with it for several months now, so what are you gonna do about it? You've lost your grip. It's understandable, you know, you're getting on. Maybe it's about time you stepped aside and let me take over running the businesses. I'd make a better job of it.'

Billy could see his father's temples pulsing with anger. It didn't worry him; after all, what could he possibly do to him? The belt would never be used – his mother wouldn't allow it.

'You've got some fucking nerve,' his father said. 'I blame meself. I made you like this, you cocky little dipshit. Just you remember, I built you up to what you are today, and I can take you back down.'

Did his father really believe he was the making of him and could destroy him? 'Sounds like you're threatening me,' he taunted.

Billy watched wide-eyed as his dad flew across the room and grabbed him round the neck. As his father's fingers clenched around his throat, Billy didn't react or even flinch. In fact, he struggled to keep a straight face.

'Don't push me, boy,' his father growled before releasing him.

As his father walked towards his drinks table, Billy decided to make him a fair offer. His mother would tell him it was the right thing to do and he'd always intended to, but he enjoyed winding him up. 'Tell you what. I'll stick to the rules. You allow me to carry on with my own small enterprises, and I'll give you a cut of the earnings. That's how it works, ain't it?'

'You don't get it. Yes, I take a cut of anything that goes down in Battersea, but I also give it the go-ahead first. No-one goes behind my back and sets up against me. This was the last thing I expected from you. You've let me down, Bill, and you've let down the family.'

'Oh, I see. You've got the 'ump 'cos I never asked permission from *Daddy*. You can't stand it, can you? You hate the thought that I might be better than you.'

His father poured himself a whisky from the crystal decanter and quickly downed it. Billy noticed his father's knuckles had gone white from gripping the glass.

'I knew you'd be defiant, but I thought I might at least get an apology from you. Get this in your head, Billy – you'll *never* be better than me. Now, this is how we're going to resolve it. You will hand over all your books to me. I will oversee your operations, but you will still run them. I'll give you a payment for your initial set-up costs, then fifteen per cent of all profits. I can't say fairer than that.'

'What if I don't agree to your terms?' Billy asked,

knowing full well that he wouldn't comply. Still, it was fun to tease his dad.

'You will, if you know what's good for you.'

'I don't think so, Dad. I don't want to work for you, end of story.'

'You have no choice. See, if I allow you to go unchecked it undermines my authority and before you know it, I'll have every Tom, Dick and Harry nipping at my heels, thinking they can get one over on me. This is how it has to be, so don't make it any more difficult than it should be.'

Billy had listened to enough and was bored of the conversation now. He jumped up and stomped towards his dad. It was time to lock horns, like stags jostling for territory and control. 'If you want my business, you'll have to fight me for it, 'cos I ain't handing it over,' he spat menacingly. He callously glared at his father, hoping the man would accept the challenge. There'd been many times when Billy had envisaged snuffing the life out of him, and now that thought flashed through his mind again.

As he scowled at his dad, he was sure he saw fear looking back at him and he sneered. He'd known the man was weaker than him and now he'd shown it.

'I'll give you until tomorrow to calm down and think about what I've offered. I know what a bad loser you are, so you don't want to fight me, Billy, because believe me, you *will* lose and none of us want to look at your moody mug.' With that, his dad prodded him in the chest.

Billy immediately went from bored to infuriated. He felt his father was trying to belittle him.

'If you want to play with the men, Billy, you'd better stop acting like a brat. I'd have more respect for you if you'd been man enough to come to me instead of hiding your brothel like a naughty little boy. Is that it, Billy, are you nothing but a naughty little boy who needs his arse spanked? Do I need to put you across my knee like I did when you was seven?' As his father goaded him, he began to unbuckle his belt.

Billy took a deep breath and felt as if he physically grew in width and height as his shoulders came up and he leaned towards his father. He could feel his cheek twitching and his face contorting as his eyes became empty. He no longer saw the man stood before him as his father – he was now Billy's adversary, a feeble irritant that he wanted rid of.

In one swift move, he swung his arm out and thumped the side of his father's head. The powerful blow knocked his dad to the floor. Billy stood over him and looked down at the man's bewildered face. He tilted his head to one side as he studied his father's expression that had changed from one of shock to terror now.

'What have you done?' his father whimpered, clearly disorientated.

'You said you made me what I am, Dad... This is me,

the powerful man you reckon you created. I ain't no-one's lackey and I never will be.'

His father attempted to get on his feet and grabbed hold of the armchair to pull himself up, but Billy found it amusing as he pushed the chair away and his dad slumped to the floor again.

'All right, Son, you've proved your point, now help me up.'

His father held out his hand, but Billy was enjoying his supremacy and instead of aiding the man to his feet, he leaned into a heavy punch that left his father laid flat out.

Billy grinned when his dad groaned in pain. He would have been satisfied, but his father still dared to affront him.

'You've just made a very big mistake, my boy. I would have let you get away with one punch but now you're taking the piss.'

As his father pushed himself onto his haunches, Billy hissed, 'I ain't your *boy* and I don't make mistakes,' and though his knuckles hurt, he punched him again, this time between the eyes.

The breath seemed to come out of his dad and his head snapped backwards, yet still, though seeming dazed, he slurred, 'You're fucking dead, Billy... dead to me and dead to your mother.'

His mother! Billy couldn't abide the thought of losing her love. After what he'd just done, he knew his father would force her to disown him, but he couldn't, not if he rendered the man unable to speak. Not if he was dead.

Billy walked purposely across the room and grabbed a cushion from the sofa. As he approached his father, the man hit out, but his strength had waned, and his fists only hit air. Where he'd been moderately entertained at his father's fight, now the sight of the man bloodied and defeated left him feeling nothing but revulsion. His father, who Billy had once admired, was now desperately failing to defend his life and Billy despised him for his faintness. He hated seeing the man's fragility and he detested him for threatening to take away the one and only good, pure thing in his life.

Billy straddled his father's chest, pinning him to the floor, and pushed the cushion into his face. His dad struggled but it was futile and as he gasped for oxygen, Billy pushed against the cushion harder. His dad's legs began to jerk, and he stopped struggling. As his arms dropped to his sides, Billy was sure he'd almost killed him and pulled the cushion away. He wanted to see his father's face when he took his last breath. He wanted his own reflection to be forever in the man's eyes.

He placed the cushion to one side and whispered, 'Any last requests?'

He hoped his dad wouldn't plead and beg for his life – that would just be too predictable and tedious – but

Billy was pleasantly surprised when his father answered hoarsely, 'Hide my body well. Don't let your mother ever know you killed me.'

His father's final words had impressed Billy, and for that, he decided to take his life quickly and to not prolong the torture. He placed his large hands round his dad's throat and squeezed as hard as he could, all the while staring intently at his own image in his father's swelling eyes.

It wasn't the first time Billy had killed, but murdering Mr Peterson hadn't been nearly as enjoyable. As the old man had fled, Billy had whacked him with a spanner on the back of his head. He'd never got a chance to see the fear in the man's eyes.

This had been different and as Billy climbed off his dead father's body, he said, 'Don't worry, Dad, I'll honour your last wish... Mum will never discover that it was me who killed you.'

23

Joan heard a hammering on the front door and glanced out of the window to see Norman's car outside and Hefty on the doorstep.

'What's the matter, Hefty?' Joan asked as she opened the door.

'I can't find Norman. I was supposed to pick him up at ten this morning but he ain't at home.'

'So? Big deal, you can take the rest of the day off.'

'Nah, something ain't right, Joan, I know it.'

'Did you tell him about Billy?' she asked.

'Yeah, and he weren't too happy.'

'What's he doing about it?'

'I dunno. He said to leave it to him. I can't think where Norman would be without the car. I'm his driver, but I haven't got a clue where to start looking for him.'

'Don't worry, Hefty. I'm sure he's just having some family time.'

'Not without his car. I can smell a rat and I'm sure Billy has got something to do with it.'

'Well, there's nothing you can do 'til you know where Norman is,' Joan said as she patted her new short curled hairstyle.

'I could take a drive up to Billy's whorehouse and see if he knows anything.'

'You could, but I don't think that's wise. I mean, you don't know what's been said between him and his dad.'

'Yeah, well, it's my job to look after him and I can't if I don't know where he is. I'm gonna check out Billy's brothel. See ya, Joan.'

Hefty left Joan's, and though she was sure the man appreciated her input, she thought he was silly to ignore her advice.

Dulcie's legs were feeling warm from the fire, but there was a terrible draught whipping around the door and making her neck ache. Her hips had stiffened up quite badly, and she found it was a painful effort to push herself up from her chair, but she had a thick woollen scarf under the stairs. It was a gift that Ruby had knitted her many years ago. It was all she had left of the woman and treasured the item dearly. Dulcie would never forget the day when she'd discovered what had happened to Ruby. She'd first thought that the girl had fled and assumed Ruby must have been in fear of how Jack would react to Georgina's kidnapping. Dulcie could have lived with that, but it had broken her heart when she'd learnt Ruby's body had been washed up on the banks of the Thames. Suicide apparently. Such a shame and such a waste.

The scarf was neatly folded on a shelf at the back, and as she reached in the cupboard for it, she heard the front door fly open and felt a cool breeze on her back. She hadn't been expecting Jack or George home for ages yet, so when she heard the door slam shut it made her jump, causing her to bump her head on the cupboard doorframe.

Jack dashed past her and into the kitchen. He seemed breathless and was as white as a ghost. She followed him into the kitchen to find him frantically yanking on the back-door handle.

'Jack, what's going on?' she asked.

'It's the Old Bill, Mum, they're after me. Where's the fucking key?'

'I don't know, George must have locked the door. Check under the mat. What have you done, Son?'

'Not now, Mum, they're right on my heels. I've got to get out of here.'

Dulcie could see her son was in a panic. She began rummaging through the kitchen drawers looking for the key. But before either of them could find it there was a heavy hammering on the front door, and a loud voice called, 'Police. Open up.'

'Shit, what shall I do?' Jack asked, his hands shaking.

'Upstairs… go… get under my bed.'

Jack flew from the room and up the stairs. Dulcie gave him a minute to settle. The police were pounding on the door and threatening to break it down. She braced herself before opening it. 'What's all this fuss about?' she asked, looking at the four policemen on her doorstep.

'Where is he?'

'Who?'

'You know who. Jack Garrett. We know he's in here.'

'My Jack? I ain't seen him for weeks. Now bugger off, go on, clear off,' Dulcie said, and went to close the door.

A copper placed his foot in the way and pushed against the door. His strength forced Dulcie backwards, but the wall saved her from falling. The copper looked at her scathingly as he said, 'We'll search the place from top to bottom. I know he's in here somewhere.'

'You can't do this... Get out of my house,' Dulcie yelled, but it was too late. Two of the policemen had already raced upstairs; one was in her front room whilst the other stood guard at the front door.

Then Dulcie hung her head as she heard a deep voice from upstairs shout, 'We've got him, guv.'

Her heart sank. It was bound to happen someday, but her son had been nicked right on top of Christmas. She had no idea what they had on him and could only hope it was something petty.

'Your dad's pet Rottweiler is at the door,' Knuckles said to Billy.

'Let him in. You never know, I might adopt him,' Billy replied, then took a seat behind a large mahogany desk that he'd had placed in front of the downstairs bay window. The brothel now also served as his office.

Hefty entered the room with his cap in his hand. Billy couldn't help noticing he was fumbling with it, obviously nervous. And so he should be, Billy thought. Hefty's massive size didn't bother him. He had Knuckles who was equally as large but a good twenty years younger than Hefty. He wasn't a betting man, but if he had to lay money on it he reckoned Knuckles would be favourite to win.

'What can I do for you, Hefty?' Billy asked. His hands were spread open on his desk, but just below it he had quick access to a pickaxe.

'I'm looking for your dad. Have you seen him?'

'Yes, as a matter of fact we had a few words last night.'

'He told me to pick him up this morning, but he ain't at home. Do you know where he is?'

'Yes, Hefty, I do,' Billy answered. He was enjoying teasing the giant.

'Where is he then?'

'At this moment in time, he's in the basement. I expect he'll be there for a while.'

'Oh... right. Is it all right if I go down and have a word with him?'

'Feel free,' Billy answered. 'The door is in the hall, but I don't think he's feeling very talkative.'

Hefty looked puzzled, but then headed for the basement. Billy smirked and sat back in his large, black leather chair. 'Pour me a drink, Knuckles – this is going to be amusing.'

Billy waited a couple of minutes, then he heard the expected cries from Hefty, followed by the man's heavy footsteps coming back up the stairs. The door burst open, and a purple-faced Hefty stood there.

'He's dead! You fucking killed him!'

'Well done, Hefty, you managed to work that out all by yourself,' Billy said, and sipped on his whisky.

'How could you? He's your father! You sick fucking bastard!'

'Now, now, Hefty, let's not start throwing insults around.'

'What about your mother? And your sisters? Please God, don't tell me you've done them in too?'

'Why would I want to do that? I love my mother, Hefty, she's a very special woman, and now it's my job to look after her.'

'She'll go fucking mental when she finds out what you've done!'

'She's not going to find out, is she, Hefty? If she does, I'll know it came from you, and then you'll be keeping my dad company.'

'You won't get away with this. It ain't right. Your dad looked after you, gave you everything you ever wanted, and this is how you repay him. You must be off your fucking rocker!'

'All right, that's enough! Knuckles, get Hefty one of these,' Billy said, holding up his glass. 'I think he's had a bit of a shock. Hefty, take a seat.'

The man accepted the drink and sat down, though he looked as if he was ready to rip Billy's throat open.

'With my father gone, it's only right that I'll be taking over. Now, you can either work with me, or against me… and you've seen what happens if you choose the latter. So, what's it to be?'

Hefty threw Billy a filthy look, but he gave him another chance and repeated his question. 'With me, or against me?'

'I've worked for your dad all my life. He was a good man. Fair. You… you ain't nothing like him. I can't work for you, but I won't work against you either.'

'See, that's not how it goes. If you're not working for me, then I must assume you're against me. Those who are against me will be destroyed. Is that what you want, Hefty?'

'No, Billy.'

'Good, I thought not. Your first job is to set up a meeting with the Portland Pounders. I want them to know I'm in charge now. Then gather all my father's men here for ten on Friday morning. Do you think you can do that?'

'I suppose,' Hefty answered.

'Right. Now leave the car here. I'm gonna be using it so it'll be shanks' pony for you from now on. Of course you could always get yourself a bike. Now FUCK OFF! And if you value your life, keep your big gob shut.'

Hefty meekly placed his empty glass on a side table as he left the room.

'Keep your ear to the ground, Knuckles, and one eye on him. If you hear or see anything, even so much as a whisper, bury him.'

'Will do, Billy,' Knuckles answered, flashing his boss a smile. The man's teeth were rotten and the sight of them turned Billy's stomach.

'And from now on, you call me Mr Wilcox.'

Billy swung his chair round and looked out of the window. Sid and Malc had helped him move his father's body, but they'd have to get rid of him soon before he began to stink the place out. That wouldn't be good for business. He couldn't have his dad just dumped anywhere though. No, his father merited a bit more respect than that. The least he deserved was a proper burial, even if it was in an unmarked grave in the cellar of the Queenstown Road brothel.

24

It was almost teatime when George arrived home, cold and laden with Christmas gifts, but pleased with her purchases. She'd dipped a fella at Clapham Junction and her haul had allowed her the luxury of having a blowout in Arding and Hobbs department store. From a distance, she'd secretly admired the dresses in the women's department, but had quickly dismissed any silly notions of wearing one. Even looking like a man hadn't protected her from being attacked and she shuddered at the thought of anything like that happening again. Her masculinity hadn't saved her from the policemen, but it went a long way to shield her on the lawless streets.

The festive shopping trip had been a welcome distraction from thinking about the policemen, and she couldn't wait to get to her room and wrap the presents. As she struggled with her parcels and fished for her key, the front door flew open. Her heart sank when she saw the worried look on Oppo's face.

'Thank Gawd you're home.'

'What's wrong? Is my gran all right?'

'Yes, yes, she's fine, just very upset.'

'Why? What's happened?' George asked, frantic with worry now.

'It's your dad. He's been nicked.'

George dumped her shopping at the bottom of the stairs, then rushed through to the front room, her mind whirling with worry and unanswered questions. 'Why's Dad been nicked, Gran?'

'The Old Bill were round here earlier and carted him off. I don't know what he's been done for. You'll have to get yourself down the station and see what you can find out.'

'But… I… Oh, Gran. I can't!' George protested, finding herself at a loss for words. The thought of having to visit the police station filled her with dread. She wasn't sure if she could face seeing any of the policemen who'd abused her. Not yet. Not until she'd got her own back.

'What do you mean, *you can't*? Of course you bloody can. You're not going to leave your father in there to rot, are you?'

'No… but… can't Oppo go?'

'No buts, go on, get yourself off. They won't tell Oppo nothing 'cos he ain't proper family.'

Her gran was a formidable character and not one to argue with. George studied her lightly lined face. The woman's lips were set in a grim and determined line. Though she'd rather have stuck pins in her eyes, George knew she had no choice other than to go to the station. She felt light-headed and could feel her pulse quicken as a wave of nausea washed over her. She couldn't tell her gran the reason why she didn't want to go. Unaware she was doing it, she twisted her mother's wedding ring and reluctantly nodded. 'I'll be as quick as I can,' she said, then pulled her coat around herself before stepping back out into the cold.

A short while later, George stood outside the police station and took a moment to compose herself. Though outwardly she appeared calm, her clenched fists betrayed how she really felt. It was so cold, her cheeks burnt, and a drip of snot hung from the end of her nose.

She had to get this over and done with, but she hated the thought of walking back into the station. She went to step forward but stopped, rooted to the spot. She couldn't do it. What if one of her abusers was behind the desk? Her stomach knotted, and she thought she was going to throw up. 'Come on, George, you can do this,' she told herself and reminded herself of why she was there. Her dad had got her out, and now she had to be brave and do the same for him.

George braced herself, then purposefully marched up the steps outside and pushed through the front entrance. Her confident manner masked her insecurities, but she was relieved when she didn't recognise the copper behind the desk.

The policeman looked over the top of his glasses as George stomped towards him. He wasn't one of her abusers, but he was still filth, a dirty lying copper.

'Can I help you?'

'You've got my dad here, Jack Garrett,' George answered, and her eyes flitted around hoping she wouldn't come face to face with one of *them*.

'That's right. You needn't bother wasting your time though. He's not allowed any visitors, and he'll be up before the judge on Monday morning.'

'You're keeping him here all weekend? What's he been charged with?'

'You know I can't divulge that sort of information,' the policeman answered.

George could tell her aggressive manner was getting the copper's back up, so instead, she switched on the charm, hoping to manipulate him to get the information she wanted. 'Please, sir, I'm beside myself with worry. My mum's dead, and my dad is all I have. Can't you give me just an indication of what's going to happen to him?' She looked through the top of her dark lashes, pleading with her violet eyes.

The copper leaned forward, and after a quick glance round, he whispered, 'He got caught with the Vauxhall mob turning over a building depot where that new power station is being built. I'm not sure what they were after, but your dad was the driver. He's been charged with aiding and abetting a robbery. Between you and me, I don't think he's got a hope in hell of getting off and will probably go down for one to three years. That's as much as I know. Now clear off, young man, before you get me in trouble.'

George's eyebrows knitted together as she digested what the policeman had told her. Driving for the Vauxhall mob? That didn't make sense. As far as she knew, her dad couldn't drive. She'd never seen him behind the wheel of a car, and what was he doing knocking about with the Vauxhall mob?

Without a word of thanks to the copper, George hurried away. She'd discovered all she could and wanted to get out of the building as quickly as possible. The police must have made a mistake. It was the only explanation she could think of, and she knew it wasn't the first time the Old Bill had nicked the wrong person.

Twenty minutes later, after an anxious walk back, George was home. She found her gran rocking back and forth in her chair and wringing her hands with worry.

'I've never seen her like this before. She hasn't said a word since you left,' Oppo whispered, clearly concerned about Dulcie.

George knelt beside her gran and relayed what she'd been told. She saw her gran's expression change from desperation to confusion.

'But the Vauxhall mob are all well past it now. They ain't done any jobs for years. Anyhow, I don't think your father even knows them.'

'That's what I thought, Gran, and he's never mentioned driving before. I reckon they've got the wrong bloke.'

'Maybe, but he was up to something yesterday, I could tell. Oh, George, what are we going to do?'

'I dunno, Gran. But whatever happens, you don't need to worry. I'll look after you.'

'I know you will, love. You're a good girl and as much as it irks me to admit it, your father taught you well. Dear oh dear, I hate to think of him banged up behind bars. There must be something we can do. You know my thoughts on that Norman Wilcox bloke, but he might be our only chance of getting your father off.'

George didn't like the idea of her dad in prison either and had already considered paying a visit to Norman to see if he'd be willing to help. After all, he'd managed to get her off the charge of murdering Mr Peterson. 'Yeah, I'll go and see him,' George replied, adding, 'He is my dad's mate, and I'm sure he'll do what he can, but that doesn't mean we have to like him.'

Dulcie nodded in agreement. 'Go on then, as quick as you can. We've got to get him out of that cell before he's in court. After that, it'll be too late.'

'I'll stay here, George. We'll be all right, won't we, missus?' Oppo said and winked at Dulcie.

George kissed her gran on the cheek before heading back out. 'Don't worry. He'll be home before you know it,' she said, hoping her words were true and that Norman would help them out again.

*

Joan answered the door to Hefty for the second time that day. He didn't seem to notice that her face was now made up, and Joan was oblivious to the fact that her pan-stick was applied too thickly, which emphasised her wrinkles, and her red lipstick was bleeding into the lines around her thin mouth.

'Still no sign of Norman?' she asked, blowing smoke rings into the air, and flicking the ash from the end of her cigarette into the palm of her hand.

Hefty didn't answer but bundled Joan back into her room.

'What are you doing, Hefty? Get orf me, you bleedin lump.'

Hefty stared at her but didn't say anything.

'Something's happened, hasn't it?' Joan asked as she eyed him suspiciously.

He walked to the window and seemed to be scanning the street. Joan thought he looked jumpy and became worried. 'Hefty, what's going on?'

The big man spun round and looked at her, then placed the palms of his hands on his bald head. 'He's dead, Joan. Billy's killed his own father.'

'Don't be ridiculous. Where did you get such an idea?'

'It's true. I saw Norman's body with my own eyes, and Billy, well, he was gloating about killing him and reckons he's taking over the business. Fuck, Joan, I can't make head nor tail of this. He's mental... fucking mental!'

Joan walked slowly to a chaise longue at the end of her bed, and sank onto it, shaking her head in disbelief.

'What do I do, Joan? He said I work for him now and he told me I'd be dead too if I don't do as he says. Shit. That means you work for him and all – we all do!'

'Yes, I realise that,' Joan snapped, then added, 'Sorry, Hefty, it's just a bit of a shock.'

'I know, I still can't get my head round it. Honestly, Joan, I wanted to kill the sly fucking cunt. How could he do this? What sort of person could kill their own dad?'

'A person that ain't right in the head, Hefty. I don't think any of us are safe now. If he can murder his own flesh and blood, then just think what he could do to us.'

Hefty sat himself down next to Joan and leaned forward with his head in his hands. 'I thought the world of Norman. I know people thought he was a difficult man, but he was always good to me, Joan. I can't stand by and let Billy get away with this.'

'No, he shouldn't be allowed to, but I don't see what you can do about it. You can't get near him, at least not safely. He's got too much protection around him. I don't know what to suggest, but one thing's for sure, we can't work for him.'

'We might not have any choice.'

Joan scratched her head, then closed her eyes, deep in thought. 'Hefty, get the girls together. I've got an idea.'

Once everyone was gathered, Joan stood behind the

bar and poured herself a large brandy. She looked at the women sat on the sofas, then to Hefty who only just fitted in the armchair. He looked nervous, drumming his fingers on his massive thigh. Carol, Vi, Annie and Hilda stared back at her, obviously waiting for an explanation for the sudden meeting. Someone rapped on the front door.

Joan knocked back the brandy before speaking. 'Ignore it.'

The women exchanged a bewildered glance. It was Carol who asked, 'Are you going to tell us what's going on, Joan?'

'Norman Wilcox is dead. He's been killed by his own son, Billy,' Joan answered, then paused as Carol gasped.

Vi jumped to her feet and spluttered, 'Jesus Christ! If Billy Wilcox is at the reins, we've got to get out of here! I've heard all about him and how he treats his Russian girls. Annie and Hilda might be all right – they're young – but us three... well, I dread to think.'

'Sit down, Vi,' Joan ordered. 'Yes, you're right, we've got to get out of here, but we're not leaving Annie or Hilda behind. We'll do this together, but it's going to be risky.'

'What have you got in mind?' Carol asked.

'We've got a few days' takings in the safe, enough to get us started. We need to pack a small suitcase each, then Hefty can run us down to Portsmouth. We'll be out of Billy's reach there, and we can set up a new business by ourselves. As far as I know, there ain't no-one running the South coast, so we shouldn't be stepping on anyone's toes.'

'Portsmouth... are you having a laugh?' Vi said in a high-pitched voice.

'What's wrong with Portsmouth?' Joan asked.

'It's a bloody Navy town. The place will be over-run with whores and strippers. And them sailor blokes... well, they can be a bit rough. No, I ain't going to Portsmouth. You'd better think again.'

'I don't know anywhere else. Portsmouth is the only other place I've ever been to outside of London. Anyone else got any suggestions?' Joan answered sharply, irritated at Vi for putting her idea down.

'I've got a cousin in Wales,' Annie offered, her voice quiet.

Joan rolled her eyes. 'Thanks Annie, but we ain't emigrating.'

'I can't drive you to Wales or anywhere else. I ain't got Norman's car now. Billy's got it,' Hefty said, and lowered his head.

'Oh, for fuck's sake,' Joan swore, then sucked in a deep breath. 'Right then, wherever we're going, we'll have to travel by train, but we'd like you to come with us, Hefty. We could use a minder.'

'Yeah, all right. If I stay around here I might just throttle Billy Wilcox, but I don't want to risk swinging for the likes of him.'

Carol said, 'I've got an idea. Bernie… he's my brother. He lives in Aldershot. He stayed there when he came out of the army. I ain't seen him for a few years, but we keep in touch. He's the henchman for Marve the Mad Axe. From what Bernie has told me, Marve is a bit of a face in Aldershot, but as far as I know he ain't got any girls working for him. Maybe we could persuade him to diversify his business. What do you think, Joan?'

Joan poured herself another brandy. Carol's suggestion didn't sound too bad.

Vi huffed, and folded her arms. 'But Aldershot is an army garrison. It wouldn't be any better than Portsmouth.'

Joan drank the brandy quickly, then said firmly, 'Vi, stop bloody whinging. We've got to do something, and it would help to have a bit of clout on our side. No offence, Hefty, but your skills don't lie in running a business. Carol, girls, get your stuff packed. We're going to pay Bernie a visit.'

George had first checked the pub that Norman was known to frequent, then after running all the way to his house she hammered on his door, breathless and desperate to find the only man who could save her father. It was nearly four, and it wouldn't be long before the sun would set. The time was quickly ticking past, and all the while her dear dad was imprisoned in that stinking shitpit, a foreboding place that she was all too familiar with.

There was no answer at Norman's, so she banged harder. Still nothing. She knew he had a place on Livingstone Road, a whorehouse that she'd been warned to stay away from. Her dad wasn't a judgemental man, but he was always outspoken about his detestation for prostitutes. She had no other option: she had to track down Norman, and on this occasion, she thought her dad would turn a blind eye to her calling at the brothel.

It took George fifteen minutes to get to Livingstone Road. She had run for so long that she felt sick, but after catching her breath she knocked hard on the door. Once again, there was no answer. Norman had to be here – he just had to be! She banged again and would have called Norman through the letterbox, but it was sealed. Instead, she tapped on the downstairs window, hoping that she wasn't disturbing a bloke on his vinegar stroke. She stepped backwards, and shouted, 'Mr Wilcox. Norman Wilcox,' then went back to the door and pounded on it.

At last, it opened, and George found herself staring at the irritated-looking face of an older woman wearing so much make-up that George had a job not to laugh.

'What do you want?'

'Mr Wilcox. I know he's here. I need to see him,' George replied.

'Well he ain't here so clear off.'

'He is. He must be!' George insisted. She wasn't going to let this ridiculous-looking woman stand in her way so she shoved past her into the hall.

'What do you think you're playing at?' the woman snapped, looking furious. 'You ain't got the right to barge in here. Hefty... Hefty...' the woman yelled.

To George's relief, Hefty appeared in the doorway. If he was there, then Mr Wilcox must be too. He looked surprised to see her and asked, 'What are you doing here?'

'Oh, you know her then?' the old crone said.

'Yeah, she's Jack Garrett's girl.'

'Oh, so *you're* George! I can see why everyone thinks you're a bloke,' the woman said as she eyed George up and down, then turned back to Hefty, adding, 'Huh, well, no doubt she's a chip off the block and just as stuck up her own arse as her old man. I'll leave you to it. Just make it quick.'

'OK, Joan,' Hefty answered, before turning his attention back to George. 'I can see you're in a bit of a state. What's wrong?'

'It's my dad. He's been arrested. I was hoping Mr Wilcox would work his magic and get him out of the nick.'

'Sorry, George, but Mr Wilcox won't be able to do anything. In fact, it's best you get off now,' Hefty said as he moved past her to open the front door.

'Hang on a minute, Hefty. You can't just fob me off.

Where's Mr Wilcox? Let's see what he has to say about it. Is he in there?' George asked as she moved towards what she hoped was the lounge.

Hefty's huge arm came out, blocking her path. She could see the skin on his thick neck looked red and his face was clammy as he said, 'You've been told Norman isn't here. He can't help you or your dad. You'll have to sort this out for yourself.'

'Come on, Hefty, you know my dad is Norman's friend and he'll want to get him out. Just give me a couple of minutes with him... please.'

George saw Hefty's body slump, and his cheeks begin to twitch. He wouldn't make eye contact with her and she could tell he was on edge. She realised then that something wasn't right. 'What's going on, Hefty?'

'Trust me, George, you really don't want to know.'

'But I do... please, Hefty, Norman is my dad's only hope. He could be looking at doing a three-year stretch.'

Hefty seemed to crack and threw his arms in the air. He walked two steps forward, spun, then three back, and then forward again, all the time muttering, 'He's dead... he's fucking dead...'

George could hardly believe what she was hearing. Hefty was ranting. Dead? Norman Wilcox dead? He couldn't be – she needed him. Her father needed him.

The heavily made-up woman appeared in the hallway again and grabbed Hefty's arm. In the dim light she looked like something from a horror film.

'It's all right, calm down, Hefty,' she said firmly, then turned to George and added spitefully, 'Are you happy now? See what you've done?'

George glanced at Hefty's crazed eyes, then at the scary-looking woman. Never mind about this being a whorehouse, it's more like a bleedin' madhouse, she thought to herself.

'Don't just stand there gawping, girl,' the woman barked. 'Help me get him through to the lounge.'

George took Hefty's other arm, and between them they tried to pull him towards the room, but he yanked free from their grasp. His arms began to flail around wildly and George, along with the woman, had to step out of harm's way. Both stared in stunned silence as Hefty then began to repeatedly punch the door, all the while moaning, 'He's dead. Billy fucking killed him. It ain't right. It ain't right.'

George gulped in shock and turned to the woman. 'Is it true?' she asked. 'Has Billy killed his father?'

The woman nodded. Then three younger-looking women appeared in the hallway, and all seemed horrified at seeing Hefty in such a state. The wooden door was now in splinters and blood from Hefty's fists dripped onto the parquet flooring. Eventually, probably exhausted, he fell to his knees and began to howl and cry.

'Help me get him to my bed,' the woman ordered the three younger ones.

George watched as they gathered Hefty up and encouraged him along the passage to a room near the end. When they disappeared inside, it went quiet for a few minutes, and during that time George realised she'd forgotten about her father. Her mind was filled by the enormity of what Hefty had said.

The women came back along the passage again, and the older one spoke. 'Right, you've heard the truth now and I suggest, if you know what's good for you, that you keep it to yourself.'

'I'm not gonna blab,' George told her and meant it. Billy Wilcox was a dangerous man, a madman; she realised that now. She was afraid of him, but if they crossed paths, she'd never let him see her fear.

Joan had thrown some essentials into a battered suitcase, and gently nudged Hefty. 'Get up, big man, time to go.'

Hefty slowly opened his eyes, looking befuddled. After his hysteria earlier, he'd fallen into an exhausted sleep, and now Joan hoped he'd wake calmer.

'Where... what...?'

'It's all right, Hefty. You've had a bit of a snooze, but we've got to get going. Come on, get yourself up.'

Hefty sat up, still looking dazed. 'Shit, I lost the plot,' he said sheepishly.

'Yes, you did, but we ain't got time to muck about. The girls are ready, let's go.'

'I'll need to shoot back to my place to pack some clothes.'

'There's no time for that. You can buy some new clobber when we get to Aldershot.'

'But that will leave me skint.'

Joan had taken what money was in the safe and knowing it now belonged to Billy, she was eager to get away. However, she didn't want to leave Hefty behind. With no idea what was in front of them, she needed a bit of muscle around and Hefty fitted the bill. 'Look, we can't risk hanging around, so I'll help you out until we get on our feet.'

'All right then,' Hefty agreed as he climbed off her bed and she opened the door to find Carol, Vi and Annie waiting in the hallway and looking anxious.

'Where's Hilda?'

'Probably in her room. I ain't seen her.'

'Annie, go and tell Hilda to get a move on. There's a bus due that'll take us to the station.'

Hefty emerged from Joan's room as Annie came running down the stairs. 'She's gone,' Annie called. 'She ain't in her room. It's empty and her bag has gone. She's scarpered.'

'This is all we need,' Joan said through gritted teeth. She'd been right never to trust that girl. She had no doubt that Hilda had done a runner straight into Billy's hands. 'The two-faced bitch. She'll be telling Billy what we're up to, and that we've pinched his money. There's no time to hang about. Come on, we've got to leave right now!'

Carol was obviously thinking the same. 'But what if she tells Billy that we've gone to Aldershot? He's bound to come looking for us. Joan, I think you should put the money back in the safe.'

'With his father gone, Billy's going to be too busy to worry about coming to Aldershot looking for us. He'll have enough on his plate, and anyhow, a few quid missing won't hurt him. We need this money. Now, let's get out of here.'

Joan was the last one out, and as she closed the door behind her, she felt sad to be leaving. All the years of living in the house and working for Norman, she thought she hadn't liked the man. But now she realised she was going to miss the security he'd provided, and ultimately, she'd miss him too. 'God rest your soul, Norman Wilcox,' she whispered. 'And God help us.'

25

The following morning, Billy sat in his father's armchair with his legs stretched out in front of him and his hands placed behind his head.

'Very comfortable,' he said out loud to himself, 'and this will be my chair from now on.'

Now that his father was out of the way, he was savouring the thought of being the man of the house. But first he had to tell his mother that his dad would never be coming home again. He wasn't looking forward to it. He'd considered saying that his dad had run off with one of the Livingstone Road brasses, but Billy didn't want to see his dear mother hurt. He loved her and would do all he could to protect her from any unnecessary pain. He thought about telling her there had been an accident, but it left too many questions, and his mother would want a proper funeral. In the end, he decided on gently breaking it to her that the Liverpool gang had killed him. It was the kindest way he could think of.

She'd been gone for the weekend, but he was sure she'd be home soon, and hoped it would be in time to cook his dinner. He always looked forward to a Sunday roast, though there'd be one less place setting at the table today. He imagined the scene: he'd be carving the meat in place of his father and his mother would be looking at him adoringly. The only blot on his landscape was Sally. Perhaps he'd carve her up instead of the roast beef!

Billy heard the front door open, then Sally came into the lounge, closely followed by his mother. Sally eyed him up and down, then gave him a filthy look before stomping back out and up the stairs. He detested her, and just her presence alone irritated him. He only tolerated her for his mother's sake.

He thought his mum looked elegant in a black wool coat that draped loosely over her slender shoulders, edged in thick fur round the neck and wide, open cuffs. He could see she was wearing a crimson dress with a black lace hem, and she wore a set of long ebony beads. She was surely the most glamorous woman in Battersea, a cut above the rest.

'Sally, come down and take your sister upstairs with you please,' she called, pulling off her red gloves, then turned to Billy and asked, 'Where's your father?'

Billy stood up from his dad's armchair. 'Sit down, Mum.'

'I don't want to sit down. Just tell me where your dad is.'

He could tell she'd sensed something was wrong. 'I've got something terrible to tell you,' he said gently. 'Dad's been killed. The Portland Pounders finished him off. I'm sorry, Mum, there was nothing I could do.'

He saw his mother's legs buckle and hurried forward, grabbing her under her arms as she began to drop.

'No... no... no, Billy. You've got it wrong... Where's your father?'

Billy gently pulled her towards the sofa and eased her down. She sat stunned, and stared up into his eyes, searching for answers.

'He's gone, Mum. It was quick – he didn't even know it was coming. They shot him from behind. He wouldn't have felt a thing. But they warned me. We've got to keep it quiet or they'll come after Sally next, then you.'

His mother sprang from the sofa and began to pound his chest with her fists, crying, 'No, no,' over and over. Billy gripped her arms, and held them to her sides, then pulled her close to him as he embraced her. He could feel her body judder as she cried into his chest. He looked over her head and noticed his sisters had come back into the room. Sally's eyes were wide as she looked at her heartbroken mother, and her brow was creased.

'What's going on?' she asked as his baby sister toddled towards them.

His mother pulled away from him and dashed away her tears, her voice breaking as she said, 'Come here, love,' and scooped her daughters to her.

Billy watched with contempt as his mum cuddled

his sisters. He hated to see her affections lavished on anyone but him.

'Your dad's been... he's... there's been a terrible accident...'

Billy impatiently interrupted. 'Dad's dead,' he said coldly, and hid a smile as he watched Sally's face pale then crumple.

'How? How did my dad die?' the girl asked as tears rolled down her cheeks.

His mother looked at him. She wanted him to answer. Yes, this was his verification. His place as head of the household was affirmed in that moment. All that had once belonged to Norman Wilcox was now under his rule, including his sisters, and anyone who dared to defy him would be aptly punished.

Molly shivered. She had dressed in several layers, but the cold felt like it was in her bones and the icy wind had numbed her cheeks. Ethel didn't seem to mind the freezing weather as she ran through the park with Charlotte giggling and chasing behind her. Molly would much rather have been at home with her sisters, but their father was in one of his moods again, and she could tell he was itching for an excuse to lump their mother one.

She thought it would be best if she kept moving to help keep warm, but she had a blister on her heel that had burst and was red raw. She winced in pain with every step. Her second-hand boots were a size too big, but at least they didn't have holes in the soles and kept her toes dry.

After a further half an hour, she decided to rest her foot and sat on an ornate iron bench. Her nose was running, and water streamed from her eyes. The sky was gradually becoming a darker grey and she knew it would rain soon. They'd have to find shelter, but she daren't risk taking them home this early. They'd have to hold out until early evening at least – then their father would either be out or in his bed.

Charlotte skipped up to the bench. Her coat was a size too small for her, and she was wearing one of Ethel's hand-me-down knitted hats, which kept slipping over her eyes.

'I'm hungry, Molly,' she moaned.

'Me too, sweetheart, but we can't go home yet.'

Ethel ran over. She was wearing their mother's coat, but her knee was poking through a large hole in her stocking and had turned a purple-blue colour.

'Charlotte said she's hungry,' Ethel said. 'I am too, but I told her it ain't time to go home yet. Ain't that right, Molly?'

'Yes, Ethel, that's right,' Molly answered and forced a smile. 'Ethel, take Charlotte over to the big oak tree. Do you remember there's a rope swing that some boys left there last week?'

'Oh yes,' Ethel answered, her face animated. 'Come on, Charlotte, I'll push you and then you can push me.'

The girls ran off, leaving Molly in awe at her older sister's childlike demeanour. Apart from Ethel's womanly body, she acted and played like Charlotte who was just six years old. Ethel would be forever young in her mind, and in some ways, Molly thought it was a blessing. After all, ignorance is bliss. Ethel would never be able to look after herself properly, but Molly would always take care of her.

Her eyes followed her sisters as they darted towards the big oak, then she spotted a familiar figure walking along the path towards them. Her face broke into a wide smile, and she jumped up from the bench.

'Hello, George, you braved the cold then?' Molly greeted her friend.

'Yeah, it's blinkin' taters,' George replied, though Molly thought she looked quite snug in her oversized donkey jacket.

'I can't feel my cheeks. The girls are over there playing on a rope swing, but to tell you the truth I'd much rather be at home under me blankets. It's safer here though, 'cos me dad's got the right hump today.'

'At least your dad's at home. Mine's been nicked.'

'Oh, no, George. What for?'

'Some trumped-up charge. He's at the station now, but he'll probably be going to Wandsworth prison tomorrow.'

'I'm so sorry, that's awful for you and your gran. Any idea how long he'll be away?'

'Dunno, a couple of years, maybe three.'

'Blimey, George, that's not good. How will you manage without him?'

'We ain't got much choice so we'll just have to. Actually, I wanted a favour from you.'

'Anything I can do, I'd be happy to help,' Molly answered, though she couldn't think what she could possibly offer George.

'Tell you what, let's go back to my place and we'll talk there. My gran will have the fire going, and being as it's Sunday, I'll lay odds on that she's baked an apple pie.'

Molly's stomach growled at the thought of apple pie, and she yearned to be inside in the warm. 'All right,' she answered, and called her sisters. She liked it at George's house. It was more welcoming than the dump she lived in. She wasn't embarrassed about her abode. Theirs was no different from hundreds of Battersea families that lived in similar conditions, or worse. She just wished her dad would leave... forever.

'Gran, it's only me,' George called as she opened the front door. 'Come in,' she said over her shoulder to Molly and her sisters.

The hallway was chilly, but much warmer than

outside, and George immediately noticed the pleasant aroma of freshly baked bread. She led the girls through to the front room and was pleased to find the coal fire roaring and Oppo in an armchair fiddling with the clock from the mantel. 'Hello. It's too cold out there so you'll have to put up with us,' she said to Oppo, then to Molly, 'Sit down, make yourself at home,' and she indicated to the plump green sofa.

Oppo jumped up and placed the clock back where it belonged. George noticed Ethel was looking round the welcoming room with her mouth gaping as usual. The girl always seemed to be in awe whenever she visited the house. Charlotte had tucked herself into the material on Ethel's coat. She was sucking her thumb and looked shy, but she usually took a few minutes to relax.

'Would you like some hot milk?' George asked.

'Yes please,' Ethel answered with gusto, and Charlotte nodded.

The door opened again, and Dulcie walked in. Her apron was covered in a light dusting of flour, and she looked surprised to see they had guests. George knew her gran was upset about her dad going to prison, and when the woman was upset, she baked.

'Hello, girls, you've timed that well. I've been in the kitchen all morning. There's enough in there to feed an army. I hope you lot are hungry?'

'Cor, yeah, we really is,' Ethel said, grinning widely. Charlotte looked more comfortable now.

'Come and give me a hand then,' Dulcie said, and hobbled to the kitchen with the girls in her wake.

'Would you mind helping gran too?' George asked Oppo. 'Only I'd like a quiet word with Molly.'

'Sure,' Oppo replied, compliant as usual.

As the door closed behind them, Molly whispered, 'He's a bit of all right,' and giggled.

'I hadn't noticed,' George answered, thinking that Molly was acting very silly.

'Has he got himself a girlfriend yet?'

'No, I don't think so. Stop drooling over Oppo. Bloody men are more trouble than they're worth,' George snapped. She had far more important things on her mind.

'Sorry. What's this favour you want from me then?'

George bit her lip as she twisted the ring on her little finger. She knew it was a big ask, but Molly was her friend and she hoped she'd agree. 'I need you to pinch something for me. Something from where you work.'

'Like what? There's nothing much in the factory except matches.'

'But the matches are made in the factory, ain't they?'

'Yes,' Molly answered, looking confused.

'I'm glad that woman in your street took a shine to you and taught you to read 'cos I need one of the chemicals. I want you to get me a box of potassium chlorate.'

'Eh? What do you want that for?' Molly asked.

'You don't need to know, but will you get it for me?'

'I... I dunno, George. It ain't that easy. Mr Nelson has the keys to the chemicals store and he brings the stuff out on a trolley every morning, just what we'll need for the day. If I see a box with that name on, I might be able to shove it up me skirt, but if he catches me...' Molly trailed off.

'Don't put yourself at risk. Only nick it if you're sure you can get away with it.'

'Yeah, all right, but what do you want it for?'

'Let's just say, them coppers who have got my dad are gonna get a surprise,' George answered. Her plan was audacious, and it would take a lot of nerve, but she was determined to get her vengeance. She couldn't get her dad released, but if he was going down, he'd go down with a bang – one that the police would never forget!

26

O n Monday morning, George tried to look inconspicuous as she waited outside the factory for Molly. It was still dark, yet the early morning rush to work was in full swing. They'd arranged to meet, but if Molly didn't show during the next hour, she'd know the girl hadn't managed to steal the chemicals. Thankfully it wasn't long before Molly came back through the gates, though George muted a smile when she noticed how oddly her friend was walking.

'Round 'ere,' Molly said, and limped into a dark corner. 'I've gotta be quick. I'm only supposed to be going to the bog.'

George followed, then Molly rummaged under her skirt and pulled out a small box of chemicals. 'That was bloody uncomfortable! I hope you know what you're doing, George. This stuff can be dangerous,' Molly said as she handed over the stolen package.

'Don't worry, I ain't stupid.'

Ezzy had a safe cracker working for him, and he'd told George all about how he made explosives to blow open the doors. She had a pretty good idea of what she was doing.

'Maybe so, but you're bloody reckless. Whatever it is

you're up to, just be careful. I've gotta go, before they notice I'm missing. Good luck, George, see ya later.'

'Thanks, Molly,' George said, before Molly dashed off.

She already had sugar, string and matches, and with the potassium chlorate, she now possessed everything she needed.

Hilda had always fancied herself as a gangster's moll rather than a prostitute, and something about Billy Wilcox appealed to her. Joan and the others had said they'd found him creepy and repulsive, but she secretly liked him. Now, she just had to get him to notice her.

Once she was sure the women and Hefty had left on Saturday, she'd sneaked back to the house and unpacked her bag. She'd ignored any punters that knocked on the door during the day and kept the front of the house in darkness in the evening to keep them away.

Now, as the sun rose on this Monday morning, she hoped today would be the day that Billy would come to check on his newly acquired brothel. Oh, she couldn't wait to tell him all about Joan stealing his money and running off to Aldershot. It was sure to grab his attention, and if she played him well, she hoped he'd reward her by handing the running of the brothel over to her. No more sleeping with the punters. Instead she hoped to be sleeping with just one man – Billy Wilcox. Who knew what that might lead to, she mused. Perhaps even the title of Mrs Hilda Wilcox. Yes, she liked the sound of that. It had a nice air about it, and the name Wilcox was both greatly feared and respected in Battersea.

Hilda sat at her dressing table and finished reddening her lips, then stared intently at her reflection in the mirror and admired her bleached blonde hair. Her drunken mother had drummed it into her that she'd never amount to anything, but she had plans. Big plans, and Billy Wilcox was paramount in them.

As though the woman was in the room, she said, 'Mother, you want to watch yourself. Billy is going to love me. Oh yes, he's going to love me all right, and then you'll need to be careful about what comes out of your disgusting mouth.'

She scraped back her stool and rose to her feet. 'Can you hear me, Mother?' she shouted to her room, spinning round.

In her head, she heard her mother's laboured breathing and raspy voice. 'I hear you,' the voice said slowly. 'I hear you.'

'Billy killed his father, so if I ask him to, he'd think nothing of getting rid of you,' she screeched, then her cackling laughter filled the room.

Hilda Murdin was mad. It was inherited, but so far, she'd managed to hide it well. She'd been twelve years old when she'd witnessed her mother set herself alight. Hilda had burnt her hands as she'd tried to pull her screaming baby brother from her mother's arms, but both had perished in the flames. She'd never forget her brother's cries. It triggered her insanity, which had recently begun to manifest as the voice of her dead mother. In Hilda's head, it was real, and she was sure that Billy Wilcox would finally rid her of her spiteful mother once and for all.

Billy gently tapped on his mother's bedroom door. She was normally an early riser and was always up to prepare Sally's breakfast before school. But this morning it was after eight and there was still no sign of her emerging.

He heard a grunt, and slowly pushed open the door before walking into the darkened room. His mother was in bed with the blankets pulled up under her chin. A sliver of light peeped through a crack in the curtains, and though dim, Billy could see his mother's eyes were swollen.

'I've brought you a cup of tea,' he said, placing the cup on a small cupboard by the side of her bed.

The room smelt of his father and there were reminders of him all around. A black suit hung on the front of the wardrobe. His braces were draped over the back of a deep blue velvet-covered chair, and his shoes were tucked underneath. The one thing that wasn't lying around was his father's belt. That was neatly secured round Billy's waist.

'Are Penny and Sally OK?'

'I've told Sally she can have the day off school today, and I've given her some toast and jam. She's keeping an eye on Penny. You don't have to worry about anything, Mum. I'll make sure you're all looked after.'

His mother sat up in the bed and reached out for Billy's hand. 'You're a good son,' she said.

Billy had never seen his mother's hair looking dishevelled, or make-up smudged under her eyes. She always appeared immaculate. He found it was quite shocking to see her in this state and he looked away in distaste. 'You should get up and dressed, Mum. I know it's hard, but we've got to carry on and act like nothing has happened. We don't want people asking questions. So far, the Pounders have no reason to come after us, so let's not give them cause to.'

'What do you mean? Are we in danger?'

'No, Mum, as long as there are no repercussions for them. That means nobody must ever know they killed my dad. If anyone asks, we'll say that he's working away for a while, and in the meantime, I'll be running the business.'

'All right, but I can't face going out today,' his mother answered, her eyes brimming with tears again.

'You don't have to, but you need to talk to Sally and make sure she doesn't say anything.'

His mother nodded. Billy kissed her cheek, then

picked up the tea, handing it to her. 'Drink this. I'm off out to sort out the business. I'll see you tonight.'

Before Billy left the room, he drew open the curtains. The window overlooked the front street. His father's car was parked outside where he had left it, but no, not his father's, it was his now. He knew how to drive it, but like his father, he decided he'd have a minder to ferry him round. He considered Hefty, but he had been too much his father's man, and instead settled on Knuckles. If ever anything turned nasty, he was the perfect muscle to have around.

George took a deep breath and tried to calm her shaking hands. She had to be steady for this. She was fully aware of how unstable her home-made explosive device could be, and if something went wrong, the implications didn't bear thinking about. She had made the bomb by mixing the potassium chlorate with some sugar in a paper bag, and coating a length of string with the mixture. This would be the fuse.

It was ready, and so was she. It had taken all her nerve to come back to the station, but this time, it wasn't her who was going to be hurt. Though anxious, the right side of her mouth turned upwards at the thought of what she was about to do. This was no more than they deserved, and she hoped her bomb would make an impact.

If she could have, she would have thrown the bag straight into the face of the copper who had used his truncheon on her, but this was the closest she could get to him and it would have to do. It was better than sitting back and doing nothing, letting them get away with it. They'd never know why their station had been blown up, but she would and that was satisfaction enough. She just wished her dad wasn't in there, though she knew he'd be in the basement and out of harm's way.

George stood behind a corner on the opposite side of the road from the building. There was no way she was going to back out now. All she had to do was light the string and throw the bag through the main doors. It had seemed so simple when she'd planned it in her head, but now a worrying thought flashed through her mind and she feared getting caught. She couldn't cope with being back in the cells again and if she did get banged up, what would happen to her gran? She realised if she started worrying about the consequences, she'd never go through with this, so quickly told herself to stop being a wimp and returned her focus to the task in hand.

A horse and cart passed her. George pulled her flat cap down, and the collar of her coat up. She glanced up and down the street. It was clear. With her blood pumping fast she hurried across the road, then knelt as if tying her laces. Two policemen came out of the station and George froze, but thankfully they passed her.

Her hands were still shaking, but she managed to

strike a match. The fuse lit easily and burnt quicker than she'd expected. She thought the bloody thing was going to explode in her hand and panicked. As fast as her legs would move, she charged towards the main door, pushed it open, then launched the paper bag inside.

She noticed there were several uniforms in the room, and as the door had flung open, a few of the coppers had turned their heads and looked directly at her. She didn't care. It was too late. The bomb had been thrown, and though she'd have liked to hang about and seen the effect of the explosion, she knew she had to get away, fast.

There were only several strides between her and the station when George heard a muffled boom. It had worked. She smiled, satisfied, as she ran along the street and into a maze of terraced houses. She'd done it. She'd blown up Battersea Police Station. She didn't know how much or little damage her small concoction had caused, but at last she felt she had one over on the Old Bill.

'That'll bloody teach 'em.' She smiled as she slowed her pace and tried to look discreet. She knew the memories of what had happened to her in that dreadful place would always haunt her, but at least now, justice had been served. She just hoped none of the policemen in the reception room could identify her.

27

The next day was Tuesday and Billy arrived at his office early. He'd been busy since taking over, sorting out his father's many business enterprises: the two poker houses, the books of the private loan scheme to review, and the insurance customers to see. The insurance was of course a racketeering scheme, but his father hadn't liked to call it that. He hadn't been so eager to see the books at the only legitimate company under the Wilcox name, but the bicycle sales and repair shop was a good front and cover for the illegal dealings.

'Good morning, Mr Wilcox,' Knuckles greeted his boss.

'Yes, Knuckles, it is indeed.'

'What have you got planned for us today?'

'There's just the Livingstone Road brothel left to sort out so come on, let's get going,' Billy ordered, marching out with Knuckles behind him. 'I'll have to teach you to drive, but for now I'll take the wheel again.'

'Yes, boss,' said Knuckles.

Billy smiled. Boss. He liked the title. It showed respect. His mood was mellow as they pulled up outside Livingstone Road. He had a key and walked in, surprised to find it unusually quiet. 'Joan... Carol...' he called.

'Oh, Mr Wilcox, I'm so glad you're here,' Hilda said as she sauntered down the stairs wearing an almost see-through black lace negligee.

'Where's Joan and the others?'

'I've been desperate to tell you, but I wasn't sure how to get hold of you,' Hilda answered. 'They've done a runner, Mr Wilcox. All of them, and they took the takings from the safe.'

Billy felt a surge of fury, aware of a small tic under his right eye that had begun to jerk. It always did when he was worked up. He saw that Hilda had noticed and was looking directly at his twitch. How dare she! He stepped forward and grabbed a handful of her loose blonde curls on the top of her head and forced her to look down. She yelped in pain. Billy enjoyed that noise and gripped harder as he growled, 'If you value your pretty face, never look directly at me again. Is that clear?'

'Ye... yes, Mr Wilcox, but please, let me go. I didn't do a bunk with them. They wanted me to... but I stayed... to work for you if you'll have me.'

'Good,' he said. 'I'm glad to hear you had the sense to make the right choice, and yes, you can work for me now.'

'Th... thank you.'

Billy released Hilda's hair and shoved her away from him. She stumbled in her heeled slippers and landed in an undignified heap on the stairs. Her ruffled hair was draped across her fair skin, and her dark eyes were glistening. Her negligee had ripped, revealing a long bare leg with a toned thigh. She was visibly shaken and her submissive look momentarily aroused Billy, but he quickly reminded himself that she was a whore.

'Get up,' Billy ordered.

Hilda used the newel post to pull herself to her feet and smoothed her hair before pushing her shoulders back. Her ample breasts were provocatively almost busting over the top of her nightdress.

'I'll send new girls to work here. You can have Joan's room and as a reward for not doing a bunk with the others, you will be in charge. However, unlike Joan, you'll still be taking customers. Are you the dancer?'

'Yes.'

'Yes, Mr Wilcox,' Billy spat.

'Sorry. Yes, Mr Wilcox,' Hilda repeated meekly.

'Good girl. Now, entertain Knuckles while I look at the books.'

Billy knew the books were kept in the safe, and he doubted Joan had taken them. She'd have only been interested in the money. He was right and taking them from the safe he glanced through the columns of scrawled figures, while overhead he could hear the bedsprings making a racket and he rolled his eyes. If

Knuckles wasn't careful, it sounded like he'd be coming through the ceiling.

He had to hand it to Joan. She'd kept tidy accounts and ran a tight ship. Livingstone Road had been turning a good profit. Billy wanted more though. He thought his dad had been weak and too soft on the girls. But things were going to be very different from now on, Billy would see to that.

Knuckles had finished, and was smoking a cigarette as Hilda douched herself, then straightened her clothing. The inside of the tops of her legs were hurting. Knuckles was a big man and had pounded her hard. She was sure she'd have bruises appearing soon.

She headed downstairs and cautiously slipped into the lounge and bar room. Billy had finished scanning the books and was helping himself to a whisky.

'Everything in order, Mr Wilcox?' Hilda asked, nervously. She was desperate for his attention but didn't want to rile him again.

'It will do, for now.'

'Can I get you anything?' she asked, drawling her voice and fluttering her eyelashes.

'Leave it out, Hilda. I ain't interested in going where Knuckles has been,' Billy answered, making no attempt to hide his revulsion.

This wasn't going the way Hilda had envisaged it, so

she changed tactics. 'I can turn my hand to just about anything, Mr Wilcox, and I've proven my loyalties are with you. I was thinking that a man in your position should have a personal assistant. Someone to look after the paperwork, appointments, correspondence, all that sort of stuff.'

To Hilda's delight, Billy's face softened, and his eyes glinted. She'd found a way to get round him. Appeal to his ego.

'I'd be honoured to work closely with such an esteemed man, Mr Wilcox,' she continued, 'and I understand the delicacy and sensitive nature of your work. I can be trusted, and I believe having me at your beck and call will only go to enhance your image.'

Billy finally smiled. 'There's no doubt, Hilda, you are a damn sight better-looking than Knuckles. I suppose you could come in useful, but I need someone I can trust to look after this place.'

'I can find you a tart to trust, with the necessary brains, but you need someone with a bit more refinement to work in your office.'

'All right, Hilda. You find me a girl for here, and you can be my assistant.'

'Thank you, Mr Wilcox. You won't regret it.'

Hilda was right, Billy wouldn't regret taking her on in a new role. Unfortunately, as Hilda would discover in time, she was the one who would eventually come to rue the day.

*

The noise in the match-making factory was almost deafening, and a pungent smell lingered in the air. Molly had become used to it, and hardly noticed any more. She sat in a row with a dozen other women. They didn't chat much as it was difficult to be heard over the sound of the machinery. And anyhow, Phyllis, the woman she sat closest to on her right, couldn't speak.

Phyllis had worked in the industry since she'd been thirteen years old, and now at sixty-two, she was the oldest lady in the factory but refused to hang up her apron. Working practices had changed since Phyllis had first begun, but the changes had come too late for her. Years of handling phosphates had caused phossy jaw, a condition that had been extremely painful and resulted in her having her jaw removed. Her face was now severely deformed, and she was incredibly thin. It wasn't easy for the woman to eat.

Even with no voice, she revelled in a bit of gossip and had learnt to read and write to communicate. However, as there were very few women in the factory who could read, Molly was unsurprised when Phyllis nudged her forearm and indicated her written note. It said that yesterday there had been an explosion at the police station, and she thought Mr Nelson had been taken in for questioning. Apparently, chemicals from the factory had most likely been used in the bomb.

Molly read the note and gasped.

Then Phyllis discreetly scribbled that three coppers had been killed and two badly injured. The floor above had been unstable, and the explosion had caused the ceiling to collapse.

Instantly, Molly could feel her heart pounding, and the room begin to spin. She tried to hide her fear and horror, praying that her face hadn't given any clues away to Phyllis. There was a reward, a big one, and she had no doubt that Phyllis or any of her co-workers would be first in line to claim it if they knew that she'd been involved.

She'd been a part of this! Murdering policemen. She'd stolen the chemicals and if they found out, she would hang in the gallows. Oh, George, she thought to herself, what have you done? After what her friend had told her about how the policemen had attacked her, she couldn't blame George for wanting to get her own back, but she could have kicked herself for not seeing this coming. George was the gutsiest person she knew and wasn't the sort to let things be.

Molly thought back to their conversation when George had asked her to steal the chemicals. She'd said something about the police getting a surprise. They'd got that all right. George had done a good job, but Molly felt physically sick and prayed they'd both be safe.

*

Every customer that came into the greengrocer's could talk of nothing else except the Battersea Police Station explosion. Oppo hadn't read the papers, but he'd been told every small detail. No-one seemed to suspect George as the bomber, but he *knew* it was her. It had to be! And he assumed Molly was also involved.

'Oppo!' Mr Kavanagh shouted.

Oppo heard the man's booming voice and jumped. 'Eh? Sorry, I was miles away,' he answered.

'Yes, I noticed. Concentrate on your job or I'll be docking your pay come Friday.'

'Yes, sorry, sir. I'll fill up the carrots – they look to be getting a bit low.'

'You do that, and whilst you're out the back, you can sweep the yard.'

Oppo was quite happy to clean up outside. He liked Mr Kavanagh well enough, but the man had something to say about everything and his opinions sometimes got on Oppo's nerves.

He'd been in the yard for about ten minutes when he heard his name being whispered.

'Psst, Oppo, over here.'

He looked round and saw George's head poking over the top of the fence. 'What you doing here?' he asked as he walked towards her with his broom in his hand.

'I had to see you,' she answered.

'You could have come in the shop like a normal person,' Oppo joked.

'Yeah, I know, but Kavanagh always listens to everything we say.'

'You're lucky you caught me out here then, but if he sees me talking to you and wasting more time, he'll keep me money short this week.'

'Don't worry, I'll be quick. Have you heard about Battersea nick?'

'Yeah, everyone's talking about it,' Oppo answered. 'It was you, weren't it?'

'Maybe,' George said with a teasing smile, 'but let's just say, I've been having a blast!'

'I knew it! George, this ain't funny. If you get caught, that'll be it for you!'

'I ain't gonna get caught, but I do need a favour.'

'What?'

'Get rid of this for me,' George said, and threw a sack over the fence.

Oppo looked inside. It was her coat. The donkey jacket that had been described in the papers.

'Thanks, Oppo, I'll see you later,' George said.

'Hang on, I haven't said I'll help you.' Of course, he would. He'd do anything for her. But by the time Oppo had looked back up at the fence, she had gone.

George had dashed to Mrs Peterson's shop and now with the daily newspaper tucked under her arm, she picked up her pace again, eager to read the main story. She had to refrain from reading it right there in the street, desperate to find out more about the outcome of the explosion.

She'd hardly slept again last night; adrenaline and excitement still kept her awake. Her father's trial had been delayed and he'd been moved to Clapham along with several other detainees. At least the coppers at Clapham were known to be a little more agreeable than their Battersea colleagues, and there was a possibility that they would allow her to see him.

Finally, back home, she took the stairs two at a time, then slammed her bedroom door closed before jumping onto her bed and laying the newspaper out in front of her.

There it was, on the front page. The headline story. Three policemen killed, and the hunt was on for the bomber. She really hadn't expected that small paper bag to have had such an enormous impact, but she couldn't have been happier with the outcome. There were pictures of the dead coppers and she recognised one of them. He'd been in her cell. This was the sweetest revenge!

She quickly read the rest of the story. They were looking for a young man in a black donkey jacket seen fleeing the scene. *A young man!* George chuckled to herself. She was in the clear. She wasn't a young man, nor did she possess a donkey jacket. She'd gotten away with murder and felt elated. She'd slain the enemy and it was a glorious sensation of victory!

As the euphoria subsided, George found herself deep in thought and twisted her mother's wedding ring. She looked at the gold band and wondered what her mother would have done. Would she have fought back? George realised she'd learnt something about herself today. She was strong and different from the other women she knew. They seemed to put up with their lot and take all sorts of mistreatment from men. Not her. She wouldn't allow it. She wouldn't stand for it. She was proud of herself for what she'd done and only wished she could brag about it to her dad and gran. She knew her father would be proud of her too. He'd taught her to be tough and she'd proved she was that all right!

The Old Bill had shaken her confidence, but now she'd shaken them, and she smiled again at the picture on the front page of the slain copper. She'd slaughter any man who dared to ever wrong her, just as she had the policeman, and if Billy Wilcox wasn't careful, he'd be next.

PART 4

GEORGINA GARRETT'S FIGHT

28

March 1933. Three years later.

George was glad the sun was shining on the day of her father's release from prison. She'd waited over three years for this, and they'd been long, arduous years, but she and her gran had got through them. The country was in the grips of something they called the Depression and though it had always been a daily struggle for survival for the poor, it seemed more and more families were now living in poverty. Many had turned to crime to fill their children's empty bellies, some more successfully than others. George considered herself lucky. She was experienced at thieving and managed to evade the law and provide well for her gran.

She stood outside the prison gates. The building was large, and had an ominous atmosphere surrounding it. Her father hadn't allowed her to visit him during his time, and she'd missed him terribly. She couldn't imagine what it must have been like for him, and the thought of him locked up in a tiny cell had kept her awake on many nights. George jigged impatiently from foot to foot. Any minute now, he'd be coming through the huge, wooden doors. Apart from being a bit taller, she hadn't changed much and still looked more like a man than a woman.

The minutes dragged by, but then the doors opened and at last, George saw her father. She wanted to cry tears of happiness but bit her bottom lip as she held back her emotions.

'Hope we don't see you again, Garrett,' she heard a guard call as Jack passed through the gates.

'You won't. You'll be stuck in this shithole for the rest of your working days... but me, I'm out of here!' her dad replied jovially.

She was relieved to hear that prison hadn't broken him. He sounded the same cheeky, confident bloke that he'd been before his incarceration. George stepped out into her dad's eyeline. He immediately spotted her, and his face broke into a big smile. She wanted to run towards him, to jump into his arms and smother his scarred and roguish face in small kisses, but instead she remained rooted to the spot.

'Hello, George. It's so good to see you,' he said, holding out his arms.

George at last ran into them, pleased to be in his embrace, though she was sure she felt his body stiffen and he winced. Maybe he was injured, but if he was, he hid it well.

'I can't wait to get home and have meself a decent cuppa and a bit of cake. How's your gran?'

'Everything's fine, Dad. Gran is like a cat on a hot tin

roof. She's been up since the crack of dawn, baking as usual.'

'Ha, sounds about normal. Have you coped all right without me?'

'Yeah, no problems. Ezzy had me doing the Manchester runs, and I've been lifting a few bits here and there to keep the cupboards full. Oppo's been helping out where he can.'

'Well done, I'm proud of you. It couldn't have been easy. You were just a kid when I went down, but look at you now, all grown up! You'll be voting soon!'

'Dad, I'm eighteen, not twenty-one!'

'Yeah, well, you're more grown up than most youngsters of your age. Cor, it's good to be out of there. I tried getting hold of Norman to get him to look out for you, but I heard he's copped it and Billy is running the show.'

'Yes, that's right, and did you hear it was Billy that did him in?'

'It was rumoured, but I didn't believe it. Is it true then?'

'Yep, when it happened, Hefty told me. I've stayed out of Billy's way, and Hefty did a runner out to Hampshire.'

'Fucking hell, who'd have thought it, eh! Oops, sorry about my language. It's that place – it gets under your skin.'

George wasn't bothered about her father's bad

language. She often used worse herself, though never in front of her gran.

'You do understand why I didn't want you coming up here to see me?' her dad asked, his face showing concern.

'Of course. If I had a kid, I wouldn't want them seeing me locked up in a place like that either. Was it really bad?'

'It was all right, but I wouldn't want to go back. Anyway, enough about that. What's all this talk about kids? I hope you ain't got yourself a fella?'

'Don't be daft.'

'Good,' said Jack, "cos if you had, I'd want to check him out first to make sure he's up to scratch and all that.'

He was feigning seriousness, but George could tell her father was mocking about. 'Dad, the last thing I want is a husband telling me what to do.'

Her father chortled, but George noticed his jovial mood suddenly change, and his pace slowed. He rubbed his back, grimacing in obvious discomfort.

'What's wrong, Dad?'

'Nothing. Just me old kidneys giving me a bit of gyp.'

George was worried, and asked, 'Your kidneys... why are your kidneys playing up?'

'They've been punched a few too many times, that's all. It was my own stupid fault. I forgot I ain't a young man any more and had a go at taking on a couple of geezers a lot fitter and harder than me. That'll teach me. I should have just kept me head down and done me time. Still, what's done is done. Don't mention it to your gran though.'

George nodded, then pointed to a red double decker heading down the street towards them. 'We should jump on this bus. I don't think you're up to walking home.'

'Leave it out. That ain't a General – that's one of them pirate buses. They're a right bleedin' rip-off and will probably charge us twice the normal fare.'

George had never heard her dad complain before about the unauthorised bus services that operated independently outside of the London General Omnibus Company. If anything, he'd always bigged up the pirates, saying a bit of initiative and free enterprise was good. Then it dawned on her that he was embarrassed about not having the money to pay for the ride.

'Twice the price or not, we're getting on this bus. Ezzy gave me a bit extra. He said it was a welcome home present for you. By the way, he's expecting you back at work next week.'

George stuck her arm out at the side of the road to indicate to the bus driver to stop. She could see her dad was looking tired, and that he was trying to hide his pain. If his kidneys had taken a hiding, she thought he probably had a few cracked ribs too.

Once seated, he smiled again. 'There's no getting nothing past you,' he said.

'No, Dad, I've been taught by the best,' George said affectionately.

'By the way, there's been something I've been dying to ask you,' Jack said, then lowered his voice to a whisper. 'That weekend when the Old Bill had me. Did you have anything to do with the police station being blown up?'

There wasn't a day that passed when George didn't recall the dead copper's face on the front page of the newspaper. The murder of the policemen had pleased her, and still thrilled her now. The only thing that had marred her pleasure was seeing how worried Molly was. The girl was terrified that she'd be implicated in the bombing but thankfully no suspicion had fallen on her. They had both got off scot-free. Now though, the mention of it from her dad caused one side of her mouth to turn up in a half-smirk.

'I knew it! I knew it was you! Soon as I heard about the donkey jacket, I thought to meself, who else but you would have the balls to carry that out.'

'Shush, Dad,' George said, looking round to see if there were any earwiggers.

'How did you do it?' Jack asked quietly.

'I'll tell you when we get home. I won't say nothing to my gran about your injuries, and you don't mention this in front of her.'

It was odd for George, but she realised how much

she'd matured, and now here she was, telling her father what to do. She was no longer the awkward little girl who behaved and looked like a boy. She'd grown into an assured adult. Her masculine appearance still caused confusion, but she was now a young woman. She inwardly chuckled to herself. She could never refer to herself as a lady, but one thing she was sure of: she'd never allow the likes of a mere man to rule over her, or her household.

There wasn't much that went on in Battersea that Billy didn't know about, and today he was fully aware that Jack Garrett was being released from Wandsworth prison. Not that it bothered him. Jack wasn't a threat. In fact, Billy had never had any veneration for him. He thought Jack was an arse-licker. After all, what sort of bloke would become best buddies with a man who had taken out his eye? Jack Garrett had done just that with Norman.

It had been fortunate timing that Garrett had been arrested the day after Billy had gotten rid of his father. The quiet, threatening word he'd had with Inspector Hendricks had worked. It had killed two birds with one stone. At the time, the Vauxhall mob had been headed up by Archie Warner, but after his retirement, the gang had disbanded. Billy had heard that Archie's son, Wayne, had been doing ten years in Pentonville, but he was due out soon and there was talk of him reforming the mob.

Wayne's turf neighboured Battersea, and Billy didn't want anyone stepping over into his patch. Stitching up the Vauxhall mob with the Battersea Power Station robbery had removed the threat to Billy, and ensured Jack wasn't around to ask any awkward questions about Norman.

It was such a shame that Inspector Hendricks had been killed in the bombing. Billy had never got to the bottom of who was responsible, but he had his suspicions. It had pissed him off though, as Hendricks had been useful to him, readily accepting bribes. Now Billy had another policeman on side, but he wasn't as highly ranked as Hendricks and didn't have as much clout. Still, Billy would bide his time. Cunningham, the bent copper, was only a constable for now, but he had a promising career in front of him and Billy would be there every step of the way.

It had been a screw on the inside at Wandsworth who'd reported to Billy that he'd persuaded a couple of new inmates to give Jack a beating. It had only taken the cost of a few smokes and a promise of a handshake to the inmates' wives. Billy had no need nor desire to waste his time ridding the world of Jack, but he hoped a few broken bones would stop the man from sniffing around. If it didn't, Billy would remind him of the reason he was battered, and if he didn't keep his nose out, a worse pasting would follow.

*

Molly sat comfortably on a small wooden footstool behind a bucket of chrysanthemums and was tucking into an egg sandwich. 'This is nice, Mum. It's not often we get the chance to have a natter without Ethel butting in,' she said with her mouth full.

'Yes, it is nice, but what have I told you about talking with food in your mouth? Urgh, it turns my stomach, it really does. And it's not very ladylike.'

Molly didn't mind being chastised by her mother. Fanny had always said that they didn't have much, but they did have manners, and good manners cost nothing. It was a shame that her father never thought the same. She swallowed her food, then said, 'George's dad gets out today.'

'Yes, I heard. I bet George is pleased. Mind you, that girl has done well to keep a roof over her and Dulcie's heads, not that I condone how she did it.'

'Oh, Mum, stop being so righteous! I've known you not to put all your takings through the books. I reckon Mrs Wilcox would have a thing or two to say about that, if she knew.'

'Shut up, Molly, you'll have me shot! But point taken, and I do feel terrible about it. After all, Jane has been good to me. If it wasn't for your father... well.'

Molly had only been teasing her mother, but it had hit a raw nerve. Her dad still helped himself to all her mother's earnings, and a good part of hers too. She'd have left home if it wasn't for Ethel and Charlotte, but she couldn't bring herself to leave them behind. It was a miserable situation, and so unfair, but neither she, nor her mother, had the guts to confront him. Instead, they chose not to discuss it.

Obviously changing the subject, Fanny said, 'Talking of Jane, she doesn't seem herself lately.'

'Oh, what makes you think that?' Molly asked, not that she cared. She'd have preferred to keep the Wilcox family a good arm's length away and didn't feel comfortable with her mother working on Jane's stall.

'Last week when I saw her, she was, I dunno, on edge. It's like she's living on her nerves.'

'I'm not surprised!' Molly spluttered. 'It's no secret that Billy killed his father. She's probably worried that she's next.'

'Really? Do you think she's heard?'

'Without a doubt. Though I don't know who would have been foolish enough to tell her.'

'Well, I hope for the sake of the person who opened their gob, Billy doesn't find out. Look, here comes Ethel. Ah, don't she look a treat in that new jacket George got her.'

Molly watched her big sister coming towards them, wearing a broad smile and full of the joys of spring. George was by her side and looked equally happy.

'Hello, Ethel. Was you a good girl today for Dulcie?' Fanny asked.

'Yes, I was, wasn't I, George? I made Dulcie two cups of tea, and I washed up. She said I'm a clever girl.'

'You are, Ethel,' George said, 'and this is for you, but I'm going to give it to your mum to look after.'

George handed Fanny two farthings and said, 'Thanks, Mrs Mipple. It puts my mind at ease to know that Ethel is with my gran when I'm out. She's not as steady on her legs nowadays, and I worry about her. The silly old woman thinks she's doing us a favour by watching Ethel. She'd have my guts for garters if she knew it was the other way round!'

Fanny chuckled. 'Ethel may be a bit backward, but she's capable of keeping an eye on your gran. You can ask her to anytime, George, and you know you don't have to pay us, though I won't deny the extra comes in handy. How's your dad? You must be over the moon,' she said, squirreling the coins away in her handkerchief.

Molly thought her mother could be quite astute at times. Her father had no idea that Ethel often sat with Dulcie, and the few coins she earned went towards feeding Charlotte. It was their secret, and even Ethel understood to keep it quiet.

'Yeah, my dad's pleased to be home. I've got to dash 'cos I want to get back to him. We've got three years to catch up on. Molly, do you want to walk back with me?'

Molly jumped from the stool. 'Yes, I will. See ya later, Mum,' she said. Her lunch break had passed quickly, but at least she had George's protection back to the factory.

Once out of earshot of her mother, Molly asked, 'Did your dad question you about… you know?'

'Yeah, but he'd already guessed it was me. You should have seen the look on his face – he was dead happy.'

'You're blinkin' mad, you lot, but I don't mind admitting that I'm jealous about you having such a lovely family.'

'You've got a smashing family too, Molly. It's only your dad who's an arsehole.'

'Yeah, and talking of which, I saw Billy Wilcox earlier. He drove past and threw his fag butt out the window at me. He stopped his car and told me to pick it up. He said it was his street and he wanted it kept clean.'

'I hope you told him to piss off?'

'I wanted to but I ain't as brave as you.'

'Don't tell me you picked it up?'

'Yes, I didn't want any trouble; then he told me I was making his street look dirty and made me walk in the road in front of his car. I was scared stiff, George, so I did, but then he speeded his car up and I had to run for me life! I saw him laughing as he drove off. I was in a right state by the time I got to work, but don't tell me mum.'

'I've had about enough of him. I should have done him in years ago,' George hissed.

'I wish you had, but I'm glad you didn't. I'd hate to think of you going down for an arsehole like him,' Molly said, and recoiled at the thought of anything happening to her friend. She loved George dearly, but she was a risk taker and had caused Molly many nights of sleepless concern.

'Don't look so worried, Molly. I've waited all this time to get my hands on Billy Wilcox, and I won't be doing anything soon. My dad's home, that's all that matters for now.'

Molly sighed with relief. When she'd seen the angry look on George's face, she'd regretted telling her what Billy had done. She knew her friend was capable of ridding Battersea of Billy, but that was one risk Molly would prefer George to avoid.

Hilda sashayed across Billy's office and ran her fingers seductively over the impressive pieces of furniture. Billy was watching her every move and she was sure she'd seen a glimmer of lust. Being his assistant made her feel special, and now she was aiming to be his lover too. He'd said he'd consider making her his assistant three years ago, and now he'd finally given her the role.

'I think I'm going to enjoy working here, Mr Wilcox. I like how my desk looks over to yours,' she purred, and lightly hopped onto the front of it before slowly crossing her legs. She reached down to her slender ankles, then slowly stroked her leg until her hands came to rest on her knee. She kept her eyes locked with Billy's, and deliberately licked her full lips. 'Are there any special perks that come with the job?'

Billy sauntered towards her, but she was disappointed to see his eyes were cold and empty. 'Oh, yes, Hilda, I can see there's going to be many perks... for me.'

Hilda smiled. She was going to get what she wanted and began to unbutton her purple silk blouse. She started at the neck but when she reached the buttons on her chest, Billy stopped her. 'Would you like me to dance for you, Mr Wilcox?' she asked and eased herself from the desk.

'No, whores dance, and that's no longer your job.'

Hilda slowly crouched down until she was face height with Billy's groin. 'What would you like me to do for you then?' she asked huskily and ran her tongue over Billy's trousers, hoping to find his manhood bulging. It wasn't, but she was confident it soon would be.

'I'll tell you what I'd like you to do for me,' Billy answered and crudely yanked her back up by pulling the hair on top of her head.

Hilda stifled a yelp. She'd had customers who liked to rough her up a bit and she realised Billy must have those tastes too.

'Take off your underwear, lift your skirt and bend over your desk,' he ordered.

At last, she'd seduced him and now he was going

to take her from behind. He'd probably slap her bum. Hilda didn't mind that, though many of her customers thought it was kinky. As she removed her knickers, she smiled wryly to herself. As far as she knew, none of Billy's tarts had ever got this far with him. This was proof she was different. He liked her, and she planned to do all she could to make him fall in love with her.

Now in position, Hilda reached for her clitoris and vigorously rubbed it. She wanted to make Billy feel welcome and ensure she was wet for him.

'Did I tell you to touch yourself?'

Billy's voice sounded gruff, so she quickly placed her hand on the desk. 'No, Billy, you didn't.'

'Have you forgotten who you're talking to?'

'Sorry, no, Mr Wilcox.'

'Just remember your place. Perhaps this will help.'

Hilda couldn't see what Billy was doing behind her, but she suddenly heard a loud crack and felt a tremendous sting on her bottom as she realised he'd thrashed her with his belt. She bit her lip to stop from crying out, then another agonising lash whipped across her skin.

'Does that hurt?'

'Yes, Mr Wilcox.'

'Do you want more?'

'Yes, oh yes please, Mr Wilcox,' Hilda lied, but in her experience, if she pretended to enjoy the pain, it would normally bring her man to a climax.

'Is that right, you want more? I'll soon have you

begging for me to stop,' Billy growled and began to furiously whip her.

The pain was too intense, and Hilda could feel her skin splitting and bleeding. This wasn't what she'd expected, and cried out, 'No more, please, Mr Wilcox, no more.' Tears smudged her dark mascara as she whimpered in distress.

'What did you say?' Billy asked breathlessly as he lashed her again.

'I said no more, please stop,' she begged, scared.

'Turn around,' Billy ordered.

Hilda slowly stood up straight, wincing in agony. Her body trembled and just the material of her skirt falling over her beaten buttocks caused her to catch her breath.

Billy had perspiration running from his temples and down his flushed cheeks. His shoulders heaved up and down as he drew in deep breaths. 'Get on your knees,' he ordered.

Though it hurt, Hilda was too frightened to disobey him and hoped he wasn't going to inflict further pain. He unbuttoned his trousers and she flinched when his engorged manhood sprang towards her.

'Suck it,' he growled.

Hilda tried to stop crying as she wrapped her lips round it, but Billy shoved himself in hard, causing her to gag. He held the back of her head and forced himself deeply in and out of her mouth. Hilda could hardly breathe and as he thrust faster and more violently, she hoped he would orgasm soon. Minutes later, she felt him lose his erection, but he hadn't ejaculated. She didn't want to disappoint him and fervently sucked to get him hard again, but Billy's penis remained flaccid in her mouth.

'Get up,' he ordered, but Hilda didn't and kept trying to pleasure him with her mouth and cupped his balls in her hand before giving them a gentle squeeze.

Billy pulled himself away. 'I said GET UP, you fucking tart. No amount of sucking is going to make me come in a whore's scabby mouth.'

Hilda's legs felt shaky, but she nervously rose to her feet. As she did, Billy slapped her round the face. She held her cheek. It felt hot, burning, but nothing compared to the pain on her backside.

'Get back over your desk.'

Hilda was quick to plead. In desperation she cried, 'Please, Mr Wilcox, I can't take no more of the belt.'

She saw a glint in Billy's eyes and a wicked look on his face. That's when she realised what turned the man on. He liked to see her beg. He got off on her imploring him to stop. She thought she was worldly wise when it came to men and had come across just about every fetish there was, but she'd never known anyone as brutal as Billy. She knew he wouldn't stop until he'd satisfied his deplorable desires. 'Please, don't hurt me again,' she said. She meant it but was pleased when she could see he was becoming aroused again. Hopefully he'd be done with her soon and the begging would be enough without the agony of the belt again. 'It hurts so much, please don't do it to me.'

'Turn around, I'll decide when you've had enough.'

Hilda sobbed and slowly turned and leaned forward over the desk, dreading what Billy was about to do again. 'I'm begging you, Mr Wilcox, please spare me the belt.'

'Lift your skirt.'

'Please, please stop,' she cried, her voice full of desperation.

'Lift your skirt!'

Hilda slowly eased it over her sore buttocks. 'Look at me, Mr Wilcox, look at the state of me, I can't take any more.'

She could hear his breathing becoming deeper and hoped he'd finish himself off, but then she felt a searing pain and screamed out in agony. 'Stop, it hurts so much,' she cried, only to scream again and again as Billy mercilessly thrashed her.

'Let me see your face,' he hissed.

Hilda felt exhausted but managed to glance over her shoulder. What she saw shocked and terrified her. Billy appeared like a man possessed. His eyes were blazing, and spittle had formed in the corners of his lips, giving the impression that he was foaming at the mouth. Her body flinched as he swung his belt across her bottom again, and this time, she pleaded with her eyes as well as her voice. 'Please… enough,' she cried, desperate for him to stop.

She couldn't take any more and slumped forwards across the desk. As she did, she heard Billy grunt and felt his warm body fluids splatter over her battered bottom. Thank God, she thought, it was over, and now she desperately regretted what she'd started.

She'd known Billy was mean, but thought he'd be an exciting lover. She'd imagined him kissing her passionately and ripping off her clothes. Not this. It wasn't fun or sexy, it was pure sadistic torture and it was only Billy who'd enjoyed it. She could hardly move and as she rested face down, sprawled across her new desk, Billy threw some money in front of her face.

'You're my assistant now – you need to look the part. Get rid of your whore's clothes and buy yourself some things with a bit of class.'

She heard Billy walk away and the door close, and finally, her broken body relaxed, and she sobbed as her heart broke. What had she done? She'd put herself at his beck and call and now there was no turning back or escaping his clutches.

'Ha, you stupid bitch, as if he could ever love you,' her mother's voice mocked.

'Go away, Mother, I haven't got the strength for you right now.'

'I'm never going away, Hilda, never. You won't get rid of me and neither will that Billy. I hope it hurts.

I hope your pretty little bottom stings and bleeds. It's exactly what a disgusting creature like you deserves.'

Hilda closed her eyes and tried to ignore her mother's jibes, but the woman was right. She'd brought this on herself, and she realised this wouldn't be the only time Billy would use her pain for his own sick pleasure. She dreaded the thought of it, but at least she now understood him and next time, she'd know to beg and plead sooner.

29

Jack had been home for over a week, and though the sofa was lumpy, he found it was a lot more comfortable than the bed in his cell. Even so, he was having trouble sleeping. It was just so quiet. He was more familiar with the echoes of men shouting, groaning and even crying, along with the noise of metal clanging, water dripping and pipes ringing. The only sounds Jack could hear now were the birds outside chirping their morning song, and the sound of his daughter's footsteps coming downstairs. He welcomed the peace and hoped he would soon become accustomed to it.

George knocked before poking her head round the front room door. 'Morning, Dad, do you want a cuppa?' she asked softly.

Jack stretched his arms, then quickly pulled them back as a shooting pain shot through his chest. His ribs and kidneys were still sore and causing him more pain than he'd allowed George or his mum to know. 'Yes please, love,' he answered, forcing a smile.

He was due to go to Manchester today for Ezzy but dreaded the thought of the rickety train bouncing his tender torso around. But unless he owned up to how much discomfort he was really in, he'd have no choice.

George came in carrying two cups of tea. She placed one on the floor in front of the sofa, then Jack moved his legs, so she could sit down next to him.

'It's your first day back at work. Are you looking forward to it?'

'Yep, can't wait,' Jack fibbed, trying his utmost to sound sincere. 'What are you going to do with yourself now that I'm doing Ezzy's runs again?'

'Well, funny you should ask. I've had this idea in my head for a while, and now you're home, I think I might give it a go.'

Jack noticed she was fiddling with Sissy's ring. Intrigued, he asked, 'Oh, what's this idea?'

'Don't laugh, 'cos this is kosher. I'll be doing everything above board.'

'You… going straight…' Jack chortled. 'Sorry, love. Go on, tell me. I promise I won't laugh.'

George placed her cup on the floor, then her hands in her lap and looked serious. 'I want to open a fight club for women and kids.'

Jack had just taken a mouthful of tea and struggled not to splutter it across the room. He gulped hard. 'A what? A fight club? For *women*!'

'Yes, that's right. Too many of the women around here get knocked about by their old men. Not to mention the likes of Billy Wilcox and his gang. I've seen them bully women in the streets in broad daylight. It ain't on, Dad. I want to show women that they don't have to put up with it. They can fight back. I'll teach them how to box and how they can look after themselves.'

Jack breathed in deeply. 'I admire your reasons, but I think you'll be flogging a dead horse. I don't mean to put the dampeners on your idea, but I ain't sure it'll work. I can't see the blokes round here letting their wives go to any sort of fight club. Even if they were permitted to go, most of them wouldn't be able to afford to pay you.'

'I've thought about that too. See, I reckon if I run the club during the day, most husbands would be at work. I wouldn't call it a fight club. I'd use some sort of cover name, something exclusive for women and kids. I know most ain't got a pot to piss in, but I'd make it so it was contributions. I doubt it would make me a mint, so the women could do crafts too. There's a stall coming up next to Fanny's near the junction. I want to rent it, and have Ethel selling the stuff the women have made. Fanny could keep an eye on her, and I wouldn't have to pay her much. I've already managed to save a few bob to buy supplies and I've got a cupboard full upstairs that I've been pinching over the last few months. See, Dad, I've given it lots of thought, and I believe I can make this work.'

'Well, well, I've gotta hand it to you. It does sort of make sense. But you'd need premises.'

'Yes, I know. I had a word with the vicar at St

Mary's. He said that as I'm doing something to help the community, I could use the church hall. Obviously, when I was talking to him, I missed out the bit about the fighting, and I agreed to donate ten per cent of any profits to the church. It'd be a good starting place, just 'til I'm in a position where I can rent my own space. What do you think, Dad?'

George gave the impression that this was something she felt passionately about, and he had to admit he liked the idea of her going straight. Three years in prison had given him plenty of time to reflect, and he'd spent many hours worrying about George following in his footsteps and ending up behind bars too. Sissy would have turned in her grave if he'd let anything like that happen to their daughter.

He couldn't imagine her working for anyone. George was far too strong-willed for that, but this plan of hers seemed like a good one. It was certainly innovative!

'Dad… what do you think?' George repeated.

'I think it's a bloody brilliant idea! You're brainy you are, just like your mother was. And I'll tell you something else, you're the spit of her. She'd be right proud of you.'

Jack leaned forward to pick up his cup of tea, and to conceal the tears in his eyes. The thought of Sissy still evoked emotion in him and looking at George all grown up was a constant reminder of his wife. She might look like a young man, but her face was the image of her mother's. He flinched again as his ribs hurt, but if he was going to support George in her new quest, he'd have to get a move on and get the Manchester run done, pain or no pain.

Later that day, George left Ethel with her gran and set about getting her new venture off the ground. She didn't need her dad's approval, and would have gone ahead regardless, but she was grateful for his encouragement and pleased he'd agreed. She'd expected him to tell her she was being ridiculous, and to stick to what she knew. But he hadn't. His reaction had surprised her and filled her with even more determination to make it work. Not just for her, but also for all the downtrodden, oppressed women who were bullied and felt they had no voice.

Her gran had thought it a good idea too. She had compared George to Joan of Arc, the young warrior, which had made them all laugh. But it had spurred a notion. Joan of Arc was nicknamed 'The Maid of Orleans'. It was perfect, and The Maids of Battersea was born. Joan had been canonised more than twelve years earlier, so the vicar was unlikely to object to her club name.

George's first port of call was the church. After a lengthy discussion with the vicar, the church hall was secured. Three mornings a week would be turned over for her use. He also agreed to mention The Maids of

Battersea in his next Sunday service, on condition that she attended. George said yes, but a shiver ran down her spine. Church wasn't a place where she felt comfortable.

Next, she went to meet Molly on her lunch break. She knew it wouldn't be easy to persuade her friend to give up her secure and relatively well-paid job in the factory, but George needed her. After all, she knew very little herself about arts and crafts.

'Let me make sure I understand this. You want me to jack me job in and teach cross-stitch and the likes to a bunch of women you haven't yet got, and for half the pay I'm earning now?'

'Yes, that's right. When you put it like that, it doesn't sound very appealing, but think of the bigger picture, Molly. This could be huge! It could grow into something amazing. We could have The Maids of Clapham, Stockwell, Tooting… everywhere! And you'll be overseeing all the teaching. Granted, it won't be very lucrative to start with, but you know what they say, from small acorns and all that.'

George wasn't sure her pitch to Molly sounded all that enticing, so she tried a different tactic. 'Look at it this way. At the moment, you don't see the benefit of most of what you earn 'cos your dad pinches it. You work stupid hours in a job you hate, and for what? With me, once we're making a profit, I'll be in a position to bung you extra that your old man will never know about. You'll be your own boss, working half the hours you do now, and you'll be helping others. Ethel will have her own job too, which will also give your mum a bit of a break, and you'll have me looking out for you all the time. Doesn't that sound better than sitting next to old phossy jaw all day?'

Molly linked her arm through George's, and after a few moments' thought, she said, 'You're a hard woman to say no to.'

'Does that mean you'll do it?' George asked excitedly.

'Yes, I'll do it, but I think I need me head bleedin' testing!'

'Great,' George enthused. 'When you go back to work, you can hand your cards in, and tomorrow, we'll have our first official business meeting.'

She spat in her hand and offered it to Molly to shake, but Molly turned her nose up, and both girls broke into a giggle.

'The only thing that bothers me is my dad. He ain't gonna like it,' Molly tutted.

'Oh well, sod him. If he's got anything to say about it, you tell him to come and see me,' George said boldly. She wasn't worried about men like Mike Mipple. In fact, she wasn't bothered about any man!

30

Fanny had been caught up in Molly's excitement and had watched with pleasure as March passed in a flurry of activity for her daughter and George. But her husband wasn't too pleased with what was going on and missed Molly's pay packet. He'd gone to take his angst out on Ethel, but Fanny had stepped in and had borne the brunt of his discontentment. Now she was doing her best to conceal yet another black eye.

'That bunch there please.' A slim blonde woman pointed.

Fanny handed over the bunch of flowers and noticed the woman was staring at her eye. 'It looks worse than it is. I was tickling my little 'un and she accidentally whacked me in the eye,' she lied.

The woman raised her eyebrows and looked disbelieving, not that Fanny could blame her. She was running out of excuses to cover for Mike's violence.

'It looks painful.'

'It's not too bad,' Fanny answered. 'That's a lovely bunch you've chosen. I'm sure they'll be much appreciated.'

'They're for me actually. A little present to myself for my birthday. I thought they'd brighten my desk.'

'Oh, they will that. Happy birthday.'

'Thank you,' the woman answered and dug in her purse and paid for her flowers.

Fanny smiled politely, and slipped the tuppence in her pocket, then bid her farewell. She felt terrible about stealing from Jane Wilcox but reasoned a few pennies here and there wouldn't hurt. After all, Jane could afford it, which was more than could be said for herself. Mike was pretty much taking all her wages, which left little or nothing for Charlotte's needs. The odd few coins she pocketed wouldn't be missed by Jane, and with them and Ethel's earnings from sitting with Dulcie, it went a long way to feeding the Mipple household.

Still, it wouldn't be long before Ethel would be working full-time. Molly had told her that The Maids of Battersea had created enough stock to open for business, and this was Kate's last week on the basket stall next to hers. From what Fanny had seen, Kate had never turned over much business, and had been moaning for months that the rent was more than she took. The end of Kate's lease had been perfect timing, and once Ethel took over the stall, Fanny felt assured she would no longer have to steal from Jane.

In between customers, she took the opportunity to rest her weary legs. She sat on her stool and looked at her dear innocent child. Yes, Ethel had all the physical attributes of a woman, but her mind had always been that of a child. She was smiling now, happily playing with a peg doll, but Fanny recoiled as she recalled the memory of Ethel's petrified face the night before.

Mike had never gone for any of the kids before, so it had come as a shock to Fanny when her husband went to give Ethel a back-hander. Luckily, Fanny's screams had stopped him, but Ethel had been left standing in a puddle of her own urine. When Fanny had knelt to clean it up, Mike had kneed her in her face, hence the shiner she was now sporting.

Fanny gently touched her swollen eye. She could take the slaps, the kicks and punches, but she'd never allow that man to beat any of her children.

Hilda walked away from Fanny's stall admiring the bright yellow daffodils. She planned on putting them on her desk, exactly in her eyeline of Billy. She'd much rather look at the pretty spring flowers than his evil face.

She'd once believed that working in his office and having a desk would make her respectable, but now she'd come to loathe her desk for the insufferable pain it represented. Billy's office had become her torture chamber.

'You saw her, didn't you? You witnessed that woman put the money in her pocket.'

Her mother's voice was in her head again, but Hilda tried to ignore it.

'I know you saw her steal that money... You won't tell Billy though, will you? No, of course you won't, you coward!'

'Shut up!' Hilda shouted. She didn't want to hear it. Yes, she'd seen the woman pocket the money and though she didn't know her, she knew the stall belonged to Billy's mother.

'Coward... coward... that's your problem, Hilda, you always betray the people who look after you.'

'Billy doesn't look after me, he hurts me.'

'Coward... coward... yes he does! It's what you wanted. You wanted Billy, just like you wanted your father. You seduced them both! You didn't care that it was me who fed you, me who clothed you... Betrayal! You betrayed me when you threw yourself at your father.'

'I was a child – it wasn't my fault!'

Hilda hadn't realised she was shouting to herself until she noticed a man pass her and throw her a peculiar look.

'I'm not talking to you any longer,' she whispered, and was pleased when her mother didn't answer.

After fifteen minutes of silence, Hilda arrived back at Queenstown Road and, thankfully, Billy's car wasn't parked outside. She could relax, for now at least, but the dread of his next attack was never far from her mind.

Her relief was short-lived when her mother spoke again.

'Tell Billy what you saw! Tell him... tell him... tell him... tell him... tell him...'

The voice was relentless. 'Tell him... tell him...'

Hilda tried singing to drown it out, but her mother's raspy voice filled her head. 'Tell him... tell him...'

If she told Billy, it would shut her mother up, but she'd be sending that poor woman on the flower stall to a terrible fate.

'Tell him... tell him... tell him...' it went on. And on. And on.

The Maids of Battersea had been up and running for four weeks, and already the membership numbers had gone from two participants in the first week to a dozen now. The contributions the women paid barely covered Molly's wages, but George was confident that once the stall was operational, the money would start rolling in.

'Hold your hands higher, Mildred, protect your face,' George shouted.

Mildred responded and lifted her clenched fists.

'Good, well done. Ruth, your right foot should be at the front. It'll give you better balance. Stood sideways on like that, you'll get knocked clean off your feet and will end up on your arse!'

The women had made a room divider from pallet wood and discarded cardboard boxes and decorated it with material flowers cut from cast-off bits of fabric from the blanket factory. George had positioned it towards the far end of the hall and held her boxing lessons behind it. The screen protected the class from any prying eyes that happened to pop into the hall for a nose.

'I can't do this, George,' Ruth moaned. 'Boxing is for men, not for the likes of us women.'

George pursed her lips. She was sick to the back teeth of hearing the women whine. She understood that they had hard lives, but she didn't have the patience for their defeatist attitudes. 'No-one's forcing you, Ruth,' she snapped. 'If you don't want to learn how to stand up for yourself, then bugger off. Go and join Molly's lace-making class. I'm sure she'll be glad to have you.'

Ruth lowered her head, then slipped from the class. George glanced round and studied the faces of the remaining women. A few of them looked anxious, and she'd already witnessed how edgy and jumpy they could be. But the idea of them attending boxing lessons was to build their confidence. 'If anyone else wants to leave, I suggest you do so now.'

The women exchanged worried looks but stayed put.

'Good. Right, I won't have any wimps in my class. We are The Maids of Battersea. Strong warrior women! From now on, if you ain't prepared to fight back, then don't waste my time coming here. Are you ready?'

The women didn't look as sure as George would have liked, but at least they all stayed and put a good effort into the lesson. She'd make fighters out of them yet!

Once the class had finished, George helped Molly clear away.

'You know, you shouldn't be so hard on the women.'

George shot Molly a look of surprise. Of all the people, Molly was the last person she would have expected to hear this from.

'Most of them who come here have been knocked about. They're scared, George, and have you considered that if they go home and hit back, they could end up getting battered a lot worse or even killed?'

'Don't be soft, Molly. What's the point of me teaching them to fight if they ain't prepared to stand up for themselves?'

'I dunno… maybe it just makes them feel a bit more confident. I'm sure they'd all love to be like you, but none of us are. Just go a little easier on them, eh? We want them coming back, don't we?'

George chewed the inside of her cheek. She didn't have empathy for weakness. If anything, it repulsed her.

'I know what you're thinking but look at me. I've had you looking out for me for years. Remember how I was picked on?'

Yes, George did, and she reminded herself that part of the reason for setting up the club was due to witnessing how Molly had been bullied. She just wished the women's feebleness didn't get on her nerves so much.

But reluctantly, she sighed and said, 'All right, you win. I'll try to be nicer.'

'That's what I like to hear. Actually, there's something I should tell you.'

'Spit it out then.'

'It's me mum. She's had another hiding off my dad, only, when you see her, don't mention it. She gets embarrassed and covers for him.'

'Bloody hell, Molly! Is she all right?'

'Yeah, she is now, but it was horrible at home last night.'

'What happened?'

'You know how my dad is pissed off 'cos he ain't got my wages from the factory no more?'

'Yes,' George answered, thinking that if he tried to take the earnings she paid Molly, she'd chop his thieving hands off.

'Well, I ain't sure what Ethel said, but he suddenly started shouting at her, calling her the thickest bastard under the sun, and then lifted his hand to whack her one. Anyhow, Mum jumped in and Dad backed off, but by then Ethel was so scared she wet herself. Mum got a boot when she was cleaning it up.'

'Fucking hell, Molly, it ain't right! None of you should be putting up with that!'

'I know, George, but what are we supposed to do? I can't move out and leave my sisters there. Mum won't go nowhere. She said my dad would find her and drag her back.'

George shook her head. She was fuming, but this was Fanny's family, not hers, and she knew she shouldn't get involved.

'He's never hit any of us before; it's always been my mum who cops it. I reckon last night was a one-off, but I'll keep an eye on Ethel.'

'Men like him make me sick,' George said scathingly.

'Yeah, but enough about me dad. Can you give me a hand with these boxes? This is all our stock for the stall next week.'

George tried to dismiss her anger at Mike Mipple, but she was seething.

'George, please. I can see you're upset. I wish I hadn't told you now,' Molly said, close to tears.

'Sorry. It seems a bit bloody ironic that here we are, teaching women how to look after themselves, but your own house ain't in order.'

'I know, but it's been like that at home for as long as I can remember. It ain't gonna change now. It's too late for my mum, but it might not be for someone else, so don't give up on what you're trying to achieve.'

George nodded, but she felt so frustrated and wished Fanny would be a Maid of Battersea. For Molly's sake, she hid her temper and focused on the stock for the stall. She hadn't realised that Molly and the other women had been so industrious. There were piles of boxes overflowing with rag-rugs, hand-made stuffed toys, lace doilies, crocheted blankets, cross-stitched artwork and knitted hats. 'Credit where credit is due,' she said, 'they ain't good at sticking up for themselves, but they're gonna make us a packet with this lot!'

*

Hilda now had a telephone on her desk. It was the only line in Queenstown Road, and rarely rang, but Billy liked to brag about it. This was another aspect of his character that she'd come to despise. She no longer found him dangerously attractive and rued the day she hadn't run off with Joan. She wished she'd listened to the old bat, but it was too late now. She was trapped with a sadistic tormentor.

Hilda heard Billy's wicked laugh in the hallway and shuddered. Another voice was still screaming in her head, and she stiffened. 'He's coming for you... He's going to hurt you again... It's what you deserve... You're useless, you stupid bitch! Tell him... tell him... tell him... He might leave you alone if you tell him... Useless betraying slut... Tell him... tell him...'

Hilda squeezed her hands hard up against her ears to block out her mother's voice, but no matter how much she tried, she couldn't mute the evil taunts. 'Leave me alone,' she screamed, but her mother's gravelly breaths were still sounding in her head.

The door opened, and Billy breezed in. He had a familiar look in his eyes, and her heart sank.

'Who are you shouting at?' he asked, licking his lips fervently.

'Myself, Mr Wilcox. I was clumsy and spilled my tea,' Hilda answered.

'Good. I don't want anyone disturbing us.'

Hilda hated what was going to happen to her next yet didn't protest. As Billy would expect from her, she pulled out a piece of black cloth from her drawer. She then walked round to the front of her desk and, feeling numb, she lifted her skirt and pulled down her knickers before reluctantly stepping out of them. She then placed the black material across her eyes and secured it with a knot behind her head. Leaning forward over her desk, she pulled her skirt over her waist and held her breath as she heard Billy's footsteps coming towards her.

His walk was slow and deliberate. He seemed to like looking at her naked flesh, though her buttocks and thighs were covered with purple bruising and scabby welt marks. She thought most men would be repelled, but not Billy Wilcox. He adored studying her wounds and enjoyed it even more when he was inflicting them. Causing her to bleed, and hearing her cry used to be the only thing that seemed to bring him to a climax. She'd soon discovered his brutal and perverted preferences and had quickly learnt to turn on the waterworks. It made him finish quicker, but then Billy had seen through her act. Now he'd only orgasm when he saw fear in her eyes. That's why he kept them covered and made her wear the blindfold. It prolonged her suffering.

Her mother was there again, her raspy breath intensifying, leaving Hilda feeling as though she was battling for space in her own head. She wanted to scream out, to tell Billy he was a crank, a bloody nutcase and wasn't normal, but the sound of her mother's cackling drowned out her own voice.

'Tell him... He's going to make you bleed... Tell him...'

Over the din in her mind, she heard Billy's trousers drop to the floor, and the sound of his belt buckle land on the polished boards. Some small amount of tension instantly left her aching body. She was at least going to be spared the strap.

He'd only used it on her twice, but on both occasions, she'd required medical attention afterwards. The doctors hadn't asked how she'd acquired her injuries. Billy paid for their silence. And for hers. Not that she was bothered about the money. The scars were reminder enough of how fierce Billy Wilcox could be. She was just grateful they were on her behind and not across her unblemished, heart-shaped face.

31

'George, sorry to interrupt, but have you got a minute?' Molly said, sounding uncomfortable.

She'd popped her head round the makeshift screen but looked like she was waiting for George to bite it off!

George instructed her class to carry on, then walked to a quiet corner with Molly. 'What's wrong?' she asked, wondering why her friend was looking so worried.

'It's Oppo. He's here, asking to see you.'

'Is that all?' George said, relieved.

'Well, it's not really on, is it?' Molly commented snootily.

'What do you mean?'

'He shouldn't be here. This is a club for women and kids. If we start getting blokes coming in, it'll make the women feel uncomfortable. I've told him to wait outside for you.'

'You're probably right, but Oppo is harmless enough,' George said.

'You know that, and I know that, but the rest of the women here don't. No, George, I don't think it's acceptable and you need to tell him he can't come here again!'

Molly actually stamped her foot as she spoke, and it was all George could do to refrain from laughing at her. 'All right, madam, don't get your knickers in a twist. I'll have a word with him.'

As George walked across the hall, she wiped her brow, then stepped outside into the bright sun. She squinted her eyes and saw the silhouette of Oppo and noticed he had a young woman with him.

'Hello, George. I hope you don't mind me coming here. I don't think Molly was too pleased to see me.'

'Don't worry about her, she's having one of her girlie moods.'

'This 'ere is Eunice. She'd like to have a look at what goes on here and as I've heard so much about it from you, I thought I'd take a look for meself. Is that all right?'

In one glance, George could tell Eunice was shy and judging by the bruises on her jawline, the woman had probably taken a beating from her husband. 'Yes, it's fine. Come in,' George said, and led them into the hall.

Molly looked up from her table and when she saw that George had brought Oppo in, she threw her a look of scorn, but her face softened when she saw Eunice behind him.

'Eunice, this is Molly. She'll show you round and tell you all about what we do here.'

'Hello, Eunice,' Molly said sweetly, 'come with me

and we'll get you a nice cup of tea, then we can have a chat.'

Eunice followed Molly away, then Oppo said, 'Sorry, George. I'd never have come but I didn't know how else to get her here.'

'It's fine, Oppo, really.'

'No, it ain't and I understand why Molly was pissed off to see me here. Mr Kavanagh ain't happy with me either. The old git says I'm always skiving off and is threatening me with losing me job again. I had to bring Eunice here though. She was in a right old state. She lives upstairs from me and last night, I heard her and her husband having a row. She says he ain't been the same since he was at the Battle of the Somme. Then today, she came in the shop, so I mentioned to her about your club. That was it – she broke down!'

'You did the right thing, Oppo. Leave her with us, we'll look after her now.'

'Thanks, George.'

'Do you want to have a look round now that you're here?'

'Err... no thanks. You lot frighten the bloody life out of me! I'd better get back to the shop and hope Mr Kavanagh ain't replaced me yet.' Oppo laughed.

George saw him out and watched him hobble up the street. She wished there was something that could be done for his leg, though it never seemed to bother him. In fact, not much ever got to Oppo. He always had a cheery disposition and a kind word to say. She'd known him for as long as she could remember and cared for him like one of her own family.

It had been a week since Hilda had bought the daffodils from Mrs Wilcox's stall and now they were wilted. Hilda sat at her desk and covertly glanced past Billy to look out of the window. The sun was shining, and April was living up to its reputation of being the month for rain showers. She'd have liked to walk past Billy's desk to the window and pull the net curtains to one side. She was sure there'd be a rainbow. But instead Hilda sat motionless and silent, hoping not to attract Billy's unwanted attention.

She was finding it difficult to concentrate as her mother's incessant ramblings had given her a pounding headache.

'He should kill you... I wish I'd killed you instead of your brother... Tell him... tell him... tell him what you saw...'

Billy slammed his coffee cup down, which made Hilda jump. She'd become so jittery lately, but it was no wonder, considering the abuse she was suffering at his hands.

She sneaked a glance at him and was relieved to see he looked engrossed in his newspaper.

'You're so thick... If he finds out you knew, he'll cut

your throat... Tell him... tell him... He'll slash your pretty face with his belt buckle... Tell him...'

Hilda couldn't take it any more, and she pushed her chair back then walked towards Billy's desk. Billy looked up and folded his paper away.

'I... erm... I don't know if this is anything or nothing, but last week, when I bought some flowers from your mother's stall, I... erm... I...'

'You what, Hilda?' Billy asked impatiently.

Hilda's mother was laughing, jeering her. 'Tell him...' she heard, over and over.

'I think I saw the lady who works there pocket the money I gave her.' There, she'd said it, but she hated herself for it, though at last, her mother fell silent.

'Fanny Mipple, stealing from my mother?'

Hilda recognised the name. She didn't know Fanny but knew Mike Mipple well. He'd been one of her customers at Livingstone Road. The man had stunk. Having sex with him had turned her stomach, and she'd always felt sorry for his wife.

Hilda looked at Billy's face. It was clear that he was furious at what he was hearing. She wanted to scream that she'd made a terrible mistake and retract what she'd told him, but it was too late now. Her heart thumped hard. She hated Billy being in a bad mood. There was always a chance he'd take it out on her. She could have slapped herself, punched herself in the head and scratched her own eyes out. She'd grassed on Fanny

Mipple for her own peace of mind, and now realised it hadn't been worth it.

Billy called for Knuckles who quickly appeared. 'It seems Fanny Mipple is ripping my mother off. I want you to pay a visit to her. Tell her I want to see her here in my office tomorrow at midday. Don't tell her why but let her know I'm not happy. Make the bitch stew for a while.'

Hilda lowered her head and scurried back to sit behind her desk. Poor Fanny, she thought. She dreaded to think what Billy would do to the woman and it was all Hilda's fault.

Then she heard his chair scrape back and all thoughts of Fanny's awful impending fate were forgotten as Billy walked towards her. Hilda closed her eyes and fought back tears. It would be her who would suffer for now.

Once the club had finished and the hall had been tidied, Molly gathered the goods the women had made.

'I'll leave you to lock up, George,' she called.

Jack had acquired a punchbag for George, which she'd been practising on earlier and was now hiding in a cupboard that housed a water tank. 'OK. I'll see you Friday. Say hello to your mum and Ethel.'

'Will do,' Molly answered, then with her arms full, she headed for Clapham Junction. This was now her regular routine, and every evening, she'd help Ethel to pack up. The stall came with a large wooden barrow and a small storage lock-up adjacent to the railway arches.

Light rain fell, and by the time she arrived at the Junction fifteen minutes later, she was damp right through. Ethel was having a joke with a customer, and once Molly had unloaded the new stock, she went over to her mother's stall.

'Hi ya. How's Ethel been today?'

'Yeah, all right,' her mum answered, but avoided eye contact.

Molly's brow knitted. Her mother was acting out of sorts.

'Is everything all right, Mum?'

'Yes, fine,' Fanny said sharply.

It was obvious to Molly that something was wrong, and she pushed further. 'No it isn't. I can tell. What's going on, Mum?'

Fanny slumped onto one of two small wooden stools and looked at her daughter. Molly could see her mum's eyes were full of despair. 'I'm in trouble. It's bad. Really bad.'

'Tell me,' Molly said gravely.

'I've had a visit and been summoned to see Billy Wilcox tomorrow. I don't know exactly what for, but I've got a pretty good idea it's about me pinching a few pennies.'

Molly hated seeing her mother in this state. Fanny's

hands were shaking, and she looked deathly pale. She had the same wild look of fear in her eyes that she always had before a beating from her father. 'I doubt Billy would know about that. I'm sure it must be something else.'

'Nah. That Knuckles bloke was here. He said Billy wants to talk to me about his mother's losses. It's got to be that. What else could it be?'

Molly gasped, though she tried to hide it from her mother. This wasn't good. Billy talked with his fists, or worse.

'It's bad, ain't it?'

Molly could see her mother was on the verge of crying.

'Don't upset yourself, Mum. I'll sort this out. Leave it to me, everything will be all right.' She tried to sound reassuring and was putting on a brave face.

'How? How are you going to sort it out? I'm not having you going anywhere near that nutter!'

'Don't worry. Let me go and see him and find out what this is all about. It may not be as bad as you think.'

'No! Absolutely not. This is my problem, Molly, and I won't have you fighting my battles. You stay away from him, you hear?'

Molly could see her mum was adamant and nodded her head. She knew it would be a waste of time to try and change her mind, and though she didn't like to defy her mother, she felt there was no choice. If she was to see Billy Wilcox, it would have to be behind her mother's back.

Jack had fallen asleep on the train and almost missed his stop at Manchester. Luckily, he had woken just before the train had pulled away from the platform and he'd managed to get off. He didn't know what was wrong with him lately. He was always so tired, and the Manchester runs were really taking it out of him.

Once outside the station, he found a bench to rest on. Rest, he thought. He'd just spent six blinkin' hours sat on his arse on a train. Why on earth did he feel the need for more rest? But his feet were aching, and his shoes pinching. He stretched his legs out in front and saw that his ankles had blown up to twice their normal size. No bloody wonder his shoes were hurting him! He leaned forward, and loosened the laces, grimacing at the pain in his ribs. Oh, what he wouldn't have given to be at home, with a good cuppa and a slice of his mum's cake.

Unfortunately, home was a long way off and there was work to be done. The rent was due, and the gas meter was almost empty. He'd promised George his support whilst she got her 'club' going, and though she seemed to be doing well, she wasn't yet able to contribute to the bills.

Heaving himself up from the bench, Jack slowly made his way to Ezzy's cousin's jewellery shop, but every step felt as if he had dead weights at the ends of his legs, and he noticed he was struggling for breath.

'Come on, man,' he mumbled to himself, 'pull yourself together.'

A wave of nausea washed over him again. He'd been feeling sick for days now but had put it down to a bit of dodgy fish. However, he was beginning to think that this was more than food poisoning, and it began to dawn on him that he was seriously ill.

He'd seen it happen to the Baron in Wandsworth nick. The bloke had run D wing but was getting too big for his boots. He'd started showing less and less regard for the screws, so had received a mattress job from the batter squad. The thin mattress had muffled his screams as the guards had attacked him mob-handed, though everyone knew the mattress was really used to protect the wardens' uniforms from blood.

A few months later, the Baron had dropped dead. There was no official connection to his untimely death and the attack by the screws, but everyone knew his kidneys had packed it in. Several blows to the organs had irreparably damaged them. Now Jack feared that his kidneys were letting him down, and he would suffer the same outcome as the Baron. He just hoped he would make it back home to Battersea.

32

George yawned as she walked into the kitchen to see her gran filling up her bucket again, probably to wash the already clean kitchen floor. The sun shone through the back window, and as her gran turned away from the sink, she jumped when she saw George stood in the kitchen doorway.

'Sorry, Gran, I didn't mean to startle you,' George said, stifling a giggle.

'My giddy aunt, you nearly gave me a bleedin' heart attack. And it ain't funny, you wicked cow!'

'I ain't laughing,' George protested.

Her gran smiled affectionately, then said, 'Put the kettle on if you want a cuppa but keep the noise down. If your dad got back last night, he's still sleeping.'

George walked across the room and went to take the bucket from her gran. 'He isn't here so must have stayed in Manchester overnight. 'Ere, give me that bucket. I'll do the floor,' she offered.

'No, no thanks. I like to do it,' Dulcie protested. She placed the bucket on the floor and dipped the mop into the steaming water. George thought about telling her that the floor didn't need cleaning again, but she knew it would make no difference. Whether it needed scrubbing or not, her gran would do it, and would clean it again in a few hours.

'Why's there a pile of veg peelings on the side?' George asked as she spooned tealeaves into the pot.

'I've saved 'em for Mary. Her old man is only doing a couple of days a week labouring and can't find any more work. She said she asked for dole money, but some bloke came round and means tested her. They failed her, on account of that stupid bloody polished table she's got. The silly woman refused to sell it, said it had been in her family for years and they all ate their dinner round it. I told her what I thought: they wouldn't be having any dinner if she couldn't afford to feed her brood and that table will end up being used as firewood. Anyway, she asked me to keep me peelings so she can make a broth. I'll throw in a cabbage or what I can and Oppo is gonna save any veg that's on the turn.'

'Can't Aileen help out? She must earn a packet in that salon.'

'Mary's a proud woman, love. I don't think she wants her kids to know how much they're struggling.'

George felt sorry for her hard-up neighbours, but most people in the area were barely surviving in similar circumstances. She was more concerned about people closer to home. 'I'm worried about my dad.'

'Oh, why's that?'

It wasn't out of the ordinary for her dad to stay

overnight in Manchester. He rarely got there and back in the same day, but he hadn't seemed himself when he'd left. 'He didn't look very well. I think he's hiding something from us. Have you noticed anything?'

Her gran wiped a section of the floor, and then plopped her mop back into the bucket. She arched her back and leaned on the handle. 'Now you come to mention it, he does seem to be spending a lot of time on the sofa. It ain't like him – he's normally dashing about like a blue-arsed fly.'

'Perhaps you should have a word with him, Gran? If there is something wrong with him, he won't tell me.'

'I doubt he'd tell me either, but I'll have a go.'

George kissed her on the cheek. 'I'm gonna get washed and dressed. I've got a busy day today.'

'But it's Thursday. The club ain't open.'

'I know, but I've got to see a man about a dog,' George called over her shoulder as she left the kitchen, hoping her gran wouldn't question her plans.

'Just a minute, young lady. Get yourself back in here.'

George turned and walked back into the kitchen. Her gran was like a dog with a bone when she got something between her teeth.

'What exactly are you up to?'

'It's a long story, Gran.'

'Good job I've got plenty of time then. Come on, out with it.'

With a resigned sigh, George pulled out a kitchen

chair and sat down at the table. 'It's Molly's dad, that Mike Mipple.'

'What about him? From what I've heard, he's a right piece of work.'

'Yes, he is, and that's just it. He went for Ethel the other day. Fanny got it instead, but to think of him hitting Ethel... I can't stand the man!'

'Oh, George, that's awful!'

'I know. I've kept out of it, but he's stepping on my toes now. He's overheard Molly and her mum talking about the boxing lessons. He doesn't like Molly working in the club 'cos he takes all her earnings, but she ain't getting paid what she was at the factory. Anyway, he wants me shut down, and he's going round the pubs telling all the blokes that their wives are learning how to fight. A few of the women have mentioned that their old men don't want them coming no more.'

'Can't your women just say you're all doing a bit of keeping-fit exercising?'

'They have been, but I don't want him stirring up problems. And I don't want Molly or Fanny to know that he's being a pain in the ar... backside.'

'What are you going to do about it then?'

'I'm going to make sure he shuts up... and for good,' George answered with a steely coldness in her violet eyes.

Her gran gasped. 'George Garrett, you are not getting up from this kitchen table until you've told me exactly how you intend on shutting him up.' She pulled out the chair opposite, and slowly eased herself onto it.

George relayed her intentions. As she spoke, she thought it sounded sickening, but it was no more than the man deserved. What surprised her the most was how her gran didn't look shocked and didn't try to talk her out of it.

'Are you helping your sister on the stall today?' Fanny whispered to Molly. 'Only if you are, I'll need you to keep an eye on my stall when I go to see Billy Wilcox.'

They were in the shared scullery, both washing from the same bucket of cold water. It was the only place in the house where, if alone with the door closed, they could talk in private.

'I'll be there later, but I've got a few things to do first. And I've already told you, you're not to go and see Billy,' Molly said firmly.

Fanny was taken aback at her daughter's commanding tone, but she was the parent and it was her duty to protect her child, not the other way around. 'And I've already told you I don't want you getting involved. The man killed his own father, for Christ's sake! You're to stay away from him. I've got something in mind so leave him to me,' Fanny insisted, trying not to let her daughter see how worried she was. She just hoped Molly couldn't see through her act of bravery.

'Mum, please. You can't go and see Billy either.'

'I'm not. I'm going to have a word with Jane. I thought if I own up, tell her how sorry I am and offer to pay every penny back… well, she's a charitable woman and might forgive me.'

'Do you think she will?' Molly asked doubtfully.

'I'll beg on my knees if I have to, and it wouldn't be the first time. How do you think I fed you kids before Mrs Wilcox gave me the job on the stall? Oh, Molly, I wish I hadn't been so stupid! I've gawn and mucked up everything now,' Fanny said, fighting tears. She'd done enough crying during the night. Not that her husband had noticed. And now, looking at the dark rings circling Molly's eyes, she knew her daughter hadn't slept much either.

'It might not be that bad, Mum. Like you say, Mrs Wilcox is a good woman. I'm sure if you explain the circumstances, she'd understand. But do me a favour? Don't go and see her until later?'

'I can't, not 'til you come and look after the stall for me. But please promise me you're not going to see Billy.'

'I promise,' Molly said, though Fanny felt sure her daughter was lying.

Jane had seen Sally off to school and was now preparing Billy's breakfast as Penny played happily with her rag-doll. Her son rarely put in an appearance when Sally

349

was home, but she knew the minute he heard the front door close, he'd be down the stairs.

She was an only child herself but had heard about sibling rivalry so assumed the contempt her children had for each other was perfectly normal. Of course, she wasn't aware that Billy often fantasised about watching all the blood seep from his sister's body, while she begged for her life, her voice no more than a gargle. If she'd known the butchering thoughts Billy harboured, she'd have taken her daughters and they would have run for their lives.

Billy always had a deliberate walk. There was never anything light and breezy about him, and this morning was no exception. He came into the kitchen, and though Jane loved her son, his presence always left her feeling sombre.

'Good morning,' he greeted, and smiled intently.

'Morning, Billy. Scrambled eggs?'

'Smashing, thanks, Mum.'

Jane took two eggs and cracked them into a pan before whisking them. She could feel her son watching her. When she'd first heard the rumours about him murdering his father, she'd dismissed the malicious gossip. After all, she knew the truth, but it wasn't something she could ever repeat. She'd have liked to scream from the rooftops that the Portland Pounders had shot her husband in the back of his head, but through fear for her daughters' safety, she kept her knowledge to herself.

'Any plans for today?' Billy asked.

'Nothing special. I thought I might pop over to see Alma later. Her Ronald got mugged last week. Two blokes jumped him on his way home from the Dukes Head. I hear he's in a pretty bad way.'

Billy reached into his inside pocket and pulled a wad of notes from his jacket. He skimmed off the top two five pounds and threw them onto the table. 'Give that to Alma, with my regards.'

Jane picked up the money, folded it and then pressed it into her apron pocket. She'd been hoping Billy would cough up some cash. It was the right thing to do, seeing as it was his boys who'd jumped Ronald. The man had been silly, trying to cheat the poker game and thinking he could get away with it, but Billy was no fool and Ronald had learnt his lesson.

Unknown to her son, Jane knew all about Billy's business, or at least she thought she did. Every man could be bought for the right price, and Knuckles came cheaper than most. But Knuckles was selective in what he told her, and he'd never mentioned what happened to Norman, or what Billy did to Hilda. There are some things a mother is best off not knowing.

Billy had taken to wearing glasses lately, though the lenses were clear glass. He thought the specs gave him more of an air of sophistication and made him look clever. He also practised speaking well, and eloquently, unlike most of the riff-raff in the area. When his office door opened, he looked over the top of his frames and refrained from smirking as Molly Mipple nervously approached his desk.

'Take a seat,' he offered, not surprised to see her.

Molly looked uncomfortable but sat opposite him.

Billy dismissed Hilda and waited for the door to close behind her before speaking again. 'I suppose you've come on behalf of your mother?'

Molly nodded and squirmed in her chair.

This pleased Billy. 'Are you aware that your mother has been stealing from mine?'

Molly nodded again and opened her mouth to speak, but Billy quickly jumped in. 'After everything my mother has done for your scummy family, out of the goodness of her heart she extends the gracious hand of charity, and this is how she's repaid?'

'I... I... I'm sorry, Billy... but...'

'Mr Wilcox,' Billy said calmly.

'Sorry, Mr Wilcox...'

'You understand my position, Molly? You see, I can't have the poor folk round here thinking that it's acceptable to help themselves to my family's good fortune. As much as it hurts me, I'm afraid your mother will have to be punished.'

'Please... Mr Wilcox... let me explain.'

'There's no explaining required. Your mother stole

from my mother, end of story. It's now just a matter of deciding what punishment is suitable. You are welcome to offer any suggestions.'

Billy could see tears pricking Molly's eyes, and she was wringing her hands on her lap. He hoped she would beg for her mother's forgiveness. The thought of her on her knees and pleading to him caused a stirring in his groin.

'I'll pay back all the money. It isn't much, but I'll pay back double,' Molly offered, her voice cracking.

'Yes, you will. But what about your mother? In some countries they chop off the hands of a thief. Do you think that would be fair? Or maybe several lashings with the whip?'

'No, please, Mr Wilcox. Don't hurt her. She only did it for us, to feed her children.'

Good, thought Billy as tears began to streak down Molly's rosy cheeks. She wasn't as tall and slender as he liked his women. In fact, she was a bit on the podgy side, and her mousy brown hair was clipped behind her ears. He preferred blondes, but there was something about her that aroused him.

'I'm not interested in her reasons. However, there is a way out for your mother. Would you be prepared to pay for her crime, Molly? Are you willing to accept your mother's punishment?'

Molly's eyes widened, and the fear Billy saw further excited him. He was sick of whores and tarts. They were too easy. But an untouched virgin. She'd be tight, and it would hurt her. Images of him breaking Molly's hymen flashed through his mind. He wouldn't be gentle. She was bound to scream.

'Yes, I... I'll do whatever it takes,' she stammered nervously.

Good, he had her where he wanted her, and he unbuttoned his trousers as he stood up, revelling in the terror he saw on her face.

George glanced up and down the street as she waited for Mike Mipple to answer his door. It was mid-morning and she knew enough about the man to realise he'd still be in his bed. There was no answer, so she knocked again, and on the pallet wood covering the front window.

A gruff voice from inside yelled, 'Fuck off.'

Undeterred, she rapped harder on the door, and eventually it opened. George gazed at the revolting-looking man who stood bleary-eyed, gawping back at her. His greyed vest bore the evidence of everything he'd eaten over the past week, and even from a couple of feet away, George could smell his vile body odour.

'Yeah?' Mike spat.

'I'd like a word, Mr Mipple.'

'Piss off,' he answered, and went to slam the door.

George jumped forward and pushed Mike backwards. He stumbled, then bounced off the hallway wall, but grabbed the newel post to save himself from falling. Her actions hadn't intimidated him and with a sneer he said, 'I know who you are, and I don't want you in my house. You're a fucking aberration. A right queer fish. Get the fuck out and if you lay a hand on me again, I'll flatten you.'

'I'm not going anywhere, Mr Mipple. Not until we've had a few words. Oh, and believe me, your words will be few.'

Mike looked confused, but then charged towards her. George reacted quickly, and as Mike approached she shot her arm out in front. Her fist hit him in his throat and stopped him in his tracks.

'You fucking bitch,' Mike rasped, holding on to his neck. He staggered backwards, then sat on the stairs. 'I can't breathe,' he said, gasping as his ruddy face paled and his eyes bulged with fear.

This wasn't the plan. George hadn't come here to kill him. She dashed towards him, but he put his hand up.

'Stay away from me,' he managed to croak, but then it sounded as though he was choking. It was clear he was struggling. He gasped, short, fast breaths but no air appeared to be reaching his lungs.

George watched helpless as Mike fell to one side, then he rolled off the stairs and onto the hallway floor. His mouth began to open and close, and George was sure he was pleading for help, but no words came out. She'd done this. She hadn't intended to kill him, but if she was honest, she wasn't worried that he was dying. It was no more than he deserved, and now she just hoped he lived long enough to hear what she had to say. George lowered herself and knelt beside him then leaned over his dying body. With her face just inches from his, she whispered in his ear, 'I came here to cut out your tongue, you filthy bastard.'

Mike was powerless to respond and as she sat up, she could see the shock and horror in his eyes. 'Yes, that's right. I wanted to slice your tongue out. Look,' she said, pulling her father's cut-throat razor from her pocket. She waved the blade in front of his face. 'I could cut it out now, while you're dying. You wouldn't be able to scream.'

Mike frantically shook his head in very small and narrow movements.

'Oh, don't worry, Mr Mipple. I shan't bother now. It'll save me having to clear up the mess,' she said flippantly. 'You haven't got long. A minute, maybe two, and during your last moments, I'd like you to think about your wife and children. You'll never be able to hurt or scare them again. They will be free of you and I'm sure your wife will dance on your grave with joy.'

George stood up to leave, satisfied that Mike would die alone and frightened on the hallway floor. The rats and cockroaches that infested the house would soon be crawling over his corpse. As she opened the front door, he fell silent, and without looking backwards, she knew he was gone.

33

Molly couldn't face going to the stall and seeing her mum or Ethel. At least not until she'd washed away the sickening feel of Billy Wilcox all over her skin. She didn't care that there'd be no hot water. Cold would do. Sore and bruised she rushed home, cringing at the flashbacks of what had just happened, then she sobbed in shame when she realised she'd left her knickers behind.

The journey home felt like a long one, but when she finally reached her street, Molly realised she'd have to pass the Wilcox home. As she ran past her heart ached at the thought of having to see Billy's house every day. Each time she stepped out of her front door, she knew she'd be reminded of him pinning her to his desk, and the searing pain as he violently took her virginity. She'd never forget the look in his eyes, or the depraved way in which he got his pleasure. Bile rose in her throat. She could still taste him.

Relieved to be home, she fumbled in her bag for the front door key. Her hands were shaking, and her vision was blurred with tears, but at last she opened the door. She closed her eyes and inhaled a long, juddering breath, relishing the familiar musty smell. She was safe.

But then her eyes opened, and she stepped into the dark hallway to see her father sprawled on the floor. She'd thought he'd have been out by now and stepped over him with little regard. That's when she noticed his eyes were open. He looked strange, staring into space. She nudged his thigh with her foot, and said, 'Dad.'

Nothing. There was no response and Molly wondered if he was dead. She crouched down and waved her hand in front of his eyes. They were unflinching. She nudged him again, this time his shoulder. Still nothing, but his head rolled to one side.

'Oh my God,' she gasped and ran to the scullery. She grabbed a piece of broken mirror that her father used when shaving, then hurried back to him and held it close to his mouth and nose. It didn't mist. He was definitely dead.

Molly rose to her feet. She didn't care. She had hated him, and now she loathed another man, Billy Wilcox, and she wished he was dead too.

Dulcie was so worried she couldn't even bring herself to bake. She should have tried to talk George out of her plan to rid Mike Mipple of his tongue, but having discovered that the man had gone for Ethel, Dulcie had told George she'd have done it herself if she'd been well enough.

Nearly an hour had passed. George had promised

she'd come straight back home, but there wasn't any sign of her yet.

Dulcie walked through to the kitchen and filled the kettle. As the water poured, she looked into the yard, and spoke to Percy. 'Seems I'm not the only woman in this family who won't put up with any nonsense!' she said. She placed the kettle on the gas stove and a thought crossed her mind. George was a clever girl and a beautiful one too. She'd inherited it all from Sissy, but if brains and looks could be passed on through family, could killing too? Could murder go through the blood of families?

Just then, the front door opened, and George came into the kitchen.

'Thank goodness you're home!' Dulcie said with relief.

'I told you not to worry, Gran.'

'What took you so long? Are you all right? Did you do it? You know, cut his tongue out?'

'I didn't get a chance. The stupid idiot started a fight and I accidentally punched him in his throat. A couple of minutes later he dropped dead, right there in front of me!'

'Oh, George, no! Did anyone see you? Where did this happen?'

'Don't worry, I'm pretty sure no-one but you knows I was in his house. I've left him in the hallway where he fell.'

Dulcie sat down at the table. It was almost as if history was repeating itself. She'd sat here once before discussing murder with Ruby. God, she missed the girl terribly. 'So nobody knows he's dead yet?' Dulcie asked, wondering if they should think about disposing of the body.

'No. Molly or Fanny will probably find him later, but I doubt there'll be any tears for the man. He was horrible, a right pig.' George went to the sink and washed her hands. 'Do you think I'm a monster, Gran? I don't feel bad about killing him. Actually, I'm pleased he's dead. What does that say about me?'

Dulcie had asked herself the same question many times over the years. 'No, love, you're not a monster. You're brave and strong. You only did what Molly and Fanny probably wished they had the guts to do themselves. If Mike had been a better husband and father, I don't think you'd have been gunning for him for just talking about your club.'

'I suppose, but it ain't normal to go round murdering people, is it? There must be something wrong with me. People have always said I'm weird... They were right,' George said as her eyes welled with tears.

Dulcie didn't like to see her granddaughter upset and killing Mike Mipple had obviously distressed her. 'Now you listen to me, George Garrett... there is nothing weird about you. Mike Mipple had it coming to him and if it hadn't been you, I don't doubt he'd have copped it from someone else. The man was not only a wife beater, he had a big mouth, and one that was sure to have landed him in it one way or another.'

'Gran, do you believe in God? Do you think there's a heaven and a hell? If there is, do you think the devil has got my soul?'

'Oh for Gawd's sake, girl! This is what happens when you hang about in church halls! That's enough of that sort of silly talk. Heaven and hell, my arse!' As far as Dulcie was concerned, God and the devil had nothing to do with George killing Mike Mipple. It was down to her. They shared the same blood. She'd committed a murder, and now her granddaughter had too. 'There's something I should tell you, but you have to promise never to tell your father. This will always be our secret.'

George agreed, and Dulcie confessed to killing Percy. 'So you see, it's a Garrett trait,' she said, hoping that once George had gotten over the shock of what she'd been told, she'd feel better about herself.

George stood up and walked to the sink. 'He's out there? In the yard?'

'Yep, right next to the coal bunker.'

'Blimey, Gran, that's one hell of a secret! I get what you're saying, but if it's a Garrett trait, how come my dad ain't killed anyone?'

'How do you know he hasn't?'

'I don't,' George answered.

'There you go. See, you ain't the only Garrett with

blood on your hands. You can't help being who you are, George. You was born that way.'

Ezzy stood outside the Garretts' front door. After he'd taken a call from his cousin, Fanny had given him their address and now he crossed his fingers, hoping it would be George and not her gran who opened it.

'Ezzy! What are you doing here?'

'Hello, George. I need to talk to you…'

'Sorry, where's my manners? Come in.'

George opened the door wider, and Ezzy walked in. He was impressed with the internal décor. He'd expected to find them living in squalor like the rest of the thieves he knew.

'Come through to the kitchen. We're having tea,' George said. 'Ezzy, this is my gran, Dulcie.'

'Pleased to meet you, Dulcie. I've heard a lot about you.'

'All bad, I hope,' Dulcie chuckled.

Ezzy instantly liked her. She was a game old bird and made him feel comfortable.

'Sit down, son, there's a fresh brew in the pot. George, get Ezzy a slice of my sponge.'

Ezzy accepted the plate of cake but placed it on the table. His stomach churned at what he had to tell them, and he stumbled over his words, 'I… I'm sorry to be the bearer of bad news, but it's err… err, about Jack.'

'My dad? What about him?' George asked, instantly looking concerned.

'He was taken quite poorly in Manchester and collapsed outside my cousin's shop.'

Dulcie's face paled, and she cried, 'Oh Gawd, is he all right?'

'Yes and no. He's alive, and he's being looked after, but he is a very sick man. My cousin had him admitted to the Manchester Royal Infirmary. He was taken in as an emergency.'

'What's wrong with him?' George asked.

'It looks like kidney failure. I'm sorry, I know it's not what you want to hear.'

'You'll have to go to him, George. I can't get to Manchester, but you can, and I don't want you leaving him,' Dulcie said. 'You'll have to find somewhere to stay close to the hospital and oh blimey, what about the money to pay the hospital bills?'

'Don't worry, I'll sort it out. I'll get on the first train out of London tomorrow morning. But what about you, Gran? I can't leave you alone.'

'I'll be fine. There's no need to worry about me. Ethel can come and stay while you're away. I should be with Jack though. I'm his mother, but I'm flaming useless nowadays.'

'You're not useless, Gran. You're just not fit to travel, that's all. You'll be able to look after my dad when he comes home.'

'Yeah, I suppose so,' Dulcie said. 'What about your club though? What will happen to it while you're away?'

'It'll be all right. Molly is more than capable of looking after it. Anyway, my dad comes before the club. Ezzy, thanks for letting us know. How much do we owe Seth?'

'Nothing. As an emergency, he was taken in free, but I don't know what his treatment will cost. The Manchester Royal is second to none when it comes to renal care. They're pioneers in that field. Try not to worry, I'm sure he'll be fine.'

Dulcie looked shaken and white with shock, and George didn't look much better. Ezzy felt helpless and made his excuses to leave. He liked the Garretts, they were a good family, but he didn't want to find himself in an awkward situation where he'd be left coughing up the money to pay for Jack's hospital bills.

Fanny had been distracted all day. It was well past lunchtime, but Molly still hadn't turned up. She hoped her daughter hadn't been stupid enough to confront Billy. She'd missed her meeting with him and was worried sick that this would only make things worse.

'Molly… Where have you been?' Ethel called.

Fanny spun round and sighed with relief, though Molly didn't look very happy. She heard her say to

Ethel, 'I had stuff to do. I'll be back in a minute, but I need to speak to Mum.'

Fanny watched as her daughter walked towards her, and from the look on her face, she wasn't about to impart good news.

'Mum, sit down a minute.'

'I don't want to sit down. Just tell me.'

'Please, Mum, this is going to be a bit of a shock.'

'Molly, stop pussyfooting around and bloody tell me! Is Billy Wilcox out to get me?'

'What? No… forget about Billy, that's all been sorted. You won't be having any trouble from him.'

'So what is it?' Fanny asked again. If everything was fine with Billy, why did her daughter look so tense? 'I can guess you went to see him. What happened?'

'Nothing,' Molly barked.

Fanny didn't believe her. She felt her daughter was hiding something, but any more thoughts of Billy Wilcox flew from her mind at her daughter's next words.

'It's Dad… he's dead.'

Fanny stared at her daughter, unsure of what to say. She wanted to laugh but held back as she knew that would be very inappropriate. 'How do you know he's dead? How did it happen?'

'I dunno. I found him on the floor in the hallway. He's definitely gone, but there weren't no blood or nothing.'

'Blimey… are you sure he's dead?'

'Of course I am!'

'Perhaps we should call the doctor to him?'

'What bleedin' good is the doctor going to do now? It's a bit late for that,' Molly answered, rolling her eyes.

'Is he still on the floor?'

'Yes, but in the bedroom. I managed to drag him through, but I couldn't get him on the bed. I just wanted him moved out of the way in case the Wests upstairs came in.'

'Good girl, Molly. Are you all right? It must have been a shock for you to find him like that.'

'Yes, Mum, I'm fine. To be honest, I'm glad he's gone.'

'No doubt,' Fanny said, 'but you mustn't let anyone hear you say that. For all he was or wasn't, he was still your father and you must never speak ill of the dead.'

Molly answered, 'Sorry,' but the way she said it lacked any sincerity.

Fanny's eyes narrowed. Molly sounded and looked different, her eyes cold and hard. Surely she hadn't had anything to do with her father's death?

Soon after Ezzy left, George set off to the Junction, but all the way there, instead of worrying about her own dad, she was considering whether she should tell Molly the truth about what had happened to Mike. In the end, she decided not to.

A young lad, no more than seven or eight years old, passed by. His feet were bare, and his shorts ragged. His thin arms looked like matchsticks. It wasn't an unusual sight, yet he was pushing a small barrow filled with beer bottles. His strength impressed George and she asked him where he was off to.

'Round the dosshouses, mister. Me mum puts me out to the tavern on Green Lane and I flog this lot to the down 'n' outs. Do you wanna buy one? I can do you a deal.'

'No, thanks, but give this to your mum,' George answered and gave the skinny lad a coin.

'Cor, thanks, mister!'

'Why are you up this end of town? You're a long way from Green Lane.'

'Me little sister turned up to help me out but me mum don't like her working round there 'cos she says the blokes are bad 'uns. I took her back to me mum – she hawks peg dolls up near the station. Now I've gotta lug all this bleedin' lot back. I couldn't leave it, could I? It'd be empty if I did and then me guv would have given me a right good hiding.'

George's heart melted for the poor lad. He reminded her a lot of Oppo when he'd been younger. She gave him another coin and smiled as his grimy face lit up. 'Tell your mum to come and see me. The Maids of Battersea, in St Mary's church hall. Do you think you can remember that?'

'Yeah, course, mister. You gonna give me mum a job in service?'

'Something like that,' George answered, 'just be sure to tell her.'

She said goodbye to the lad and hurried until she arrived at the flower stall to find the three Mipple women gathered together and talking closely. George had a good idea what they would be discussing!

'George, hello. You'll never guess what's happened!' Ethel blurted.

'No, go on, tell me.'

Molly reached across and patted Ethel's arm, a signal to tell her to be quiet. Then she looked at George and said, 'Me dad's dead.'

George could see there was no sadness in her eyes when she spoke, but there was something wrong, a hardness in her features. She wondered if Molly knew the truth about how her father had been killed. 'What happened to him?' she asked, testing the water.

'We're not sure. Perhaps his body just packed up.'

Thankfully, George couldn't detect any hint of accusation in Molly's answer, so whatever it was that was bothering her, it wasn't anything to do with Mike's death.

'I'm very sorry for your loss,' George said, though everyone knew she didn't mean it. No-one was sorry for the loss of Mike Mipple! 'There must be something in the water. My dad's ill too. He's in hospital in Manchester, and from what I know, he's in a bad way. I've got to go to him, but I can't leave my gran.'

'Don't you worry about that. Ethel will stay with her and sleep at your place until you come home, won't you, love?' Fanny said.

'Yes, I like cooking things with Dulcie,' Ethel answered, her face beaming with delight.

'And don't worry about the club either or the stall. I'll make sure things tick over smoothly, though there won't be any boxing lessons,' Molly said.

'Thanks. I'm not sure how long I'll be away, and I'll have to work whilst I'm in Manchester.'

'What do you mean? What work?' Molly asked.

'You know, go back to my old ways and do a bit of dipping and lifting. There'll be accommodation to fork out for, not to mention me dad's hospital bills.'

'Oh, Christ, George. You be careful!' Fanny said.

'Yeah, I will. Can Ethel come round first thing in the morning?'

'Yes, of course she can.'

'Thanks. I'd best be off, I've got to pack a case, and sorry I won't be around for your husband's funeral,' George offered.

'To tell you the truth, George, as far as I'm concerned he can go in a pauper's grave. It's no more than he deserved.'

Fanny certainly wasn't grieving; in fact she looked as if a weight had been lifted from her shoulders. George had felt a bit guilty for killing Mike Mipple at first, but she wasn't sorry now. However, when she looked at

Molly, there was something in her friend's demeanour that worried her. 'Are you all right, Molly?'

'Yeah, and I'm not sorry that my dad's dead.'

George frowned. Molly was trying to act as if nothing was wrong, yet she knew her well enough to recognise that something clearly was. Unfortunately, there was nothing George could do about it... for now.

34

It had been three weeks since Molly had visited Billy, and in that time, Billy had only demanded sex from Hilda the once. Even then, he hadn't climaxed and complained that she was loose because she'd had too many dicks. It suited Hilda. She much preferred it when he left her alone. Yet still, she felt she was his prisoner.

It was too early for Billy to be in the office, and Knuckles was still upstairs sleeping in one of the Russian girl's beds. He alternated between the two so could have been in either room.

Hilda took advantage of the solitude, and cautiously opened Billy's 'private' drawer in his desk. Ever so carefully, and with her heart pounding, she lifted his handgun out of the way and began to search. She wasn't sure what she was looking for. Anything. Something that could bring him down.

'Stupid cow, stupid cow, stupid cow! You're not as clever as Billy Wilcox.' It was her mother's voice goading her again. She tried to ignore it and listened for sounds of movement from upstairs.

'You're dumb, Hilda Murdin, just like your father. And you're a wicked tart! You thought I didn't see you throwing yourself at your dad? Sitting on his lap, flirting with him, being Daddy's girl… You tempted him. You asked for it.'

'No I didn't!' Hilda whispered. 'I was only six years old. I didn't know anything about what men and women do. How could it have been my fault?'

Before her mother could answer, Hilda heard the stairs creak. Her head shot up and she held her breath. This was risky. If Billy found out she'd been snooping, she'd end up in the cellar with his dad. Then she heard Knuckles clear his throat.

'Shit,' she cursed quietly, then quickly, though gently, closed the drawer and locked it, returning the key to its hiding place under a cactus pot on the desk. She darted across the office and sat, trying to look innocent at her own desk. She was disappointed that she hadn't found anything to use against Billy, and her mother's voice filled her mind again.

'Told you,' she said. 'Stupid cow, stupid cow, stupid cow.'

Hilda's throat felt as if it was constricting. All hope had diminished and been replaced with a depressing realisation – there was no escape from Billy Wilcox, or her mother.

'I'm a bloody miracle, I am,' Jack chirped. He was sitting up in bed, and clearly feeling much better. Against all the odds, Jack had defied the doctor's prognosis and was on the mend.

'Yeah, well, maybe so, but you've still got to take it

easy,' George said as she poured him a glass of water.

'Thanks, love. There I was, on death's door, and now look at me. Three weeks later and I'm like a new man! There's no need for you to hang about now so you may as well get yourself back home to London. I'll be out meself in a day or two. Cor, I can't wait. This bloody place is nearly as bad as prison.'

'Oh really? I don't think so, Dad! I've seen the way you muck about with the nurses.' George laughed. She wouldn't call it flirting, but her father's easy charm had won them over.

'Not all of them. There's one who's got a face like a smacked arse. I call her the sergeant major, but not to her face, mind.'

George pulled up a seat and sat next to her dad's bed. She'd been worried sick she was going to lose him. When she'd first arrived in Manchester, her father looked to be on death's door, and now it was so nice to see him almost glowing with health. 'If you're only going to be a couple of days, I may as well wait for you.'

'Don't be daft. What's the point in paying out for that B and B? I thought you'd be in a hurry to see your gran?'

'She's all right,' George said. 'Ethel is with her, and Ezzy has made sure she ain't been going without.'

'So much for them Jews having a reputation for being tight! Seth has been more than generous in what he pays you, and it's been good of him to send some of the money to Ezzy for your gran. I don't know what we would have done without them.'

'Yeah, you're right there, Dad. He's been telephoning Ezzy too and giving him updates on your condition. I know it's helped to ease me gran's mind.' George felt a pang. She had missed Dulcie. 'I suppose it would make sense to go home. I ain't got nothing for Seth to buy unless I do another job.'

Jack leaned forward, closer to George, and lowered his voice. 'There you go. It ain't worth the risk of getting caught up here, not for the sake of staying with me. I'd hate to see you banged up in a Northern prison. Go on, sling your hook. If you get the train now, you'll be home by dinnertime. Anyway, I can't think why you'd wanna stay up here. The place is even more bleedin' dismal than London.'

George decided that her father was right, and she felt assured that he wouldn't be long behind her. She'd been away for most of May, and had a lot of catching up to do, along with a few people to thank. She'd be eternally grateful to Ezzy and his family, and of course to Oppo who had been regularly popping in to check on her gran. Not *all* men are bad, George decided, just most of them.

It wasn't long before George was heading home. Secrets, secrets, secrets. The sound of the Manchester to London train reverberating on the tracks seemed to ring out the words in George's head. Secrets, secrets, secrets. The sexual assault on her by the policemen, blowing up the station, the dead coppers, murdering Mike Mipple, and her gran being a killer too!

George had so many secrets to keep, but one troubled her more than most – her gran burying her husband in a barrel in the backyard. The thought of it unnerved her. Her bedroom window looked directly over his final resting place, and as a child she'd played on that patch of ground, unaware that a dead body was just a couple of feet below her.

She could understand why her gran had killed Percy. She'd never known the man herself, but from what Dulcie had told her, he'd been a complete waste of space. But she couldn't get her head around the fact she was living in a graveyard! Something would have to be done about it, though at this moment in time, she didn't know what.

And now there was Molly to worry about too. She had a secret that was obviously distressing her. She was being unusually stubborn, and no matter how hard George pushed her, she refused to share it. George had seen the strain on Molly's face. Her heart went out to her friend, but there was nothing she could do to help unless Molly was willing to disclose what was upsetting her.

Yes, Molly had it in her to be stubborn, but George was more dogged, and she would keep on at Molly until the girl gave in and opened up. Whatever was bothering her, George thought it must be bad; after all, they'd shared each other's secrets for most of their lives.

35

Jane had heard a rumour. Apparently George Garrett was running some sort of club that taught women how to defend themselves. Had the gossip been about anyone else, then she wouldn't have believed it, but she wouldn't put something like this past George. After all, the girl was tough and had been fighting from a very young age.

Jane thought it was a fantastic idea, and something she'd be keen to support. However, she'd like to check things out for herself first, and was on her way to the church hall.

When she arrived, she was greeted by a beautifully hand-painted sign above the door, which read, 'The Maids of Battersea.' She wondered if she was in the correct place. The Maids of Battersea didn't sound much like a self-defence group. If anything, it put her in mind of service women. She could easily envisage George boxing, but she couldn't imagine the girl as a servant to anyone. Undeterred, and more curious than ever, she entered the hall and was surprised to find Molly Mipple holding an audience of at least a dozen women, seemingly showing them how to make lace.

The door caught the wind and slammed shut behind

her. It caused a large whooshing noise and one hell of a bang. The class fell silent, and Molly's head flew round, but when she spotted Jane, instead of appearing pleased to see her, Jane noticed she looked mortified.

'Hello, Molly. I'm sorry to disturb you, but can I have a word please?'

Jane noticed that Molly's eyes were like saucers, and she was sheet-white. As she slowly pushed her seat back, Jane was sure she saw Molly wobble unsteadily as she walked up to her.

'I've heard some talk, rumours of a women-only club being run by George. Is this it?'

Molly nodded.

'Good, I'm in the right place then. So where is George?'

Molly remained mute and pointed to a screen near the back wall.

'Thank you,' Jane said, and walked to the other end of the long hall, wondering what was wrong with Molly. The girl's behaviour was most peculiar.

George suddenly appeared from behind the screen. She was dressed in her usual attire, looking more like a man than a woman and asked abruptly, 'What do you want?'

'Hello, George. I hope you don't mind me calling in like this?'

'That depends on why you're here.'

'I've come to see what you're doing.'

'It's none of your business,' George said.

Jane realised she'd made George suspicious. 'I'm sorry, I didn't mean to offend you. It's just that I've heard you're holding some sort of class to teach women how to defend themselves. I think it's a smashing notion and I'd love to know more about it.'

George eyed her doubtfully, but asked, 'Did you want to join the class?'

Jane nearly laughed. She couldn't punch her way out of a paper bag and had no desire to learn. God forbid, she'd break a nail! And she had no need to fight. Norman had always looked after her, and now she had Billy. 'No, but thank you all the same,' she answered humbly. 'However, I would like to offer you my support.'

'Thanks, Mrs Wilcox, but we're doing all right,' George said. 'Now, if you'll excuse me, I have a class to teach.'

She turned to walk away, but Jane called to her, 'Wait, George. I've got an idea I'd like to run by you.'

George looked impatient but stood with her hands on her hips and waited for Jane to continue.

'I've heard that some of the men don't like the idea of what you're doing, and to be honest, it's got a few of the women talking rather unfavourably too. If people's perceptions could be changed, I believe you'd have the ladies in these parts hammering down your door to join your club.'

'Probably,' George said, 'but I don't see how I can change their minds.'

'Well, I was thinking… I have quite a bit of influence in the area, and one of my late husband's trusted colleagues runs the local newspaper. I'd be happy to write an article to promote the club. You'd have the final say, of course, but if I put my name to The Maids of Battersea, I'm sure people would be less scathing, and you wouldn't have to operate so guardedly.'

'What's in it for you?' George asked.

'Nothing, really. I'm just an advocate of promoting power for women. Too many wives and daughters are abused. It must stop, and this is a step in the right direction. By the way, why call it The Maids of Battersea?'

George snorted, and said, 'It was inspired by Joan of Arc.'

'Oh, I see,' Jane fibbed, not grasping the connection. 'So what do you think? Would you like me to get involved?'

'I'm not sure. If we go public with this, I would lose the use of this hall. I can't see the vicar allowing me to teach boxing to women.'

'Oh, I hadn't thought of that. But where there's a will, there's a way. Who knows, maybe a quiet word from me would change the vicar's mind. After all, he'll be wanting another donation for the church roof again soon, not that I've ever seen that roof re-leaded.'

The women smiled at each other, and Jane was pleased to see George had dropped her guard.

'I know you're busy now,' she said, 'so let's meet for tea later and we can discuss it further. Say half past four at Pinkie's?'

'Pinkie's?' George baulked.

It flashed through Jane's mind that George might feel out of place in Pinkie's teahouse, especially as the prices were just as extravagant as the art deco interior. 'Or you could come to mine if you'd prefer?' she quickly offered.

'No, Pinkie's is fine.'

'Great, I'll see you later then,' Jane said, and trotted off.

She waved goodbye to Molly, and as she made her way home her mind went into overdrive. She was so pleased that George had agreed to allow her to be a part of her club. Since Norman had been killed her life had felt empty, and her days endlessly boring. This was just what she needed to get her teeth into. It was exciting, and fresh, but most of all, a challenge.

Now that George was back, and word had spread, Molly had been chuffed to see the participant numbers of The Maids of Battersea increase again. Some of the women had slumped off whilst George had been away, not that Molly could blame them. She was sure they found boxing far more exciting than rag-rug or lace making!

She was halfway through her craft class but finding it difficult to concentrate. Seeing Mrs Wilcox had sent her into a panic. She was the last woman Molly expected to walk through the door. Thankfully, she hadn't stayed long or spoken much to her, but all sorts of crazy thoughts had passed through Molly's mind. The encounter had left her speculating about the possibility of Mrs Wilcox knowing what she was trying to desperately hide.

It was bad enough that she knew to expect another interrogation from George later. Her friend wouldn't let the matter drop. George seemed to instinctively know that something had upset her, and it was clear she was determined to get to the bottom of it. Molly kept assuring her that everything was fine and dandy, but she knew it wouldn't be long before she'd crack and tell her the terrible truth.

She'd allowed Billy Wilcox to have sex with her. The act had been violent and humiliating, but she only had herself to blame. She could feel herself shrinking in her chair at the recollection of that awful day. The memory would never go away, and to make matters worse, she had a constant reminder – a bastard child growing in her belly.

36

George woke up the next morning and smiled to herself as she climbed out of bed. She still couldn't believe what a fool Jane Wilcox had been. The woman had more money than sense and was practically throwing it at her. George didn't mind, she was happy to use it, and it felt like she was getting one over on Billy.

The summer air smelt sweet, and George was in a good mood. It had been a while since she'd been excited about anything, but Jane's big ideas had her all fired up. 'Good morning,' she greeted Dulcie as she almost skipped into the kitchen.

'Morning, love. Your dad's already left for Manchester. Is Winnie coming in today?'

A woman from the club had told George about her middle-aged neighbour, Winnie, who had recently lost her husband. George had approached the woman, and she'd agreed, for a small price, to sit with Dulcie on the days when Jack went to Manchester. The arrangement freed Ethel up to work on The Maids of Battersea stall.

'Yes, Gran, she'll be here later. How are you getting on with her?'

'Fine. She's a bit quiet though. I think she's scared of me, but I don't know why.'

'Have you been nice to her?'

'Of course I bloody have! What do you mean by that?'

'You can be a bit... sharp sometimes,' George answered.

'Well, if people weren't so stupid... Anyway, you must have been late home last night. I didn't hear you come in.'

'No, I wasn't, Gran, but you was fast asleep in your chair. I didn't want to disturb you, and Dad was snoring on the sofa, so I went to bed.'

'Oh, I hadn't realised you was in your room when I went up. You must have had a good night's kip 'cos you're full of the joys of spring this morning.'

'I am, but it's nothing to do with sleep.'

Dulcie handed George a fried egg sandwich. 'Get that down your neck and tell me what's made you so bleedin' cheery.'

George hungrily ate the sandwich and spoke in between mouthfuls. 'I've struck a deal with Jane Wilcox, and it's a bit of a win-win situation for me.'

Immediately, George noticed her grandmother's face fall. 'Don't look like that. She's all right – nothing like her son.'

'I wouldn't be so sure. You've got egg on your chin,

and I hope for your sake you don't end up with it all over your face. So, what's this deal then?'

'She likes the idea of the Maids, and for some unknown reason, she wants to back it.'

'You've still got egg on your chin,' Dulcie said, and pointed.

George laughed, and rubbed the dripping yolk away. 'You mean I really do have egg on my chin? Anyway, she's gonna write some snazzy piece for the newspaper about the club, which will be free advertising as well as a good endorsement from her. You know what they're like round here, but they'll soon change their minds once Jane gives it the thumbs-up. She has this notion that all women, now that we can vote, should have free choice. She said she's seen too much repression of women, and it's about time we all learnt to stick up for ourselves.'

'Personally, I wouldn't give her as much credence. She's nothing more than a jumped-up gangster's missus, but you're probably right. A lot of folk in Battersea will follow her viewpoint. But what about the vicar?'

George leaned back in her chair. 'I ain't worried about him,' she said, "cos first Jane said she'd bribe him, but then offered to cough up the readies to lease some premises for the club. After all, the vicar will probably throw us out, which will be her bloody fault for sticking her oar in.'

'Are you sure you've thought this through, love? I'm

sure she'd stand to her word and lease you a place, but then what? You could be stuck with somewhere and no money to pay the rent.'

'Gran, I ain't silly. I made her agree to pay six months in advance. And she said she'll kit it out with some training equipment. Cor, picture it, Gran... A proper boxing ring and everything!'

'Smells a bit fishy to me,' Dulcie said, and folded her arms firmly across her body.

'Not 'alf as fishy as them bloody kippers you cooked yesterday! The house still stinks of them,' George said, wrinkling her nose.

'I can't believe she's gonna do all that out of the goodness of her heart.'

'You're ever so cynical sometimes. It's straight up. We've agreed that the whole thing is going to be run as a legit business. Entrance to the club will remain on a voluntary contribution basis, but all the women must participate in craft making, and not just come for the boxing. Jane's also gonna stump up for some proper equipment for that too. She only had one stipulation.'

'I knew there'd be a catch somewhere,' Dulcie said, and her eyes narrowed.

George tutted. 'All she wants is ten per cent of all profits to go to a worthy women's charity, and any money she puts in to be paid back with no interest. And before you jump in and say anything, I think the charity thing is a good idea too.'

'It's your lookout, but I'd never trust a Wilcox. I hope I'm wrong and I'll have to eat my words, but watch your back, girl.'

She knew her gran only had her best interests at heart, but George was far shrewder than the old woman gave her credit for. Admittedly, she'd been reluctant to trust Jane at first, but as they'd spoken, she'd found herself warming to the woman. She couldn't quite understand the reasons for Jane wanting to put so much in and get nothing in return but concluded that some people were just soft in the head.

George thought that if Molly was well-off, she'd do something nice like Jane. There were folk who were like that. Just nice. Maybe it was better to be nice, rather than cruel, but she thought that was something she'd never know.

There was no mistaking it, Fanny could hear Molly throwing up in the yard, but it was obvious the girl was trying to hide her sickness. Full of despair, Fanny slumped onto her bed. She thought her daughter had more sense!

Molly crept back into her room, but Fanny leapt from her bed and was ready to confront her. She pulled the curtain dividing their rooms to one side. 'A word,' she said sternly.

Molly looked sheepish, but Fanny had no sympathy and said abruptly, 'You're in the family way then?'

Molly's head dropped.

'Answer me!' Fanny barked.

Molly's body jerked and stiffened. 'Yes,' she answered, her voice barely audible.

'How could you? How could you have been so stupid? Who's the father?'

Molly lowered her head again.

'I asked you a question.'

'Billy. Billy Wilcox,' Molly replied, avoiding eye contact.

Fanny frowned. There had been no sign of them seeing each other. 'Does he know?'

'No, and I don't want him to.' Molly looked up pleadingly and was beginning to blubber. 'Please, Mum, he can't know!'

Her daughter's tears did nothing to soften Fanny. She thought the girl should be grateful that her father wasn't alive. He would have beaten the unborn child out of her. 'He has to know. He'll have to marry you. Either that or pay for an abortion.'

'No... No, Mum! I can't see one of them backstreet butchers! Look what happened to Sarah Hook – they used the needles on her and she bled to death!'

'Calm down, Molly, and keep your bloody voice down! We don't want them upstairs hearing about this. How far gone are you?'

'I've only missed one monthly,' Molly snivelled.

'Good. At least we've got a bit of time to get this sorted before you start showing. But if you refuse to get rid of it, then you'll have to marry Billy. The child needs a name, and I ain't having no grandchild of mine being born on the wrong side of the blanket. Have you got any idea what'll happen to you as an unmarried mother? For a start, if the doctor comes when you're birthing that child, and he needs to stitch you, he won't give you nothing for the pain. They don't think mothers without husbands are deserving of it. And that's just the start, so you'd better marry Billy, or else!'

'But I don't want to marry him. I hate him… hate him!'

'You should have thought about that before you opened your legs,' Fanny scorned through gritted teeth.

Molly ran from the room in a flood of tears. Fanny could hear her sobbing from the scullery, and her sisters trying to console her.

Fanny had said her piece without thinking clearly. She'd never allow her daughter to see a backstreet butcher. It was far too risky. They could try the tin bath with boiling water and a bottle of gin, but she'd attempted that herself and it had failed. No, there was only one solution – Billy would have to do the right thing.

*

Ezzy's new security system meant that the door to his shop was no longer open to the public. A push-button electric bell had been installed, and instead of the commonly used buzz sound, his bell played musical chimes. Ezzy took great pleasure in listening to it, and several times a day, he would pop outside to ring it. He'd had it for over a week now, but the novelty hadn't yet worn off.

It was approaching lunchtime and Ezzy was thinking about closing for an hour when he heard the bell chimes ring. There was a large window in the shop door, and as he walked towards it, his hackles rose. Two men were waiting outside, and they didn't look like potential customers.

'What do you want?' he called.

'Open up,' one of the men answered.

'I'm closed. You'll have to come back later.'

'Open the door,' the man repeated.

'No, I'm closed,' Ezzy said, and turned to walk away. He was halfway across the shop when he heard glass shattering. He spun round to see the man had broken the window and was now reaching through to open the door.

Ezzy ran towards him. He was short and stout and no match for the two muscly men, but it didn't deter him from having a go. He bashed at the man's arm, but by now the door was opening, and he was thrown to one side.

The first man loomed over him. Ezzy had always feared being robbed and kept a cricket bat behind the counter. He was too far away. It was no use to him now.

'Oops, looks like your door has broken,' the largest of the men said sarcastically.

Ezzy didn't answer. His mouth was dry, and he could feel himself trembling. If his heart didn't slow down, he thought he might die of fright.

'Shame about that. It'll cost you a few bob to get it mended. 'Ere, Malc, look at this lovely glass counter,' the other man said as he ran his hand along the worktop. 'It would be a travesty if this got broken too.'

Ezzy began to question if the men were in the shop to rob him. After all, surely they'd be demanding he open the safe?'

'It would, Sid, it'd be a pity. How much do you think it would cost to get a new glass counter?'

Sid spoke again. 'You've got a lot of valuable items in your store, Mr Harel. I would strongly recommend that you take out our cover to protect them.'

'Co... cover... What sort of cover?'

'Insurance, but me and Malc are very busy men, and we don't have time to stand around here discussing the pros and cons of our policy. Malc, show Mr Harel an example of how easily accidents can happen, just in case he hasn't got the message.'

Ezzy watched helplessly as Malc threw over a large grandfather clock. It had been in Ezzy's family for years, but now lay smashed on the floor. 'All right... all right... stop now,' he pleaded. 'How much do you want?'

Sid smiled. 'That's a very sensible question, Mr Harel. We'll take two pounds as a down payment, then fifteen shillings a week.'

Ezzy climbed to his feet, and with hunched shoulders he went to his cash register. It had been a busy morning in the shop, and as he took the money out, he hoped they wouldn't demand more.

Malc hovered over his shoulder, intimidating him. But to Ezzy's relief, although the man must have seen the full till, he accepted the two pounds, and then as though it was a normal business transaction, he shook Ezzy's hand.

'Mr Harel,' Malc said, 'you are now under the protection of Billy Wilcox. This business arrangement is to be kept discreet, and as long as you pay up every week, Mr Wilcox will ensure your safety. Good day to you.'

They were gone, but Ezzy's heart was still racing. He'd heard all about Billy Wilcox and his insurance and knew exactly what would have happened if he didn't give them the money. And now, like it or not, he'd be bitterly paying for his wellbeing for the rest of his working life.

37

The weekend arrived, but Billy wasn't relishing the idea of spending any time at home. He loved his mother but couldn't stand the sight of his younger sisters.

He sat in his father's chair, and lit Norman's old pipe. 'Where's Sally?' he asked his mother.

Jane looked up from the table she was huddled over. 'Is that your father's?'

'What, this?' Billy asked, holding up the pipe. 'Yes. You don't mind, do you?'

His mother looked as if she was going to object, so Billy quickly added, 'It makes me feel closer to him.'

Jane didn't respond, and her attention returned to whatever she was doing at the table.

'Where's Sally?' Billy asked again. He was hoping she wouldn't come barging into the lounge and disturb his peace.

'She's at Trudi's. They had a sleepover and Penny's having an afternoon nap. She had a bad dream last night that kept her up, poor thing.'

Billy drew on the pipe, and as the sunlight caught the smoke, he watched it swirl and curl into fascinating shapes. 'Does the mellow smell of this remind you of Dad?' he asked.

His mother seemed distracted, but half-heartedly answered, 'Er… yes, I suppose.'

'Have you made any tea?'

Again, Jane didn't appear to be listening, and Billy could feel himself becoming agitated. He liked to have her full attention.

'MUM…'

'What, Billy? You can see I'm busy.'

'What are you doing?'

'I'm writing an article for the *Lambeth Gazette*. I've already spoken to Jonathan Penning, and he's agreed to run it on the third page.'

'What are you writing about?'

'The Maids of Battersea. Have you heard about them? It's a club that George Garrett has set up.'

There had been some talk in the brothel about it, but Billy hadn't taken much notice. Whatever stupid club thing George was up to didn't affect his business. 'Yeah, but why are you writing about it?'

'I've agreed to help. I think the whole concept is fabulous. George is teaching the women boxing skills, and when they're not training, they make arts and crafts that they sell for funding and profit.'

He thought it sounded ridiculous, and women shouldn't be boxing. But he knew George could hold her own. It had been a few years back, but she'd given some of his boys a bit of a pasting. 'Why do you want to be connected to something like that?'

'Do I really need to explain myself? Can't you see the benefits in it for women?'

'To be honest, Mum, no. A woman's place is at home looking after the house and kids. Not in a boxing ring!'

'Things are moving on, Billy, and you should keep up with the times. In fact, I think it would be a good idea for you to send your girls to the club. You know I don't like you having those... places, but if someone's going to make money from it, it may as well be you. And it's common knowledge that prostitution is the oldest career in the world. However, they must meet all types of men, maybe some violent ones, and I should think it would be good for them to be able to defend themselves.'

Billy roared out laughing. 'You have got to be kidding me? The girls are working. They're too busy pleasing men to be worrying about bashing them!'

'I'm sure you could spare them one morning a week?'

'Forget it, it's never going to happen,' Billy answered. 'It wouldn't be good for business.'

'All right, but what about that girl you have working in your office? She may have to deal with difficult men at times.'

Billy gave it some thought. He rather liked the idea of Hilda learning a few fighting skills. It might provoke a bit of aggression in her. He'd found her boring lately, and the thought of her fighting back turned him on. 'All right,' he said, deciding this would also humour his mother and please her. 'She can take the classes, but only one a week.'

'I was thinking, the club will be requiring new premises, and as you're not using the shop your father acquired for the expansion of the bicycle hire business, perhaps George could take the space?'

'No, absolutely not. I won't support her in any way whatsoever, and if my father was alive, he'd forbid you from getting involved.'

'No he wouldn't, your father was a very reasonable man. But fine, if you won't allow George to take on the shop, she's a very resourceful woman; I'm sure she'll find something suitable.'

Billy scowled at his mother, though she didn't notice as she'd turned her attention back to writing the article. He didn't think George was in any way similar to how his mother had described, especially the term 'woman'. There wasn't anything womanly about her, and setting up this stupid fight club just went to prove his point.

Molly had taken her sisters to the park, but this time it was because she wanted to, and not because she was keeping them out of her dad's way. Things at home had been more relaxed now that he was dead, and her mother was finally feeling the benefit of her earnings.

Everything would have been great, but she'd ruined it by getting herself pregnant!

She unconsciously rubbed her stomach. It was still flat. Apart from the nausea, there were no signs of her condition. But she knew she wouldn't be able to hide it for much longer.

'Hey.' She heard a shout, and turned round to see George jogging towards her.

'I thought I'd find you here,' George said when she caught up with her.

'You know me,' Molly answered, trying to sound cheerier than she felt.

'Yes, I do, and I still know something is wrong. I'm sorry to keep harping on about it, but I don't like to think of you upset.'

'Let's sit down,' Molly said, leading George towards a bench. It was about time she told her friend the truth. A white fluffy cloud momentarily covered the sun, and Molly shivered as she began to relay the details of what had happened with Billy.

'The filthy bastard! I'll kill him!' George seethed.

'That's not the worst of it,' Molly said, fighting to hold back the sobs that had caught in her throat. 'I'm pregnant.'

George's head snapped around, and she stared wide-eyed at Molly. 'You have got to be fucking kidding me!'

'I wish I was. I thought it would be safe 'cos it was

my first time, but it wasn't, and now me mum said I've got to get rid of it or marry Billy! What am I gonna do, George? I'm too scared to have a backstreet job done on me, but I can't face marrying Billy.'

Molly buried her face in her hands as she cried, and George put a comforting arm across her shoulders, saying, 'I can't believe your mum expects you to marry him after he forced you into it.'

'She... she doesn't know.'

'What! Why not?'

'I daren't tell her, George. She's like a bloomin' lioness when it comes to protecting her kids. She always took the brunt of me dad's temper to keep him away from us, so Gawd knows what she'd try to do to Billy Wilcox. He's mad, a nutter, and I don't want her going near him.'

'He deserves to have his fucking balls chopped off.'

'I know, but George, you won't tell her, will you? Promise me you won't tell her.'

'I'll keep schtum, but there's no way you can marry the bastard.'

'As I said, me mum's insisting, and it's either that or a backstreet butcher.'

'I ain't having this. I'm gonna sort Billy Wilcox out once and for all.'

'No! No, George. I don't want you going near him either. You don't know what he's capable of and if anything happened to you I'd never forgive myself.'

'Nothing is going to happen to me.'

'You can't be sure of that. It's not just him. He's got muscle around him too and you wouldn't stand a chance. Please, George, I'm begging you to butt out of this. If anything happened to you I'd have it on my conscience for the rest of my life. Anyway, maybe it won't be so bad being married to him. His mum is all right, and if we live with her Billy won't treat me badly with her around.'

George hung her head, then at last said, 'It's your life, Molly, you've got to make your own choices, and live with them, but he'd better treat you right.'

Molly felt sick with relief. She'd managed to talk George out of going up against Billy, and as long as her mother was kept in the dark, she'd be safe from him too. She didn't want to marry him, but it seemed she had no other options. Her fate was sealed.

Fanny knocked nervously on the Wilcox's front door, and Jane opened it with a friendly smile, though Fanny thought after hearing what she had to say, that smile would soon be wiped off her pretty face.

'Hello, I wasn't expecting you,' Jane said.

'I know and I'm sorry to turn up unexpectedly, but can I have a word please, Mrs Wilcox?'

'Yes, come in. Go through to the lounge, I'll bring us some tea.'

Fanny walked into the opulent front room, and her heart sank. Billy was sat in an armchair and didn't look pleased at her intrusion.

'What are you doing here?' he asked, his voice barely more than a whisper.

'I think you know,' Fanny answered. She was scared, but for Molly's sake she was determined to hold her ground.

'No, actually, I have no idea, so why don't you enlighten me?'

'Let's wait for your mother,' she answered firmly, her shoulders back and her head held high.

Billy aggressively folded his newspaper, then threw it to one side. She flinched when he jumped to his feet. All of Fanny's instincts were screaming at her to run, but she remained where she was and before she knew it, Billy was towering over her.

With his face close to her own, he sniggered, 'She begged me for it.'

Fanny held her breath. She knew he was trying to bait her, but then Jane walked into the room and Billy sprang backwards. Fanny detested him and hated the idea of her daughter having to marry him. But it was better that than bearing a bastard child.

'Sit down, Fanny,' Jane offered, and handed her a cup of tea in a fine china cup. If Fanny hadn't been so distressed, she may have appreciated the quality tea service and fine décor of the room, but instead, she was trying to stop herself from shaking and causing the cup and saucer to rattle.

'So, what can I do for you?' Jane asked.

Fanny's eyes flitted apprehensively to Billy then back to Jane. He was glaring menacingly at her, and she could feel his eyes boring into her. She wanted to say she'd made a terrible mistake by coming round, and run for the door, but that wouldn't have helped Molly.

'It's about my daughter, Molly... and Billy.'

'Oh, what about them?' Jane asked, glancing briefly at her son.

'This is a bit delicate, so I'll just come straight out with it. She's in the family way. Your Billy has got my daughter pregnant, so I'll be expecting him to do the decent thing.'

Jane gasped, and Billy closed his eyes. The news must have come as a shock to him.

'Is this true, Billy?' Jane asked.

'I doubt it. It could have been anyone so what makes you think I'm the father?'

'Don't try to insinuate that my daughter is a tart. You're the only man who has touched her, so you know full well that it's you,' Fanny said firmly, though she was sure she was trembling.

'Yeah, well, it's her word against mine.'

'Is it true, Billy?' Jane asked again.

The room was in silence as Billy paced towards the

window to stand with his back to them. The atmosphere felt explosive, and Fanny feared it was about to ignite.

'Well, is it?' Jane asked again. 'Did you lay with Molly Mipple?'

'Yes,' Billy snapped, and spun round, 'but that doesn't mean it was me who got her pregnant. She's probably been with half the blokes in Battersea.'

'How dare you,' Fanny said, leaping to her feet. It was bad enough that he was denying the child, but suggesting she slept around added insult to injury.

Jane jumped up too and held her hand on Fanny's arm. 'Please, let me deal with this,' she said and faced her son. 'Billy. I don't want to hear you saying such vile things, especially about the girl who is potentially carrying your child.'

'There's nothing potential about it!' Fanny added with derision.

'I ain't having this. You can't stitch me up for getting her pregnant. It was only the once, and she weren't no virgin,' he shouted, then stormed out of the room, slamming the door behind him.

Fanny finally felt as though she could breathe again and slumped back onto a chair.

'I'm sorry about Billy, but it's probably the shock. I'll wait for him to calm down, then I'll speak to him. In the meantime...' Jane grabbed her purse from her handbag by the side of the sofa. 'Take this,' she said, and handed Fanny some coins.

'I don't want your money, Mrs Wilcox. I want your son to do the right thing by my Molly. You know what her life will be like as an unmarried mother. Believe you me, and I say this with the greatest respect, I don't want to see Molly married to Billy any more than he wants to marry her, but would you see your first grandchild born a bastard?'

'No, I don't want that. Molly's a good girl, and I've no doubt that my son is responsible for this situation. I'll make sure Billy sees sense, trust me.'

Fanny did trust Mrs Wilcox, though the same couldn't be said for her son.

'Come back this evening and bring Molly. Try not to worry, we'll get this sorted.'

Fanny left and headed for home. If she hadn't been so angry with Molly, she may have felt sorry for the girl. At least there was one small consolation in marrying Billy – as his wife, Molly would never be poor.

38

Two months had passed since Molly had told George she was pregnant, and though she tried to hide it, George could see her friend's stomach beginning to swell. Not that Molly would have to keep it a secret for much longer. Much to George's dismay, Molly was due to marry Billy next month. George had tried to talk Molly out of it, and from what she'd heard Billy wasn't keen on the union either. But Molly had refused to listen. She'd been adamant that she'd made her bed and would have to lie in it. As far as George was concerned, Fanny Mipple and Jane bloody Wilcox had a lot to answer for. If they hadn't pushed for this marriage, it wouldn't be happening.

George felt sweat dripping down her back. She'd arrived early at the gymnasium and had been jumping rope for fifteen minutes. She threw her rope down and surveyed her growing business. The large upper room was perfect for the fight club and the shop downstairs had a back room attached where the women held their craft-making sessions. When she'd first viewed the premises, she'd known it was exactly what she was looking for, but the landlord had turned her away. It wasn't until Jane used her Wilcox name that he'd changed his mind and couldn't hand over the keys quick enough.

It was the same when George went to purchase the gym equipment. The bloke in the warehouse had laughed at her request for boxing gloves, but Jane's influence had him almost begging for George's custom. Now she regretted accepting the woman's help in spite of the benefits. She should have known better than to work with Billy's mother.

Molly's voice drifted up the stairs as she heard her call, 'Are you up there, George?'

'Yes,' she answered, 'I'll be down in a minute.'

She returned the skipping rope to the equipment cupboard and grabbed a towel to wipe her face. It wasn't quite nine in the morning, but already the balmy August weather was making the gym hot and leaving her feeling sticky. The Maids of Battersea were in for a torturous training session today!

Molly came upstairs, and George was grateful to see she was carrying a large jug of water.

'I thought you might need this.'

'I said I'd come down.'

'I know, but Ethel is downstairs, and I wanted a word with you, in private.'

George poured herself a much-needed glass of water and sat on a long wooden bench that ran the length of the room.

'It's about me and this place. You know I love it, but

I've been talking to Mrs Wilcox, and she doesn't think Billy will want me working, not when we're married, and especially not once the baby is born.'

George still couldn't believe that Molly was going to marry the man who blackmailed her into having sex. How could she? It only made sense if Molly hadn't told the truth; maybe she'd lied and cried rape as she was too ashamed to admit that she'd willingly slept with Billy. Now it seemed she wouldn't be working in the club, but she'd been expecting this and said, 'Fine, suit yourself.'

'Don't be like that, George,' Molly said, sounding hurt.

'Listen to yourself. You and Mrs Wilcox are all for promoting the Maids when it suits you, but you're just like all the fucking women who come here – weak!'

'Be reasonable! I'm having a baby, George. I can't be a working woman. And as for Mrs Wilcox, you should be grateful. If it wasn't for her the Maids would still be in the church hall and selling on the market. Thanks to her you've got a proper gym, and a bloody smart shop downstairs!'

Apart from her gran, Molly was the only other person who could talk frankly to George without her getting narked. Most people watched what they said around her, but not Molly.

'I was doing just fine by myself! Yes, she and that fancy newspaper have boosted numbers, and yes, she's kitted out this place, but thanks to her interference I'm running more of a bloody fitness club than a boxing club! I don't need her, and I don't need you. If you want to walk out on this, then fucking well go!' George threw her glass across the room. 'Now go on, fuck off!'

Molly looked horrified as it smashed against the wall, but she held her ground and said, 'No, George. I won't go like this. There's things we need to arrange.'

Ethel poked her head round the door, looking tentative. 'Is everything all right?' she asked.

'Yes, Ethel, it's fine. Go back downstairs and stay there like I told you to,' Molly answered impatiently.

Ethel quietly closed the door behind her.

'Sorry, I didn't mean to worry Ethel,' George said, calmer now. She was quick to anger, but quick to calm down too. She felt guilty for raising her voice and smashing the glass. After all, Ethel had the mind of a child and had witnessed enough violence in her life.

'Funnily enough, Ethel is one of the things we'll have to discuss. You won't be able to keep an eye on her in the shop while you hold your lessons up here.'

'Don't worry about Ethel, she'll be fine. I'll get her an assistant,' George said with a wry smile, and both women laughed. 'I'll miss you,' she added.

George now felt awful for even considering that Molly had lied to her about Billy forcing her to have sex. Molly didn't have a bad bone in her body, and George knew what Billy was capable of.

'Me too, but we'll still see each other all the time.'

George nodded, but bit her tongue. She wasn't convinced that Billy would allow Molly to remain friends with her.

'I wish you'd change your mind about coming to the wedding,' Molly said.

'No, sorry, Molly. I can't stand by and watch you make the biggest mistake of your life.'

Molly's eyes filled with tears. 'But I'm not marrying him because I want to! I have to, you know that.'

'Don't start bawling again. You don't have to marry him. I told you, I'd help you with the baby. I'd make sure the child never wants for anything.'

'I know, but it wouldn't be fair on the baby. It needs a father, and can you imagine the terrible life it would have being a bastard? I'm marrying Billy for the sake of the child, not my own. Anyhow, I couldn't back out now, even if I wanted to.'

'Of course you could!' George said, hoping that there was a slim chance that Molly was having second thoughts.

'No, I couldn't. I had dinner a few weeks ago at Billy's house. Mrs Wilcox wanted to go through some of the wedding arrangements. She was busy in the kitchen when Billy threatened me.'

George instantly saw red but hid her fury. 'What threat?'

Molly began to cry again and through her tears, she answered, 'I told him I wasn't sure that I wanted to marry him, and he went potty. He said he believes the baby is his, and if I didn't go through with the wedding, he'd take the child from me and have me thrown into an asylum.'

'He said what?'

'He told me he hadn't wanted to marry me but could now see it had its advantages. I think he means about the marital bed. Oh, George, the thought of sharing a bed with him... I don't know what I can do. He's not taking my child. I'll have to marry him... but I can't stand him!'

Molly collapsed into a heap, her body racked with tears.

'For fuck's sake, Molly. Why didn't you tell me any of this before?'

'I couldn't... I'm so ashamed.'

'You've got nothing to feel ashamed about. Get up, pull yourself together, and make my excuses for my class today. Leave this to me, I'll be back later.'

'No, please, George. Leave it... just leave it.'

Determined, George ignored Molly's pleas as she stomped out to head for Billy's office. Molly was scared of Billy, but George wasn't, and she planned on putting a stop to this sham of a wedding once and for all.

*

Hilda's head shot up when the office door flew open. She was surprised to see George Garrett barge in.

'Get your hands off me,' George shouted at Knuckles as he tried to bar her way.

'It's all right, Knuckles, let her in, and get me a drink,' Billy ordered.

As Knuckles left the room, George threw him a filthy look then walked straight up to Billy's desk. She didn't seem to have any fear of the man, and Hilda wondered if she realised that Billy kept a gun in his drawer.

'I take it you're not here to ask if you can be the best man at my forthcoming wedding?' Billy mocked.

George leaned forward and placed her hands wide apart on Billy's desk. She stared him straight in the eyes, and answered, 'There isn't going to be a wedding.'

Hilda saw his eyes darken, and his cheek begin to twitch. He was furious. She admired George's courage, but thought the woman may have underestimated how vicious Billy could be.

His voice a menacing growl, he said, 'I can assure you, there is.'

'Molly's too scared to tell you, but I'm not. The wedding is off. Molly won't be marrying you, and the child will be raised as a Mipple. Her mind is made up, so that's an end to this farce.'

George straightened up, her chin held high and Hilda thought she looked magnificent, like some kind of warrior, part man, and part woman. She held her breath, waiting for Billy's reaction, but then George turned round and walked boldly out of the office.

Billy slammed his fist down on his desk, and Knuckles rushed back in. 'Sorry, boss. I tried to stop her, but...'

Billy's lips were set in a straight thin line. 'I want her dead,' he said.

'How, boss? Do you want me to cut her throat?'

'No... I want her and that fucking club gone. The Maids of Battersea, huh? Well, I'll have it burnt to the ground, and give her a death like her French heroine, burnt at the stake, just like Joan of fucking Arc!'

Hilda quietly gulped. Billy didn't make idle threats. She liked George, and her weekly lesson at the club, but now the place was going to go up in smoke. It would be a pity for it all to end in ashes and the harrowing memory of seeing her baby brother burn to his death flashed through her mind.

'*London's burning, London's burning, fetch the engines, fetch the engines. Fire fire! Fire fire! Pour on water...*' Her mother's voice filled her head again, spitefully singing a nursery rhyme that always left Hilda's blood running cold.

'Flames, Hilda, scorching flames... look at your hands, you stupid bitch... you couldn't save your brother and you can't save George!'

Hilda turned her shaking hands over and stared at the faded scars on her palms. She squeezed her eyes closed, trying to get rid of the image of her brother's charred body. You're wrong, Mother, she thought, inspired by George's courage. She could save George and she would.

39

It was a bright and sunny Wednesday morning in mid-August, but Ezzy's mood didn't match the weather. A dark cloud hung over him. He resented paying Billy's gang, and today the insurance was due. With a heavy heart he opened the shop as usual, but was on tenterhooks, waiting with dread to see Malc and Sid's ominous faces outside the newly glazed door.

Customers came and went, and by eleven Ezzy's nerves were jangled. Every time the bell chimes played, his body stiffened, and his blood pressure increased. He thought he'd have a heart attack at this rate and hoped they'd arrive soon so he could get it over and done with. There were only a couple more hours to go as like most of the businesses in town, the shop closed for half a day on Wednesdays.

Ezzy was stood in his doorway saying goodbye to a regular customer, when he noticed the two thugs approaching. His face dropped, and his customer must have noticed because she finished midway through a sentence to make a hasty exit.

'Mr Harel, I believe you've been expecting us,' Malc said.

Ezzy couldn't bring himself to greet the men. They followed him into the shop and up to the counter.

'I trust you have your scheduled payment ready?'

Ezzy cleared his throat. 'I wanted to talk to you about that,' he said uncertainly. His mouth felt dry.

'All discussions have been concluded... unless you'd like a reminder of our terms?' Malc sneered.

Ezzy quickly replied, 'NO... no. But I was wondering if we could negotiate the terms, only I'm struggling to meet them. Surely it would be better for all concerned for me to stay in business? With what you're asking from me, I may have to shut up shop.'

'Who are you trying to kid, Mr Harel? We both know that what you are paying is affordable for you. You just don't like giving us any of your profits. Well, tough! Like I said, if you'd like a reminder of the terms, Sid here will be happy to oblige.'

Before Ezzy answered, Sid elbowed a framed piece of expensive artwork hanging on the wall and it fell to the floor.

'Oops, my arm slipped,' said Sid, and snickered.

'Here... please... take the money,' Ezzy urged, placing the coins on the counter.

Malc picked up the cash and doffed his flat cap. 'Good day, Mr Harel. See you next week,' he said, and they left.

Ezzy's heart sank at the sight of his antique oil painting. It had belonged to his father but had clearly been damaged. There were small fragments of glass scattered on the shop floor. Hugely disappointed, he went through to the back of the shop to get a broom but jolted when he heard the bell chimes. He prayed Billy's ruffians hadn't returned and felt a surge of relief when he saw it was Jack Garrett.

'Hello, Ezzy. Are you all right, mate? You look like you've seen a ghost.'

'Yes, yes, I'm fine,' Ezzy lied.

'What's happened here?' Jack asked, surveying the broken glass and the broom.

'Oh… erm… I… nothing, just a bit of an accident.'

He noticed Jack's eyes narrow. 'You can tell me it's none of my business, but I've known you a long time, and though it may be wonky I've got a good nose for when something ain't right.'

'Billy Wilcox's heavies have just left. They come here once a week and demand money from me. If I don't pay up, they'll smash up the shop… or worse,' Ezzy blurted out. He felt better for sharing his burden, though he knew there was nothing Jack could do to help.

'Bloody hell, mate, that's rough. Trouble is, once they've got their claws in, there ain't much you can do about it.'

'Yes, I know. I'll just have to grin and bear it,' Ezzy said, faking a smile.

He couldn't go to the police, not with all his dodgy dealings in stolen goods. He'd simply have to cough up and hope they didn't tighten the thumbscrews for more.

Molly had rushed round to George's, but she hadn't been in and she was frantic with worry. Had she been to see Billy? Had he hurt her? Was she lying injured somewhere, or worse, dead? She hadn't dared to let Dulcie see how frantic she was and made an excuse for calling, asking the woman to tell George she needed to see her.

George hadn't come around, which caused Molly to worry even more! She'd lain awake half the night imagining the worst, until she had fallen asleep in the early hours of the morning. All too soon, the morning light woke Molly with a start. Her first thought was of George and she rushed to get dressed. She hurried as fast as she could to the gym, hoping and praying to find her friend there. She was desperate to see her – desperate to find out if she was all right.

When she ran inside, George looked up from what she was doing and smiled. The tension left Molly's body and she slumped. 'Oh, George, I was so worried about you. Did you go to see Billy?'

'Yes, and I told him you're not going to marry him.'

'What did he say?'

'Not much. He can't force you to marry him if you don't want to.'

George's world may be black and white, but Molly didn't think it was as simple as that, and she couldn't believe Billy would be so amenable. 'He must have said something.'

'No, Molly, he didn't. That's it, job done. The wedding is officially off.'

Molly ran to George and affectionately threw her arms round her. 'Thank you... thank you so much! I don't know what I'd do without you.'

'Get off me, you soppy mare,' George said, jokingly squirming. 'I've got to go upstairs. Are you coming?'

Molly let go of her friend, then a worrying thought dampened her jovial mood. 'No, I'll have to go and tell my mother. She won't be too pleased.'

'You've got to be honest. Tell her you only agreed to marry Billy to protect her and I'm sure she'd understand.'

'Maybe. Anyway, thanks again, George, and I'll see you tomorrow.'

Molly turned to leave, but then Hilda came in. It wasn't her usual day for the club, so Molly assumed Billy had sent her with a message and she tensed.

'Is George here?' Hilda asked.

'Yes, she's just gone upstairs,' Molly answered curtly.

'Good. Is it all right if I go up and have a word? In private.'

'Does this have anything to do with me marrying Billy?'

'No... well, not directly. He doesn't know I'm here. Look, it's really important, and I'm sure she'll tell you all about it.'

Molly was curious to know what was so important that Hilda had sneaked away from Billy to come and talk to George, but whatever it was would have to wait. She had far more pressing things on her mind – such as telling her mum that she was going to be an unmarried mother.

Billy threw a cigarette butt out of the car window and blew smoke rings in the air. He'd known Hilda was up to something, so he and his henchmen had followed her.

'The two-faced, scheming whore,' he said slowly. 'But that's fine. She'll be going up in smoke along with her new best buddy.'

''Ere, boss, do you think her and that George are... you know... lesbians?' Knuckles asked, snorting like a pig as he chuckled to himself.

'Don't be so fucking disgusting,' Billy snapped. Then he saw Molly leaving the shop. A light breeze caught her cardigan and blew it away from her body, exposing the small swell of her stomach. That was his child growing in there. She was his incubator and he was going to marry her, regardless of George Garrett.

'Sorry, Mr Wilcox,' Knuckles said.

'What's the plan now then?' Sid asked.

'Exactly the same as before,' Billy replied nonchalantly.

They waited a few minutes, and once the street had cleared, Billy, Knuckles, Sid and Malc climbed from the car. Malc carried a can of petrol.

Billy had thought about executing his victim in the dead of night, but Wednesday afternoons were always quiet. Anyway, even if he was seen, he doubted there'd be many people who'd have the bottle to grass on him.

Once outside the double-fronted shop, Sid threw open the door, and once inside Malc immediately started to splash petrol around.

'Don't use it all. Save some for her,' Billy said, and looked around for the stairs that led up to the gym. The smell of petrol made his nose twitch, but he smiled at the thought of George Garrett being doused in it. He could imagine her screams, and the smell of her flesh burning. He wondered if it would have the same aroma as roast pork.

He'd only planned on killing George, but if Hilda was stupid enough to be disloyal to him, then she'd be getting burnt too.

'Shush...' George whispered.

Hilda had briefly told her about Billy's notion to kill her, when she was sure she'd heard an unfamiliar noise downstairs.

'What is it?' Hilda whispered back.

'Don't move,' George said, and tiptoed quickly across the gym.

She quietly opened the door at the top of the stairs and could hear muffled voices. She thought one of them was Billy's.

She closed the door, and fished around in her pocket for a key, then locked it. For extra measure she grabbed a wooden seat and wedged it under the handle. 'They're here already,' she said quietly.

Hilda looked terrified and whimpered.

'It's all right, just stay right behind me,' George instructed.

'But… they're going to torch the place. Oh my God, George, he's going to burn us alive!'

'Shush… calm down. It's all right, we'll be OK.'

The door began to rattle. Someone was kicking it from the other side. Both women stood frozen and stared at the door. Then they heard Billy's sinister voice.

'I know you're in there, George Garrett, and you, Hilda. Make it easier on yourselves and open the door.'

'Piss off, Billy,' George shouted.

She heard him laughing, and then he said, 'Come on, open this door and let's talk.'

'We've got nothing to talk about.'

'Have it your way then. I'm going to burn this place down, with you and that tart inside. It's not going to be an enjoyable way to go. If you open this door, I might be kind and make it quicker for you. Either way, you're going to die.'

'Fuck off, Billy. I ain't opening this door for you to get the gratification of seeing my face when you kill me. If you're gonna do it, just fucking do it.'

There was a minute of quietness, then George heard a whooshing noise, and dark, black smoke began to seep under the door.

Hilda began screaming hysterically.

'Shit, he's fucking done it,' George said, then spun and whacked Hilda round the face with the flat of her hand. 'If you want to get out of here alive, you've got to stay calm.'

The shock of the slap seemed to work, and Hilda stopped screaming while George ran to the equipment cupboard and grabbed two towels. She threw one at Hilda and told her to wrap it round her head.

The smoke was getting thicker, and she could hear the flames crackling. It wouldn't be long before they burnt through the floor.

She grabbed Hilda's hand and pulled her to a small skylight at the back of the gym.

'It's too high up – we'll never get up there,' Hilda said frantically.

'Yes we will. I'll give you a bunk-up. You'll have to reach up to open the window, and then climb outside.'

'We'd have a better chance at the front windows,' Hilda said.

'No... I haven't got the keys on me and even if I did, they're barred. We wouldn't get through. This window is our only way out.'

Hilda looked up at the small skylight. 'How are we going to get up there?'

'I told you, I'll give you a bunk-up. You'll have to reach up and pull yourself up. Do you think you can do that?' She had to shout over the sound of the roaring fire.

Hilda shook her head, and George could see the anguish in her eyes. 'Come on,' she urged, 'we haven't got long. Climb on my shoulders.'

'It'll never work... even if I can get onto your shoulders... it's too high,' Hilda said hopelessly.

George could taste the smoke now, and it began to irritate her lungs. She coughed, and then her eyes fell on something that gave her an idea. It wasn't easy in the smoke – it stung her eyes – but she managed to get back to the other side of the large room and grabbed the long wooden bench. It was easily the length of a large church pew and could be used as a sort of makeshift ladder. As she dragged it across the gym, she heard Hilda's panicked voice, 'Smash the window with it George. Let some air in.'

George was worried the fresh air would fan the flames, which were now licking around the door and flickering through the floorboards. She dashed back to the small window and leaned the bench vertically against the wall. It didn't quite reach the window, but she was sure they could shimmy up and escape.

'Oh my God, we're going to die,' Hilda cried as the flames intensified.

'Shut up! This is our way out. Take your shoes and stockings off and you'll get a better grip. Grab each side of this bench and push yourself up with your legs, while you pull with your arms.'

'I can't... I can't, George.'

'Just do it. It's that or die in here!'

Hilda did as she was told, but she wasn't acting as quickly as George would have liked. 'Hurry up,' she barked, looking behind her to see the fire had now breached the door. The heat was intense, and she was struggling to breathe.

Hilda had managed to scramble about halfway up the bench, but George could see her strength was waning. 'Hold on, Hilda, you're nearly there,' she yelled, and began to climb the bench too. 'I'm right behind you – keep going.'

'I want my mother to burn again too,' Hilda screamed back.

George thought she must have misheard her and carried on climbing. She felt she was making good progress, but her eyes were closed against the harsh smoke. Then she heard Hilda shouting again.

'You're going to be destroyed, Mother. You've burned once in the flames and now your soul will burn in this world. Hell will engulf you!'

George looked up just in time to see Hilda let go and she tumbled down, screaming as she fell. She tucked herself in tightly against the bench but felt Hilda's body thump against her as the woman hurtled past.

Hilda abruptly stopped screaming. George looked down and through the smoke she could see her lying in a very unnatural position. There was nothing more she could do. She continued to climb, and hoped that Hilda was dead, or that the smoke would get her before the inferno did.

40

'Are you going to see if you can get your old job back at the match factory?' George asked. It had been a week since the fire, but her voice was still croaky.

'Erm... I dunno... I mean, I don't think they'd take me on in my condition,' Molly answered.

They were sat in George's front room, eating a Victoria sponge that Dulcie had made. The old woman was in the kitchen making a fresh pot of tea.

'What about you, George, will you reopen the club somewhere?' Molly asked.

'No. I never bloody liked it. I thought I was going to be coaching boxing, but I ended up doing more star jumps than throwing punches. I think me dad was right – it ain't really what the women round here want.'

'The crafts shop worked well though,' Molly said, trying to sound upbeat. 'It was making a good profit.'

'Yeah, maybe, but I ain't a shop sort of girl. I dunno what I'm gonna do, but I know I won't be working for no-one else,' George said, and began coughing.

Molly thought George's cough sounded chesty, probably the effects of the smoke from the fire.

'Something will come up, it always does,' George said. 'I'm just glad you wasn't there when the fire started.'

Molly slowly nodded her head. 'Me too. Poor Hilda. She was only my age. That's young to die.'

'Well, it wasn't exactly natural causes!' George blurted.

There was a loud clattering from the kitchen. The sudden noise made Molly flinch. Dulcie must have dropped a saucepan lid or something.

George was giving her a strange look. 'Are you all right? You seem a bit jumpy,' she asked.

'Actually, George, I'm scared shitless! I ain't seen Billy since you told him that I didn't want to marry him. He tried to kill you, so it's pretty bloody obvious that he ain't taking it lying down. What if he comes after me next?'

'He won't. And I'm still here, so stop worrying.'

'But it's a blinkin' miracle you're alive! Hilda didn't make it out and I hadn't long left the gymnasium, so it could have been me. I don't believe this is the last of it. If I don't marry him, I think he'll keep on 'til we're all dead!'

'Hang on, what do you mean, "if"? Please don't say what I think you're going to say.'

'I have to do it, George. I ain't got a choice. I've got to think about my baby. Marrying Billy is the only way to keep us all safe.' Molly hadn't wanted to cry, but she couldn't help herself.

'For Christ's sake, Molly! You don't have to do anything you don't want to. You know what I think about the police, but if it makes you feel better I'll go to them. I'll tell them what Billy did.'

'What's the point? He's got too many of them in his pocket and that'll just make matters worse. No... my mind is made up. At least me mum will be happy.'

Dulcie came into the room carrying a tray. 'Quick, take this,' she urged George.

George jumped up and apologised as she took the tray. 'Sorry, Gran, but you should have called me to carry it.'

'What's going on in here? Molly, why are you so upset?' Dulcie asked.

'She's going to go through with the marriage to Billy,' George said, answering for her.

'Can't say as I blame her,' Dulcie mused. 'He's a dangerous man, and you know what they say about keeping your enemies close. I think you and that baby would be a lot safer married to him than you would be otherwise.'

'How can you think such a thing, Gran? The man's a nutter!'

'Exactly,' Dulcie answered, 'and that's why Molly needs to keep him sweet... and close.'

Molly hadn't expected to get any support from

George's gran, but the woman appeared to understand how she was feeling. She had to protect her child, even if it meant sacrificing her own happiness. At least she and her baby would both be alive, and her mum, along with her sisters, and George too.

George saw Molly out, then sat in the front room with her gran. Dulcie had plenty to say to the girl, none of which could be said in front of Molly. She drained the last of her tea, then turned to her granddaughter who was staring blankly into space. 'You're not going to let him get away with destroying your business, are you?'

'Eh? Sorry, Gran, what did you say?'

'I said, you won't let him get away with it, will you?'

'No,' was George's simple yet solid answer.

'I thought not. Have you got a plan?'

'I'm working on it.'

'Are you going to kill him?'

George's eyes widened but Dulcie didn't know why the girl looked surprised.

'Yes... it's what he deserves, but is that wrong of me, Gran?'

'No, love. You're a Garrett woman and the bastard needs to know he shouldn't have crossed you.'

George smiled at her grandmother.

'Having said that, I'm not sure you're supposed to enjoy it so much.' Dulcie laughed.

'I can't think of anything that will give me more pleasure than watching Billy Wilcox die.'

'You've got to be shrewd, my girl. You don't want to swing for the sake of his worthless life.'

'Yes, I know. I'm not sure how I'm going to do it. He's always got his heavies around him and at home Jane and his sisters are there. Even when I do manage to finish him off, I'll have to find somewhere to hide his body.'

'Bury him in the garden with Percy,' Dulcie said with a chortle, though the thought sent a shiver down her spine.

'No way! It's bad enough living with one dead body outside my bedroom window, let alone two!'

'All right, calm down,' Dulcie said, surprised at George's reaction. 'I was only kidding.'

'Sorry, Gran, but it gives me the creeps.'

'You are a funny one.'

'I just don't like it being so close to home... literally.'

'Oh well, he's been there years now and it ain't hurt you,' Dulcie said, and huffed.

'I suppose, but I still don't want Billy Wilcox in that grave! Anyway, I'm going to bide my time on this.'

Dulcie's brow furrowed. 'Why?'

'Well, if Molly is determined to marry him, then so be it. If I knock him off after the wedding, it'll mean that she'll be a widow instead of an unmarried mother and the child won't be a bastard. And as his widow, she'll be all right for money.'

'I've said it before, but you're clever, just like your mother,' Dulcie said, thinking that brains and the ability to kill were a potent combination.

Ethel was working back on the flower stall with her mother, but her persistent questions about the fire were driving Fanny up the wall. Fanny tried to remain patient with the girl, but it wasn't easy. Especially as she was worrying so much about Molly. She'd lain in bed at night, wide awake with the same thought going round and round in her head – was she sending Molly to live in misery by forcing her to marry Billy? Each time she asked herself, she came to the same conclusion. The child needed a name, though she'd have preferred it not to have been Wilcox.

Billy was a murderer. A cold-blooded killer and she asked herself what sort of mother would put her daughter in danger, but she reasoned Molly would be safe. Billy wouldn't hurt the mother of his child, and they would never want for anything. Billy had the power and resources to protect them and as long as Molly played ball, she was sure Billy would look after her. The wedding would go ahead, and she'd been to see Jane, telling her to pass on the news to Billy.

*

Billy paced the floor of his office. Knuckles stood quietly against the wall. Hilda's desk was gone.

'I'm not fucking happy about this. I want George Garrett incapacitated before I get married. I can just picture her turning up and gobbing off.'

That morning, his mother had assured him that she'd spoken to Fanny, and there was no question about the certainty of the wedding. He didn't want George putting in an appearance. The bitch was like a fucking cat with nine lives, or just very lucky, but either way, he wanted her out of the picture. He was resolute that the wedding would go ahead without a hitch. Not that Molly meant anything to him, but he wouldn't have any child of his growing up as illegitimate.

'You could shoot her, boss. Put a bullet between her eyes.'

The same thought had crossed Billy's mind on more than one occasion, but he already had the Old Bill sniffing around about the arson attack and asking questions about Hilda. He could do without drawing any more unwanted attention to himself. After all, there was only so much his blokes on the force could do to cover for him. 'No, that won't do.'

'What do you want me to do then, boss?' Knuckles asked.

'Get Sid and Malc to stake out her place. When she

comes out, tell them to beat the fucking bitch to a pulp, enough to keep her out of action for now without killing her. I'll see about finishing her off when the Old Bill have stopped nosing around.'

As Knuckles hurried from the office, Billy added, 'And make sure she knows it's from me.'

41

'Gran, I'll see you later. Dad should be home soon, but I'll be back within the hour,' George said, and kissed Dulcie lightly on her cheek.

'Where are you off to?'

'Just up to Mrs Peterson's shop. It's Ethel's birthday tomorrow, so I thought I'd buy her a bag of sweets.'

'Take some money out of my purse and get her something from me, please.'

'Yes, will do,' George said. She called into Mrs Peterson's shop, but every time she did it reminded her of the woman's husband and the man who'd killed him. Billy had been a thorn in her side for years now. She clenched her jaw at the thought of him marrying her best friend. But if things panned out as she planned, it wouldn't be long before Molly would be at his funeral.

George was about to step into the shop, when she got the feeling that someone was watching her. She looked over her shoulder, but the street was quiet. Perhaps she was just being paranoid, she thought, and shrugged it off.

Having purchased the sweets and Fry's chocolate, George ambled back towards home. It was such a pleasant morning. She wasn't in a rush, but once again, she got the feeling of being watched. Suspicious, she stopped and checked around her. It had only been just over a week since the attack on her life, so she couldn't be too careful. There was a lady behind her pushing a pram, another outside a house cleaning the front window, and two small boys chasing after each other.

Then she spotted a car parked on the corner of the street. It looked out of place, like it didn't belong there, but it was too far away to see if anyone was inside. It could be Billy's car, but she couldn't tell. They all looked the same to her.

To be on the safe side, George turned round and cut through an alley, which brought her out on to the main road. She was relieved to see it bustling with shoppers, but kept her eyes peeled and wits about her. Billy Wilcox was brazen. He'd razed the club to the ground in broad daylight. She wouldn't put anything past him.

A man bumped into her, seemingly by accident. Her guard was up but she thought she recognised his face. She just couldn't put a name to it.

'George? George Garrett? It is you, ain't it?'

'Yeah, what of it?' she answered warily.

'It's me, Alfred Linehan. I lived upstairs when you was born. I haven't seen you in years, but I'd recognise those eyes anywhere. Just like your mother's.'

'Oh, hello.'

'How's your father?'

'He's fine, Mr Linehan. Shall I send him your regards?'

'Yes, please do. Nice seeing you, take care of yourself.'

'You too,' George said, and carried on walking. He wasn't the first person to tell her how alike she was to her mother, but she'd have to take people's word for it. She wished she had a painting or photograph of her. The chance encounter with Alfred and thinking about her mother had been a distraction and she was soon just a couple of streets from home. All thoughts of the mysterious car had been forgotten. Until she saw it slowly pass her.

It was Billy's car. She recognised Malc driving it and was sure Sid was sat next to him. They stared at her as they passed. Sid gestured with his finger across his throat, making no secret of their intentions.

George wasn't afraid. Malc and Sid were thugs, nothing more. Malc was a big bloke, but his movements were slow. She'd already clouted them once before, though it was many years back. Still, she didn't think she had anything to worry about, unless they had weapons.

The car pulled up, and the men climbed out. They swaggered towards her, doing their utmost to look intimidating, and between them, shoulder to shoulder, they managed to block the pavement.

'Get out of my way,' George said.

'Ask nicely,' Malc replied.

'All right. Get out of my fucking way, wanker... please.'

Malc stepped forward. He was toe to toe with George

but she refused to back away. 'Get in the car,' he sneered.

This was going to be a challenge, but she still felt confident. 'Make me,' she said, and clenched her fists, ready to lash out.

'I will if I have to, but it'd be much better for you if you came quietly.'

George considered the idea. They'd probably take her to Billy. 'I ain't going nowhere with you, so either let me by or try and make me get in the car... but I'm warning you, one of you is gonna get hurt.'

Malc looked at Sid, and just as George had anticipated they went to grab her. She punched upwards and caught Malc under his chin. His head jarred back, but he stayed on his feet. She managed to get a good blow to Sid's stomach. She'd winded him and he groaned. It was the opportunity she needed, and she raised her knee sharply, catching him in his groin. He let out a yell, and she was about to punch him again when Malc seized her right arm. She lashed out with her left fist at him, but he had a firm grip.

'Grab her,' Malc yelled at Sid.

Before she knew it, they'd overpowered her, but she still refused to give in and fought against them as they bundled her into the back of the car. Sid placed a muslin bag over her head. She couldn't see a thing and waved her arms and legs around furiously. 'You fucking bastards! I'll have you for this!'

'Quieten down, George, no-one is listening to you.' She recognised it to be Malc's voice.

She heard the car engine churn, and felt Sid grasping her arms. Panic rushed through her as she realised he was tying her wrists together, but she stopped fighting, deciding to conserve her energy for what was to come.

'When my Molly marries your Billy, we'll be related, won't we?' Fanny asked.

Jane was scanning the accounts for the stall, but briefly looked up. 'No, I don't think so. But I think it's about time you called me Jane.'

'All right, Mrs Wil... I mean Jane,' Fanny said, looking a little disappointed.

They had their weekly meeting every Thursday morning in the small café next to the station. So far, Jane had never discovered the discrepancies in the takings that Billy had uncovered.

She closed the books and handed them back to Fanny. 'That all looks in good order. How's Molly? I haven't seen her since the... erm... fire.' Jane had read all about it in the papers and dealt with the police when they'd called to question Billy. He'd denied any knowledge of the incident and, thanks to her, he had a watertight alibi. She had her suspicions, and deep down had a niggling feeling that her son was responsible. She'd never condone what he did, especially Hilda dying. She was also irked that he'd destroyed a flourishing business that she had a vested interest in, but she would always protect him. After all, you never grass on your own.

'She's well, but the fire was a terrible shock for her. She couldn't stop crying for a couple of days afterwards. I suppose it was the thought that she could have been in the building too.'

'I don't think there would have been a fire if Molly had been there,' Jane said. She knew Fanny would know the truth about that terrible day. There was so much gossip and talk surrounding it, nearly all of Battersea knew Billy was behind it.

Fanny looked surprised at Jane's comment but chose to ignore it. Instead, she leaned closer and lowered her voice. 'Her belly is getting bigger. Good job the wedding is only two weeks away.'

'Indeed.' Jane nodded. 'And considering the circumstances, I think the decision to hold the ceremony in the registry office with only immediate family present was absolutely the right one.'

'Yes. I don't think Molly wants any fuss.'

'Good.' Jane fumbled in her purse under the table and took out some coins. She handed them to Fanny. 'Give this to Molly. With the Maids out of business now, she'll be short of funds. There's no point in her looking for an alternative job. She'll be a married woman soon, and Billy won't allow her to work.'

Fanny took the money and quickly squirrelled it away. 'Thank you, I'm sure she'll be grateful for this.'

'Have there been any suggestions from George about reopening?' Jane asked.

'No, according to Molly, she's adamant that the place will remain closed. Shame really, I think it was doing a lot of good for loads of the women round here. She's quite the innovator, that George!'

'Yes, she is, and it's about time sports were more accessible to us ladies. Maybe once the insurance claim is settled, she'll reconsider.'

'Maybe,' Fanny said, 'but don't hold your breath.'

They finished their tea, and Fanny went back to work on the stall. As Jane meandered through Clapham Junction, she mulled over their conversation. It was obvious Fanny knew that Billy had burnt down the club. In doing so, he'd killed Hilda and George had only had a narrow escape. No-one could say whether Billy had deliberately set out to kill the women, or if he just had a grudge against the club and what it stood for.

Either way, her son was a killer, yet Fanny Mipple was willing to permit her daughter to marry him. Jane questioned what sort of mother the woman was. She'd never tolerate Sally or Penny marrying anyone like Billy. He was a son only a mother could love, and regardless of his crimes, she loved him dearly.

'It's only me, Mum,' Jack called as he came through the front door.

As soon as she heard his voice, Dulcie hurried from the kitchen. 'Is George with you?' she asked, concerned.

'No, I ain't seen her since the day before yesterday. Why?'

'She went out this morning, and she hasn't come home yet. She was only popping up the shop and said she wouldn't be long. That was over three hours ago!'

'Don't worry. She's probably bumped into someone she knows and gone off to do something with them.'

Dulcie followed Jack into the kitchen, where he asked, 'Are you gonna put the kettle on, Mum?'

She stood on the spot where her husband had lain dying, and wrung her hands. 'Something's wrong, Jack. I've got a bad feeling – I can feel it in me water.'

'You know you're not always right about these... feelings you get. What about when you thought you could read the tealeaves and told Mrs Winterbottom that her old man was having an affair with their next-door neighbour? You was wrong about that and look at the bloody trouble it stirred! Face it, Mum, you ain't no Florence Cook.'

'Florence who?' Dulcie asked. 'Never mind. George knows I'm alone today and she wouldn't have stayed out this long unless, well, unless... she had no choice.'

'Do you think something has happened to her? Do

you reckon Billy Wilcox has got to her?' Jack asked worriedly.

'It's a possibility. George said he started that fire deliberately, and I believe her. He wants her out of the way for some reason. He's tried to kill her once and failed. Who's to say he wouldn't have another go? Oh, Jack, I should never have let her go out alone.' Dulcie could feel tears pricking at her eyes and turned away from her son.

'Try not to worry. I'll find her and if Billy fucking Wilcox has harmed one hair on her head, I'll kill him.'

The front door slammed as Jack left to look for George. Dulcie walked across to the sink, and gazed out of the window, muttering quietly, 'I hope he finds her. Oh God, I hope he does. If you're there, Percy, do some good for a change and help my boy find George.'

George felt as if she was waking up from some sort of bad dream, only she couldn't remember what the dream was. She was bumping around, but unsure of where she was. She wanted to go back to sleep, but the sound of horses' hooves disturbed her.

In a state of confusion, she tried to open her eyes, but they seemed to be stuck. Her body ached. Her head was throbbing. She wondered where she was and if she was still dreaming.

Cobbled streets. She recognised the rhythm. The

sound of wooden wheels on cobbled streets. The movement stopped and so did the sound of hooves. Then she heard a man's voice. 'It's all right, love, you're home now.'

She wanted to sit up, but her weak body wouldn't move. Sleep. She'd go back to sleep. But it hurt. Everything hurt. Where was she? Oh yes, she remembered. The man said she was home. Then she heard her gran. 'No... oh no... George... George... Can you hear me? Is she alive? George?'

Yes. Yes, Gran. I'm alive, she thought, but her mouth wouldn't open. I'll go back to sleep now, she thought again, then drifted away.

Jack ran up to the cart, breathless and frantic with worry. He'd heard George had been found. Someone had told him that Tubby Hawkins had taken her home on the back of his cart. They said it was bad. As he'd raced off, he'd been warned to prepare himself.

When he reached home, he found a throng of people outside his house, and apart from his mother's anguished cries, there was an unsettling silence.

'Jack... look what they've done to her. Look what they've done to our beautiful girl,' Dulcie was sobbing unashamedly, and pulling at Jack's jacket.

He approached the cart, praying he'd find his daughter alive.

'She's been roughed up real bad, Jack. I've untied her hands,' Tubby said, his voice breaking. 'I'm sorry, mate.'

Jack didn't notice Tubby weeping. He barely took in the sight of the neighbours having a nose and he didn't see his mother bawling as she held on to the cart for support. It was as if the world around him had stopped. Time stood still. His senses had numbed. He heard nothing. All he could see was the horror of his daughter's battered face, smothered in blood, and her lifeless-looking broken body. A cry caught in his throat. Then he jolted into action. 'Help me get her indoors,' he said to Tubby.

Two elderly brothers from a house over the road appeared, carrying a door between them. 'Use this,' one of them offered.

Another man stepped forward to help, and they managed to move George onto the door to carry her inside. She didn't make any noise, which further worried Jack.

'I've sent for the doctor,' Mary from next door said in her broad Irish accent. She was hovering in the front room doorway.

'Thanks,' Jack replied. He'd have liked to have told her to go away, but Dulcie was in a flap and might need the woman's help.

'Did you see who did this to her?' he asked Tubby.

'No. Some young lads found her round the back of

the coal yard. It don't take much working out though, do it, Jack?'

'No, it doesn't and he ain't getting away with this. I'll kill him, Tubs. I swear, I'll fucking kill him.'

George whimpered. Jack hadn't been aware of Mary moving away, but now she appeared again, carrying a bowl of water and a cloth. She knelt beside George and wiped the dried blood from her eyes. 'It's all right, lass, the doctor is on his way,' she soothed.

It was more than Jack could bear to watch. He barged past Dulcie and went into the kitchen. He knew his mother always kept a bottle of whisky in the larder and grabbed it before slumping at the table. After several large gulps from the bottle, his nerves had calmed, but his heart was breaking. It hurt him to see his daughter so severely beaten.

He drank several more glugs of whisky, then wiped the back of his hand across his mouth. 'I'm sorry, Sissy,' he cried, 'I've done my best by our girl, but it wasn't enough.'

The kitchen door flew open. 'The doc's here and George is awake,' Dulcie exclaimed.

Jack leapt from his seat and hurried to his daughter's side. She was still lying on the door in the middle of the front room floor, with Mary bandaging her head.

The doctor gently pulled Jack to one side. 'Mr Garrett, a word,' he said. 'George has suffered a vicious and prolonged attack. I can see no evidence of sexual assault, but she has endured several severe blows to the head. I'm afraid, if she survives, we won't know the long-term effects of this for some time yet.'

Jack could hardly pull his eyes away from his daughter's swollen face. 'What do you mean?' he asked. George was alive, her eyes were open, so surely she was going to be fine.

'You have to be realistic and aware that your daughter may not pull through, and if she does, she could have brain damage.'

Jack stared blankly at the doctor, then shook his head in denial. 'No, no, she's gonna be fine. Her eyes are open.'

'At the moment, but she isn't responding to any stimuli. When and if she comes round fully, your daughter may have difficulty with her memory, or slurred speech. With these severe head injuries she may suffer from some brain damage and have problems with muscle control, leaving her unable to walk. I hope it doesn't come to that and there are many possible outcomes, but hold on to hope as there is always the chance of her making a full recovery.'

Jack baulked at the doctor's words. He felt sick to his stomach but didn't know if that was the effect of the alcohol or the hideous possibility of his daughter ending up like a cabbage. He fled from the room, grabbed the remaining whisky, pushed past Tubby who was in the hallway, and ran from the house. He felt he had to escape and get away from the unbearable situation. He knew he should be with George, but he couldn't bring himself to sit and hold her hand and tell her everything was going to be fine, when really he knew it probably wouldn't be.

He'd watched Sissy die in front of him. He couldn't face seeing his daughter's life ebb away too.

42

Molly stood at the foot of the bed and nervously looked at her new husband. She'd been dreading this moment more than the actual wedding ceremony.

It had been a week since George had been badly beaten, and though Molly had begged for the wedding to be postponed, Billy had insisted it went ahead. So, earlier that day, she'd grudgingly become Mrs Billy Wilcox.

Fear of becoming Billy's next victim had made her go through with it, even though in the light of what had happened to George, her mother had relented and told her she didn't have to marry him. But Molly had. Terror had overpowered her ability to make a reasonable decision and she was now a married woman living in a house her husband had purchased in Clapham.

She had hoped to live in the same house as his mother – it would have made her feel safer. And now, despite this upmarket area, and the luxury of this house, she longed for the squalor of her family home.

Billy was stretched out on the bed with his hands folded behind his head. He was wearing his trousers, but his body was bare. Molly felt embarrassed and didn't know where to look.

'It's late. Get in,' he told her.

She shuddered, hating the thought of him touching her. In fact, she hated everything about him. He'd nearly killed her best friend. It still wasn't known if George would ever recover, yet now she had to share a bed with the man responsible for the attack.

Slowly, Molly slipped off her dressing gown. She didn't look at Billy but could feel his eyes scrutinising her. She folded back the blankets and sat on the side of the bed.

'You don't have to worry,' Billy said. 'There will be no consummation of the marriage whilst you are with child.'

Molly sighed with relief. She was glad he couldn't see her face.

'I'm not vain enough to think you wanted to marry me today, but you've done the right thing for the child. That being said, you are now my wife and I will take my conjugal rights after the baby is born. In the meantime, I will have a mistress and I don't want to hear you complaining about it.'

Molly wouldn't complain! Finally, some good news and now she felt she could breathe easier. She climbed into bed next to Billy but lay close to the edge with her back to him. Her nightdress was long, and she'd kept her underwear on.

It had been a long day and she was exhausted, but she couldn't relax. How could she sleep soundly knowing she was lying next to a killer? Every time she closed her eyes, she thought about her best friend, battered beyond recognition. She rested her hand on her stomach, thankful for the baby inside her. It would keep her safe... if only for the next four months.

Jane didn't know what her son had against George Garrett. It was obvious he detested her and always had. She'd heard the whispers about Billy arranging the assault on George, and though when she asked him he'd denied it, she knew by the way that he avoided her eyes that he'd ordered it. First the fire, and now this.

Years ago, she'd learnt to turn a blind eye to her husband's business dealings and chose to ignore the fact that people who crossed him were often hurt or killed. Jane knew all about Norman's sharpened belt buckle, but her husband had morals and standards. She thought he'd passed them down to Billy, but clearly not. Her son was out of control. She didn't like to admit it, but the gossip, along with the latest events, had aroused her suspicions about Norman's death. It couldn't be true though, she thought, and shook her head. Once again, for the sake of her sanity, she dismissed her misgivings.

She was on her way to visit George. The Garretts lived four streets away and as Jane knocked on the door she hoped the olive branch she had to offer would be accepted. If Billy was responsible for what had happened to George, as his mother, it was down to her to make amends. She thought the wad of cash she had wrapped in brown paper would be a good start.

When there was no answer at the Garretts', she scribbled a quick note on the paper, and pushed the money through the letterbox. She knew someone must be home but could understand why they wouldn't come to the door. It wasn't the first time Jane had paid guilt money to a victim's family and she knew it wouldn't be the last.

Satisfied her conscience was a little clearer, she went to walk away but then Dulcie came to the door. Jane turned round and saw the woman scowl. She instantly knew she wasn't welcome.

'You've got some bloody nerve,' Dulcie said, her lips curling in disgust.

'Please, Mrs Garrett, hear me out,' Jane pleaded.

'I ain't Mrs Garrett and haven't been for years. Get your facts straight. Anyway, I ain't interested in anything you've got to say. You and yours ought to be ashamed of yourselves. Look at you, walking round here like lady fucking muck, but we all know what you really are.'

Jane stood her ground. She'd been expecting a frosty reception. 'Slate me as much as you like, but I haven't come for an argument.'

'I don't care what you've come for, but whatever it

is, you can poke it up your arse and sling your fucking hook.'

Dulcie stepped out of the doorway, causing Jane to take several steps backwards. She noticed the old woman look up and down the street before rolling her sleeves up. Dulcie was a daunting woman, but surely, she wasn't going to punch her?

'Listen here, Mrs erm… er, Dulcie,' Jane said firmly, but she was trembling inside. Dulcie's impressive stature dwarfed her own small frame.

'No… you listen to me,' Dulcie shouted, 'your lot have always been trouble. Your old man took my Jack's sight in one eye, and now thanks to your son, my granddaughter is lucky to be alive. It weren't enough that Billy tried to burn her to death, he then had her kicked from here to kingdom come. And I ain't forgot how she nearly ended up doing time because your Billy killed Mr Peterson. An innocent man paid for that crime with his life. How does that make you feel, eh? You might think you can lord it over Battersea, but I ain't scared of your lunatic fucking son. You should be though. Do you sleep with one eye open at night?'

Jane suddenly forgot everything she'd prepared to say and found herself speechless. Dulcie's booming voice had caught the attention of the neighbours and now they had an audience.

'You look worried, Mrs Wilcox,' Dulcie said

sardonically, 'but then if my son had murdered my husband, I think I'd probably look worried too.'

Jane gasped. She could hear people muttering around her but felt too ashamed to look. She saw Dulcie glance round with a smug expression. The woman seemed to be enjoying verbally tearing strips off her, though if what Dulcie had said was true, and she thought it probably was, this was no more than she deserved.

'You can turn a blind eye to what's going on right under your nose, but I don't believe you're fucking innocent in all of this. What sort of woman are you? How can you let him get away with killing your husband and now this? Who's next, eh? You? Your daughters?'

Jane bit her bottom lip as her eyes began to well with tears, but she wouldn't cry, not in front of everyone. Dulcie had said everything that Jane had tried to deny. But she couldn't allow herself to believe it. 'I'm sorry,' she said quietly, then spun on her expensive designer heels and ran towards home. Despite what had been said, and her fears that it was true, she loved Billy with all her heart. He was her son, her flesh and blood, and she refused to believe she'd given birth to an atrocity... a monster.

George had stayed in the front room all week, though she'd lost track of time. They'd attempted to move her to her bedroom, but when they'd picked her up she'd moaned in pain. She heard the doctor say it was because of her broken ribs. Now, still drowsy and in a world of her own, the sofa had become her bed.

She wasn't sure if it was night or day and had become confused with reality and her dreams. But when she heard the front door slam, she was pretty sure she was awake and had heard her gran shouting at someone, but now her gran was softly calling her.

She opened her eyes and tried to focus. Dulcie was leaning over her and spooning something in her mouth. It tasted sweet. She liked it. Next, she felt herself floating again and began to see strange lights and vivid bright colours. Then she saw her dad chasing a frog with the head of a horse. The frog jumped out of the window and her dad turned into a daisy. She must be dreaming.

Voices again. More shouting. It sounded like her gran and dad were having a row. Snippets of their conversation registered with her. Dulcie was calling him useless and telling him he needed to sober up. He was telling her to mind her own business. They talked about her. She needed more medicine, her gran said, and her dad had to stop drinking whisky. They needed him.

George's eyes opened, and she dropped her head to the side. Her vision was fuzzy, but she could see her dad slouching in the armchair. Her gran was stood in front of him wagging her finger and telling him off. Then she saw the whisky bottle and realised her father was drunk.

She opened her mouth and tried to speak. Nothing came out. Desperate for her gran's attention, she tried to lift her arm. It wouldn't work. What had happened? She felt trapped. She panicked but couldn't scream. Her mind was shrieking, begging for help, but they couldn't hear her and didn't know she was awake.

In a state of confusion, darkness began to descend.

It was two weeks later when George finally spoke, and her voice was heard.

PART 5

THE EMERGENCE OF GEORGINA GARRETT

43

Three weeks had passed since George had been set upon by Malc and Sid. Her bruises were almost faded but she'd be left with a scar on her forehead and two teeth missing from the side of her mouth. It still hurt to take deep breaths and to move around, but as everyone kept reminding her, she was lucky to be alive.

Friends and neighbours had been popping in and out, and Oppo called in daily after work, but she hadn't seen Molly. Her gran had updated her and told her the wedding had gone ahead and Molly was now living in Clapham. She guessed Billy had control over her friend, which explained the lack of visits.

Their neighbour Mary's daughter had dropped in a few magazines. Aileen worked in a swanky beauty salon in Chelsea and would call in every Sunday to see her mother. Her weekly visits always caused a stir in the street. Curtains would twitch, and women would emerge on their doorsteps to get a glimpse of the glamorous Battersea girl who'd made good from the slums. They'd all be talking about her outfits and hairdos for days after.

George winced as she reached across to the side table and picked up a copy of *Vogue*. She began to flick through the pages of the fashion magazine and chuckled to herself. She couldn't believe women paid a shilling for this drivel!

'How are you feeling today, love?' her gran asked as she walked into the front room with two cups of tea.

'Great, thanks. I might venture outside today.'

'Erm, not so fast, young lady.'

'Why? I'm not going to spend my life hiding away from Billy Wilcox!' George said angrily.

'I'm not suggesting that you do, but I think you should wait until you've got your strength back properly.'

George rolled her eyes, but she had to admit her gran was right.

'Did you hear your father come home last night?'

'Yeah, he stumbled in and went straight upstairs to bed. I would imagine he had another skinful, so I'll doubt we'll see him 'til much later.'

'I don't know what's got into him,' Dulcie said, pursing her lips and shaking her head. 'He's never been able to handle his drink and I thought he was a better man than my Percy. Turns out he's just like all the bloody rest of them... useless.'

'That's a bit harsh, Gran,' George said, though she was disappointed to see her dad always drunk lately.

'It's the truth! I know it was hard for him to see you hurt, but it was for me too and you don't see me drowning me sorrows. Blinkin' men! So much for them being the tough ones. George, take it from me, love. If you can get by without a man, then do it. They ain't worth the newspaper that they wipe their arses on.'

George gulped her mouthful of tea and laughed. 'I get what you're saying, Gran, but they do have some uses.'

'Like what? Name one.'

'Having babies,' George answered.

'Well, yes, but apart from that?'

'Security,' George said, deep in thought and twiddling her mother's wedding ring.

'Security... You've got to be kidding me!'

'No, Gran, I ain't. I reckon if I'd had a husband to look out for me, Billy wouldn't have tried to kill me.'

'But you're tougher than most men I know.'

'Probably, but there's only one of me, so do you see what I mean?' George asked. She hadn't realised it herself before now, but she'd be much safer with a man in her life.

'Yes, I see, but he'd have to be special to win your heart.'

'Maybe,' George answered, 'Or maybe just big and strong,' she added, and winked at her gran.

The magazine was open on George's lap, and she noticed her gran squinting across the room from her armchair to look at it.

'My eyes ain't what they used to be, but from here, that woman looks just like your mother.'

George picked up the magazine and studied the model. She was beautiful. 'Really?' she asked.

Dulcie got up from her chair and leaned over George's shoulder.

'Yes, she's taller than your mum and her hair is shorter, but she's the double of her. Your mum was a stunner, just like you. I love my Jack, but I never understood what she saw in him. I mean, he's lovely, at times, but I think he fell out of the ugly tree and hit every one of the branches on the way down.'

George looked closer at the model. She was striking, with dark make-up that made her eyes jump out from the page. 'I bet she'd have no problem getting herself a husband.'

'No, and neither would you,' her gran said.

George wasn't convinced. 'If I looked like her, I wouldn't!'

'That's my point, love, you do look like her. You just need a little help to enhance it.'

George screwed up her face quizzically.

'Take them fancy clothes off her and wipe away her make-up, and honestly, that could be you splashed across that magazine.'

George had never really paid much attention to her appearance. She'd become accustomed to acting and dressing like a man – it was all she'd ever known. It had never occurred to her that she could be beautiful. 'Do you really think so, Gran?'

'Yes, I know so. Tell you what, it's Sunday, so Aileen will be next door visiting her mum. How about I have a word with Mary and see if Aileen will pop in here and make your face up for you?'

'Oh, I dunno, Gran,' George said.

'Go on, it'll be fun. And what have you got to lose? If you don't like it, you can wash it off.'

George nodded, though she didn't think it sounded much like fun. If anything, it sounded more like pure bloody torture. Still, if she was going to bag herself a man, then it was about time she made herself look more like a woman.

It was ten minutes later when George heard her gran return and by the sound of it, Aileen and Mary were with her.

'Hello, George. Your gran tells me you're feeling much better and fancy a bit of glamming up. Well, you've got the best person for the job here. My Aileen does all the top stars, don't you, darling?' Mary said proudly.

'Pack it in, Ma,' Aileen said, and pulled an exasperated face.

George looked Aileen up and down. She didn't look much like her mother. Mary had bright red curly hair, as did Mary's four other girls. Even Mary's husband had strawberry blond hair. They all had the same green eyes too and a sprinkling of orange freckles. Aileen stood out as different. Her hair and eyes were chocolate brown, and her skin was much darker. Jack had always joked that Aileen looked like the rag and bone man, and now George could see it too.

'Do you have any cosmetics, George?' Aileen asked. Her accent was soft, not like her mother's thick Northern Irish twang.

'No,' George answered.

She liked Aileen, though considering they'd lived next door to each other their whole lives, she didn't know her very well. Aileen was only a few years older, but they'd never really played together growing up. Aileen had always been a girlie girl and liked dolls and clothes, where George had preferred to get dirty and play with toy guns.

'Not to worry. I always carry mine with me. You're not that different in skin tone to me, so I'm sure mine will suit you.'

George realised they were all staring at her and she suddenly felt clammy.

'Don't look so nervous.' Mary laughed. 'She's going to make you look a treat. Come on, Dulcie, let's have a cuppa and leave them to get on with it.'

George relaxed and felt better without all eyes on her, and Aileen got to work.

'You know, I hear all sorts in the salon and apparently, it's very fashionable in Paris to be a lesbian.'

'Is it?' George asked, wondering why Aileen was talking about women who love women as men do.

'Yes, they say there are women in Paris who have taken to wearing men's clothes and openly hold hands with their female lovers.'

'I'm not a lesbian, if that's what you're getting at.'

'Really? So why have you always dressed like a man?'

'I don't know, it's how me dad raised me.'

'Haven't you ever wanted to wear a skirt?'

'Yeah, when I was younger, sometimes.'

'Don't talk now and keep still. I don't want to poke your eye out.'

Nearly an hour later, Aileen handed George a mirror. 'There you go, you look stunning. I wish I had your eyes – you're so lucky.'

George took the mirror and slowly lifted it to her face. She gasped at her reflection. 'Is that really me?' she asked.

'Yes, George, it's you. Who'd have thought it?'

'I... I... Wow, Aileen. It feels a bit weird, but I love it! I look...'

'Beautiful,' Dulcie said. She'd walked into the room and had tears in her eyes at the sight of her granddaughter.

Mary followed in behind Dulcie. When she saw George, her eyes widened, and she gushed, 'Jesus Christ, George, you look amazing, like an angel sent from heaven from the good Lord above.'

'Blimey, it's only a bit of make-up and a new hairdo,' George said, feeling embarrassed at all the attention.

'But it makes all the difference,' Dulcie sniffed. 'We'll have to get you some nice dresses to go with your new look.'

'Will you be keeping it?' Aileen asked.

'Yes, I think I will,' George answered. She was looking at herself again and beginning to get used to her more feminine appearance.

'In that case, I'll leave you a few bits 'cos I've got plenty in the salon. If ever you're over Chelsea way, you must call in.'

'Yes, I will. Thanks, Aileen.'

Dulcie saw the neighbours out, while George sat studying herself. Yes, she was just as beautiful as the model in the magazine. She was tall like her too. She'd never imagined herself looking like this. It felt good and liberating to finally acknowledge herself as a real woman.

Her gran came back into the room and sat in her armchair. 'When you're up to it, we'll go shopping up the Junction and see about getting you some new clothes,' she said.

'We won't be able to afford that for a while, not with me dad drinking like he is.'

'Yes, we can. We don't have to worry about money.'

'How come?'

'That Jane Wilcox woman came round here when you was ill. I told her to bugger off, but she shoved some money through the door. It was a fair old whack too, only don't mention it in front of your father – I don't want him pissing it up the wall.'

'You can't take money from her!'

'Why can't I? That doctor and his concoctions don't come cheap, and how else would I have paid the rent? You was unconscious and your father... well.'

George bit her tongue. She could see her gran's point, but they weren't bloody charity cases. She couldn't believe they'd taken money from the Wilcoxes. The thought of it grated on her. It was humiliating.

'As soon as I get back on my feet, we're going to pay her back, every penny.'

Before her gran could answer, the door opened, and her dad walked in. He looked bleary-eyed, and his hair was sticking up. 'Morning, ladies,' he chirped, then his body jerked, and he jumped backwards, his face draining of colour. 'Sissy! What? How?'

'Dad... it's me, George.'

'Fucking hell! What have you done? You look just like your mother! For a moment, I thought that was her sitting there!'

'Sorry, I didn't mean to startle you. Aileen popped round and made my face up. Do you like it?'

'Oh, George, yes love, you look stunning. But I don't know if I'm happy with you going about like that. You'll get all sorts of unwanted attention.'

'Leave it out, Jack. You've had her looking like a boy all her life. She's grown up now, a woman, and it's nice to see her looking like one for a change.'

'Yeah,' George added, and grinned at her dad.

'I can see I ain't got a chance against you two and I

must admit your mother would have loved to have seen you looking like that.'

George could hear the sorrow in her father's voice and hoped he wouldn't break down in tears. He left the room before she could see, but she knew he'd be reaching for the bottle again.

'I've got something you might like,' her gran said. 'On top of my wardrobe, there's a brown leather case. Get it down and have a look inside. The stuff will be a bit dated now, but I'll bet it'll look smashing on you. Go on, go upstairs and have a look, then come back down here and show me.'

George was intrigued. She found the suitcase, though it hurt her body when she lifted it down. She placed it on her gran's bed and opened it. She carefully peeled back the tissue paper to reveal a cream lace dress, a pair of silk high-heeled shoes to match along with gloves, a handkerchief and a small hat. She laid the outfit on the bed and realised, from a photograph she'd seen, she was looking at her gran's wedding dress. Dulcie had asked her to put it on, but she couldn't. The man her gran had married when she'd worn this was now buried in their backyard!

She walked back into the front room to see her gran's face drop.

'Sorry, it didn't fit,' she lied.

'No, of course not. I wasn't thinking,' Dulcie said, 'but I'm determined to see you in a pretty dress to match your pretty face. I know Mrs Barker at number thirty-seven. Come on.'

'It's Sunday, Gran. Mrs Barker won't have her shop open.'

'Exactly. She'll be at home with her twenty-odd cats, but she always has a load of stock in her spare room.'

'I ain't being funny, but everyone knows her stuff stinks of cats' piss, and it's all second-hand.'

'And since when have you been too proud to wear hand-me-downs? Come on, just humour me. I'd just like to see you looking like a proper woman. Whatever we get from Mrs Barker's can be thrown out once I've seen you dressed up.'

George half-heartedly agreed and helped her gran along the street. Mrs Barker was pleased to see them, and even more so when they said they'd like to purchase some second-hand clothes from her. They rummaged through the goods in the upstairs back room and found a couple of things to buy. George couldn't wait to get out of the house. She thought it stank, and the flea-bitten cats were making her itch.

'Go on then, use my room,' Dulcie said enthusiastically when they got home.

George went upstairs, closed her gran's bedroom door, and held the clothes at arm's length as she stepped into a blue dress embellished with black beads and tassels that ended just below her knees. She slipped on the black heeled shoes, which tied on the front with a ribbon, then pulled on a pair of long, blue gloves that matched the dress perfectly. Her make-up complemented the outfit as well.

She looked in the mirror on her gran's dressing table. She couldn't see her whole image but what she saw took her breath away.

'Hello, Georgina,' she said out loud, 'and goodbye, George.'

Georgina Garrett had emerged. Like a caterpillar from a chrysalis. She was now a beautiful butterfly and was ready to spread her wings.

44

It was still warm for October. Molly was bored and fed up with being cooped up inside the house. And she missed her mum and George. Billy refused to allow her to visit them. He said they were scum, and now that she was a Wilcox she was better off without them. He didn't want his child associating with those sorts of people. Molly had been offended but had kept quiet. They hadn't yet been married for two months, yet she'd already learnt that anything she said to upset Billy would result in an angry outburst. He'd warned her that if she wasn't pregnant, she could have expected a swift back-hander across her face!

She looked at the clock on the mantel. It was only half past ten. The morning was dragging by so slowly. The house was clean, the laundry done, and dinner was already prepared. She thought about calling on her neighbours, but when they'd introduced themselves, their well-to-do manners had made Molly feel inferior. She was a working-class girl from an impoverished family, and though when she was younger she'd dreamt of living in a big house in a nice area, she now found herself feeling out of place.

It was Friday, Billy's poker night. He wouldn't be

home until late. If she snuck to Battersea, she'd have plenty of time to get back before him, but it was a long walk without any money for a bus. He would only give her enough cash for housekeeping, and she'd have to show him receipts and account for every penny spent. But there must be some money somewhere in the house, she thought, longing to see her family, and desperate for news of George.

'Sod it,' she said, and dashed up the stairs. She rummaged through Billy's wardrobe and searched through his jacket pockets for any loose change. She didn't need much for a bus ride. But there was nothing. So she tried his drawers. She found two flick knives, a knuckle-duster and a policeman's truncheon. She was about to give up, when underneath a grainy photo of his father she found a small leather purse with several coins inside. Perfect. She took what she needed and hoped Billy wouldn't notice.

It was a fraught bus journey to Battersea, and once she was there, though she'd have liked to have seen her mum, she decided it was too dangerous. Billy knew people, and if she was seen at Clapham Junction, it was sure to get back to him. Instead, she hurried to see George.

By the time she reached George's house, her heart was hammering and she'd broken out in a nervous sweat. She knocked several times on the door. When it opened, she was close to tears.

'Molly... come in,' Dulcie said, ushering her through with a sense of urgency. 'You're taking a risk, ain't you? We've guessed that Billy ain't letting you out.'

'Yes, but I had to come. How's George?'

'You can see for yourself in a minute. She's upstairs; she'll be down in a tick. Go through, take a seat and I'll put the kettle on.'

Molly sat in the front room and caught her breath. She felt the baby kick and smiled. It felt good to be in familiar surroundings. When she heard George coming down the stairs, her fears were replaced with excitement, but when her friend walked in the room Molly gasped in shock.

'Molly, I can't believe you're here! It's so good to see you,' George said, holding her arms open.

Molly would normally have embraced her friend, but she was speechless and couldn't take her eyes off her.

'Are you all right, Molly?'

'Erm, yes, sorry. It's just... you... you look so different!'

'Do you like it?' George asked, doing a quick spin.

'Yes! Goodness, George, I'd hardly have recognised you. Amazing. Absolutely bloody amazing!'

'Oh, by the way, I'm not George any more. The new me is called Georgina.'

'Georgina. It suits you,' Molly said.

'Anyway, enough about me. Does Billy know you're here?'

'No, he'd go mad if he did.'

'I thought as much. Have you seen your mum?'

'No, but can you get a message to her? Tell her I'm all right and I miss her. Are they all right?'

'Yes, but I know they've been worried about you. Billy told your mum she's not to come and see you, so for your sake, she's stayed away. She'll be over the moon to know you're well. And how's the baby?'

'The baby's fine. Kicking hard. I reckon it's gonna be a boy. I just hope he don't take after his father.'

'You don't have to stay with him, you know. You could always come here. It'd be a squeeze, but we'd make room for you.'

'I know, thanks, George, I mean Georgina, but I wouldn't want to bring any more trouble to your door. I'll work it out, don't worry.'

The next few hours sped by, and before Molly was ready she found it was time to leave. Saying goodbye was heart-breaking, but she did her utmost to hide her sorrow from Georgina.

As she climbed aboard the bus, a feeling of foreboding overwhelmed her. She dismissed her worries and put it down to being upset about returning home. But her instincts had been right, and later that week, Molly's fears would be recognised.

*

It had taken some getting used to, but Georgina now liked the greasy feeling of lipstick on her lips. And more so, she liked the way it made her look. She flounced downstairs with her newfound confidence.

'You look a picture, Georgina. Are you off out somewhere nice?' her gran asked.

'I'm taking Ethel to the fair. I saw them setting up yesterday.'

'That's nice. It's a shame Molly can't go with you.'

'Yeah, I know. Still, it was great to see her.'

'You haven't mentioned her bastard of a husband. What's going on in your head?'

'Nothing, Gran. I'm just biding my time. Don't worry, I ain't forgotten or forgiven. He'll get what's coming to him soon enough.'

'Be careful, love. Your father's in no fit state to look out for you and I don't suppose you've heard the last from Billy.'

'Probably not, but he'll be hearing from me... when I'm ready.'

'Like I said, be careful. From what I've heard, he's stepping on toes close to home.'

'What do you mean by that, Gran?'

'Something your father said when he was pissed. He let slip that Ezzy is having to cough up to Billy's gang. The blokes who beat you up have been calling into Ezzy's every week for money. Diabolical it is, a bloody cheek. I dunno what makes them think they've got the right to go around threatening people and taking their hard-earned money.'

'Oh, they have, have they? That's another one to chalk up for them.'

'Yeah, well, don't say anything. I don't think Ezzy wants anyone to know what's going on. He's a proud man, by all accounts.'

'I won't say a word. Anyway, that's enough about Billy and his thugs. I'm off out. I won't be late, see you later.'

She had no doubt that Billy Wilcox would be coming for her again soon, but she refused to be intimidated. She'd survived his attacks, and now, if anything, it should be him who was scared of her!

Heads turned as Georgina walked self-assuredly to Ethel's. She wasn't used to receiving so much attention and couldn't help smirking when two chaps on a motorbike passed and gave her a wolf-whistle.

'You looks lovely,' Ethel exclaimed when she opened her front door.

'Thanks. Are you ready to go?'

'Yes. See ya later, Mum,' Ethel called over her shoulder. As they began walking, she said, 'I ain't never been to the fair before.'

'You're in for a treat, but make sure you don't wander off without me.'

Once they arrived, Ethel was keen to ride on the

Spinner, but the colourful frontage of the boxing booth drew Georgina.

'The match is about to start, Ethel. I promise you, we'll just watch the main fight and then you can go on all the rides.'

Georgina didn't notice Ethel pouting. She was too intent on getting a good view of the boxing ring. Two old-timers were having a bout. One of them had been a champion in his day. Georgina forgot her new ladylike demeanour and roared and cheered with the crowds. The champion swung a left hook and knocked out his opponent. The fight had only lasted two rounds. Georgina thought she could have done better herself. Then the showman climbed into the ring and called to the audience for any brave volunteers to come and challenge the champion. The winner would receive the nobbings.

'Go on, Georgina, you could beat him,' Ethel urged.

'Shush, no. They won't let a woman in the ring, and I ain't dressed for fighting.'

The showman asked for some encouragement. The crowd responded by throwing coins into the ring. The champion jeered. Then a man stepped up and received a rapturous cheer. As he climbed under the ropes, he peeled off his shirt to reveal a tanned and muscular torso. The sight took Georgina's breath away. She'd never seen such an attractive body and he had a handsome face to match.

The challenger and the showman exchanged a few words then the showman announced, 'Ladies and gentlemen, I give you Lash, the bare-knuckle Gypsy King.'

Some of the crowd booed but most applauded. They were only interested in seeing blood.

Lash stepped into the centre of the ring and touched gloves with the champion. Georgina didn't realise but her fists were clenched by her sides as she silently willed Lash to win.

The fight began, but within a minute Lash had floored the champion and it was all over. He'd impressed Georgina. The crowd began to bay for more, while Georgina stood transfixed amid the racket with her eyes firmly fixed on Lash. He seemed to sense that she was watching him and scanned the faces in front of him until he saw her. For a moment their eyes locked and Georgina felt a tingle, like an electric current had passed through her.

'Can we go now?' Ethel asked, breaking Georgina's thoughts.

'Yes,' she answered, but kept her gaze firmly on Lash.

He jumped from the boxing ring and Georgina lost sight of him, but she instinctively knew he was coming to her.

'Come on then,' Ethel said, and pulled on Georgina's sleeve.

She turned to leave, then felt a hand on her shoulder. Her stomach knotted, and her pulse quickened. She hesitated, giving herself a moment to compose herself before slowly turning back to face the man who'd had such an unexplained effect on her.

'If you don't mind, I'd like to make your acquaintance, ma'am. I'd tip my hat if I was wearing one.' Lash smiled.

Georgina was enthralled by his courtesy, but found she couldn't answer. She peered up, mesmerised by his black eyes.

'I'm Lash, but you already know that. It's a pleasure to meet you.'

Georgina swallowed hard and managed to say, 'Georgina... Georgina Garrett.'

'I'd like to show you the fair in a way you've probably never seen it before and if that appeals to you, meet me at the coconut shy in twenty minutes. Please, don't be alarmed. I'll ensure we are chaperoned.'

Georgina nodded. She thought she probably shouldn't agree to be meeting an unknown man, but she had a yearning to be near him. He smiled and then he was gone.

'What about the rides?' Ethel asked.

'You heard the man. He's going to show us the fair.'

Georgina found it all very intriguing and the idea of being chaperoned amused her. She tried not to get flustered and hoped her calm exterior hid her excitement.

Lash's dark and mysterious looks had beguiled her and for the first time, passion stirred. She found his black hair and olive skin seductively striking.

She didn't know it, but Lash's gypsy aunt, his *Bibio*, had read the stones and foreseen the fate of her nephew. She'd told him he'd marry the *gadji* (non-Romani) girl with violet eyes, but *prikaza* (bad luck) would be bestowed upon them.

However, it was meant to be, and today was the first day of the rest of their lives.

45

Billy unlocked the door to the attic. As soon as he opened it, the stench hit him. Since he'd discovered that Molly had been to Battersea, he'd kept her prisoner in the loft and had even boarded up the window. It had been a week, and from the overpowering smell emanating from the bucket he'd left for her, it was clear it needed emptying.

'Get up,' he snapped in disgust.

It would have been so much easier to have given her a slap, but he couldn't harm her, not whilst she was carrying his child.

Molly heaved herself up from the mattress on the floor, and pushed her lank, greasy hair behind her ears. 'Please, Billy. I'm sorry. It won't happen again. I'll never see my friends or family again,' she pleaded.

'Too right you won't. Just so you know, because of your little pleasure trip, your mother has lost her job. And if you dare defy me again, I'll see to it that Ethel, your backwards fucking sister, is locked up in an asylum for good.'

Molly's eyes widened. 'No, Billy, no. I promise I'll do what you say.'

'Good. Now I'll get you a bowl of water. You fucking stink and need a wash.'

Billy grabbed the bucket with distaste, and quickly emptied it. He then took Molly a bowl of water, soap and a towel. While she cleaned herself, he went to get her some food and water before locking the attic door again. He was sick to the back teeth of having to show consideration for his wife's welfare and couldn't wait for the baby to be born. As he left the house, slamming the front door behind him, he gritted his teeth in frustration. Once that child was out of her, he'd make sure she never disobeyed him again.

Georgina looked up at the clouds and tried to make pictures from the patterns they formed. She was feeling relaxed, lying on her back on a horse blanket with Lash beside her. 'There, that one there... it looks like a fish,' she said, pointing upwards. The fair and the rest of the world felt far off in the distance as they idled hours away on top of a small hill.

Lash rolled over to his side and supported his head with his muscular arm. The long piece of grass he was chewing tickled her cheek and she smiled as she brushed it away.

'How did you get this scar?' Lash asked as he tenderly ran his finger across the light purple mark above her eyebrow.

Georgina's breezy mood changed as she felt herself tense at the memory. 'I... erm... I was attacked. Two men, they jumped me and beat me. I was trying to protect my friend and they didn't like it.'

'You know who did this?' Lash asked, sounding outraged.

'Yes, local lads, working for Billy Wilcox.'

Lash took the piece of grass from his mouth and threw it to one side as he sat upright. 'Billy Wilcox, I know his name... I'm going to make sure he never forgets mine.'

'No, it's all right, Lash, this is my problem, not yours.' Georgina looked up at his profile and could see the anger in his jaw. She liked the idea of having a strong man to protect her, but she wanted to exact her own retribution on Billy.

'You're my woman, Georgina. I'll see to it that Billy Wilcox never hurts you again.'

'Please, Lash, leave him to me.'

'I can't do that – it's not our way. In my clan, if a woman wants to punish a man, she won't pick up a stick or use her fists, she'll throw her skirts at him, contaminate him with *marime*. Some say it's superstition but it's our belief. Billy Wilcox needs more than to be soiled.'

'Oh, don't worry, I intend to do a lot more than throw my skirt at him!'

'You don't understand, Georgina. My family isn't

pure Roma blood, but we live our life as many of our ancestors did. First, I will meet with the elders and then Billy's fate will be decided. You must not interfere, you're in my world now.'

Georgina could feel her frustration rising and pushed herself to her feet. She didn't believe in all the hocus-pocus rubbish that Lash talked about, though she kept her thoughts to herself. Instead, pleading with her eyes, she said, 'All right, you deal with Billy Wilcox, but in the meantime, I'm scared, Lash. Can you get me a gun or something to protect myself?' She'd quickly learnt how to get what she wanted from Lash and felt sure he'd fulfil her request.

Lash reached out his hands and grabbed her, then gently pulled her down towards him. Georgina knelt in front and held her breath. She wanted him to kiss her again, to feel his musky breath against her skin, to run her hands over his back and feel his taut muscles. But most of all, she wanted him to agree to give her a gun.

'Yes, my love, if it makes you feel safe, I'll give you a pistol this evening and I'll show you how to use it, but you have nothing to fear, not any more.'

Georgina smiled and closed her eyes as she felt the softness of Lash's full lips pressing against hers. She'd got what she wanted, a gun and her man's lust.

After a few minutes, he breathlessly pulled away but Georgina felt concerned as she saw his face take on a serious expression.

'The men who attacked you, did they defile you?'

Georgina understood his question. She knew her purity was important to him. No, Malc and Sid hadn't done anything like that but the policemen had abused her and Georgina wasn't sure if she was still a virgin. She lowered her eyes as she struggled to find the right words.

'Have you laid with a man, Georgina?'

Thankfully, she could answer this question truthfully and vehemently shook her head. 'No, and I won't lay with any man unless I am married.'

Lash's seriousness softened and she saw a mischievous twinkle in his eyes as he smiled. 'You're a good woman,' he said, 'and as much as I'd like to, I won't try and change your mind.'

He held her until the sun began to set, telling her of his life and travels. She enjoyed every moment in his arms and his soft gypsy twang almost sent her off to sleep.

'Come now, it's getting late,' Lash eventually said as he jumped to his feet and helped her up. 'When you are invited to sit at my family table, you'll be offered a seat reserved for *gadji*. Don't worry, one day you'll have the seat next to mine.'

Georgina said nothing but allowed Lash to lead her down the hill and to where the caravans were settled on the edge of the fair. She felt a little nervous about entering Lash's community and feared she wouldn't be welcomed. As if reading her mind, Lash gently squeezed her hand.

'Don't worry, my family have mixed blood. My grandfather took an outsider for his wife. You may be greeted with some mistrust at first, but never with hate.'

Georgina swallowed hard and followed Lash as he weaved around the tents and wooden caravans. Some were beautifully painted with ornate detail, but others looked decrepit. Children playing stopped to look at her and Georgina tried not to stare back at the women in long skirts who shadily ogled her.

'Here, come in,' Lash said, when they came to the caravan he'd grown up in.

Georgina slowly followed him up the wooden steps and hesitantly went inside. She wasn't sure what to expect and couldn't see much past Lash's broad frame. She glanced round, taking in the polished china proudly on display, then Lash stepped to one side and Georgina saw a middle-aged woman sat at a table. She guessed the woman was Lash's mother as the family resemblance was striking.

The woman looked her up and down, then barked, '*Besh!*'

Georgina wanted to flee, but Lash pulled out a seat and said, 'My mother insists you must sit.'

'Oh,' Georgina said, surprised, and smiled nervously at the woman as she sat.

Lash's mother then rattled off something that Georgina didn't understand, and Lash answered, '*Bori*.'

Again, the woman spoke and once she had finished, Lash told her, 'Speak in English, as your own mother did.'

To Georgina's relief, the woman finally smiled, saying, 'I'm sorry, I like to tease. It's very nice to meet you, Georgina, and you are welcome. Would you like some nettle tea?'

'Thank you, that would be nice,' she answered. Georgina wasn't sure it would be but didn't want to appear rude.

'You call me *Sackra*,' Lash's mother said as she went to the stove.

'That's a beautiful name,' Georgina answered.

Lash leaned forward and whispered, 'It's not her name. It means mother-in-law.'

Georgina could feel her cheeks flush and whispered back, 'I heard you say the word *Bori* to your mother. What does it mean?'

'Daughter-in-law.'

Georgina said nothing but raised her eyebrows. It seemed she really was being welcomed as part of the family though she'd only known Lash a matter of weeks and there'd been no mention of marriage.

'I'll be back soon. I'm going to get the thing we spoke of earlier.'

Georgina nodded. She now felt comfortable with his mother and understood that she wouldn't be allowed into Lash's caravan without a chaperone.

Moments later, Georgina sipped on the hot nettle tea. The earthy taste wasn't as bad as she'd expected and now she plucked up the courage to ask Sackra if she could read the leaves.

'No, but Lash's aunt, my sister, she reads them and foretold of you. I fear my son's fortune but he will make his own fate.'

Georgina wasn't sure what Sackra meant but sidestepped the comment to ask about the caravan. As the woman went on to tell of its history, Lash appeared and indicated with his head that it was time to leave. 'I'll see you, *may angle sar te merel kadi yag,*' he said to his mother.

'Yes, my son, and Georgina, remember, *kon del tut o nai shai dela tut wi o vast* – if my son willingly gives you one finger he will also give you the whole hand.'

Lash helped Georgina as she stepped down from the caravan, her mind still contemplating Sackra's words.

'I'll walk you home now.'

'What did your mother mean about the finger and the hand?'

'She likes you and it was her way of telling you what a good man I am.' He laughed.

'I already know that.'

Once out of sight of the prying eyes of the clans, Lash

handed Georgina the small pistol and several bullets. He showed her how to load the gun and how to fire it, then told her, 'Only use this if you feel your life is in danger.'

'I know, thanks, Lash. I feel better knowing I have this close by.'

They were soon outside Georgina's house but she didn't want to leave him and as he pulled her into his arms, she husked, 'I wish you didn't have to go.'

'Me too, but I told my mother I'd be back before the fire burns out.'

'I wondered what you'd said. I hoped it wasn't something about me.'

'I'd never talk bad of you, Georgina. I'll teach you my tongue, and our children will know the Roma ways.'

Georgina felt her stomach flip. He'd referred to marriage and children again! It was too soon. He didn't know her. He had no idea of the things she'd done. She'd never felt this way about a man. She must love him but could he still love her if he knew she was a killer? Would he forgive her for using the gun and killing again? She hoped so, but was too afraid to ask for fear of losing him.

The next day, Georgina wrapped a black lace shawl round her shoulders and studied her reflection in the gilt-framed mirror on her bedroom wall. She looked good, she knew she did, and smirked to herself at the thought of her face being the last thing that Billy Wilcox would see before she blew his brains out.

She picked up her purse and opened it. The small hand pistol she'd managed to persuade Lash to give her was safely tucked inside. She liked that he was chivalrous and though she could have left Billy for Lash to deal with, this was something that had festered within her for years.

'You look smashing, love. Are you going out with Lash again?' her gran asked when she went downstairs.

'Yes,' she answered, but first she had some unfinished business to attend to.

'Have a good time. Will you be back late?'

'No, Gran. I'll only be out for an hour or two. Lash is coming here for his dinner tonight. Is that all right?'

'Yes, that'll be nice. I'll make us a nice bread and butter pudding.'

Georgina kissed her gran then set on a determined march to Queenstown Road. She knew that was where she'd find Billy. She'd have preferred the element of surprise but now that she had the gun in her possession she couldn't wait any longer. Molly was due to give birth soon, and Georgina worried what would become of her friend once the baby was born. Billy should have died a long time ago.

When Knuckles opened the door, Georgina turned on the charm. It worked. She was shown through to

Billy's office where he was sat looking smug behind his desk. He looked her up and down, then ran his tongue over his lips. 'Well, well, you scrub up well,' he drawled, sarcastically adding, 'Have you come here for a job?'

'I want to talk in private so get rid of Frankenstein.'

Billy nodded to Knuckles to leave them, and once the door had closed, he said, 'Let's hear it then.'

'Actually, I don't have anything to say to you. I've come to kill you,' Georgina said calmly and reached into her purse.

She guessed that Billy kept a gun and was surprised when he made no attempt to go for it. She wanted him to make the move, intending to shoot him as he went for his gun. Instead, he stared her out with an ironic look. She stepped towards him, holding the pistol at arm's length, just as Lash had shown her.

'Before you shoot me, there's something you should know,' Billy said, showing no sign of fear that a gun was pointed at his head. 'See, the thing is, I've been expecting something like this from you. I've always suspected it was you behind the police station explosion and I've got to say, that took some bottle. And so does this. That's why I've taken out insurance.'

Georgina ground her teeth. She wanted to see Billy's grey matter splattered across his ridiculous ostentatious desk, but something wasn't right. He was too cool.

'If I'm harmed in any way, there will be repercussions. Contracts are in place to ensure your grandmother and father are killed. You'll be left alive, I've made sure of that, but their deaths will be of your making. It's down to you. Kill me if you like but be prepared to bury those you hold dear.'

'I don't believe you!' Georgina said.

'Do you want to take the risk?'

Georgina gripped the gun tightly. She wanted to annihilate Billy, but what if he was telling the truth? She couldn't kill him if it meant her family would be murdered.

She dropped her arm to her side. 'You cunt,' she spat.

Billy sneered. 'Knuckles will see you out.'

Georgina left deflated, but not defeated. She couldn't kill Billy but somehow, she had to exact her revenge. She just had to think of a way, and until she did, she wouldn't rest.

46

Dulcie opened her front door to find Fanny on her step, looking perplexed.

'You look like you've got the woes of the world on your shoulders. What's wrong?' she asked as she invited the woman in.

'It's Molly,' Fanny replied. 'I haven't seen or heard from her for three weeks now. Not since she came here to see Georgina. Do you think Billy found out and has done something to her?'

'Go through to the front room and sit down. I'll put the kettle on and then we'll have a chat.'

Dulcie rubbed her sore hip as she waited for the kettle to boil. She hadn't mentioned it to Fanny, but she'd been wondering the same thing, especially as Molly had said she'd sneak back for another visit before the end of the month. Well, it was now midway through November and there was still no sign of her.

Dulcie carried the tea through. 'I shouldn't tell you this, but Georgina has been worried too. When she knew Billy wouldn't be there, she went round to their house in Clapham yesterday but there was no answer.'

'Oh, Dulcie, what if he's... you know... killed her?'

'Nah, I shouldn't think so. He wants that child born.

She'll be safe until then. She's due any day now, ain't she?'

'Yes.'

'There you go then. She'll be proper heavy and resting with her feet up.'

'I hope you're right, Dulcie. But I should be with her. I hate to think of her giving birth all alone.'

'I'm sure she won't be. You know what a flash git that Billy is! He'll probably have some expensive doctor there making sure that the baby's fine.'

'I do hope so. But what if something has happened to her and he ain't told us?'

'Fanny, stop worrying, you'll do yourself a mischief. Jane would know if something was wrong, and granted she sacked you, but she wouldn't keep you in the dark about your own daughter, now would she?'

'No, I suppose not,' Fanny answered, though Dulcie didn't think the woman sounded convinced.

'Tell ya what, Georgina is out grafting but when she gets home I'll tell her how worried you are and send her round to Jane's. How's that?'

'Oh, would you, Dulcie? That would be such a weight off my mind. It's bad enough worrying about how I'm going to pay the rent, let alone this as well.'

'No luck with finding work then?' Dulcie asked, though she already knew what the answer would be. Billy Wilcox seemed to control everything.

'No. Word has spread that it was Billy who got rid of

me. It means nobody will touch me with a barge pole now. We're just about managing though. Ethel's been doing a bit of babysitting, and I had a few bob saved. I'll have to find something soon though, 'cos my measly savings won't last for much longer.'

'Your Ethel is always welcome to come and sit with me, and I'll pay her for her time, though it won't be much.'

'Jack still bad then?'

'Yeah. There's no talking to him. He's fallen to the bottom of the whisky bottle and I can't pull him out. Georgina has done a few Manchester runs for Ezzy, but he doesn't want her doing them any more. He reckons her new look makes her stick out like a sore thumb. She's gone back to lifting to fill the cupboards, but I don't like to see her breaking the law, not since my Jack did time.'

'She's a clever woman, Dulcie, I'm sure she'll be careful. I hear she's got herself a new fella?'

'Yes, Lash. Nice bloke, but he's one of them gypsies from the fair. I weren't sure about him at first, but he treats her like a blinkin' queen, and she lets him! I ain't said nothing to her 'cos she'd do her nut, but he slips me a couple of bob here and there. I wouldn't be at all surprised if she marries him.'

'Blimey, Dulcie, I didn't realise it was that serious.'

'It is, and it's nice to see her happy.'

'How do his family feel about it? They don't normally like outsiders,' Fanny said.

'Apparently not, but they seem to have taken to Georgina.'

'That's good. Will she go travelling with them?'

'No, of course not,' Dulcie answered huffily, but in truth it was a possibility, and one she hadn't considered.

'We're moving on, Georgina, following the fair East,' Lash explained.

They were sat facing each other in the long grass on the edge of the field watching as the rides and stalls were packed away.

'I wish you didn't have to go,' Georgina said, and pulled her jacket closer around her.

'Are you cold?' Lash asked.

'A bit.'

'Come here, I'll keep you warm,' he offered, and pulled her in to his brawny body.

Georgina enjoyed the closeness. She felt safe with Lash. They sat quietly for a few minutes, then he said, 'Come with me.'

'Where?' she asked.

'On the road with us.'

The thought appealed to her, but she knew it would be impossible. 'I can't, Lash. I need to be here to look after my gran.'

'I understand. I realise the importance of family.'

She could hear the disappointment in his voice. 'Will

you be coming back this way soon?' she asked hopefully.

'I doubt it, not for at least six months.'

Georgina nestled her face deeper in to Lash's chest and breathed in, wanting to hold on to the memory of his masculine scent. She wanted to tell him she'd miss him but couldn't bring herself to show any sentiment.

'I could stay... if you'd marry me. I know it's only been a few weeks, but you're the woman for me. What do you say, Georgina, will you be my wife?'

She pulled away from his embrace and looked deeply into his dark eyes. 'Really? You'd leave your family and your way of life to be here with me?'

'Yes, I would. I love you, Georgina.'

She loved him too, but she carried deep secrets and wasn't sure if Lash would want to be her husband if he knew the truth about her.

'I love you too, Lash, but there's stuff you don't know.'

'I'm sure there is, but whatever it is, it won't change how I feel about you.'

Georgina wasn't convinced.

She stood up, but Lash grabbed her hand and said, 'I won't let you go, no matter what you've done; as I said, it won't change the way I feel about you.'

'But what about your family? They'd hate me if you stayed here because of me.'

'Don't talk soft, woman. They've already hinted at it. My mother said you've got good child-bearing hips, and my dad said he'd be pleased to see the back of me. I know he's only kidding, but it's his way of letting me know. They can see the love I have in my heart for you, and they want me to be happy. I choose you, but that doesn't mean I have to sacrifice my kin. They'll always be there for me, as I will for them, but my life will be with you.'

Georgina looked over to the caravans and questioned if it was really fair to allow Lash to leave it all behind. 'I'm going to tell you something, then I want you to walk away and think about everything. When you come back in six months, you can tell me if you still want me to be your wife.'

It was a long afternoon but after Georgina had told him about the murdered policemen and Mike Mipple, Lash had taken her in his arms and passionately kissed her. During that moment of wanting, as their bodies entwined, he told her he'd do anything to protect her… and on his return, he'd sort out Billy Wilcox before taking her as his wife. Little did he know she'd already confronted Billy to kill him. It hadn't been possible but she intended on deeply hurting him and she wouldn't wait six months for that pleasure.

After promising she'd be here for him on his return, she'd left him in the field and headed home. As she walked, she licked her lips. She could taste Lash. Yes, she believed she did love him. He stirred passions in her body that she'd never experienced before. Best of all, he offered protection, something she'd come to realise she needed.

47

Molly rubbed the small of her back as she slowly paced the tiny attic room. This was the second pain she'd had in the last ten minutes. She'd seen her mum give birth and knew it started like this. She just hoped she could hold on until Billy got home, though she knew that would be a few hours yet. The thought of pushing out the child alone terrified her.

She lowered herself onto a wooden chair and picked up her crocheting. It wasn't easy to see what she was doing as Billy had boarded up the only window, but she tried to concentrate on the baby blanket she was midway through making. Another pain gripped her. She gritted her teeth and held her breath as she waited for the aching to pass. That had come on faster than the last.

'Oh, God… BILLY,' she screamed, though she knew her cries for help wouldn't be heard. 'I want my mum,' she whimpered, giving in to another wave of agony.

The baby was on its way, and Molly had to prepare herself for giving birth without any help. She'd never forgive her husband for this. Never.

*

'I'm thrilled for you, love, I really am,' Dulcie said, and clapped her hands together.

'Calm down, Gran. If I marry him, it won't be for ages yet. The fair is off travelling again, and he won't be back this way for months.'

'Well, that'll give us plenty of time to sober up your dad before the big day.'

'Lash has got a plan for that. He said he'll lock him in a *vardo* until his blood is red and clean. They did the same with their cousin.'

'Well, something needs to be done,' Dulcie said, pursing her lips. 'By the way, I forgot to tell you. Fanny popped in yesterday. She's worried about Molly 'cos she ain't had word from her for weeks now. I said you'd call in to see Jane and find out what's going on.'

'No problem, I was going to see her today anyway. I'll go now. Will you be all right by yourself for a couple of hours?'

'Yes, love, I'll be fine, don't worry about me,' Dulcie lied. Her hip was aching more than usual, which she put down to the change in the weather.

'If you see my dad, don't mention anything about Lash. Nothing's set in concrete yet and we've only known each other for two minutes. I don't want an ear-bashing, though I doubt he'll remember it by tomorrow.'

Georgina hurried out of the house, obviously thrilled at receiving a marriage proposal. Dulcie smiled to herself as she picked up her reading book. It was nice to see her granddaughter so happy. She'd had a rough time of it lately, mostly thanks to Billy Wilcox. But Dulcie thought things would be different soon. Georgina had a man by her side, a tough bare-knuckle fighter. A gypsy from a strong travelling family. Billy Wilcox would be a fool if he thought he could get to Georgina now, though it was still a worry that Lash would be away for the next six months.

'Hello, George, come in,' Jane said when she opened her front door. 'You're looking fabulous.'

'Thank you,' Georgina replied, admiring Jane's lilac cashmere jumper that she wore with a fitted black velvet skirt. 'You do too.'

'Can I get you anything? A tea, something stronger, perhaps?'

'No, thanks. I was hoping you'd have some news of Molly?'

'Molly… yes, she's doing well. Billy has informed me that the doctor is calling in on her twice weekly, and I saw her a couple of weeks ago. She's as big as a bus! Her ankles are a little swollen, but that's to be expected.'

'Good. I'm glad to hear she's all right, but a lot can happen in two weeks. I'll call in on her later. Where's Sally?'

'She's at school and Penny is upstairs with new chalks.

She loves to draw, it keeps her quiet for ages. Are you sure I can't get you anything?'

'Erm, all right, I'll have a lemonade, please,' Georgina answered. The room felt warm yet there were only embers glowing in the hearth.

Jane left and moments later, returned with two glasses. When she walked back into the room, the warm smile she offered was friendly and genuine, yet it didn't cause Georgina to have second thoughts about what she planned to do. 'Jane, please sit down at the table.'

Jane looked bemused. 'Why?'

'Just do as I tell you,' Georgina ordered and pulled the small pistol out of her purse to point at the woman. It was the same one she'd held at Billy's head.

Jane gasped, and white-faced she dragged out a chair. She sat down and asked tremulously, 'Why are you threatening me with a gun?'

'I have to do this, Jane. I'm sorry.'

Jane looked terrified and begged, 'No... please... Georgina... don't... don't hurt me.' Tears began to stream down her face and she was unconsciously fiddling with her long ebony beads. Her black eye make-up streaked down her cheeks. Georgina thought it was odd to see the woman looking anything but perfect.

'Your son has left me no choice. Billy has to pay for what he's done, and as he's seen to it that I can't kill him, the only way to get to him is through you. Believe me, I wish there was another way, but you have the unfortunate burden of being his mother. You should have drowned him at birth. He's not right in the head, and I think you know it.'

'I do... I know he's ill... and I'm sure he murdered Norman, his own father.'

'Of course he did, and you could have told the police. Instead you did nothing and it's time for you to pay for letting your son get away with murder.'

'George, please, don't kill me. What about my daughters? You wouldn't want them to grow up motherless. I know you did, and I'm sure there's been many times when you wished you had a mum.'

Georgina glanced at the gold ring on her finger. Her mother's wedding ring.

'Please, George, don't leave Sally alone with Billy. Anything could happen to her without me to protect her! Think about it, George, for Sally's sake!'

'Huh, did you think about the women that your son abused?'

'What women?'

'Don't come the innocent with me. I was one of them. You knew he tried to burn me alive. You must have known he had me beaten up too because you came round with blood money.'

'George... please...'

'Georgina. My name is Georgina! Where do you keep your writing paper?'

'It… it's in the bureau,' Jane said nervously, pointing.

Georgina kept her eyes on Jane and the gun pointed at her as she rummaged through the walnut cabinet, then she placed a pad and pencil on the table. 'Write this down,' she instructed.

Jane picked up the pencil. Georgina could see the woman's hands were shaking.

'To whom it may concern,' Georgina begun.

Jane stared at her.

'Write it!' she shouted.

Jane scribbled down the words. 'I cannot live with the knowledge of what my son has done. Following a visit from Malcolm Henderson and Sidney Bell, I now know the facts of my husband's death, and to hear that my son killed his father is too much for me to bear.'

Georgina noticed that Jane had stopped writing. 'This isn't a game. If you don't do as I say, I swear, I'll tie you to that chair and make you watch while I shoot Penny, then I'll blow your fucking brains out before I pick Sally up from school, and after I've shown her the mess a shot-up head makes, I'll kill her too.'

'You wouldn't… you wouldn't hurt an innocent child.'

'Wouldn't I? Do you want to test that?'

Jane shook her head.

'I thought not. Write down exactly what I tell you and I give you my word that Penny will be safe and Sally will come home from school to find your dead body. It's gonna be a shock, but at least she'll still be alive. If you want to do it the hard way, I'll make sure she dies… in agony.'

'Please, Georgina, don't kill me for Billy's mistakes.'

'Mistakes? Was it a mistake that I wasn't burnt to death? Was it a mistake that I wasn't left a fucking vegetable when his thugs jumped me? Billy's mistakes have cost you your life. I want the man destroyed, so you are going to blame *him* for your suicide. I hope he feels real pain until the day I can kill him too. Now pick up the fucking pencil!'

'I see. So, this is a suicide note. You want me to write my own suicide note?'

'Yes, Jane, that's right. And when Billy reads that Malc and Sid grassed him up, that'll be their downfall too. Billy will terminate his own gang, the very men who tried to terminate me. It's ironic really, don't you think?'

'I think you must have gone mad, Georgina. This isn't you,' Jane said bravely.

'That's where you're very wrong. Now, shut up and write!'

Molly screamed. She thought the pain was going to kill her. She'd removed her underwear and was on her knees, holding on to the wooden seat for support. Her waters had broken and now the contractions were coming every couple of minutes.

She panted, half hoping to hold back the inevitable birth, half hoping to get the child out as quickly as possible. She'd never felt so scared, not even when her father had been in a rage and beat her mother.

'Argh… oh, Mum,' she cried in agony.

Beads of sweat perfused her brow. She gripped the seat and arched her back.

'I hate you, Billy Wilcox, hate you,' she ground out through gritted teeth.

She reached between her legs and could feel the top of her baby's head.

Jane had finished the letter and had left her tears splashed on the paper. She'd signed and dated it. Now, Georgina held the pistol to Jane's temple as she checked the words.

'Perfect. You've done the right thing, Jane. You've secured your daughters' lives.'

'Please… just make it quick.'

As though she'd resigned herself to her fate, Jane sounded surprisingly composed, which impressed Georgina. Even with a gun to her head and knowing her life was about to be snuffed out, she remained a lady. 'Close your eyes,' she told her.

Jane did as she was instructed then spoke softly, 'Please make sure nothing bad happens to my girls.

Penny won't remember me but tell her how much I loved her.'

Those words. *Tell her how much I loved her.* The same last words her own mother had uttered. Georgina turned her head and caught sight of herself in the mirror. What was she doing? Jane was right – she had gone mad! Suddenly disgusted with herself, she dropped the gun to the floor, then staggered back until she was up against the wall on the other side of the room. 'I'm sorry, Jane... I'm so sorry... I don't know what I was thinking.'

Jane's body seemed to slump with relief, then she burst into tears again. She held her head in her hands as she cried. 'It's all right. I realise my son has driven you to this. It's a miracle you're even alive after everything he's done. I don't blame you for wanting to get your own back.'

'This isn't the way. It's him I want dead, not you! I thought killing you would be punishment for him, but you don't deserve to die... it's not your fault. God, I can't believe I went this far.'

Georgina looked at the pistol on the floor. Her legs felt weak and she thought she might throw up. Revenge had blinded her and marred her judgement. She had been just moments away from killing an innocent woman, something she'd have never forgiven herself for.

'So, it is true? All the things you said... He killed Norman?' Jane asked.

Georgina nodded, but her mind was still whirling at the shock of what she'd nearly done.

Jane stood from the table and dabbed her wet cheeks with the tips of her fingers. Then, she moved towards the gun and picked it up. Georgina thought she may turn it on her and braced herself for the bullet.

'Billy murdered my husband. Will you show me how to use this gun?'

Georgina blinked hard disbelievingly.

'If anyone is going to kill my son, it will be me. I brought him into this world and it'll be me who takes him out of it. He's done nothing but leave a trail of pain and destruction behind him and he'll keep doing it until he's stopped.'

'No, Jane, you're not thinking straight. You can't do this. If you kill your own son, it'll destroy you,' Georgina said, and slowly walked towards Jane hoping to take the gun from her.

'But you're right, George, someone has to. It should be me... I made him. I must have done something wrong... I don't know, maybe I made mistakes when he was growing up... It was a difficult birth, perhaps he got damaged... but he can't be permitted to carry on like he is. I have to think about my girls.'

'Jane, give me the gun,' Georgina gently said, worried that the woman could turn out to be as mad as her son.

'No. Don't worry, I know what you're thinking, but I'm nothing like him. I'm just seeing things clearly for the first time. I think I've always known that Billy isn't right, but I've never accepted it. I love him, George, he's my son, God knows I love him… but what if he decides that he wants to kill Sally? He hates her, you know. He can't stand to be around her. I wouldn't put it past him to murder her next, and there's Penny to think about.'

Jane stuffed the barrel of the pistol into the waistband of her skirt. 'I'm going to have a large brandy. Care to join me?'

Georgina felt confused. She couldn't quite work out what was going on. 'Yes,' she answered, and watched as Jane went to a cabinet and poured two drinks into crystal glasses. She handed Georgina a brandy, then said, 'Bottoms up,' before downing her drink. 'Ah, that's better.' She smiled, though Georgina could see that her smile didn't reach her eyes.

Georgina sipped on the potent alcohol. It burned her throat as she swallowed it.

'You're a tough cookie, George. I'm going to be more like you.'

'I'm not tough. I just won't let men take advantage of me.'

'Good on you, that's what I say.' Jane sat on the arm of the sofa and crossed one elegant leg over the other. 'But what made you like this?'

Georgina walked over to the table where she'd forced Jane to sit earlier. She looked out onto the quiet street.

Two small girls with pigtails were playing hopscotch whilst a little boy threw stones up against the kerb. The world outside was carrying on as normal and seemed a million miles away from the madness that was going on in the room.

'People aren't born tough. Life makes them that way. What's happened to you, George? What has made you the woman you are?'

Georgina twisted her mother's wedding ring. A kaleidoscope of images flashed through her head. Distant, vague memories of a man with red hair holding her down and hurting her. Being locked in a dark cupboard, her hands tied together. The policemen, more pain, more humiliation. Defiled again. The fire, the feeling of being terrified for her life. Malc and Sid beating her unconscious. Men... Men had made her tough and she'd suffered in the process. Surprised at herself, she gasped as all the awful memories flooding her mind forced tears from her eyes. She'd been through so much but cried very little.

'Are you all right?' Jane asked softly.

Georgina hadn't realised but she was sobbing now. Except for her anger, she'd suppressed so many emotions but allowing a few tears had unleashed the floodgates. Years of hidden misery tumbled out. She cried until she couldn't cry any longer.

Finally, all her weeping spent, she turned, drained, and looked at Jane.

'Better?'

'Yes,' Georgina said, and drew in a long juddering breath. 'Blimey, I don't know where that came from. I feel a right pillock now.'

'There's no need to be embarrassed. It's better out than in. Do you want to talk about it?'

'There's nothing to talk about,' Georgina answered defensively.

'There obviously is but have it your way.'

'You're quite a remarkable woman, Jane. I came here with every intention of killing you. I held a gun to your head and made you write your own suicide note. Yet you offer me a shoulder to cry on. I take my hat off to you.'

'There's nothing remarkable about me. I'm ashamed of myself. I've let Billy get away with murder. No more though – that's it. I have to ensure Sally's safety.'

'Molly!' Georgina said.

'What?'

'How do we know Molly is safe? She hasn't been seen for a while now. Christ, Jane, we've got to check on Molly.'

'Don't panic, I'm sure Billy wouldn't harm her.'

'How can you be sure… are you forgetting that he killed his father?' Georgina shrieked.

'Right, let's go. Let me write a quick note for Sally. I'll tell her to wait with my neighbour until I get home.'

Jane quickly crumpled up the suicide note, then left instructions for Sally. Both women marched to the kitchen and splashed cold water on their faces. Jane grabbed a light coat and threw it on, rushed upstairs and came running back down with Penny, then grasped her handbag and they dashed out of the door.

After dropping Penny with the neighbour and ensuring that she'd look after Sally, she said, 'Let's get to the Junction and grab a taxi cab from there.'

Georgina agreed it would be the quickest way to get to Clapham. There was no reason to think that Billy had done anything to hurt Molly, but the man was unpredictable, and even his own mother agreed that no-one was safe, not all the while her son had breath in his body.

Molly faintly heard someone knocking on the front door. She screamed with all her might, not to be heard, but in excruciating agony.

'Please, help me,' she yelled once the pain passed, but she was sure whoever had been at the door would have gone by now. If she could have got to the boarded-up window, she would have hammered on it in the hope of someone on the streets hearing her.

She managed to lay herself down on the bare floorboards, exhausted and scared for the life of her soon-to-be-born child and her own. Anything could go wrong. The baby could get stuck or she could bleed to death. As she pushed, she cried again for her mum.

*

They'd heard Molly's screams and Georgina had managed to pick the front door lock.

'Quickly, the bedroom,' Jane said, running up the stairs as Georgina followed closely behind taking them two at a time.

'She's not in here,' Jane said coming out of one room.

Georgina searched the other two, but Molly was nowhere to be seen.

'Did you hear that?' Jane asked.

'What?'

'Shush… there… it's coming from the attic!' Jane exclaimed.

Georgina ran to the end of the hallway, shouting out Molly's name. She found a small door and behind it, a dark narrow staircase that led to another door. She flew up the stairs, but the next door was locked.

'MOLLY,' she called.

'George?'

'Yes… can you open the door?'

'No… I'm locked in. Please… help me… the baby.'

'Stand back, Molly,' Georgina said, and kicked the door.

It didn't budge, and she'd hurt her ankle but she kicked again and again.

'Argh,' Molly cried from the other side.

'Hurry up, George,' Jane said.

'I'm trying,' she grunted, and rammed the door with her shoulder using all her force.

At last, the door gave way. The room was almost in darkness, but Georgina could see Molly looked petrified and was holding a baby in between her legs. The sight was shocking.

'Oh, love, what has he done to you?' Jane said as she darted past Georgina and crouched down beside Molly and the baby.

'He locked me up... I was so scared...' Molly cried.

Jane stroked Molly's matted hair off her face. 'It's all right,' she soothed, 'we're here now and we won't let Billy hurt you or the baby.'

Then Jane turned to Georgina. 'Go downstairs and find me scissors or a sharp knife. Get me water and towels.'

Georgina stood transfixed.

'GEORGINA!' Jane snapped.

'Er... yes, sorry,' she answered and flew into action. She ran round Billy's house collecting the things Jane had told her to. How could he have done this to Molly? God, she wished she could kill him.

Jane had cut the umbilical cord and cleaned up mother and baby. Molly held her son in her arms and looked at him adoringly. All the fear and horror she had felt melted away. Her child was perfect. Beautiful. She instantly fell in love, and though exhausted, she held him to her breast. The baby instinctively suckled.

'Hello, little man. I'm your mummy,' Molly cooed.

She'd have liked to name him Edward after the king but knew Billy would want to have his way and call the child Norman. It gave her the creeps.

As the baby fed, Molly offered a silent prayer. 'Please keep my boy safe and don't let him have his father's evil traits.'

'Can I have a word?' Jane whispered discreetly to Georgina.

They were downstairs now with Molly resting on the sofa. Once they were in the hallway and out of Molly's earshot, Jane said, 'I want to take them back to my house.'

'I'd rather they were at mine,' Georgina answered.

Jane came back with, 'I've got more room.'

'I know, but you've also got a headcase son. No, I think they'll be safer at mine.'

'Come off it, Georgina. No offence, but what protection can your gran and drunken father offer? I've got this,' Jane said and pulled the pistol from the waistband of her skirt. 'I think this beats yours.'

'I can't argue with that, but the gun belongs to me.'

'It did, but it's mine now,' Jane said firmly.

Georgina wasn't in a position to argue with the

woman; after all, Jane was the one holding the gun. She would never have thought Jane would have it in her to use it, but now saw the woman in a different light.

'Your house it is then.' Georgina shrugged. But they still had to deal with Billy. They all knew that once he discovered Molly was gone, he'd go on a rampage looking for them.

As the taxi cab drove into Battersea, Molly could sense the thick tension in the air. 'I'm not sure about this,' she said worriedly, 'Billy won't tolerate it – he'll come looking for me. The first place he'll go is to my mum's house. What if he hurts her or my sisters?'

'Don't worry, we'll pick them up. In fact, Jane, we'll have to go to mine 'cos he's sure to look there too and I don't want my gran left alone.'

'Yes, you're right. We'll drop Molly off, you stay with her and I'll fetch Sally and Penny and Fanny and the girls.' Jane squeezed Molly's hand, then said, 'Don't worry, darling, everything will be fine.'

But Molly was worried. How would everything be fine?

When the cab pulled up outside Georgina's house, Dulcie came out on the doorstep.

'What's going on?' she asked, ushering the women indoors.

'I'll explain everything soon. Look after Molly, Gran, she's just had the baby.'

'My goodness, what's she doing up and about? She should be resting! Molly, go and sit yourself down. I'll put the kettle on.'

Molly sat on the sofa and held her child protectively to her. She rocked gently back and forth, petrified that at any moment Billy would come charging through the door and rip the baby from her arms. She wanted to cry but held herself together. She was a mother now. She had to be strong.

Jane and Georgina were in the hallway, and though their voices were low, Molly could hear their conversation. She heard Jane say, 'Keep an eye on them. I'll get Sally and Penny and I'll send word to Fanny. Billy will still be working. He won't realise what's happened for a few hours, so we've got plenty of time.'

'OK, but we really need to come up with a plan to sort Billy out.'

'I've got that in hand,' Jane said solemnly.

'What do you mean?'

There were a few moments of silence, then Molly heard Georgina say, 'Are you sure that's what you want to do?'

Jane then answered, 'Yes. It's the only way. I'll bring my girls here and then I'll go back to his house and wait for him.'

Molly heard the front door close then Dulcie asking

Georgina what had happened. Georgina gave the woman a condensed version then walked into the room.

'Right then, let's have a proper look at this little bundle,' she said, holding out her arms for the baby.

Molly handed him over.

'He's a handsome chap. What are you going to call him?'

'Billy wanted Norman for a boy...'

'You have got to be kidding me! Is that what you want?'

'No... I like Edward.'

'Yes, it suits him. Hello, Edward.' Georgina smiled. 'I think he wants his mummy back now.'

'Give him here,' Dulcie said as she came in with a tray of tea. 'You're not really the maternal type, are you, love?'

'I like babies... as long as I can hand them back.' Georgina laughed.

Molly was grateful for the sweet warm tea, and the slice of cake that came with it. Dulcie fussed over Edward whilst Georgina looked out of the window. It was obvious that she was keeping her eyes peeled for Billy, but she was trying to do it covertly. They were doing their utmost to behave normally but she knew it was all an act. Everyone was on edge, and though no-one said it, Molly knew they were all frightened too.

48

Jane fidgeted nervously on Billy's navy blue and cream sofa. She checked the clock on the mantel again. It was five minutes past six. Molly had told her he was normally home by six. The barrel of the gun dug into the top of her thigh. She stood up and paced the room, hoping she'd be more comfortable.

Another ten minutes passed. Jane tried not to think of what she was about to do. Then she heard a car pulling up outside. She looked out of the window and was filled with dread. It was Billy. At last, he was home. She drew a deep breath and took a firm stance on the cream rug in the middle of the lounge.

'Mother!' Billy said surprised when he walked in and saw her. 'What are you doing here?'

'I know everything,' Jane answered gravely.

'What are you, an encyclopaedia?' Billy said with an uncomfortable chuckle.

He walked past her to an onyx and gilt table and poured himself a drink. 'Would you like one?'

Jane could feel her heart hammering hard. She felt giddy with nerves but tried to keep her voice calm. 'No, thank you. Sit down, Billy,' she said.

Billy walked back past his mother and sat in an

oversized armchair. He looked relaxed with his legs up on a small stool, a glass in one hand and his father's pipe in the other. There was something in his eyes though. Was he goading her?

'It's nice to see you.'

'I wish I could say the same, Billy.'

'Do you want to tell me what this is all about? I suppose you know Molly is upstairs?'

'Actually, she isn't. How could you have locked her up there like that? She and the baby could have died!'

'Baby? Has she had the baby? Where is she?' Billy said, jumping to his feet.

'Yes, as a matter of fact, she's had a little boy but you're never going to see your son.'

'Where are they, Mother?' Billy growled.

'Don't you dare take that tone with me. SIT DOWN!'

Billy's eyes widened, and his brows lifted, but he did as he was told.

'I get it. You're going to give me a good telling-off, and I probably deserve it. It was wrong of me to keep Molly upstairs, but I thought she'd be all right. I'm calling him Norman, my son, what do you think about that?'

Jane couldn't believe her son was smiling as if nothing was wrong. 'You're a sick bastard! That's what I think about that. You killed your father, Billy. My husband, dead, because of you.'

Billy stepped towards her, so Jane quickly pulled the

pistol from her skirt and pointed it at him. He stopped in his tracks and held his hands up.

'Whoa, Mum... take it easy...'

Tears pricked at Jane's eyes, blurring her vision. 'Sit back down,' she said, hoping to keep a distance between them.

Thankfully, Billy slowly stepped back and lowered himself onto the armchair. He didn't look quite so relaxed now.

'Why? Why did you kill your father? How could you have?' Jane asked, hoping at least to get some answers.

'I didn't want to, but he pushed me to it. He knew how to wind me up and he kept on until I snapped. It was his own fault... he bloody asked for it.'

'Even now, you're still blaming your dad. You're not man enough to own up to it. Norman was a good father and husband. Something you'll never be!'

'I'm sorry, Mum, I never wanted you to be upset.'

'Upset? I'm devastated! And I'm scared, Billy!'

'You've got nothing to fear. I'd never hurt you – you know that. I love you, Mum.'

'I thought you loved your father. And what about Sally? How could I ever trust you around her?'

'I promise I'll never touch a hair on that girl's head. I know she means the world to you. Put the gun away, Mum. You don't need it. I'll always look after you, honest.'

Jane noticed her hand was shaking and tears were streaming down her face. Her voice was shaky, but she said, 'Norman meant the world to me too, but you killed him. I'll never forgive you, Billy... never.'

A dark look descended in her son's eyes and his face twisted. 'Do you think you're going to shoot me then, Mother? Is that your plan? Rid the world of Billy Wilcox?'

'Yes... it's my responsibility to destroy the evil I created.'

'Ha, don't flatter yourself. You had *nothing* to do with who I am. Look at you... you're weak. You can't even hold the gun steady, let alone pull the trigger. Killing isn't as easy as you'd think, is it? You need strength, Mother... and you don't have what it takes.'

Jane squeezed the trigger. She wanted to do it. She felt she *had* to do it. But Billy was right... she couldn't and cried out in anguish.

'It's all right, Mum, don't upset yourself,' Billy said softly with a wicked leer. 'It's good that you can't murder your own. Now, hand me the gun.'

He stood up and slowly walked towards her again. But she couldn't let him have the gun. He was mad enough to use it to shoot her. She wouldn't put anything past him. Then if she was dead, Sally would be next and then Penny.

Resolute, she closed her eyes and, BANG, fired it.

The noise was almost deafening and left a ringing in her ears. She didn't want to look but forced herself to open her eyes.

Billy had fallen at her feet and was holding his shoulder. He looked up at her with a ridiculous grin on his face. 'You did it, Mum. I can't believe you actually bloody did it!'

Jane dropped down beside her son and took his head in her hands. 'I'm so sorry,' she cried. 'God forgive me, but I had to do it.'

'I know, Mum... I love you.'

Billy's eyes closed. Jane gasped. 'NO,' she shouted. 'Don't die, Billy... please don't die.'

She placed her hand over the gunshot wound and tried to stop the warm sticky blood from oozing out. Someone was knocking on the front door. The noise must have alerted the neighbours.

In a faint voice, Billy said, 'Go, Mum... get out the back door.'

'Oh, thank God, you're alive! Hold on, Son, keep breathing.'

'I'll be fine, it's only a flesh wound. But get out before the police arrive. I'll lie for you – tell them it was an intruder. I'll always protect you, Mother... always. You and my son... We'll all be together, just the three of us.'

Jane caught her breath and realised she'd made a terrible mistake. He'd said just the three of them. Sally and Penny would never be safe, not all the while Billy lived. She stood up and looked down at the creature bleeding onto the immaculate cream rug. She pointed the gun and fired again, this time aiming directly at his head and with her eyes open. The blood of her only son splattered across her face. He was dead, and she'd rectified her mistake.

49

Georgina saw Jane almost running down the street and opened the front door. She immediately noticed the woman had blood on her and hoped it was Billy's.

'You did it then?' she asked and closed the door behind them.

Jane nodded but appeared to be unable to speak. She was clearly traumatised by the experience.

'Go upstairs and clean yourself up. There'll be a stiff drink waiting for you down here, along with your grandson, Edward. Keep him in mind, Jane. You did this for him, and your girls, for all of us.'

Again, Jane nodded but said nothing, but as she walked up the stairs, she turned and mumbled, 'Edward... you said my grandson, Edward?'

'That's right. Molly named him Edward.'

Jane half-heartedly smiled and carried on up the stairs.

As Georgina walked back into the front room, she hoped the woman would one day come to forgive herself. The room was silent and all eyes were on her, waiting for an answer. 'It's over,' she said quietly.

Everyone sighed, as if they'd all been holding their

breath. Even Sally look relieved and Fanny exchanged a reassuring glance with Molly.

Minutes later, Jane walked in sheepishly and knelt in front of her daughter. She took the girl's hand and spoke softly. 'I'm really sorry, Sally, but your brother is dead.'

To everyone's surprise, Sally said, 'I know. Good.'

'I realise you didn't get on very well, but it's OK to be upset. You don't have to pretend.'

'I'm not. Oh, Mum, I should have said something to you, but I was so scared of him. He told me what he did to Dad and threatened that if I ever told you, he'd do the same to me. I hated him. He was always hitting me behind your back. I'm glad he's dead.' Sally broke down and Jane comforted her.

'Good riddance to bad rubbish. Now, we'll have no more talk of... him. We've got a new life to celebrate, and I for one reckon we ought to wet the baby's head. Anyone fancy a whisky?' Dulcie offered, sounding cheery.

'Am I allowed?' Sally asked as she wiped away her tears.

'No, young lady, most definitely not!' Jane answered.

'Oh, go on Jane, it's only the one and it's not every day the girl will get to become an aunt.'

'OK, she can have the one but make it small.'

'If Sally's having whisky, can I have one too?' Ethel chirped.

Fanny was quick to answer, saying, 'No, and before you ask too, Charlotte, you're not having one either.'

'Give me a hand, love?' Dulcie asked Georgina, beckoning her to the kitchen.

Once they were out of earshot from Jane, Dulcie whispered, 'Do you reckon she'll be able to live with what she's done?'

'It won't be easy for her, but she insisted on doing it. She said it was her responsibility. I don't know, Gran, I'm sure taking the life of her son will leave her feeling guilty for the rest of her own, but I think she knows it was the only way she could protect Sally and Penny. It's not like she could have gone to the police. Half of them were on Billy's payroll.'

'And what about his henchmen, the two that jumped you?'

'Well, without Billy, they're nothing. I don't know if they'll turn up at Ezzy's again, but if they do, I'll be ready and waiting for them.'

'And what if they don't?' Dulcie asked, eyeing her granddaughter suspiciously.

'Ha, don't look at me like that – you know me too well! But I know what you're thinking and you're right... I'm not going to let them get away with what they did to me. But if they leave Ezzy alone, I'll leave them alone, for now. Then when Lash comes back, I'll let him sort them out.'

'Good on you,' Dulcie said, and poured several

drinks. Georgina carried the tray through, and Dulcie handed round the whisky in china cups. 'To Edward,' she said.

Georgina leaned against the mantel and surveyed the scene. Sally pulled a face of disgust at the taste of the alcohol, whilst Molly gazed lovingly at her newborn son. Her gran got up to pour herself another drink, which was sure to make her tipsy. Fanny, Ethel and Charlotte were sat on the floor with a game of draughts between them. Jane looked in shock as she pulled Penny onto her lap. It wasn't any wonder that the woman appeared dazed after what she'd just done.

Georgina knocked back the dregs of her whisky, then said, 'Seeing all of us together like this has got me thinking.'

'Oh no,' Molly joked. 'This could be dangerous.'

'I think I know what you're going to say,' Dulcie said, and looked proudly at her granddaughter.

'We've all been hurt, one way or another, but I won't stand for it, and neither should you! None of us should ever have to put up with any more crap. And we're stronger together, as we've proved. For that reason, I'm going to re-form the Maids of Battersea, and you are now all principal members.'

Acknowledgements

With special thanks to my agent, Judith Murdoch. The wonderful team at Aria and Hannah Smith for championing my book.

Thank you to my family and friends for their encouragement. My mum, Brenda Warren, for her belief in me. My husband, Simon, for doing everything in the house so that I can write.

About the Author

SAM MICHAELS lives in Spain with her family and a plethora of animals. Having been writing for years *Trickster* is her debut novel.

Hello from Aria

We hope you enjoyed this book! If you did let us know, we'd love to hear from you.

We are Aria, a dynamic digital-first fiction imprint from award-winning independent publishers Head of Zeus. At heart, we're committed to publishing fantastic commercial fiction – from romance and sagas to crime, thrillers and historical fiction. Visit us online and discover a community of like-minded fiction fans!

We're also on the look out for tomorrow's superstar authors. So, if you're a budding writer looking for a publisher, we'd love to hear from you. You can submit your book online at ariafiction.com/ we-want-read-your-book

You can find us at:
Email: aria@headofzeus.com
Website: www.ariafiction.com
Submissions: www.ariafiction.com/
we-want-read-your-book

f @ariafiction
🐦 @Aria_Fiction
📷 @ariafiction